broken sky

Also by Chris Wooding:

The Haunting of Alaizabel Cray
Poison
Storm Thief
Broken Sky: The Twilight War

CHRIS WOODING

broken sky

ACT 2

COMMUNION

■SCHOLASTIC

This omnibus edition first published in the UK
in 2008 by Scholastic Children's Books
An imprint of Scholastic Ltd
Euston House, 24 Eversholt Street
London, NW1 1DB, UK
Registered office: Westfield Road, Southam, Warwickshire, CV47 0RA
SCHOLASTIC and associated logos are trademarks and or registered
trademarks of Scholastic Inc.

First published by Scholastic Children's Books as
Broken Sky: Part 4, Part 5 and Part 6 in 1999

Text copyright © Chris Wooding, 2000
The right of Chris Wooding to be identified as the
author of this work has been asserted by him.
Cover illustration © Kanako Damerum & Yuzuru Takasaki
Inside illustration © Steve Kyte

10 digit ISBN 1 407 10408 X
13 digit ISBN 978 1407 10408 9

Printed by CPI Bookmarque, Croydon, CR0 4TD
Papers used by Scholastic Children's Books are made
from wood grown in sustainable forests.

3 5 7 9 10 8 6 4 2

www.scholastic.co.uk/zone

KING
MACAAN

MORACQ

TOCHAA

PRINCESS
AURIN

1

Too Many Mirrors

The corona of Kirin Taq's dark sun was mimicked by the sea below, the rippling waves tearing the hoop of slowly writhing fire into a shivering circular smudge on the black water. The air was the temperature of a cool summer's night, tempered by a sharp breeze that sliced along the coast. But it was not summer; nor was it night, even though the world turned under a velvet-blue sky, and the glow of the sun was barely more than that of a bright moon. Kirin Taq – the dark mirror-world to the sun-washed lands of the Dominions – knew neither seasons nor the cycle of day and night. The sun was a depthless hole in the sky, outlined by its ring of lazily coiling flame, and it never moved.

Crouched along the black-sand beach, the village of Mon Tetsaa threw shimmering blobs of torchlight into the sea, a net of man-made stars that reflected the sprawling outline of the busy fishing port. It was nestled in a large inlet, where two thick arms of land reached out from the coast and formed a natural harbour. Within the sheltering embrace of the cliffs, the beaches were crowded with long, straight jetties studded with tethering-posts and torches mounted on high poles.

The shallow-bottomed boats of Kirin Taq were in profusion all around, black shadows of all shapes and sizes, rocking gently against their moorings. At the harbour mouth, a double-masted ship with a long, narrow keel was slowly ploughing out to open water, almost invisible except for the bright torches along its hull and prow.

Along the waterfront, the inns never closed. Music drifted through the air, the throaty sound of a boneholler clashing with the raucous, jagged chords of a jing vaa playing a little further along. Both were accompanied by the thumping of feet and clapping of hands, different rhythms coming from different inns. The scent of frying fish and heavy spices was thick in the air, and there was sweetbread baking nearby. But for the two strangers who trod the rickety, moisture-warped planking of the waterfront, there was no time for merriment. They had an appointment to keep.

They followed the inns along the main strip, keeping the black beach and the sea beyond on their right. The girl glanced up at the inn signs as they passed; the boy kept a wary eye out from beneath his heavy hood, watching for the cold gleam of Guardsman armour. Eventually, the girl grabbed her brother's arm. "That's it," she said.

He didn't acknowledge her statement, but she knew he had heard her. They continued to walk, making their approach towards the curving, horseshoe-shaped building. In common with most Kirin architecture, it had no hard edges, and the corners were blunted. In the planking of the forecourt stood a tall pole with a banner depicting a striking symbol that furled and rippled in the biting breeze. It was a twisted pictogram, painted in dark slashes of black on a white background, with the lines seeming to curl around and behind each other in a curiously three-dimensional way.

"What's that supposed to be?" the girl asked. The only reply was a shrug. She glanced at her hooded companion, his face deep in shadow. "Chatty today, aren't we?" she observed brightly.

"I shouldn't have come with you," he said. "I stand out too much."

She blew derisively through her lips. "This is a town full of Marginals. Coastal folk. They must get all sorts through here. I bet it's so *exciting*."

The boy sighed. "Are we going in?"

"Oops, better not keep him waiting," she said, and they stepped inside.

The interior of the inn was lit warmly by the glow from a deep fire-trench that ran along the centre of the floor. A triple railing of black wood kept people from falling in, except when it lunged across the trench at one of the many short bridges that spanned the fiery gap. Mirrors on the ceiling spread the light across the room. All around, wicker mats were placed for sitting, and low, teardrop-shaped tables made of a black, reflective stone stood between them.

The boy drew the hood of his cloak closer over his

head. He was aware that hiding his face in such an obvious manner would draw just as much attention as if he showed it. It didn't matter. He couldn't take all their eyes bearing down on him, despite his sister's assurance that they would not notice. The hood stayed on.

"There he is," she said, squinting at someone on the far side of the fire-trench. She looked back at her brother, and gave him a reproachful glance as she saw his hood still up. Sighing to herself, she let it pass without comment. "Come on."

They stepped through the clusters of Kirins, sitting cross-legged on their mats, eating and talking in their lilting, lyrical tongue. The fine bones of the Kirin kind were roughened in the Marginals, generations of hard workers replacing elegance with strength. Their skin was a lighter shade of grey than the deep ash of the purebreeds, and their brows were slightly wider; but the eyes were the same, cream irises on a white background, flicking this way and that as they conversed and gesticulated.

The boy closed his own eyes for a second as if in shame, as he and his sister walked across one of the short bridges that spanned the firepit. A dry, hot updraft billowed up to meet them from the bed of glowing coals beneath, racing under the hems of their cloaks and crawling up their backs. And then it was gone, and they sat down at one of the teardrop tables opposite the man they had come to meet.

"Show me the halfbreed," he said.

4

The boy arranged himself on the wicker mat, and then briefly slid back his hood, exposing his face. His skin was coffee-coloured, a warmer shade than the Kirin grey. His nose was blocky, and his lips a little thicker than usual. But it was his eyes that gave him away; for his irises were a saffron yellow. He pulled his hood over his face again. Half Kirin and half Dominion stock. Half shadow and half light.

"I apologize," the Kirin said nervously, glancing around in case anyone had seen. "You understand I wanted to be sure. Your . . . um . . . face is proof of who you say you are."

"That's alright," the girl said. "And we know *you*'re who you say you are."

"Taacqan," he said tersely, by way of introduction.

"My name is Peliqua, and this is my brother Jaan," said the girl. She was older than the other, seventeen winters by Dominion-time, with red cornrow braids that fell down her back.

"Your brother?" Taacqan queried, his eyes flicking from one to the other. Unlike Jaan, she was a purebreed Kirin.

"Half-brother," she corrected. "But it's only a term. We've always thought of ourselves as brother and sister. We just happen to have different fathers. His was from the Dominions."

Taacqan relaxed a little. Somehow he felt more comfortable talking to her, and avoided meeting her hooded companion's gaze.

"Um . . . would you like drinks?" Taacqan offered.

"It's better if we don't," Peliqua replied apologetically. "We shouldn't stay. You should come and meet the others." She looked up briefly at the mirrors on the ceiling, and frowned imperceptibly. "It's not safe here."

"It would look strange if we came in here to meet this man and didn't stay for a drink," Jaan pointed out in a low, cautious monotone.

"Of course, you're right," Peliqua said, a smile springing to her face. A moment later, her smile faded, one emotion chasing the other off her features. "One drink. And don't mention. . ." she trailed off suggestively. "We could be being watched."

"Um . . . very well," Taacqan said. "I'll get them. What will you have?"

"It doesn't matter," Jaan said, as his sister drew breath to reply. She gave him a look of pique, as if to say: *it mattered to me!*

Taacqan nodded slightly and left. The bar had a room off the main area where drinks were mixed to order, and that was where he headed. He returned a short while later with three wooden cups of jewelberry wine, a clear, blue liquid distilled from the crystalline plants of Kirin Taq. Setting it down on their table, he seated himself and they began to act out the charade of pleasant conversation.

"That sign, out in the forecourt," Peliqua asked cheerily. "What does it mean?"

Taacqan looked around warily. He was putting on a poor display of being at ease. "That? It's for protection."

"Protection against what?"

Taacqan took a shaky swig of wine. "We're on the coast *and* on the borders of civilized society. North of here are the Unclaimed Lands. It's protection against *anything*. The Marginals are a superstitious sort."

"And you're not a Marginal?"

"No. My brother was, but not by birth; he fell in with the ships and never really got out."

"Was?" Jaan queried, surfacing from his habitual quietness for a moment.

"He died," Taacqan replied. "Actually, no, he was *taken*. By the Jachyra. See, he was a Resonant, he just wanted to stay out of the way and go where they couldn't find him but they—"

"Oh! Oh! We shouldn't be talking about *that* here," Peliqua said, flustered and waving her hands.

Taacqan stopped. Was she *really* the one he was supposed to meet? Seventeen winters or so, with such a lighthearted, scatty manner? The other one seemed more reliable, with his spare conversation . . . if he had been a little older, and if he hadn't been a halfbreed. Because after all, who could trust a halfbreed? They had Dominion blood in them.

There was a minute of silence, during which they all sipped at their drinks, the cold, sweet taste in their mouths turning to blooms of glowing heat as it slipped down to their stomachs.

"What's out there?" Peliqua chimed suddenly, making an expansive gesture to indicate that she meant the sea.

Taacqan raised an eyebrow. "Near the coast, there's good fishing. Ships are the fastest and safest way of moving heavy loads in Kirin Taq. There's a lot of money in shipping. You wouldn't know to look at them, but some of the Marginals have got a lot tucked away, where Princess Aurin's taxmen can't reach it." He rubbed his knuckles uneasily. "Course, that's just rumour," he added. "I wouldn't know anything about that."

"But what about *beyond* the coast?" Peliqua asked, fascinated.

"Deepwater," Taacqan replied gravely. "Nobody goes there. No ships ever come back. There are creatures out there the size of this port that could swallow a ship whole."

"*Really?*" she breathed, her eyes sparkling.

"Really," he said. "Anyway . . . um . . . that brings me back to that symbol in the forecourt. The Marginals are afraid that one day the things from Deepwater might start coming closer to the coast. It'll never happen, of course; the waters are too shallow. But they have all kinds of folktales about the day when the Deepwater creatures come inland, though . . . um . . . it's not like anyone actually knows whether they even have *legs* or anything. Only a few people ever saw them and survived, and that was from a great distance. But that's what the symbol is there for. Well, that and the Koth Taraan, but they're a whole different set of dice."

"The Koth—" Peliqua began, but Jaan stopped her by laying his hand on her arm.

"Look," he said, and they followed his shadowed gaze to the doorway of the inn. Three Guardsmen stood inside the door, the fourth stepping in after them. In the glow from the fire-trench, their polished black armour was edged in red, slices of light that slid over them as they moved. Carrying their long metal halberds, they began to disperse, walking purposefully between the sitting groups of Kirins on the other side of the firepit.

"Don't worry," Taacqan said, though he sounded more like he was the one in need of reassurance. "It's just ... um ... a routine thing. They maintain a presence along the waterfront to discourage any—"

"It's not *that*," Peliqua said, alarmed. "It's Jaan. He's a halfbreed, remember?"

"I know," Taacqan said, and for a moment he was unable to conceal the distaste in his voice.

"I don't know if you're *aware* of this," said Jaan, suppressing his anger at Taacqan's tone, "but Princess Aurin isn't keen on Dominion-folk." He leaned closer. "Now the average person just thinks I'm a freak at first glance, but if anyone works out that I'm a halfbreed ... what do you think's gonna happen when people start asking where the *other* half came from?"

"I don't—" Taacqan began, but Peliqua spoke over him, agitated.

"Let's just get out of here," she said. "Is there a way out back?"

"They'd see us leave," Jaan said. "Just sit tight. We'll have to hope they don't look too closely."

But already, a Guardsman was crossing the firetrench, nearing where they sat. As one, they returned to their show of conversation, talking about nothing, pretending not to notice the newcomers like the rest of the inn was doing. Taacqan was sweating, his forehead glistening with moisture, and he stuttered and stumbled over his words; but Peliqua laughed readily at what he said, and she appeared entirely at ease. Jaan was silent, his head bowed beneath his hood, occasionally sipping at his cup of jewelberry wine.

The Guardsman stopped at the table next to them, and began to speak to the people who sat there. Jaan couldn't make out the words, but he could tell by their tone that the replies were civil and curt. Nobody liked Princess Aurin's Guardsmen, but antagonizing them was a sure way to make trouble for yourself. The words exchanged, the Guardsman walked over to Taacqan's table, his tall black frame looming over them as they sat cross-legged on the floor.

"You don't look like Marginals," he stated bluntly, his voice deadened by his full-face mask. His glassy black eyepieces revealed nothing of what was beneath.

"No, we're from further south," Peliqua said, a disarming smile appearing on her face. "We're up here to visit Taacqan's brother. *He's* a Marginal. Well, not by birth; but he fell in with the ships and never really got out," she added, repeating exactly what Taacqan had told her.

Taacqan started in alarm as she blithely told the Guardsman his real name, and he had to bite the inside of his lip to stop himself from making a sound as she went on.

"And I'm Peliqua, and this is *my* brother Jaan," she said, bubbling. "Would you like to join us for a drink?"

"No," the Guardsman replied simply, then turned the blank sheen of his eyepieces on to Jaan. "It's a little hot for such a heavy cloak," he observed.

"Oh, no, you see my brother has a . . . condition," Peliqua said.

"A condition," the Guardsman repeated sceptically. Then, shifting his halberd to his other hand, he reached down and pulled back Jaan's hood. For a moment, Jaan's face was exposed, his yellow eyes glazed and staring, his head surrounded by thick ropes of black hair with threads, beads and ornaments sewn through them; and then he flinched away, trying to hide himself, and Peliqua cried: "Oh! Oh! See?" as she pulled his hood back over his head and got to her feet, facing the Guardsman angrily. People in the room began to turn and stare.

"He had a bad birth, that's all!" she cried. "Our mother died delivering him, and he came out deformed! Did you need to show everyone? Haven't you shamed him enough?"

"Sit *down*!" the Guardsman snapped, lashing the back of his armoured hand across her face. She collapsed with a yelp and lay on the floor, sobbing.

The room was silent. Every eye was turned on the Guardsman, including those of his companions. He shifted awkwardly, and the silence dragged into an eternity. Then he gathered himself, turned to the Guardsmen near the door and said: "There's nothing here. We'll move on."

They left, their footsteps the only sound amid the barely contained hostility in the room. The thud of the door closing behind them resounded through the inn. And then, slowly, the mutterings started, buds of sentences that soon flowered into conversation, and the burble and chatter that was the lifeblood of the inn resumed.

"Um . . . are you alright?" Taacqan asked.

"Let's just get her out of here," Jaan said grimly, helping her to her feet. She pulled her hood over her head, and they left the inn, their steps followed surreptitiously by the gazes of the other revellers.

They had walked a little way along the torchlit waterfront, the chill breeze teasing at them, when Taacqan repeated his question. Peliqua had been sobbing softly as they walked, and he was moved to concern.

"Peliqua? Are you hurt?" he asked.

At that, the sobbing changed note, and turned into soft, gleeful laughter. She threw back her hood, and her eyes were dry. There was a bruise forming on one side of her jaw, but she was smiling.

"I'm okay," she said brightly. "Just stings a little, that's all."

"Then . . . you weren't. . .?"

"Oh, no," she said. "I had to distract him. If it had crossed his mind that Jaan was a halfbreed, he'd have arrested him like they do all Dominion folk. So I provoked him, to give him something else to think about." She felt her jaw. "Ow, but you'd better appreciate this," she said to Jaan. He didn't reply.

Taacqan glanced around, to be sure nobody was near them. The waterfront was never empty, but at the moment there were only a few figures that they could see, walking or idly driving carts of seafood pulled by pakpaks, the leathery-skinned, two-legged riding beasts of Kirin Taq. The sound of music from the inns was distant now, and they were heading into an area of warehouses and storage bays, where the hulking buildings sat quietly.

"Now can we talk about . . . um . . . why you're here?" he ventured.

"Parakka," Peliqua said, forgetting her bruise. "You want to join Parakka, right?"

The word meant much. Parakka was the organization of traitors that had attempted to resist King Macaan's invasion of the Dominions. They had failed in that, but had succeeded instead in establishing themselves in Kirin Taq, where Macaan's daughter

Aurin held the populace in a tight and cruel grip. As their legend had grown, they had become an icon for the dissatisfied; but only a few, like Taacqan, were willing to risk execution and worse by attempting to join.

"That's right," he said. "I want to be part of Parakka. And there are a dozen or so more here who feel the same."

"And how soon can you get them?"

"Within a single cycle. But first I—"

"You want to meet the others we came with," Peliqua finished.

"My associates trust me," Taacqan said defensively. "They're putting their lives in my hands. I have to be sure."

"That's okay, we understand," Peliqua said. "You know, *we* have to be sure as well. We've been watching you for quite some time."

"I guessed you would," he admitted. "But I never saw any sign of it. I suppose that's how it should be." Suddenly he changed the subject. "Why couldn't we talk inside? Too many ears?"

"Too many mirrors," Peliqua said.

"I don't understand," he replied.

"The Jachyra," she said. "Macaan and Aurin's secret police. They travel through mirrors. They *see* through them."

"Mirrors?" he said, incredulous. "But ... I thought ... they were invisible. That they could be anywhere. That they could pluck the thoughts out of your head."

"No, silly, that's just the rumour," she said, laughing. "Macaan started that a long time ago to keep people away from the truth."

"A . . . a *rumour*?"

"You leave a rumour long enough, give it the right soil, and it'll grow into a fact," said Jaan sagely.

They walked off the waterfront after a time, heading across a ridge of scrubland. On the other side was one of the many coves near Mon Tetsaa, a short beach of black volcanic sand hidden by the surrounding land, and invisible from the sea. On the beach, a small campfire burned without smoke, with four figures sitting around it.

Peliqua led them along a steep trail that dipped down to the beach, treading carefully along the rutted dirt track between the tall, night-blue clumps of bladegrass. Without taking her eyes off her awkward descent, she asked over her shoulder: "Why do you want to join Parakka, Taacqan?"

Jaan winced. The way she had said it, it was too obviously a set question. They were supposed to divine the motives behind new recruits by roundabout means, not by asking them directly. Subtlety had never sat easily with his sister. Still, he was interested in Taacqan's response, if only because he thought he'd already guessed why.

"My brother was a Resonant, like I told you," he said, his words sure and unfaltering. He had thought about this a lot. "Sometimes it's like that, you know. Resonant talent doesn't run in families. Well, I'm sure you know that Princess Aurin launched a great operation some time ago to round up any Resonants in Kirin Taq. I suspect she wasn't keen on the idea of people who could flip between the Dominions and Kirin Taq at will; too difficult for her to control."

"That wasn't the whole reason," Jaan said grimly, thinking of the stories he had heard. The Resonants from both worlds that Macaan and Aurin had captured had gone to become part of Macaan's foul living machines, the Ley Boosters. It had happened during the Integration, when the King had merged the Dominions and Kirin Taq so that he could invade the former world. But he did take Taacqan's point; beings that could jump between the two parallel worlds could not easily be bound by walls or cages.

"Anyway," Taacqan continued. "He managed to stay out of the way of Princess Aurin's cull by going to sea and becoming a Marginal. I didn't like what they were doing to Resonants, but I didn't know how to change it. Then he contacted me a few months ago, and told me about something he'd heard while he was travelling." He stumbled a little on the uneven ground, and Jaan, behind him, instinctively grabbed his arm to steady him. Taacqan flinched away from the halfbreed's touch, unable to help himself. Jaan withdrew, his face unreadable beneath his hood.

"Um . . . well," he went on. "Parakka was what he

was talking about. An organization that intended to end the tyranny of Macaan's family. I came up to meet him, but still I wasn't ready to risk everything for the sake of bucking the Princess's law, no matter how much I hated it."

"Is that when the Jachyra took him?" Peliqua asked, her arms out to steady herself as the decline steepened near the bottom.

"Not before he'd managed to contact you," Taacqan said. "But yes, then he was taken. And that was when I decided enough was enough. I met with the others he had talked into joining him, and then went ahead with the plan he had arranged, and . . . now here I am."

The trail dissolved into a short scramble down a bundle of weather-worn rocks, and then they hopped down on to the sand. The four figures by the campfire rose as they approached, leaving their own cloaks where they sat. Peliqua led Taacqan nervously into their presence, followed by Jaan. The faces of those who waited for them were expectant in the firelight.

"Taacqan," Peliqua said, beaming. "Meet Kia, Ryushi, Calica and Ty."

2

The Heartbeat of the Planet

Time in Kirin Taq was marked in a curiously similar way to the Dominions, Ryushi thought, even though there were no seasons or a divide between day and night. Strange, then, that they both operated on a roughly equal twenty-two hour clock. Elani would undoubtedly put it down to her theory of balance, reflection and connection that she used to explain the coexistence of the two worlds. It had become something of a project to her, and Ryushi found it faintly disturbing that a nine-winter child (Dominion time, of course) should be compiling information on such an abstract subject, even if she was basically just expanding on the works of the ancient philosopher Muachi. But then, she should know what she was talking about; after all, she was a Resonant, and there were not many people around today who had more experience of both worlds than she. At least, not many who hadn't already been taken by Macaan for the Ley Boosters.

Ryushi closed his hand around one of the crystalline shards of a nearby Glimmer plant and broke it off from the clump. Up here, on the side of a steep hill just on the edge of the Unclaimed Lands, they grew in profusion. He held it in front of him for a moment, watching the soft blue pulse deep inside it, winking on and off. If he watched it for long enough, it would gradually change to white, and then to yellow, then a dull green, and on through all the colours of the spectrum until it came back to blue. The whole process took around twenty-two hours. The Kirins called it a cycle, and that was how they marked their days. Of course, now he'd broken it off from its connection with the earth, its pulse would gradually fade and die over the space of a few cycles. But—

"Sometimes you are *so* deep," Calica said, sitting down next to him.

"Er . . . what?" he replied stupidly, shaken out of his reverie.

"Lost yourself again, huh?" she asked, a smile curving her catlike cheekbones in the faint light. "What were you thinking?"

"You tell me," he said with a grin, handing her the Glimmer shard.

"Okay," she said, taking up the challenge. She weighed the object in her hand for a moment, then closed her fingers around it and shut her eyes. There was a faint, almost inaudible hum as the pale white spirit-stones that were planted in her spine began to leach energy from the ground. It rose and faded again as quickly. She opened her eyes and handed him the shard back.

The milk-white spirit-stones along Calica's spine allowed her to shape the Flow – the ley energy that formed the lifeblood of the planet – in a curious form of postcognition. She could sense, just by touching an object or being in a place, the events that had occurred in the past concerning it. Sometimes she could even divine the mind of a person by contact with an object they had handled. She had done it once with King Macaan's earring; she had done it with Ryushi many times. But it was an imprecise skill, and sometimes frustratingly vague; and she never seemed to be able to divine the things she *really* needed to know.

"Treading on Elani's ground, aren't we?" she chided, teasing. "She wouldn't be happy if she caught you musing about her work."

"It's just weird," he shrugged apologetically, turning the shard in his hand and studying it. "I mean, every single one of these things pulses in the same rhythm, and in sync. It's like the heartbeat of the planet or something."

"You've got the soul of a poet," she said spuriously. "What colour is it now?"

Ryushi gave her a look. They were surrounded by clumps of the things, all pulsing a tiny light of the same colour in their core. Calica blushed slightly. "Blue," she said sheepishly.

"We're supposed to make our next rendezvous with Taacqan when it's gone red, so that's. . ." he tried to calculate, and then gave up. "I hate these Glimmer things," he stated, vaguely annoyed. "You know how many innocent women and children I'd kill just to get a glimpse of the sun again? It's been a year now. A *year*! And I only know *that* 'cause Hochi keeps a calendar going back at Base Usido."

Calica sighed sympathetically, brushing her orange-gold hair back from her face, and looked out over the Unclaimed Lands. Vast leagues of forested wetlands spread out beneath them, stretching to the horizon and beyond. Enormous, bare shoulders of cold rock humped out of the sea of leaves here and there, and beneath the pale canopy of drooping, water-fat foliage there brooded treacherous marshes. No wonder it was unclaimed, she thought. Who would want it?

She turned her head to look at her companion, watching him as he toyed thoughtfully with the broken shard of the Glimmer plant. Seventeen winters now, he was, though he'd missed the last one because he'd been in Kirin Taq. In profile, she studied his small, elfin features; the slope of his nose, the outline of his chin. In the year that had passed since the Integration, that face changed from the face of a naïve and sheltered boy into something closer to a man. The change wasn't physical; it was in the way he smiled, in the glances he threw, in every nuance of expression. His blond quills had grown longer and thicker, and now they hung about his face in short, rotund tentacles, stiffened with tree sap. The set of his shoulders was stronger, betraying a new confidence in himself that had come upon him since he had first been flung out into the world by the destruction of his home. He had changed, just like they all had; yet he was still the same. And she loved him.

Some treacherous instinct told Ryushi that her eyes were on him, and he looked up. She cast her own gaze down, flushed, embarrassed at being caught staring. He smiled laconically to himself and looked back over the Unclaimed Lands.

"Our luck's gonna run out sometime, you know," he said distantly.

"Yeah," she replied, her cheeks still hot and eager to distract herself with conversation. "But we've had more than our fair share. It's been a year, and Macaan and Aurin still think Parakka was wiped out during the Integration."

"It can't last," Ryushi replied. "I mean, we've been growing and growing, recruiting all over Kirin Taq. But it's not enough. And the more we recruit, the more chance of getting caught." He paused. "Once Aurin knows we're in her territory, she'll hunt every valley and every forest till she finds us."

"Ryushi, you *know* that already," Calica replied. "You've known that all the time. Why the sudden gloom?"

He tilted his head upwards, to where the deep blue-black of the sky was smeared with wispy clouds of light purple. "I dunno. Just a feeling." He absently tossed the shard of Glimmer down the hill. "Like things can't go on the way they are."

Calica frowned. "Well, if they can't, they can't," she said. "But we've done a lot of good here, you know. The Kirins don't *want* to live under Aurin's rule, they just didn't have any way to do anything about it until now. Parakka's given a lot of people a lot of hope. And we're getting strong again. I mean, not like *before*, but—"

"It's not *enough*, though," he said, frustration in his tone. "We could be ten times as strong as this and we still couldn't square up to Aurin's army of Keriags. If we had every Kirin in the land on our side, I'd still only give us a fifty-fifty chance. It's just—"

"You've been talking to Kia, haven't you?" she interrupted gently.

He adopted an expression of exaggerated guilt. "Yeah. She worries about it a lot. She thinks Parakka isn't solving the real problem."

"How so?" Calica asked, interested.

"Well, it's just that recruiting members is fine, but that's all we seem to be doing right at the moment. We can't win by force so why try? We need another way around the problem. We've got a good network of connections now; we should concentrate on something else. It's time to devote our time to trying other solutions."

"She should put it to the Council," Calica suggested. "They'd listen to her."

"She's going to, I think," Ryushi replied.

"Your sister's a strong character," she observed, somewhat reluctantly.

"She's got something against *you*, though," he said. It was bluntly put, but there was no point denying it; they both knew that while Ryushi's twin had long shed the frostiness that she had developed as a defence against her grief at her father's death, she made no secret of her dislike of Calica.

"Yeah," Calica said neutrally.

"What's worse is she won't tell me *why*," Ryushi said, digging the ground with his toe. "I mean, we've not been so close since . . . y'know . . . but it's so *unreasonable* of her."

Calica made a vague noise of agreement. She had her own theories on the subject.

The fire cracked and danced in the hollow, snapping enthusiastically as it stripped the branches of dark wychwood down to char. Wychwood was one of Kirin Taq's greatest natural resources; in the absence of anything like glowstones – such as were common in the Dominions – it provided a smokeless and long-burning fuel for fires and torches, and reduced down to almost nothing when it was done.

Jaan reached into the fire with a stick and poked it about a little, stirring up the already fierce blaze. Next to him, Peliqua was lying on her back, looking up at the sky. On the other side of the shallow depression in the earth, on the edge of the warm hemisphere of light, Ty sat with Kia, his arms around her waist. Since Kia and the others had rescued Ty from Os Dakar over a year ago, the two had been practically inseparable, and by now holding each other was as natural to them as breathing.

"Taacqan seemed nice," Peliqua commented suddenly, breaking the silence that had hung between them for a time.

"I think he was kinda surprised," Kia replied. "He didn't expect to be meeting Dominion-folk. Can you believe that?"

"I guess he just assumed we'd be Kirins," Ty observed.

"It wasn't *that*, it was his reaction that got me," said Kia. "I should be used to it by now, I suppose, but it still catches me once in a while. Y'know, how he got that *what have I let myself in for?* expression. And why? Just 'cause our skin is pink and we've got coloured irises. Where's the sense?"

"But his brother was a Resonant; he said so," Peliqua protested, raising herself up on her elbows and looking across at Kia. The Dominion girl was slim, tall and slightly gangly, with dark red hair in a ponytail and shockingly green eyes. "He *must* have seen Dominion-folk before."

"Old prejudices run deep, and we get scared of people that are different," Kia said. She tilted her head back so she was looking up at Ty. "Remember what Hochi was like with Tochaa?"

"Uh-huh," he said. "Besides, dear Princess Aurin has spent enough time stirring up anti-Dominion sentiment to make our job harder than it already is. She's got the whole of Kirin Taq believing that anyone without grey skin is an outlander pirate from across Deepwater, come to kill their womenfolk and destroy their way of life from within, and Macaan's done the same with the Dominions and white irises."

"Sweet girl," Kia commented. Ty made a noise of sarcastic agreement. "Using our own ignorance about what's beyond the sea to keep us apart."

"You think he'll still turn up for the second rendezvous?" Peliqua said, sounding worried. "Oh, I hope he will! We have to meet the rest of the people who want to join."

"If he doesn't, we're better off without him," Ty replied. "We have to rely on people working *together* against Macaan – Kirin *or* Dominion-born. Parakka won't work if none of us trust each other."

"That's a manifesto if ever I heard one. You're sounding more like me every day," Kia grinned, nudging him in the chest with the back of her head.

"Can I help it if my girlfriend thinks she has a monopoly on politics in this relationship? Getting on the Council has made you too full of yourself."

"You're only jealous," she teased.

Kia had sat on the Parakka Council ever since the Integration, when she had been instrumental in the assault on the Ley Warren near Tusami City. That her suicidal bravery had owed more to blind hatred of Macaan's forces than tactical brilliance didn't matter; the troops had needed something to rally around after their crushing losses in the battle, and she had been it.

Ryushi and Ty, to a lesser extent, had also been hailed as heroes; but the death of the much-respected Otomo – for which some blamed Ty – had cast a shadow on his sacrifice, and Ryushi's discovery of the Ley Booster was seen by some as more lucky chance than anything else. And while Ryushi and Ty were uncomfortable with the attention, Kia had seemed to glory in it.

When the Council reformed after the Integration, casualties had left several posts to be filled. In the midst of the acclaim, the Council could scarcely fail to offer one to Kia, and Calica had advocated that she be appointed, despite the differences between them. Since then, she had been actively involved in the politics of Parakka, and had something of a reputation as an outspoken voice in debates.

Ty, on the other hand, had retreated from public view as much as possible, preferring to keep himself to himself. While Kia had bounced back quickly from the Integration – when she had drained herself to near-death by expending her power beyond its limits – Ty had spent a lengthy period in convalescence, recovering from the wounds sustained in the crash that had killed Otomo. It had given him a taste for peace, after his hectic months as a prisoner on Os Dakar. The skin-dyed tribal colours that he had obtained there had faded over time, his wild black hair had grown back to some extent, and now he looked more like the boy Kia had left behind at Osaka Stud, so long ago. But he had not lost the lean muscle that the hardships of Os Dakar had left on him; nor the haunted look in his eyes, nor the terrible guilt at the atrocities he had committed there.

"I'm bored," Peliqua declared after a few moments, slumping back down to the ground again. Jaan shifted his weight next to her with a rustle. It was the most noise he'd made for an hour or more. "Well, aren't you?" she prompted him, as if his small movement had brought him suddenly back into the realm of conversation.

"I don't *get* bored," he replied.

"I do," she said, as if he didn't already know that. "So let's do something. What about you, Kia? Ty?"

Kia shuffled her shoulders comfortably within the circle of Ty's arms. "I'm just fine here," she said lazily.

Seeing that she was going to get nowhere with those two, Peliqua focused her efforts on her brother again. "Come on, Jaan. There's still three-quarters of a cycle before we have to meet Taacqan. Let's *do* something."

"Like what?" Jaan sighed.

"Let's explore," she said.

"Peliqua, you're such a kid. What's the point?"

28

"Because it's fun!"

"It's *not* fun, it's dangerous. We're right on the edge of the Unclaimed Lands."

"I'll protect you, little brother," she replied with a grin.

"I don't want protection, I want you to leave me alone," he said.

"No you don't," she declared decisively, getting up and dragging him up by the hand. "Come on! Let's get away from these two for a while." She winked at Kia and led her limply protesting brother away from the fire.

"What is *up* with you today?" Peliqua asked. "You've been in a mood ever since we went to Mon Tetsaa."

Jaan waved a hanging vine aside with an expression of irritation. He might have known his annoyingly mercurial sister would drag him straight into the Unclaimed Lands. Her unquenchable sense of adventure was fine at times, but at moments like this it grated on his nerves. And now they had headed into the wetlands, the ground underfoot becoming alternately squelchy and waterlogged or dry and bristly.

"Well?" she prompted, when he didn't answer.

"What did you actually hope to *see* out here?" he asked, deflecting her question.

"I want to climb that big rock," she enthused. "You know, the nearest one that we saw above the treeline."

Jaan squeezed his eyes shut and pinched the bridge of

his nose with his fingers. "That must have been a mile in from the border," he said, praying that she would reconsider.

"Too late to turn back now!" she bubbled happily.

"That's what I thought you'd say," he muttered.

They forged onward, mostly in silence until Peliqua took to talking to herself after Jaan proved unresponsive. This was doubly annoying to him, for he now had a running commentary of everything his inquisitive sister observed, punctuated by little asides to herself about how boring and dull her brother was. As they walked, the going became worse, and they sometimes had to backtrack or detour around small bogs and sections where the dark, brackish water came up above boot-level. The trees and foliage began to take on an oppressive quality, their tubular leaves drooping low and brushing their shoulders and heads occasionally. Jaan was no longer sure that his sister actually knew where she was going, but he followed anyway, murmuring slanders under his breath.

That was when Peliqua stopped, holding out a sleek, grey-skinned arm to warn him to do the same. He was immediately on the alert, his saffron eyes scanning his surroundings. At first, he could not see what had alarmed his sister; there seemed to be no pressing danger, and there was no sound but the distant, plaintive cries of marsh-birds and the stirring of the leaves.

Then he saw.

He had probably been looking right at them and not known what they were. They looked like boulders, hunching out of the wet undergrowth; and they were some distance away, obscured by trees and tall grasses. But now Peliqua pointed them out, he looked hard at them. His mother's blood had given him the Kirin low-light vision, evolved through generations under an eclipsed sun; but even so, he found it difficult to discern any detail there. If he was being logical, there would be no reason to think anything suspicious of the hulking, immobile shapes nearby. Except that they were suddenly surrounded by them, and they hadn't been before.

The boulders had moved.

"Er . . . *this* isn't good," Peliqua said in a small voice.

Jaan groaned. "This is the point where we start regretting the fact that we didn't get to ask Taacqan about the Koth Taraan," he observed dryly.

"Koth Taraan?" Peliqua repeated, breathless with wonder. "Is that what they are?"

"*I* don't know! It's just a best guess!" Jaan replied, exasperated. His gaze flicked from one blocky shape to another; but they were too far away to make out anything beyond their shadowy outlines, and then only in glimpses between the foliage. He glanced back at Peliqua. "Still want to climb that rock?"

"No," she replied. "Uh-uh. In fact, I'm kinda thinking how nice that campfire was."

"Yeah, that's what I was thinking too," he said. "Why don't we just turn round and go back there?"

"That's a good idea," Peliqua agreed. "We could . . . *Oh!*"

Her short gasp of surprise was brought on by the sight of one of the boulder shapes suddenly moving, raising itself a little and then lumbering a few metres before stopping and settling again. In that space of time, she saw that, whatever they were, they were big. At least half her height again, and perhaps more. She had thought she would be able to make out more detail as it stirred, but the poor visibility foiled her. In moments, all was still again.

"Wasn't that the way we came?" Jaan asked slowly, nodding towards the space that the shape had vacated.

"I think so," Peliqua said.

"Think they're trying to tell us something?"

"Uh-huh."

Jaan ran his hands over the spring-loaded dagnas concealed in his sleeves. They were two-foot long, serrated blades hidden inside light wooden tubes on his forearms, that could be unsheathed by knocking the tubes together hard. Their presence reassured him a little. "Come on, then," he said, and they began to walk slowly back towards the border.

The boulder-shapes lumbered aside further as they warily made their way through the gap in the surrounding creatures. Always they were just too far away to be seen in detail, displaying a surprising ability at hiding for such large-framed things. But they appeared to be keeping their distance, and that was what was important. The two trespassers were allowed to leave unharmed; and though Peliqua kept catching glimpses of something following them all the way back, she could not be absolutely certain that it was not just her imagination.

3

No One Left to Tell

Kia drew the Glimmer shard from her belt and looked at it. The pulse at its core flashed a weak browny-red. She'd had this shard for too long; it would soon be time to get another.

"Are we on time?" Ryushi asked, standing next to her.

"I'm not sure. It's so hard to be exact with these things," she replied.

Their meeting-point with Taacqan was a sheltered spot underneath a rocky bluff that hung over their heads. They were surrounded by a sparse smattering of many-armed wychwood trees, their circular blue leaves layered like scales along their limbs. The dark sun brooded in the narrow slash of sky between the treetops and the lip of the stone overhang, watching them.

"I don't like this," Ryushi commented.

"He's not even late yet," Calica said, from where she leaned against the rock wall behind them, turning her katana in the dim light and examining its edge. "You're just having a paranoid day." Calica still hadn't got out of the Dominion habit of referring to day and night; in fact, she maintained it on purpose, as if reluctant to forsake the ways of her homeland.

"We could have chosen a better place than this," Jaan said darkly. "It's well-hidden enough, but it'd be perfect if they decided to ambush us."

"You kidding?" Calica said. She tapped Ryushi on the arm with the flat of her blade. "Our little supernova here could clear the forest for half a mile in any direction if it came to a fight. Anyway, these people are sailors and fishermen, not warriors."

"You sound very confident, Calica," Peliqua said.

"Call it intuition," she replied slyly, "but I've a feeling Taacqan is going to turn up real soon. Alone. And he's picked up a bit of a cold since last time we saw him."

Nobody argued with her; her spirit-stones worked both ways, past *and* future, and she had a disconcerting habit of predicting things that were about to occur. This time was no exception; she had barely finished her sentence before they heard the sound of branches being pushed aside and the soft pad of footsteps on the turf. A few moments later, Taacqan appeared, sneezing explosively as he arrived.

"My apologies," he said. "I've picked up—"

"—*a bit of a cold since last time we saw you*," Peliqua and Ryushi chorused, grinning. Calica shrugged in the background. "Lucky guess," she said, and went back to the nonchalant examination of her blade.

Taacqan frowned, aware that there was some joke going on that he didn't understand, but he decided it

35

wasn't worth pursuing and said: "Are you all ready? The others are waiting nearby."

"Lead us, then," Kia said, pulling her bo staff up from where she had been leaning on it and casting a disparaging glance at Calica.

South of the border of the Unclaimed Lands, the wetland foliage changed to forests of wychwood and haaka, which petered out as they reached the rocky shores and cliffs of the coast around Mon Tetsaa. It was through these forests that Taacqan took them, avoiding the open land in case they should be spotted by the King's Riders on wyvern-back. As a rule, the Riders did not come this far north, tending to stay in the more populous provinces inland, but Taacqan was nervous enough as it was and was in no mood to take chances.

"What happens when you've met the others?" Taacqan asked suddenly, looking at Kia.

"Well, once they've got over the fact that we're Dominion-born—" Kia began, but Taacqan interrupted with: "Oh, I told them that already."

"How did they take it?"

"Two dropped out. They said they wouldn't trust their lives to Dominion-folk. The rest are . . . um . . . wary, but they still want to join. They'll come around more fully when they've had time to think. It was just a bit of a shock. I mean, first the halfbreed and now you four. . ."

"We can't pick and choose our members, Taacqan,"

36

Kia said, a little sternly. "All that's necessary is the will to resist the tyranny you live under. Anything else is purely cosmetic."

Taacqan was silent for a time, leading them through the trees without ever seeming to need to check where he was, sniffing occasionally because his nose was running. Then, at last, he spoke: "We want to learn more," he said slowly. "*I* want to learn more, be of use to you. Against Aurin."

"Then you're welcome," Kia replied. "And if your friends feel the same, we'll take it from there. What you can do depends on your individual skills. Some might be of use to us staying here, being our eyes among the Marginals. Others we might need at one of our sanctuaries. It depends."

The trees began to thin out now, dissolving into the jagged rocks, coves and inlets of the coast. The ground was covered in scrub and shale, and their footsteps changed from thuds to crunches as they made their way down to another cove, this one even smaller and more well-hidden than the one they had first met in. Mon Tetsaa was a distant clump of lights to the north, just visible below the horizon. Here, all was silent but for the susurrant hiss of the waves and the fitful sighs of the wind.

"What are the Koth Taraan?" Kia said suddenly, as if the question had just occurred to her.

"Um . . . why do you ask?" came Taacqan's puzzled reply.

"Well, Peliqua and Jaan said you mentioned them earlier, when you first met," she said, pretending casually to scrutinize the end of her bo staff. "And last night, they went over into the Unclaimed Lands and came across something that they think—"

"They went into the Unclaimed Lands? Why?" Taacqan asked, suddenly distressed. Kia's interest was piqued; the Koth Taraan seemed to be something of an important subject to him.

"It doesn't really matter why; the point is, they did. *Do* you know anything about them?"

"Everyone in Mon Tetsaa knows about the Koth Taraan," Taacqan said. "And the first thing they learn is that they are a *very* territorial people."

"People?" Kia queried.

"Creatures," he corrected himself. "I'm sorry, I . . . um . . . used to come up here and study them. I'd live in my brother's house while he was at sea. I suppose I've spent so much time at it, it's difficult not to think of them as people. But they're not; they're mindless, violent things. Your friends were very lucky, if they got off the Unclaimed Lands alive."

"Are we talking about the same thing here? Peliqua said they looked sorta like boulders from a distance."

Taacqan made a thoughtful face. "Yes, I suppose it would have been them, anyway. There's nothing else that lives this close to the borders that is anywhere near their size. The Koth Taraan wiped them all out. You know, a group of Guardsmen and settlers and so on went in there once; the Princess wanted to expand northward, and they were testing out the territory. They never came back, and a few days later the Koth Taraan attacked Mon Tetsaa. That was about a year ago now. Like I say . . . um . . . terrible, hostile things. Mindless."

"That doesn't *sound* mindless," Kia said. "It sounds like revenge. Warning you to stay off their land."

"Oh, no, it was a rampage. They were angry. All animals get angry if you encroach on their territory."

The descent to the cove was, if anything, even rougher than the last one. The rocks slanted sharply down towards the beach, and water runoff from the higher ground had carved shallow trenches into the stone that made the footing precarious. There was no campfire here, but Jaan and Peliqua, with their keener vision, could make out the group of waiting figures on the black sand below. Eventually, the Parakkans touched down on the beach and strode across towards Taacqan's companions. One of the figures broke away from the main group to meet them. He was unusually stocky for a Kirin, with a close-cut beard of dark blue and heavy brows above his striking white eyes.

"Taacqan," he said gruffly. "These are the Parakkans?"

Taacqan introduced them each in turn, ending with the newcomer, whose name was Aran. "I didn't think you were coming," Taacqan said to his companion. "I hoped my message had reached you."

"Not before time, either," Aran replied. "A day later and I would have been on my way south again, down the coast." He paused. "I'm sorry for your brother, Taacqan. I heard you put up a good fight before they dragged him away. How did you—"

"There'll be time for that later," Taacqan said. "For now, we have to hurry. This is a treasonous business we're on, and if we're caught. . ." he trailed off suggestively.

The other nodded. "Come, then," he said to Kia. "We must meet—"

He was cut short by a scream, tearing suddenly from the throat of one of the women in the group behind him. He whirled, a blade flashing free from his heavy belt; Kia's bo staff snapped into a ready stance; Ryushi's hand was on his sword. For a heart-stopping second, none of them could see the danger; and that sensation was perhaps worse than when their eyes finally fell on what the woman was looking at.

Rising out of the beach, sloughing black sand in a cascade from its narrow shoulders and thin back, was a Jachyra. It was a terrifying scarecrow of a figure, its unnaturally long arms and emaciated legs buried under a motley of belts and rags, sections of its body and face meshed with a dull metal so it was impossible to tell how much of it was flesh and how much was not. The feeble glow of the dark sun glimmered on the lenses of its eyes, one of them telescoping and retracting with a high-pitched whirr as it turned its head to focus on each of the traitors on the beach, settling finally on. . .

+++ **TAACQAN!** +++ it howled, its voice shrill with feedback and crackling with an undercurrent of static.

And then the others broke cover, and suddenly the beach seemed alive, the spindly monstrosities that were King Macaan's secret police rising like corpses from their sandy graves on all sides.

"Ambush!" Ty yelled, swinging his hooking-flail free from his belt. It was one of his mementoes from his time as a prisoner in Os Dakar, and the only weapon he had really learned how to use; three weighted balls on the end of three chains, connected at the junction where he held them, and each ball with a vicious edged fin of metal jutting out from its smooth surface.

Ryushi's sword and Calica's katana scraped free of their scabbards together. "I *knew* this one was gonna go wrong," Ryushi said to himself. Taacqan was wide-eyed in terror, his attention fixed on the creature that was loping across the sand towards him, screaming his name, the sound half-voice and half-mechanism.

"What's this about?" Kia shouted, shaking him roughly by the shoulder. "Did you do this?"

"I didn't betray you!" Taacqan cried, his voice thin with fear. "I didn't!"

"Well *someone* did," she grated, releasing him and gripping her bo staff instead.

And now the screaming really began in earnest, for

the first of the Jachyra had reached the group of Kirins nearby, and with a *shrik* its finger-claws slid out as one of the men ran at it with a shortblade, hoping to defend the others. But as Calica had observed, these people were not warriors. A clumsy swipe at the creature's head was easily ducked, and it raked its metal nails across the man's exposed belly as it passed without even breaking stride, dragging a spume of steaming blood with it. Unnoticed behind his killer, the man dropped shakily to his knees, his hands on his stomach, and slumped face-down into the sand.

"Run!" Ryushi shouted at the other Marginals that were assembled; but they were surrounded, penned in like sheep, and each panicked attempt to disperse only brought them face to mummified face with one of the advancing Jachyra.

"Help them!" Aran bellowed to the Parakkans, but his eyes told them that he knew it was useless. The Jachyra descended on their hapless victims without mercy, and the shrieks and howls of the would-be recruits shredded the air as the creatures set about them in a murderous fury.

It was only because Aran had met the Parakkans halfway between the main group and the edge of the cove that they had been spared the first assault; but several Jachyra had headed for them instead of the Marginals, and they were almost upon them now, with the others that had participated in the slaughter coming fast behind.

"Get out of here! Fall back!" Calica cried, her katana held before her, ready to meet the enemy. "We can't fight them!"

"I really think we *can*," Kia said blandly at her shoulder, and threw out her arms, fingers splayed. The sandy ground before her feet bulged upwards and then tore away from her towards the more distant group of Jachyra, as if some vast subterranean mole was burrowing just beneath the surface of the beach. A moment before it reached them, the bulge exploded in a stinging fountain, and something vast reared out of the earth with a roar, a huge shadow in the sandstorm. The Jachyra balked and hesitated, their lenses whirring in an attempt to see the nature of their opponent; but an immense fist smashed out of the cascade of black sand, pulverizing one of them into the ground with a sickening cracking of bones and tearing of metal.

And then the sand cleared, and they could see. Kia had created a golem out of the beach, a huge, mindless shape in a vague approximation of humanoid form. Sand poured from its arms and down its body, shaking off in great curtains whenever it moved; but Kia was constantly renewing it, replenishing its body as it diminished itself. It opened the great, ragged gash that was its mouth and then, with a bellow, it attacked.

"Kia! We've got to get out of here!" Calica cried. "They'll overrun us!"

But if Kia was hearing her, she wasn't answering. Her hatred of Macaan's forces had ceased to be the

43

controlling force in her life over the last year, but in the heat of combat she found that it still burned just as brightly, and she wasn't going to let these abominations live to massacre any more innocents.

"Ty!" Calica shouted. "Look after Kia!"

Ty nodded, his weapon still held ready. Calica outranked them all, being a former leader of the Tusami City chapter of Parakka, and they knew what a tactician she was. In battle, they bowed to her greater experience. At the same moment, those Jachyra that were not occupied with the golem reached them, led by the creature that was howling Taacqan's name, and the battle was joined.

Jaan and Peliqua leaped as one to meet the attack. Jaan clashed his forearms together, and the blades of his dagnas snapped out with a metallic scrape; Peliqua pulled free the manriki-gusari that was wrapped around her waist. It was a long, thin chain with a heavy diamond-shaped weight at each end. Still in the air, she struck out with it, hoping to entangle the closest Jachyra; the blades of Jaan's dagnas were with her, a twin strike lashing out that would have beheaded the creature had it hit. But it *didn't* hit, because the Kirins had never fought the Jachyra before, and they were completely unprepared for the inhuman speed of their opponents. Still screaming Taacqan's name, the creature dodged their double-attack without even slowing, and rushed past them as if they were not even there. A moment later, the creature's companions joined the fray, and the

Parakkans found themselves in a desperate fight for their lives.

The beach had become a battleground. Nearer the lapping edge of the water, Kia's golem fought with the Jachyra, pitching its huge strength against their far superior reactions. They darted around it as it swung at them, slashing at its legs with their finger-blades. But their attacks did no good against the black sand that was the golem's flesh; its wounds closed as fast as they could make them. Kia was keeping them occupied, preventing them from joining their companions; and occasionally, when one of the Jachyra was careless enough to allow itself to be caught, she had the pleasure of tearing them limb from limb.

Close by, the dark sun looked over the still bodies of those that the Jachyra had slain, lying in a rough heap on the blood-soaked sand.

"Help me!" Taacqan shrieked, as he was pitched off his feet and thrown hard to the sand. Aran ran to his defence, his sword upraised, but the creature that loomed over Taacqan lashed out behind itself without even looking, and opened his throat with its cruelly hooked fingers. He slumped, gurgling, to the sand, while the Jachyra crouched over the prone form of Taacqan.

"*Help me!*" he screamed again, but no one could. They were barely holding the creatures off as it was; nobody could afford to let down their guard for even a split-second.

+++ **You left me, Taacqan** +++ the creature buzzed,

its patchwork face scarcely an inch from his, one claw held under his chin.

"Wh-what?" he breathed, his voice trembling so much that the word was barely recognizable.

+++ You ran. You saved yourself. You let them take me, Taacqan +++ The creature leaned in closer until the metal grille of its mouth was touching Taacqan's lips, and he tasted oil. **+++ How could you do that to your _brother_? +++**

Taacqan's white Kirin eyes widened in horror as the Jachyra leaned back a little, allowing him to see its ragged body, the mummified fusion of metal and flesh that was its face. A short whistle of feedback escaped its mouth, and then it spoke again, a whisper that was mangled by the mechanism that was its voice. **+++ Look what they _did_ to me +++**

"You're not _him_!" Taacqan screamed, suddenly thrashing under the creature, trying to escape from the horror that held him pinned.

+++ Brother +++ it said, the word coming out like a curse. Keeping him held down with one hand, it studied the other one, flexing the dull metal of its fingers before the lenses of its eyes. **+++ You don't seem happy to see me back +++**

"_You're not my brother!_" Taacqan spat in the creature's face.

+++ Not your brother? +++ came the mock-surprised response. **+++ But I remember so well the time when you broke your arm falling from a pakpak,**

down by the tree near Mother's favourite market +++
The Jachyra leaned close again. +++ **I pushed you, don't
you recall?** +++

Taacqan's breath was locked in his throat, a vein
jumping beneath the grey skin of his temple.

+++ **I see that you do** +++ it said, and then, holding
Taacqan's jaw with one hand, buried its claws in his
belly.

Ryushi grunted as his sword bit hard into the leg of a
Jachyra, coming free in a rill of greenish fluid. He
threw his head back as a clawed hand flashed out of
nowhere and narrowly missed his cheek; the creature's
follow-up strike was intercepted by Calica's katana.
Peliqua's manriki-gusari worked alongside Jaan's
dagnas, spinning and flashing through the air, whirling
around her body, entangling and parrying while her
brother struck out with his blades. Ty's hands were also
full, his hooking-flail lashing about him as he fought to
defend Kia, who was concentrating too hard on
maintaining her golem to fight. They were trying to
retreat out of the cove, back up the rocky trail to higher
ground; but the Jachyra were so *fast*, it was impossible
to concentrate on anything beyond the job of staying
alive. Sweat sheened their faces as they blocked and
leaped and ducked; the air seemed full of the slashing
claws of their enemies.

And sooner or later, Kia was going to tire, and
the golem would crumble, and they would be

overwhelmed by the reinforcements on the other side of the beach.

"Ryushi!" Calica said through clenched teeth. "Stop holding back! We're losing here!"

Ryushi half-turned his head at her comment, and one of the Jachyra got a quick swipe at him, the tips of its nails grazing the edge of his throat and drawing a little blood there.

"Okay," he grated, swinging up his sword to fend off the next blow. "Fun's over."

The Flow swelled up inside him with a feverish eagerness, his spirit-stones drawing power from the ley lines that ran invisibly beneath the earth, storing it, regulating it . . . and then releasing it. He thrust out his hand, a cry of exultation escaping his lips, and a shockwave of energy ripped through his body and along his arm, a translucent ripple of force that smashed into the Jachyra directly in front of him and annihilated it. He swung the torrent of energy towards the other Jachyra that assaulted them, blasting them apart like leaf-piles in a gale, their mechanical screams drowned in the roar of energy that poured through his body. Those who were not hit by the first blast tried to run. Some made it away, some didn't; but by the time Ryushi managed to rein himself in, the beach was a charnel house.

All was silence in the aftermath. Ryushi stumbled weakly, his legs beginning to give, but Calica bore him up. In the dim light, the glistening lenses of the distant

Jachyra watched them warily. Even those that had been fighting Kia's golem had retreated to a safe distance, and were silent.

"Taacqan!" Ty suddenly exclaimed, and he ran to where a dark shape lay on the sand, its hand raised feebly. He knelt down next to the wounded Kirin, but one look at the horrendous gash in his stomach told him that there was nothing he could do. Taacqan looked up at him, struggling to speak, and Ty took the dying man's hand as he breathed his final words.

"I . . . was a coward," he said, labouring for the strength to form his words. "I didn't try to save my . . . my brother. I ran . . . and left him to die. I lied to the others about what . . . what I had done. Tell them!"

Ty's gaze was full of pity. "There's no one left to tell."

Taacqan gripped his hand hard. "The Jachyra . . . it was my brother . . . he knew things . . . only we knew. . ." he coughed, and there was a rattle from deep in his throat. "It . . . was . . . him. . ." Then suddenly, his eyes went wide, as if in alarm, remembering something he had so say before his essence finally left him. He clutched Ty's shirt front desperately with his free hand. "The Koth Taraan . . . and the Keriags . . . they . . . can. . ." he breathed, and then his eyes closed, and he died. The Jachyra that he had spoken of was nowhere to be seen, having retreated with its companions and cloaked itself in shadow.

For a moment, nobody moved. The Jachyra were keeping a safe distance, now with a healthy respect for

Ryushi. The golem had stilled, and was crumbling away, its arms and legs running in cascades to join the beach again.

"Back off and let's leave," Calica said. She didn't need to add why. Ryushi wouldn't be able to pull off another burst of energy for quite some time. He had been holding back because he knew he would drain himself to exhaustion if he cut loose; and if the Jachyra sensed that, they would attack again with redoubled fury, and Parakka would have another helpless fighter to defend.

In the year since the Integration, Ryushi's ability to control his enormous power had improved slightly, but not much. It was still an uncontrollable beast that, once released, would have to be manhandled back into captivity before it burned him out. He'd bluffed a Jachyra before, in the Ley Warren near Tusami City, into believing he had a greater mastery of his power than he really did. Calica was gambling that it would work again. All evidence so far had shown the Jachyra to be essentially cowardly creatures, sneak-attackers and assassins who generally only fought when they knew they would win. Ryushi had given them something to think about now, and they were not keen for another taste.

And so, slowly, with their eyes never leaving the scarecrow silhouettes of their enemies, the Parakkans began to climb the rocky trail up the cove to the high ground, leaving their dead behind them, the scent of blood rising from the beach and mingling with the sharp salt tang of the sea.

The Jachyra watched them go, motionless. None of them made any move to pursue.

For a time, there was only the sound of the sea.

And then, without a signal or a word, they turned as one and descended on the Jachyra who had killed Taacqan, and tore it apart.

4

Cold Gem Lying

The mainland of Kirin Taq was a webwork of provinces and their boundaries. The independence of the thanes – the rulers of each province – had been taken when King Macaan took control of Kirin Taq, turning those thanes that he did not execute outright from politically powerful figures into little more than caretakers for his land. Unlike in the Dominions, where Macaan had destroyed the thane system entirely, he allowed a diluted version of it to exist in Kirin Taq, to help watch over the land while his daughter grew and his attention was on the conquest of the other world.

Since Macaan had taken the throne in Kirin Taq, the provinces had remained strictly in order, with the family lines of the existing thanes gradually being replaced by Macaan's favourites. His influence stretched from the Unclaimed Lands in the north to the Iron Coast, far to the south; and through all the generations his family had ruled from the same seat of power. Standing at the nexus of six provinces, the hub of Kirin Taq; the royal palace, Fane Aracq.

It stood atop a high hill, honeycombed with roads

that led away to the surrounding lands. It was a masterpiece of Kirin architecture, a construction of soaring spires and parapets that displayed no sharp edges at all. Made entirely of creamstone, it looked as if it had been carved from cloud. Standing white and ethereal in the twilight, it had no regular shape, no symmetry at all in its construction: high walkways spanned gaping drops between towers; tiny domes like bubbles nestled at their bases in clusters; blunt needles of stone bristled out in sprays, fulfilling no obvious purpose except to add to the beautiful chaos of the palace. It was a creation like no other had been before or likely would again, and it was the home of Princess Aurin, ruler of Kirin Taq.

She stood at one of the oval wind-holes of her chambers, looking out over the land beneath her. The distant torches of a city; the beautiful blue-green fields; the banks of crystalline flowers at the edge of a river so clear that the water could only be seen by the reflection it threw of the black sun's light. All of it was hers, given to her by her father. It meant less than nothing to her. It had taken no effort on her part to attain; it was given half out of necessity and half out of guilt. Her father had needed to leave the land in safe hands, and she was his only bloodline since the death of the Queen, long ago. And it was his way of trying to make up for her childhood, the latest of his many gifts to her, as if any material possession, even one as grand as this, could make her love him as she had her mother.

She turned away from the window. Her chambers were lit by the rare white glowstones, imported from the Dominions, that sat in brackets around the curved walls. A low, smooth table rose out of the floor, carved from the very stuff of the room itself, and was surrounded by ornately-patterned wicker mats and cushions. Fragile ornaments in shades of blue sat on the wide sills of the glassless wind-holes. A huge mirror formed part of one wall, its wrought-iron frame sending writhing tentacles sewing in and out of the creamstone, meshing it to its setting. It was an exact copy of another one, a world and half a second away, in her father's sanctum in the Dominions.

For a time, she studied her own reflection. The young woman who looked back at her was strikingly beautiful. Tall and willowy, she wore an elegant white dress trimmed in turquoise, and long, tight-fitting gloves of the same colour. Her hair, in sharp contrast, was the darkest black, worn in two loose plaits at the side that coiled around to meet the rest of the silken fall in a clasp. The only jewellery she wore was a triplet of turquoise stones, a larger one flanked by two smaller ones, linked by a pair of thin silver chains around her neck. The necklace was as much a part of her as the curved lines of her eyes or the sleek bow of her shoulders. She never took it off. She couldn't. Her life depended on it.

A subtle change in the ambient pressure of the air warned her that a visitor was imminent. She took a small step back from the mirror and waited. A few moments later, a ragged, filthy claw breached the reflective surface as if breaking through a film of water – though there were no ripples as it came – and the hunched and ragged form of Tatterdemalion, Chief of the Jachyra, stepped through into the chamber.

+++ **My lady** +++ he said, dropping to one knee before her and bowing.

"You don't have to do that, Tatterdemalion," she said. "I think we have gone beyond the need for ceremony between us, yes?"

+++ **As you wish** +++ the Jachyra said, rising to his usual bent, slouching stance, his weight perfectly balanced to react to an attack from any quarter.

"You have news?"

+++ **I do, my lady. What we have long suspected has been proved at last. Parakka are here** +++

Aurin did not even blink at the information. "Tell me what happened."

+++ **We received word about a Resonant living among the Marginal community some time back. Complying with your orders to round up all the —** +++

"My *father's* orders," she corrected tersely.

+++ **My apologies. When we captured this Resonant, it was decided that he was a suitable candidate for ... conversion** +++ Tatterdemalion shifted uncomfortably. +++ **After the process was complete, he revealed that he had been a Parakkan sympathizer, and that he had arranged to meet with** them a short while before we took him. He suspected that his brother would continue his attempt +++

"And you saw a chance to locate the Parakkans and follow them back to their hideout," Aurin finished.

+++ **I misjudged the new recruit** +++ Tatterdemalion buzzed amid a crackle of static. +++ **He retained a grudge of some kind against his brother. His intention was to ambush and kill him. We hid ourselves at the rendezvous, but he broke cover and gave us away. Our hand was forced. We attempted to kill or capture the Parakkans; but we suffered losses and were forced to withdraw** +++

"And the new recruit?"

+++ **He was executed for his actions** +++ the Jachyra stated without emotion.

"Good."

Aurin turned away and went to the window, her fingers splayed across the sill as the cool wind stirred her hair. Tatterdemalion followed her uncertainly, loping across the room to stand a short way behind and to the left of her.

"Who knows of this?" she said at length.

+++ **The Jachyra. No one else** +++

"You will not tell my father." It was an order, not a question.

+++ **Understood, my lady** +++

She ran her fingertips across the cold gem lying against her collarbone. "How goes things in the Dominions?"

+++ There was a little resistance to begin with, as you know. Since then, there has been nothing. Parakka were the most potent force against us, and they failed to hold us back. The combined forces of the Keriags and the Guardsmen have subjugated utterly the mainland Dominion civilization, excepting the sparsely populated steppes in the East and portions of the southern deserts. The nomadic folk of those places are difficult to find and bring to heel, but they are an insignificant threat and apparently too concerned with their own problems to oppose your father +++

"Oh yes," she said, with a hint of a smile. "The desert folk have the Sa'arin to worry about, and the Nomen have a hard enough time just surviving. Doubtless they still prefer their primitive existence to my father's rule."

+++ **Doubtless** +++ Tatterdemalion agreed neutrally.

"And besides, he hasn't *utterly* subjugated anything," Aurin said. "The Machinists' guild remain autonomous, and the Deliverers remain free."

+++ **The Machinists are a mercenary organization, and will work for whoever pays them. Your father sees no need to waste the manpower in bringing them under his heel** +++

Aurin laughed, low and humourless. "Or perhaps he thinks he can't penetrate the Citadel? I should imagine he will find that something of a task if he tries, yes?"

+++ **Possible. I am merely reporting his words** +++

"I'm sorry, Tatterdemalion. Please go on," she said, glancing over her shoulder at him.

+++ The Deliverers remain a mystery, both as to where they come from and how they operate. The King is intending to implement a system similar to the one in Kirin Taq, to choke off the supply of spirit-stones to those not of noble blood, or in the employ of those nobles. That will make the Deliverers next to redundant, except to service his future troops and allies. He will seize the mines, and make it treason for a commoner to have stones. It will crush once and for all the chance of rebellion. But it will take time +++

Aurin was silent for some while, her eyes focused on the middle distance, looking out over the half-lit realm that she ruled. Meaningless, all of it. She cared nothing for the realm, nothing for the tracts of land that the people clutched for, nothing for the pathetic little insects that scurried about in their useless jobs and pointless lives.

+++ And the uprising in Kitika, my Lady? +++

"Uprising?" she laughed. "Please don't grace it with so grand a title. A few traitorous bandits in an insignificant little manufacturing town hardly constitutes an uprising, yes?"

+++ I informed you of its beginnings two cycles ago. I think it unwise to leave a decision any longer +++

She sighed, as if bothered by the troublesome inconvenience of a reply. "Send some of my father's Guardsmen. Take the Jachyra to be sure nobody escapes. Kill the rebels. Send their families to the mines. Then kill the ruling council for allowing the cancer of dissent to thrive in their town." She paused, then added as an afterthought. "Kill their families, too."

+++ And what will you have me do about Parakka, my lady? +++

"I will deal with Parakka," she said, the faintest wisp of a smile crossing her face.

5

Windows into the Past

The Rifts ran along the edge of the Fin Jaarek mountain range, hugging the eastern shores of Kirin Taq's waist. The name was given to a vast stretch of dense forest that hid a network of valleys, canyons and shattered terrain beneath its cool, dark foliage. Sections of land would suddenly plunge hundreds of feet to a plain many miles across, and deep, bottomless cracks zigzagged unpredictably across the ground. It was a hostile place, populated by all kinds of beasts that had thrived in the environment and adapted to be equally as hostile as their surroundings. The Kirins steered clear of it, preferring the mountains to the east or the plains to the west. Only a few isolated collectives of people lived there, those who were willing to brave the vicious world that the Rifts offered in exchange for rich land and relative freedom from Aurin's rule.

One such isolated collective was Parakka.

Hochi sat on the edge of his sleeping pallet, his huge shoulders and back outlined in the orange light of the glowstone in the bracket behind him. His face was in shadow, his heavy brow creased sternly as he contemplated the tiny object in his massive hand. It was a small silver pendant, its thin chain curled haphazardly across his palm. It was wrought in the shape of the hollow corona of the Kirin Taq sun, with a symbol set in the circular gap in its centre. Hochi had been gazing at it for a long time, studying the swirls and curves that made up its shape. Tochaa's parting gift to him, entrusted to his care as the Kirin died in his arms in the Ley Warren during Parakka's doomed battle to prevent the Integration.

A year now, and he still had no idea what it meant.

The pendant represented many things to him. Guilt, first and foremost. Tochaa had lost his own life defending Hochi from the Keriags, when Hochi had never treated him as he deserved; he had seen only the grey skin of a Kirin, instead of the man beneath, and it had taken Tochaa's death to make him see otherwise. It also represented the promise he had sworn, to introduce Parakka to the Kirin people, to help them raise themselves from under the yoke of Macaan's family. That was the job he had dedicated himself to for the past year, and he had worked tirelessly at it. But it wasn't enough. He still felt that he was missing the true nature of the task that Tochaa had given to him; and the answer was there, in his hand, if he could only see it. . .

"Hey, Uncle Hochi!" Elani chimed as she swung around the doorframe and propelled herself into the room. She entered the room at a run, but his heavy mood and lack of response caused her to slow down, her smile fading, until she came to a halt next to him.

"I'm sorry, did I bring you down, Elani?" he asked, giving her a halfhearted smile.

"Course not, Uncle Hochi," came the depressed reply. "Whatcha doin'?"

Hochi slipped the pendant back over his bull neck; it was a little too tight for him, but he was fortunate that Tochaa had worn it loose. "Thinking, I suppose."

"Careful," she warned.

"Thanks."

She sat down on the pallet next to him and huffed out a sigh. "You've been doing too much thinking recently, Uncle Hochi. I never get to see you."

"I'm busy, Elani. You know how much work it takes to keep an organization like this running? Just co-ordinating the different groups is—"

"*I'd* be busy if you'd let me go with the others when they're out recruiting," she said pedantically.

"You know you can't," he replied. "Besides, you're one of our only Resonants. You're too valuable to risk, even if I let you." Elani looked at him hopefully. "Which I *wouldn't*," he added, watching her face fall.

"Why do I have to be valuable?" she moaned. "Can't I be expendable, like Gerdi?"

"Gerdi's not expendable, he's just a pain in the—"

"Hold it, boss-man, or you'll say something you regret," came a voice from the doorway, and the subject of their conversation sauntered in, wearing a wry grin under his shock of green hair.

"Oh good," murmured Hochi sarcastically. "Just what I need."

"Hi, Gerdi!" Elani beamed. Hochi and Gerdi's weird relationship never ceased to amuse her. They both expended so much effort on disguising the affection they felt for each other, when it was plainly transparent to everyone that there was a deep respect between them.

He saluted her smartly. "How you goin', Elani?"

"I'm bored," she moaned, pulling a maudlin face.

"Then I've got just the thing for you," Gerdi declared. He cast a look over at Hochi and added: "You too, Hoch. You've been sitting on that pallet for so long it's starting to warp under you. Not that it'd *take* long."

Hochi didn't even bother rising to it. He wasn't in the mood for one of Gerdi's endless routines of jabs about his weight or his huge belly.

"Whew," Gerdi said, throwing up his hands. "If *I* got that much enthusiasm on *my* return from the north, I'd go and join Aurin instead of hanging around with you lot."

"They're *back*?" Elani cried, jumping excitedly to her feet.

"Uh-huh. Sighted on the clifftops. They'll be here any minute."

"Come on, Uncle Hochi!" she said, grabbing his hand, her small fingers dwarfed in his wide palm. He heaved himself off the edge of the pallet, wincing slightly as the wound in his leg twinged. It was a souvenir from the Integration, when a Keriag had plunged a *gaer bolga* spear through his thigh; because of the hooked serrations on the spear, it had never really healed properly. Sighing, he allowed himself to be led outside.

Base Usido was Parakka's core of operations in Kirin Taq. Given the short amount of time that they'd had to set it up, it had flourished fast over the year since its inception; but its success had been dearly bought. The Rifts were a dangerous place, and many lives had been lost during the construction of the defences that ringed its edges. Even now, they could not afford to relax their guard against the dangers of the Rifts; but it was a necessary sacrifice, for only in a place like this could Parakka have remained undetected for so long.

It was as if the ground had been stamped in by some immense, misshapen foot. An enormous section of the forest floor, spanning many leagues, seemed to have simply dropped three hundred feet down from the surrounding land and formed an inverted plateau, a great plain surrounded by miles of sheer cliffs. The perimeter of Base Usido ran out in a semicircle from one such stretch of cliffs, swallowing up hundreds of acres of the grassy blue plain that it sat on. Its walls borrowed something of their design from those used in the stockades of Os Dakar; the high stone barricade was surrounded by a lethal brace of metal stakes, angled upwards and outward.

Hochi's hut was only one of many cut from the flexible, dark red wood of the abundant haaka trees. It sat in a cluster near one of the cliffs that rose at the back of Base Usido, a wall that thrust upwards so high that it seemed to lean over the group of buildings beneath it. Its stone skin was impregnated with lifts, winches and pulleys, allowing access to the clifftop fortifications that defended the rear of the settlement.

As they stepped outside, they entered the never-ceasing atmosphere of industry that the Base operated under. Nearby, a courtyard and a group of small offices formed the wyvern-pens; three of the magnificent creatures waited there now, their double-pairs of wings folded at their side, shifting their weight expectantly on their immensely muscular legs. The riders on their backs, lying against the wyverns' bony spines in padded harnesses, were being instructed by somebody on the ground; but a high wooden wall obscured him or her from view. As they watched, one of the wyverns bunched its squat body and then lunged upwards, leaping a clear fifty feet, its split tail trailing behind it. Then it spread its wings, the huge ones at the back opening out before the smaller forewings, and propelled itself upwards with a screech towards the sky.

"When is Cousin Ryushi getting Bonded?" Elani asked, reminded by the sight. "He's always going on about becoming a rider, getting to have his own wyvern companion that only he can fly."

"Not till he comes of age," Hochi said. "Those are the rules. He only has another year to wait."

"A *year*? But—"

"Getting Bonded is not as straightforward as it looks, Elani," Hochi said, his deep voice smoothing over her high squeak. "To have a mental link that close with another creature, it's a big responsibility. Wyverns are intelligent creatures too. They have their own will. It's not just a matter of control, it's a kind of kinship. Even Bonding at your eighteenth winter is too early sometimes. Kia and Ryushi's father gave them Bonding-stones a long time ago, and I argued with him then about it. In his place, I have to look out for them. I owe him that much." He paused. "They haven't come of age yet, Elani, and until then I won't let them complicate their lives further with something like Bonding."

"O-*kay*, I just asked," Elani sighed, wearied by the long explanation.

As they went further through the Base, they passed more evidence of the self-sufficiency of the colony: a steam-driven sawmill; a small, crude hatchery; a training field; a water pump and a small reservoir; a longhouse similar to the one in Gar Jenna, their old hideout in the Dominions. Most of the metal had been cannibalized from the war-machines that had survived the battle at the Ley Warren, and assembled by those Machinists that worked for Parakka. It was not an easy life in Base Usido, but it was better than for many who lived outside the Rifts.

They reached the main gate just as it was being winched closed behind the new arrivals, screeching as its two metal halves slid together on vast rollers. Six riders were dismounting from their pakpaks, passing their tethers to handlers who waited to stable the tired beasts. They had come down to the plain via one of the many mechanical haulage lifts that dotted the edges of the cliffs, and ridden the rest of the way to the gate. Now, as Elani saw them, she let out a whoop of excitement and ran up to her "cousin", Ryushi. He was one of her wide range of adopted family members, which included Kia, Hochi and the twins' dead father Banto.

"Hey, El," he said wearily, as she launched herself into his arms and hugged him. She squeezed him tight for a few moments, before it dawned on her that Ryushi's reciprocation was only half-hearted.

"What's wrong?" she queried, drawing back so her wide eyes could search his.

"We got trouble," he said gravely. "Aurin knows we're here. We gotta call the Council."

The longhouse was silent as Kia sat down again, her red hair aglow in the flickering light. Her report of the incident at Mon Tetsaa had given everyone something to digest, both the Council members that were sat in a circle around the deep firepit and those that stood beyond the glow, where the torches had been purposely extinguished to emphasize their non-involvement. Everyone was allowed to listen to the Council; but those that had not been elected were only allowed to speak at the Council's discretion. Until then, they had to stand outside the island of light in the dim blackness.

Kia shifted herself slightly on the wicker mat that she sat on, her green eyes moving from one Council member to another, awaiting their response. Age was of no importance in Parakka – a person was judged on their merits, not on their experience – and at least a quarter of the members were under twenty winters in Dominion-time. A good proportion of the Council were Kirins, too, when there had been none before the Integration. Times had changed. Since the Dominion-folk in Parakka had been flipped to Kirin Taq after the battle at the Ley Warren, the majority of their subsequent numbers had been made up of the native people. Her eyes fell finally on Calica, meeting her gaze levelly across the sullen coals of the firepit.

"It seems, then," said the Convener, a gaunt Dominion man with lank white hair, "that our time has suddenly grown short."

"I disagree," came another voice. Unsurprisingly, it was a young Kirin called Baki who protested. He always played the opposing viewpoint, even when he did not believe it himself. It was his way of balancing both sides of an argument. "So Aurin knows we're here in Kirin Taq. I have no doubt that she suspected all along; our spies have reported much the same from what they have gathered in the cities. But she doesn't know where we're hiding. She still can't find us. We're in no greater danger here than we were before, and we shouldn't rush things. We have to be more careful, and that means *not* hurrying."

"Two seasons ago, that would have been true," Calica said, still maintaining her habit of marking time Dominion-style. "But not now. The few free Resonants that we have managed to make contact with tell us that Macaan has the Dominions well under his power now. That's largely thanks to his taking a large portion of Aurin's army of Keriags with him. Soon he won't need them any more, and Aurin can recall her troops and use them to scour every inch of Kirin Taq until they find this place."

"We should bolster our defences around the Rifts, then," said one of the other members.

"Well, that goes without saying—" someone else began, but Kia suddenly interrupted him.

"What's the *point*?" she cried, silencing everyone for the second time. "You can't defend against the Keriags. Not with what we've got. We don't even have our war machines anymore. We scrapped them all to get the raw materials to build this place. Wasting time and resources on trying to stop those things is just senseless. If the Keriags get to Base Usido and we're still here, we all die. It's that simple."

Her pronouncement took a few moments to sink in. She glared at Baki, daring him to contradict her. The other members of the Council were recalling what they knew of the creatures called the Keriags. Most of the Kirins had seen them first-hand; to the Dominion-folk, they were largely known only by their fearsome reputation. Tireless, insectile warriors, endless in number and near-unstoppable, they had been responsible for the deaths of many of Parakka's troops during the Integration.

"I assume you have a—" the Convener began. He was about to say *suggestion*, but Kia talked over him.

"Yeah, I *do*," she replied hotly. She had everybody's ear now. "We've been trying ever since the Integration to investigate Aurin's hold over the Keriags, to work out why they obey her. It's not worked. The Jachyra are too smart, and they keep our spies out of her palace. It's a miracle none have been caught trying to get in and interrogated. So we need a new angle. I want to go and try the Koth Taraan."

A murmur rippled around the darkness outside the firelight. Kia had explained what they had learned about the creatures during her report, and relayed what Taacqan had told her about them.

"But the Koth Taraan are mindless beasts. You said so yourself," the Convener stated.

"Yeah, that's what Taacqan told me. He was very clear on that point. In fact, he made a little *too* much effort to make out that they were mindless and violent. But when Peliqua and Jaan had a run-in with them, they didn't seem like either. I think he was keeping something from us, for one reason or another." She rubbed the back of her neck. "I think he might have been protecting them. I don't think I'd have realized any of this, but for what he said to Ty at the end. He said something about the Koth Taraan and the Keriags. I don't know what that meant exactly—"

"It's something of a tenuous reason for travelling all the way back to the Unclaimed Lands, don't you think?" Baki interrupted derisively.

"As an alternative to sitting on my hands in Base Usido and getting massacred, I think it's pretty good," she replied, smiling sweetly at him.

"Now hey, nobody's sitting on their hands!" protested another member.

"That's all we *have* been doing!" Kia cried. "We've been maintaining the illusion of doing a lot and getting nowhere. And there's no time for that any more. I'm gonna try something different. Alone if I have to, but I think it would greatly increase my chances if some others were to come along with me. *If*, of course, the honourable Council will allow it." She said this last sentence in a tone that suggested she was going whether they liked it or not. The motion was voted on and carried.

Other things were discussed that night, including what they had learned of the Jachyra from the events that had occurred at Mon Tetsaa. Taacqan's brother was a Resonant, that they knew. And if he was to be believed, the Jachyra that had killed him had been his brother also. What, then, had happened in the meantime? Were *all* the Jachyra Resonants? Did that explain their ability to pass through mirrors; was it some kind of twist on their natural abilities? Conjecture and guesswork, and no solid proof. There was little that could be done. Baki made a new call to send their best spies to Fane Aracq to try and infiltrate Aurin's palace, but the motion was denied. Too many chances had been taken that way already. They needed somebody on the inside, needed it *desperately*; but there seemed to be no way of *getting* there.

Days passed in the Dominions, but in Kirin Taq it was only the repetitive cycle of colours within the abundant patches of Glimmer plants that told of the passing of time. Preparations were being made for Kia's trip north, along with the multitude of other missions that had been forced into action by the incident at Mon Tetsaa. Messengers were leaving for all corners of the land; diplomats were being sent to the tribes in the Rifts to negotiate their support; the wyverns' breeding programme was being stepped up, and new blood needed to be imported, so merchants had gone to buy battle-wyverns. The defences were being shored up, also, for despite Kia's protest against that motion she had been voted down. Like the Convener had said, time had suddenly grown short, and everyone in Base Usido was keenly aware of the fact.

"Hey, sis," Ryushi said, materializing at Kia's shoulder as she adjusted the saddle on a pakpak. She jumped and swore, and the pakpak crabbed away nervously. Ryushi caught its reins, and Kia soothed it for a moment before turning to her brother.

"You scared me," she said with an embarrassed smile.

"Didn't mean to," he replied. She could tell by his

72

expression that there was something he wanted to talk to her about. They were twins, even if they hadn't acted like it for a long while, and she knew him better than anyone.

She glanced up at her pakpak. "You wanna go for a ride?"

"In the Rifts? Not too safe," Ryushi said.

"You think *we* need to be worried?" she asked, goading him.

"Not really," he admitted. "I just thought I'd say."

"Go get a ride and saddle up, then. I'll race you out."

Ryushi returned shortly with a mount of his own, and they cantered their pakpaks to the gate in silence. Once the lookouts had pronounced the plain beyond all clear, they were allowed to leave. The gate began to slide noisily shut behind them.

"When the gate closes, we go," Kia said. "First to the mottled cliff."

"I'll have a fire ready when you get there," Ryushi grinned.

The gate clanged shut, and they dug their heels into the leathery flanks of their mounts. The pakpaks' strong hind legs gave them extraordinary acceleration, and they sprinted across the plain at a staggering pace. The wind blew the twins' hair into whirls, pushing at their faces and shoulders as the blue-black grass beneath them was eaten up by the long strides of the pakpaks. Kia yelled in exhilaration as she began to outpace her brother, bent low against the neck of her mount. The

73

beasts skipped along the plain, their two-toed feet propelling them forward in low bounds, their tiny front limbs hugged close to their chests.

The race lasted only a few minutes, but to the twins it seemed longer in the rush of adrenalin. Ryushi had come to enjoy these windows into the past that he shared with his sister, when everything between them was as it had been before their father had been killed. There were precious little of them nowadays. When they eventually came to a stop, Kia had beaten him soundly, and had already dismounted by the time he pulled up next to her.

"No fair; you chose the faster one," he said breathlessly.

"Half of winning is forward planning, bro," she replied.

The mottled cliff was a section of the towering walls around Base Usido that was covered in patches of a curious green-brown fungus that held a dim luminescence in the twilight of Kirin Taq. They settled at its foot, after checking as far as they could along the plain for anything dangerous about. The only signs of life were a flock of bright wading-birds, shadowy outlines in a nearby pool.

"So, you decided if you're coming with me yet?" Kia prompted as they lay half-reclined on the grass, chests heaving with the exertion of the ride. The pakpaks, nearby, had taken to cropping grass in the way they always did when left unattended for more than thirty seconds. "You've only got a cycle left to decide."

"Yeah," he said. "I'm not."

"Oh," said Kia, sounding a little surprised and disappointed. "Okay."

There was silence.

"Is this about Calica?" she asked.

"Why should it be?" he replied.

"Well, you do spend an awful lot of time with her. . ."

"I don't seem to have anyone else to spend it with, now do I?" Ryushi was unable to keep the accusation out of his voice.

"You're sore about something," Kia said, lying back on the grass.

"Yeah, now that you mention it, I am," he replied. "Am I still your brother or what?"

"Course you are," she said, frowning. "What kind of—"

"No, you don't seem to get me. *Takami*'s our brother, but he's also a murdering, honourless bag of filth. I mean more than a biological brother, more than a brother in name only."

Kia raised herself up on her elbows and sighed. "Stop dancing around the subject and tell me what you're getting at."

"We don't act like twins any more, Kia. We'd barely pass the grade as friends. *Acquaintances* is more like it." Ryushi looked out over the plain, his eyes becoming distant. "We didn't *used* to be acquaintances."

"A lot's changed since then," Kia replied quietly. "People have died."

"*We* haven't," Ryushi shot back. "It's – oh, there's no

75

point to this. It's not like this conversation is gonna alter anything, is it? You've got Ty now, anyway. What do you need with a brother?"

"Is *that* what this is about? And what've you been doing with Calica, you hypocrite?"

"I've gotta spend my time with *someone*," Ryushi argued. "What do you expect? You've been icing me out for the last year."

"Yeah, but *Calica*. . ." she said, a hint of something distasteful in the word.

Ryushi got to his feet and turned on her, angrily. "What is your *problem* with her? You think you can shut your own twin out of your life and then reserve the right to judge what he does? Uh-uh, it doesn't work like that. You forfeited all that a long time ago."

"What do you *see* in her?" Kia cried, rising with him. Their conversation had degenerated into a shouting match by now, such as they had not had in a long time. "I mean, what is she, really?"

"She's a *friend*," he replied.

Kia laughed, genuine amusement in her eyes. "You really believe that? *Please*. Anyone can see how you are about each other."

"And how's that?" Ryushi asked scornfully.

"Figure it out," she replied.

There was a long moment as they glared at each other, challenging. Then Ryushi's lips twisted into a sarcastic curl.

"You're jealous, aren't you?" he said.

"Of her? As *if*," Kia shot back, but the denial was not strong enough to be convincing. Besides, there was something more than that, there had *always* been something more. A feeling she couldn't pin down about Calica that—

"After what you've done with Ty, cutting me out for him, you're jealous of me doing the same to you!" Ryushi accused, barging into her thoughts. "And you call *me* a hypocrite. You can't have it both ways, sis. That's pathetic. Other people have got their lives to lead, y'know."

With that, he took a few steps' run-up and vaulted on to the saddle of his pakpak, which grunted in vague surprise and raised its head from the grass.

"For the record, I think this Koth Taraan thing is a wild-goose chase," he said. "And even if I didn't, I wouldn't go with you. Back home you always made out you were the mature one, sis. I think it's your turn to grow up now."

He spurred the pakpak and was away before she could reply, racing across the plains back towards Base Usido, under the hollow glare of the dark sun high above him. His sister dwindled behind him, but he never turned back to look as she watched him go. His head was full of anger, not only at her but also at himself. He was as bad as she was. After all that he had said about leaving him out of her life, he had held something back himself. There was another reason why he wasn't going with her.

A message had arrived for him at Base Usido. The spy had brought it to Calica, and she had told him. A stranger had been travelling the towns, asking for Ryushi by name. The stranger wanted to meet him. The stranger had important information, but he would not speak to anyone except Ryushi.

The stranger said a name.

The name was Takami.

6
A Dishonest Bone

"You do know, of course, that this is a trap," Calica said, brushing the orange-gold cascade of her hair behind her ear and studying her companion.

She and Ryushi rode slowly away from the mechanical lift that had brought them up the sheer side of the valley. They spared nods for the operators and guards as they stepped off the wide metal platform, pushing through the wheezing clouds of steam that rose up from the pressure-brakes. Their pakpaks snuffed and grunted as they picked their way into the dark undergrowth, brown eyes uneasy. Whether by smell or by instinct, they knew the dangers of the Rifts, and they would soon as not leave the sanctuary of Base Usido to head through the trackless depths of the forest.

"Course it's a trap," he replied, once they had gone a little way in. "Frankly, I'm kinda disappointed in Aurin. I thought she'd try harder."

"And you're still going? Why?"

"Because the Princess knows I'm not gonna turn down a chance – *any* chance – to get to him."

"Takami? Look, I know how you feel about him, but

setting yourself up like this isn't going to get you any closer to what you want."

"What I *want* is to see his head on a burning post," Ryushi replied, his voice entirely serious. "But that's beside the point. How could I pass up this opportunity, if there's even the slightest possibility I could get to him? I'm honour-bound to avenge my father. You know that."

"Sure, I know that. And so does Aurin. That's why she's using it against you."

Ryushi made a shrug of concession, as if to say: *so be it*, and the discussion was over.

Calica turned her attention back to the trail. She knew how eaten up Ryushi was about this whole affair. Ever since he had duelled with his older brother in the dark tunnels of the Ley Warren, he had been obsessed with exacting revenge for their father's death. After all, it was Takami's treachery that had plunged them from their safe existence in the mountains into the violent reality of war in the first place. Several times Ryushi had tried to find a way to reach his enemy, to force an end to their blood-feud; but Takami was a noble now, Takami-*kos* of the province of Maar. He was too well-guarded to get near. It frustrated Ryushi, and she saw that; but it was beginning to get out of hand, if he intended to go along with such a blatant trap as the one they faced.

Bizarrely, Kia's reaction to the news that Takami was the killer of their father had been far less extreme than Ryushi's. They had waited for her to recover from the near-fatal weakness she had inflicted upon herself during the battle at the Ley Warren before breaking it to her; but even so, she did not seem to be cut nearly so deep by the revelation as her twin. Perhaps all her hate was already invested in Macaan's men. Maybe her new love for Ty had calmed her somewhat. But whatever the reasoning behind it, the idea of revenge on Takami had not become her first priority as it had with Ryushi; though Calica had no doubt that Kia would not hesitate to grasp any opportunity to get hold of her treacherous older brother.

"Look, I'm just going there to meet with this person," Ryushi said, mistaking her contemplation for sulky disapproval. "It'll be on neutral ground. There's not much chance of an ambush, and if there were. . ." he shrugged, "we can handle 'em. But all I know so far is that this guy is mouthing off about wanting to meet me, and that he has something on Takami. I can't just let it rest at that. Once I meet him, and we find out what the whole story is, *then* I'll decide if I'm gonna go with it."

Calica gave him a sidelong glance. "As if I believe *that*," she said. "Your mind's made up already."

They rode on, and the Glimmer shards that they carried in their belts pulsed from red to indigo to violet. Base Usido was close to the edge of the Rifts, but not so close that it didn't take a half-cycle or more to get on to open land. They were kept constantly wary, for even though their route was through the less dangerous areas of the Rifts, staying on the high plateaus, it was still far from safe. As their journey progressed, Calica dropped back a little, slowing imperceptibly until she was a few feet behind Ryushi and out of the range of his peripheral vision. Ryushi, keeping his eyes on the doleful trees around him, did not notice her doing it; and his attention was too focused to notice her olive gaze on him, studying the side of his face as she had done so many times before, her mind distracted by something other than the dangers of the Rift beasts.

She didn't know when it had happened. Even when she pressed herself, she could not pinpoint the moment when her friendship and respect for her companion had shifted violently to love. Perhaps there had always been a smouldering ember there somewhere, waiting to ignite the rest of her. She remembered when he came to her quarters in the canyon hideout of Gar Jenna, back in the Dominions. She remembered how he had impulsively hugged her upon their return from Os Dakar, and how the hug had seemed to hold . . . well, more than friendship. Those moments had happened over a year ago, and at the time she had thought little of them. But now. . .

It didn't matter. However, whenever it had happened, it *had* happened. And she had to deal with it.

Unfortunately, that was turning out to be the hard part.

The trouble was, she didn't know his mind. She was unable to read the signals. Eighteen winters had passed in her life, but like many in Parakka she had grown up hard and fast since she lost her parents to Macaan. She was a strong warrior, a respected tactician; she was the head of the Tusami City chapter of Parakka before she had even come of age. Her life had been a fight to be the best, and it had left precious little time for such intangibles as romance. She had been perfectly happy to get by without that particular hindrance; but she had reckoned without the overwhelming insistence of the emotions that harried her now. She had assumed that she had a choice where love was concerned, but circumstances had proved her wrong.

Her psychometry was no use, either. It gave her only surface detail; and the one thing she never seemed to be able to find out was how Ryushi felt about *her*. Perhaps it was because it meant so much to her that she could not glean it from him, in the same way that an important show could make a performer so nervous that they were unable to do what they had done a hundred times in rehearsal.

It seemed the simplest thing, just to tell him how she felt and be done with all the torture that she put herself through. The simplest thing, but somehow her pride would not allow her to form the words in her mouth.

Calica's spirit-stones worked both ways, though neither was very reliable. As well as the past, she occasionally grasped flashes of the future as they flickered across her subconscious mind. It was such a flash that interrupted her thoughts and caused her to whisper an alert to Ryushi.

"What is it?" he asked, looking over his shoulder at her, one hand on the hilt of his sword. They were in an area where the trees had become sparser, pushing their way through rocky ground, and the faint light from the dark sun filtered through the leaf canopy a little stronger than usual, painting everything a dim pastel blue.

"Something's coming," she said urgently. "Get out of sight! Over there!"

They wheeled their pakpaks together and rode them as fast as they dared to where a screen of star-thorn bushes grew on the fringe of a shallow, stony dip in the land. They pulled their mounts to a halt behind the cover, the pakpaks' feet crunching and scratching on loose gravel, and settled to wait, searching the forest for a sign of what Calica had sensed.

It was not long in coming. First there was a short fizzle of soft blue-white light, which glowed and died almost as soon as Ryushi noticed it. Then another, darting round the gnarled bole of a haaka tree and extinguishing itself, quick as an eyeblink. Then two together, wheeling in perfect formation and disappearing. Then more, and more, until finally there were hundreds of the things, fat tadpoles of light that were being slowly drawn together, appearing in the darkness and crawling towards a central core of light, which glowed brighter as more of the ghostly arrivals joined it. The air was filled with a sharp whispering noise, the sound of a thousand hushed voices in unison, but Ryushi was unable to make out any words amid the subdued clamour.

"Bane?" he asked, his eyes fixed on the congealing mass.

"Bane," Calica agreed.

And then the mass began to take shape and form, elongating and solidifying until it was almost eel-like, with a frill of ethereal energy running down its narrow sides, and a face that had no eyes but only a wide, blind mouth. Trailing sparkling blobs of blue-white light in its wake, it wound its way off through the trees, curving and arcing and rolling and diving between the boughs, until its illumination had faded from sight.

"That's the third one I've seen recently," Calica murmured gravely. "I don't like it."

"Why?" Ryushi asked. "They never go near the other settlements in the Rifts. They're no trouble."

"The other settlements are full of Kirins," Calica said, edging her pakpak out of hiding. It responded with a snort. "Base Usido has a lot of Dominion-folk. That's a lot of spirit-stones."

"So what?"

Calica scratched the back of her forearm anxiously. "There've been developments since you left for Mon Tetsaa. All the reports show that there are more Banes than ever before now, and they all seem to be heading for Base Usido. Banes only form when there's something to feed on. We figure it's the energy from the spirit-stones they're looking for."

"Yeah, but they're scavengers; they're too weak to—"

"It's not *them* I'm worried about," Calica interrupted. "It's the packs of Snagglebacks that follow them around. And with the Snagglebacks, you get the Snappers. I'm sure you remember *them*."

Ryushi made a tiny nod. He remembered them well enough; Os Dakar had been crawling with them.

"Something's brewing," she said distantly. "I'm just worried about it. Perhaps we should go back and warn the Base."

"*You* can," Ryushi said. "I've got an appointment to keep."

For a moment, Calica hesitated, caught in a choice between satisfying her niggling worries or staying with the one she reluctantly loved. But it was only a moment, for in the end there was no contest. With an inward sigh of resignation, she turned her pakpak and made ready to travel on.

The Votive Grove stood on the western edge of the Rifts, a mile or so beyond where the ground finally gave up its chaotic jumbling and smoothed itself into grassland. It stood alone, a cluster of exactly one hundred tall, straight trees that towered high and curved in on themselves to form a vast natural dome of blue leaves shot through with sparkling seams of crystal. The trunks of the trees formed the pillars to this colossal place, which had been standing for longer than any could remember. Legend had it that it was created by a great King of long ago, as a monument to the son who tried to have him assassinated. Before he was put to death, the son was granted a final request, as was customary for royalty; he asked that the King leave something marking his memory that would stand for eternity, and so the Votive Grove was planted.

That was but one legend. Many others had sprung up since then, so much so that the place was rarely visited now. It was a haunted place, where evil spirits and Banes dwelt. But evil spirits had no need for fires, and Ryushi could see the spasmodic flicker of a blaze between the pillars of bark, throwing the short, dancing shadows of the trunks on to the grass outside the grove.

"Someone's home," Calica observed needlessly.

Ryushi didn't reply. He patted the neck of his pakpak absently and then nudged it into a trot, heading towards the grove. Calica followed, her hand resting on the hilt of her katana.

All was still as they passed between the immense pillars and into the shelter of the arched canopy of knitted branches. A shallow stone firepit was in the exact centre of the Votive Grove, and a bonfire had been built up in it. The deep, gruff purring of the burning wood was the only sound aside from the animal noises of their pakpaks and the periodic clink of their scabbards tapping against their saddle buckles.

They waited for a moment, but there was no sign of whoever had built the fire.

"Is anyone there?" Calica called, her voice swallowed by the leafy dome.

"Course," came the reply from the darkness outside. "Think that fire built itself?"

They reined around and saw a shadow leaning against one of the trunks, a smaller shadow by its side. Standing just on the edge of the firelight, it was impossible to make out exactly who it was.

"Well, we're here," said Ryushi, squinting at the stranger.

"I was thinking you weren't gonna show," came the reply. "Then I thought, well, if you saw me here it might put you off and you'd turn and get before you heard me out."

I know that voice, Ryushi thought. *It's been a year, but...*

"Whist?" he queried tentatively.

"Pretty sharp, Ryushi," he said, stepping into the firelight. Blink loped along next to him, his huge, rangy grey dog. He hadn't changed much since last time Ryushi had seen him. He still went barechested, with his lean body covered in swirling skin-dye designs that crawled up his neck and around his cheeks and face and eyes. His hair was still bunched and spiked and hanging, a mishmash of styles and colours, and he still wore the thick metal glove on one hand that he used for throwing the razor discs on his belt. No, he hadn't changed much. It was just that he was *supposed* to be dead. And Ryushi wasn't certain that he wouldn't have preferred it that way.

"I thought Ty took care of you back in Os Dakar," he said, sliding his sword free from its scabbard. Calica followed suit, controlling with her knees her nervy pakpak's attempts to sidestep.

"Well, y'know, reports of my death have been greatly exaggerated, and all that stuff," Whist replied offhandedly, walking across the grass towards where they stood by the fire. "You really wanna know the details?"

"Indulge me," Ryushi replied. "And stay where you are."

"Seems I heard that line first time we met," Whist said, halting obediently and squatting down to scratch under Blink's chin. "Kirin guy, Tochaa, said that. How's he doing, anyway?"

"He's dead," Ryushi replied.

"Really? Shame," Whist said thoughtfully. "He was uptight, but I kinda liked him." He shook his head, aware that he had drifted. "Oh yeah, sorry. You wanted to know why I'm here, and not dead after falling off that stupid big machine, huh? Well, Blink here wasn't too keen on meeting the ground at that kinda speed, so he winked out to a safer spot. And seeing as we were sorta entangled, he took me with him." He nuzzled the massive dog, which licked his nose. "I'd seen Flicker Dogs like him disappear with food in their mouths before, back in the Wildlands. Guess I didn't think he could transport a whole human. Proved me wrong." He grinned at them.

Ryushi glanced at Blink, remembering Kia's story of how they had got into the Fallen Sun stockade on Os Dakar. Flicker Dogs could wink themselves over distances without crossing the intervening ground, simply popping out of nowhere.

"Anyway," Whist continued. "I hid out while the Keriags trashed the settlement. There's not much left of it now. After that, when they thought there was no one still alive, it was easy enough to get off the plateau through the Guardsmen's corridors now I knew that Blink could get me there. I'm an enterprising kid." He stood up and stretched. "So there you are. And now I'm here. Satisfied?"

"What are you up to?" Ryushi asked, naked suspicion in his tone.

"Why did I get you to come here, you mean? Ah, that's pretty much the real question, isn't it? I wanna give you a present. See, I've been round a lot this past year, and I get to hear things, and I know you and your brother aren't exactly on great terms. Since he's become a thane, stories about him are all over. He—"

"Nobody outside of Parakka knew I was alive until ten cycles ago," Ryushi interrupted. "And only Aurin knew then. You're working for her, Whist. Don't insult me by pretending you're not."

Whist gave him an apologetic smile. "Sorry, but you

haven't been keeping up on current affairs. Aurin circulated your description to every thane in Kirin Taq at least nine cycles ago. The Jachyra passed it on for her."

"So how did you find out?" Calica interceded.

" 'Cause I work for *Takami*," he replied, getting faintly exasperated. "Not Aurin."

Ryushi's face became a sarcastic sneer in the shifting firelight. "That's even better, Whist. The one person on Kirin Taq who is liable to want me dead more than Princess Aurin and you're working for him. You do know that if you try to ambush us now, I'll obliterate you and this whole grove?"

"This isn't an ambush," Whist replied. "Calm down, why don'tcha? I'm here to make you a deal. I can get you a shot at Takami." He paused for a moment, allowing his offer to sink in. "And in return, you let me into Parakka."

Ryushi's pakpak took a shifty step backwards; he automatically steadied it with the reins that were gathered in his left fist. "Come on, Whist. You betrayed my sister twice in Os Dakar. You think I'd even go along with your offer, let alone allow you to join Parakka?"

Blink growled at him, the sound low and throaty. Whist calmed his companion, running his gloved hand along the thick muscle of the massive dog's back. The two were linked by the power of Whist's spirit-stones, dog and boy in symbiosis. Ryushi had often wondered exactly how close their bond was, and its nature; but he was pretty sure that Blink's reaction reflected the emotion that Whist kept hidden.

"You're a smart kid, Ryushi," Whist said. "Obviously, I wasn't gonna expect you to agree just like that." He began to pace around at the edge of the circle of heat thrown out by the fire. "See, the thing is that you took it personal, what I did on Os Dakar. It wasn't personal. Me and Kettin had a deal; he left me alone, and I delivered any new arrivals to the plateau into his hands. It was his way of recruiting, y'know? Getting the cream of the bunch. Course, he had to find out if new kids were worth taking or not, and that was what the Snapper Run was all about. But it was just . . . that was my *deal*, see? Our arrangement." He looked up, his eyes meeting Ryushi's. "You saw what it was like on Os Dakar. We all did what we could to survive. Ask your friend Ty, ask him if *he* didn't have to compromise his morals to get by in that place."

"So what about Takami?" Ryushi asked, ignoring the reference to Ty because he knew it was true. "Why'd you choose him?"

"I didn't *choose* him," Whist replied, looking wounded. "He captured me. I had kind of a rough time after Os Dakar – the land around that place don't exactly get called hospitable, y'know? – and his guys picked me up and brought me to him."

"So, what, you got a deal going with him, too?" Calica asked.

"Like I said, I'm an enterprising kid," he shrugged.

"Better that than rotting in a jail 'cause of my Dominion skin."

"And now you're betraying him, too," Ryushi said.

"Hey, it's not like I *asked* to be in his service. It was kind of a life-or-death decision." He looked at Blink, who growled sullenly. "I don't like being put in that position," he said. "He don't deserve no loyalty from me." Then he brightened. "But *you*," he said, pointing with his gloved hand. "I know you. You don't got a dishonest bone in your body. Otherwise you wouldn't have been so easy to sucker on Os Dakar. And when I heard about you, that you were still kickin', well, I thought: if there's one person who's gonna give my boss the payback he deserves, it's Ryushi, right?"

Nobody replied for a moment. Calica was watching Ryushi for a reaction.

"Anyway," Whist went on. "A guy like me has to cover himself. And if we make a deal, and Takami bites it . . . well, you're happy, but what about me? I'm out of a job, right? I need a safety net. And I'll tell you, I've had it with Aurin and her thanes. That leaves me with Parakka. All I ask is, if I get you to Takami, you forget about what I've done before and let me in."

His speech finished, Whist squatted back down next to Blink, who was sitting to attention, watching Ryushi and Calica with interest.

Ryushi was silent.

"Tell me you're not seriously thinking of trusting this lying slime," Calica said.

Still Ryushi didn't reply, his face set in intense thought.

"I'll tell you what," Whist said, standing up. "I can see you need to work this out and make a decision. I'll be back here in two cycles. If you're not here, I'll assume the deal's off. If you are. . ." He grinned and left the sentence hanging.

"Ryushi. . ." Calica said, unable to quite believe he was giving serious credit to Whist's words.

"I'll see you both," Whist said, and with that he and his ever-present companion walked away, leaving the shelter of the Votive Grove into the twilight outside, rapidly fading from shadows into nothingness.

"Ryushi?" Calica prompted again.

Slowly, he tugged his pakpak around and began to head silently back towards the Rifts, and she could do nothing but follow.

7

Through the Gloom Until

The dank carpet of the Unclaimed Lands crept across the marshy earth beneath them. The Parakkans stood on a jutting ridge several miles to the northwest of Mon Tetsaa, their pakpaks cropping grass nearby with their flat teeth and rubbery lips. The thin clouds in the blue-purple sky held a faintly poisonous, greenish tinge, drifting across the face of the black abyss that was the sun. From somewhere beneath the wetland canopy, marsh-creatures gibbered and pipped. Rising above, knees and elbows of reddish rock slid out of the obscuring trees to dominate the landscape. A cool wind blew, swirling around them.

The Unclaimed Lands. The domain of the Koth Taraan.

"Well, it's not as if it's worse than the Rifts, is it?" Peliqua said doubtfully. Her previous experience of the place meant that she wasn't keen on going back, but that still didn't quell her habit of finding a silver lining in every situation.

"That's only because we know what lives in the Rifts," Ty said. "We don't have any idea about this place."

"We know *one* thing that lives here," Kia stated.

"You're still sure you wanna do this, Kia?" Gerdi asked, one eye closed as he checked the sights on his crossbow.

"Never mess with a girl's intuition," she replied.

"Wouldn't dream of it," he said, slinging his crossbow back into its harness on his back. "How about you, Jaan?"

"Oh, I'm just raring to go," the halfbreed replied dismally.

"Yeah, I can tell," said Gerdi.

"None of us has trekked for two days – *cycles* – just to turn back now," Hochi said, his warhammer resting on his shoulder. "Let's get down there."

"Just remember," Kia said to them all. "We're supposed to be making contact. Don't get scared and attack anything. We don't fight unless they start it. Understand?"

"Unless your intuition is all off and they pulp us 'cause they really are as mindless as Taacqan said," Gerdi replied flippantly.

"Well, yeah, there is that," Kia mused. "Oh well, I suppose we gotta take the rough with the smooth. Come on."

They made their way down off the ridge and towards the Unclaimed Lands. After tethering their pakpaks in a sheltered nook and strapping feed-bags around the creatures' leathery underbellies, they unloaded their supplies and got ready to set off on foot. The wetland ground was too unstable for riding, even for the surefooted pakpaks, and their mounts would undoubtedly end up stuck or lame if they took them in. They hesitated a moment at the border, each of them considering what they were getting themselves into; but the hesitation did not last long, and they forged on into the murky world of the Koth Taraan.

The atmosphere seemed to thicken instantly as they stepped into the wetlands. It was as if each of the knotted trees and bloated, dangling leaves sensed that they were intruders and frowned at them, weighing them down with disapproval. The high-pitched *kikiriki* of the marsh-rats was like the whine of blood in their ears, the frequency resting just on the top end of human hearing. Distantly, a repetitive booming noise heralded the presence of something they would rather not meet. Many-legged leafcreepers wound their slow and sinister way through the branches, occasionally stringing themselves across the travellers' path as they crossed from tree to tree, so that they had to duck underneath the long, furred body and its small, hook-toed legs that scrabbled uselessly at the air. All around them, the wetlands crawled with life, and the terrain veered between unpleasant, treacherous and downright lethal.

Gerdi nattered at Jaan as they walked, only half his mind on the trail. Jaan was characteristically uncommunicative, even around Gerdi, who, at thirteen winters, was only a little younger than the halfbreed. Gerdi usually tried to be friendly by bullying him out of his frequent dark moods, but Jaan would not ever really let the Noman boy near him; and while they could be called friends, they could not be called close.

"Keep alert, you two," said Hochi grouchily, after Gerdi had made a derisive comment to Jaan about the big man in a stage whisper that was loud enough to be overheard by everyone.

Peliqua couldn't be certain, but she thought that they had travelled further into the Unclaimed Lands than she and her brother had got before they made their first sighting. It was she who saw it first; she squealed excitedly and pointed before remembering that the Koth Taraan were supposed to be dangerous. It was a low shape against the background of one of the massive rocks that they had seen from the ridge, silent and unmoving. Had she not been looking out for it, she would have missed it completely. But though she tried to show the others, the only other person who could make it out in the dim light was Jaan, sharing as he did her Kirin vision.

"Are there any others?" Kia asked urgently.

"I can't see any," Peliqua said, scanning the surroundings with her cream-on-white eyes.

"Are you *sure* there's anything there?" said Hochi, narrowing his eyes as he peered into the darkness.

"I *think* I – oh!"

"What?" Ty said quickly. "What is it?"

"It just moved," Jaan supplied in Peliqua's place.

"Guess that settles *your* hash," Gerdi said to Hochi.

As the others continued talking, Hochi sidled nonchalantly over to him, with a view to clubbing him around the head; but Gerdi carefully positioned Peliqua between them so he could not get a clear shot.

"Where's it going?" Kia asked. "Is it coming towards us?"

Jaan squinted. "I think it's. . ." he began.

"It's moving away," Peliqua said. "Maybe it's going to tell the others we're here."

"Or go for reinforcements," Ty said.

Kia leaned on her bo staff. "Either way, they know we're around. We might as well keep on going. They'll come to us."

"Why do I not like that idea?" Gerdi murmured to himself.

The talking stopped after that. Everyone was far too intent on looking out for the Koth Taraan. Now that they knew they had been spotted, a confrontation was inevitable; but the real question was, would it be peaceful, or would it be a battle? Were the Koth Taraan beasts or beings? Questions and doubts preyed on their minds, for none of them were certain of anything about the creatures beyond their terrifying reputation, and none of them had any idea how they would handle the Koth Taraan if it came to a fight.

Time dragged, sucking at their feet like the swampy ground they travelled over. And still nothing happened. There was no sign of the Koth Taraan, and the Glimmer shards that they carried indicated that at least a half-cycle had passed since they had crossed the borders. The going became steadily worse, so that each new step was uncertain; stable ground could suddenly turn into a wet sinkhole, or plunge them knee-deep in cold bogwater. Vines grew thicker here, plucking at them with the tiny hooks on their leaves, attaching themselves like leeches; and the ground seemed to breathe a faint, chill mist that wound sinuously around their ankles. They were footsore and tired, covered in cold mud and soaked to the skin.

"Stop," said Kia, holding out a weary arm. They gratefully stumbled to a halt. "This is pointless. They're just letting us run ourselves ragged before they deal with us. We wait here. Make a camp."

"I don't think we're gonna need to," said Gerdi. "Look."

They were surrounded. Where the vast creatures had come from, Kia could not say; but this was their home ground, and they knew how to use it. This time, though they still kept just far enough away so that it was difficult to make out their form, they did not attempt to disguise their presence. They stood, some swaying, some hunched, some lumbering across the undergrowth; but they were there. The Koth Taraan.

"Okay, this is it," Kia said, running an anxious hand through the deep red of her hair. "Everybody stay calm. Gerdi, no tricks. We want them to trust us."

Gerdi was too busy keeping his eyes on the dark

shapes that moved slowly through the mist to bother with a reply.

"Kia," Ty hissed in warning. "Your side."

She looked, and there she saw one of the Koth Taraan moving through the twisted trunks and thick vines towards them. The others kept their distance, but this one was coming purposefully closer, gradually gaining definition as it approached. It walked awkwardly and heavily, pushing through the gloom until it stood before them, and there it stopped.

It was the first good look any of them had ever got at a Koth Taraan. It was at least ten feet high, and probably six broad, plated from head to toe with thick, lumpy armour of a dark green hue. Its enormous shoulders dwarfed the small head that was set low between them. Its face was a broad, angular shape without ears, nose or mouth, but instead dominated by two immense, teardrop-shaped eyes of the purest black. It was not the only evidence of the strange proportions in the creature's body shape. For though its torso and its upper legs and arms were small, it possessed massive forearms, plated in armour, that ended in a set of thick ivory claws over a foot long. Similarly, its lower legs were huge, terminating in a flat, elephant-like foot clad in the same lumpen hide as covered most of its body. It was as if a boulder had simply stood up and uncurled itself.

The black, alien eyes were unreadable, but for Kia they reminded her uncomfortably of the cruel gaze of the Keriags, and she thought of what Taacqan had said to Ty just before he died, linking the two species somehow.

Nobody spoke. They were waiting to see what the creature would do. For a long time, it did not stir, except for moving its eyes from one of the Parakkans to the other, an action that was only visible by the sliding of the moist glint of light on its lenses.

It did not speak, or make a sound. Silently, it watched them.

Peliqua began to fidget nervously, glancing occasionally around to see if the others had moved closer.

"Say something, Kia," she urged quietly.

Kia swallowed. Now that she faced one of the creatures, she had no idea what she had intended to say to them. After a moment, she blinked sweat out of her eyes and spoke.

"We're not here to fight," she said through a dry throat. "We're not trying to invade your territory. We just want to talk."

The creature turned its head slightly, so that it was looking at her. She felt her nerve failing under its gaze. Still it did not make a noise.

"Uh, Kia, you might want to see this," said Gerdi from behind her. She took a wary step back from the creature and looked where he was pointing. The Koth Taraan behind them were moving, ambling slowly aside to create a gap in the circle that surrounded them.

"They did that before!" Peliqua said. "It means they want us to go, I think."

An expression of fleeting anger crossed Kia's face. Ty laid a hand on her shoulder, and she composed herself again at his touch. Turning back to the creature that waited near them, she planted her staff hard into the ground in a gesture that meant they weren't going anywhere.

"No," she said levelly. "We've come this far, and we're not turning back now. We ask for an audience with you, with your leaders if you have them. We have important things we must discuss. Things that could affect the lives of both our races."

Ty looked from Kia's face to the creatures. Was she really getting through? he thought. Or was she just wasting her time, trying to communicate with something that was incapable of understanding her? And even if it could, how would it reply? They had no mouths, and their enormous claws were hardly suited to hand-signals.

The creature did not move or respond, just watched her with its alien eyes.

"I know you can understand me," Kia said stridently. "So listen to this. We have no desire to encroach on your land, but we are *not* leaving until we can talk to one of you about the matter that faces us all."

A long pause. And then, as one, the Koth Taraan that surrounded them suddenly broke from their immobility, raising their claws and stamping the ground; and each of them emitted a high-pitched screech, something that was less heard than felt, which sawed at their brains and made the Parakkans want to clutch at their heads.

They did not understand exactly what was happening, but the general signals were clear enough. Anger. A challenge.

Attack.

"Scatter!" Kia cried as the Koth Taraan that stood close to her swung a massive claw down at her. She whirled out of the way, lashing her staff at the creature's head; but it was too small a target, and too well-protected by the thick shoulder armour. Her blow cracked harmlessly into its hide.

The Parakkans broke and ran, knowing that there was no hope in a stand-up fight with these creatures. They were outnumbered, and the Koth Taraan were on home ground, as well as possessing a great physical advantage. Agility was the Parakkans' only asset, and so they split up to use the terrain to greatest effect. All except Ty, who stayed with Kia, his hooking-flail a deadly blur in his hands, and would not leave her side.

Vines lashed at Jaan's face and tangled in the thick ropes of his hair as he ran in search of decent defensive ground. All around him, the sounds of the lumbering Koth Taraan as they crashed through the undergrowth was in his ears. The earth squelched beneath his boots, threatening to give way at any moment, but something compelled him to keep going, zigzagging randomly in case he should—

"Duck!" bellowed a voice from in front of him, and suddenly he was face-to-face with Hochi, the big man's warhammer held ready for a swing. He threw himself to the mud, rolling aside as a claw the size of his upper torso carved a lethal path through the mist where he had just been, and its owner thundered out of the trees a moment later. But Hochi was ready for it, his weapon crashing into the Koth Taraan's back with a force that would have shattered most of the bones in a man's body.

The great creature staggered, stumbled . . . and then stood erect again, fixing Hochi with a black gaze of malice.

"Mauni's Eyes," he cursed under his breath in wonder, then shouted "Run!" at Jaan before following his own advice.

Gerdi threw himself aside as a massive shape barged past him, smashing into a tree and blasting a splintered dent in its trunk large enough to make it slowly topple, accompanied by the angry hiss of leaves as it went and ending in a booming splash as it hit the waterlogged ground. He hadn't even bothered to draw his shortblade or unlatch his crossbow; he knew the former would be useless and the latter would take too much time to operate at such close quarters. He was vaguely aware of Peliqua nearby, her red braided hair coiling around her body as she dodged away from the clumsy, brutal strikes that swept at her from all directions. Her manriki-gusari was as ineffective as his own weapon, and she, like him, was forced into a desperate dance of evasion, praying that something would happen soon that would turn the tables of what looked like a hopeless situation.

Kia fought like a wildcat, but even she knew that their position was untenable. There were too many of them, and they were too well-armoured to damage in any noticeable way. They were slow, but they were everywhere, and the terrain beneath her feet seemed to collude with the enemy to trip her up and wrongfoot her, laying her open to a hit. And it would only take one hit. . .

The stones in her back burned with power that ached for release, glowing dark red, six blazing points along her spine. But she could not afford the concentration that creating and maintaining one of her golems would entail; and the Koth Taraan were barely giving her breathing space to release the Flow that writhed impatiently within her spirit-stone battery.

Even amid the chaos of the fight, she could not help thinking that if Ryushi were here, this could all be over in a moment. And even as adrenalin streamed through her system, and her long-honed reflexes carried her away from the jaws of death again and again, she still felt a stab of guilt and regret that they had not parted on better terms.

Sweat ran along Peliqua's grey skin as she threw herself out of the way of another blow, moving on instinct. She hit the ground in a roll and hopped to her feet in a half-crouch as the long, vicious claws slashed through the air inches above her head. Her muscles were beginning to ache now, and oh, she could have cried with frustration that she didn't have a set of spirit-stones right at this moment, like the Dominion-folk did. But she refused to despair; despair was not an emotion she was familiar with. There was always a way, always a solution.

And then she saw it.

She tugged at the manriki-gusari around her waist, and it came free. She backflipped out of a two-clawed smash, pulling the chain taut as she sailed through the murky air, and lashed out with it as her feet struck the turf. The lead-weighted tip shot out like a whip, cracking between her assailant's shoulder armour and its huge forearms to strike the side of its head, just at the edge of one its wide eyes. It let out an ear-splitting screech, flinching backwards with its claws crossed in front of its face, and stumbled backwards in retreat.

"The eyes!" she shouted. "Go for their eyes!"

It was as if the Koth Taraan heard her words. For the briefest of seconds, they hesitated as one; and in that moment Kia had the time she needed to release the Flow. She sent herself into the earth, feeling the slip and slide of the mud, seizing it, engulfing every tiny molecule, pulling them, moulding them, shaping them. The whole process took only a split second, but it was infinitely complex, a subtle play of forces on the most microscopic level. And the ground responded to her, suddenly reaching up with four great, brutal hands and clamping on to the arms and legs of the Koth Taraan that she faced, pulling it hard, toppling it backwards to the earth and pinning it there, spreadeagled.

But it was strong. She had never felt anything strain with so much power against the bonds that she maintained. So strong, in fact, that she couldn't hold it. . .

"Ty! The eyes! Kill it!" Jaan yelled, appearing from nowhere, his dagnas jabbing and darting as he attempted to hold off another one of the Koth Taraan.

Ty's hooking-flail spun in his hand, carving an edged circle in the dim light. But he did not strike. He looked at Kia with an expression of torment; but Kia was struggling to keep the creature held down, and could not help him. It fixed its dark eyes on him, endless pools of black in its inhuman face.

"Kill it!" Jaan cried.

Hochi roared as he slammed his warhammer into another Koth Taraan. His weapon was the only one which seemed to have any kind of effect at all on the massive things, and then it was only to stagger and stun them. Now he was flailing recklessly, battle-fired, putting his great weight into every swing in the hope that he could outmatch these creatures by brute force. But he was *too* reckless, and he was suddenly surprised by a swift step back by his opponent that caused his hammer to miss by inches. The overswing left him vulnerable, and he saw the terrible claws of the Koth Taraan sweeping up to open his chest; but at the last second, he released his grip on his hammer, and the shift in momentum lent him just enough inertia to throw himself out of the way. There was a feeble tearing noise as his thin, wet shirt was ripped open in three great strips and fell in shreds around him, but he escaped with only a long scratch along his belly. Escape was a relative term, however; for he landed on his bottom in the mud, weaponless, and suddenly there were two Koth Taraan looming over him, lunging in for the kill. . .

"I *can't*!" Ty shouted, letting his hooking-flail spin to a stop in his fist and hang limply over his knuckles. "I won't be a murderer again!"

It was something he had always feared, ever since his time in Os Dakar. Then, as the Pilot of the Bear Claw, he had been responsible for the deaths of many in the fight for his own survival. The experience had scarred him, left him with a lasting aversion to killing; and though he could cope with the deaths of monsters like the Jachyra and the Keriags at his hands, he could not murder what might be a sentient being, only defending its territory.

"They're *animals*!" Jaan fairly screamed. "*Kill* it!"

But by then it was too late, for at that moment Kia cried out and fell backwards as if pushed by an invisible force, and the Koth Taraan tore through its bonds and rose to its feet, massive and powerful again. . .

And they stopped.

The claws halted mere centimetres from Hochi's exposed chest, their vicious tips suddenly arrested. The attacks on the others suddenly diminished to nothing, the creatures stepping back and reverting to a ready stance, slightly crouched, their black eyes watchful. The Parakkans held their positions, breathing heavily, wary of this sudden reprieve.

Hochi did not dare move as the Koth Taraan's claw came closer, until it was scraping the hair of his chest, and gently, delicately lifted Tochaa's pendant on its sharp tip, bringing it closer to the creature's face. Then it let the pendant fall, and stood up, taking a step backward.

The one who had first approached them, the one Kia had entrapped in the earth, tipped its head to the side in a gesture that none of them recognized; and a moment later, it spoke, though the words seemed to be coming from *inside* their ears rather than from outside.

((We will talk)) it said, and the Koth Taraan turned their backs and began to lumber away, leaving the bewildered Parakkans with no choice but to pick themselves up and follow.

8

Only the Spoils

Calica had had enough.

It seemed to her that there were two forces fighting within her, and both were to do with pride. She did not dare tell Ryushi how she felt about him, because she thought that rejection would destroy her; and yet she was disgusted with herself for not having the courage to face up to the task, and that emotion dented her self-image badly. For a long while, the former force had held sway over her; but the latter one had been steadily growing, gathering strength as she let her torment drag on longer and longer, until eventually it had overwhelmed her.

This is stupid, she told herself. Childish and stupid. You've come of age; Ryushi's almost done the same. You're responsible enough to handle this, and he's responsible enough to take it. It's time to stop messing around and get on with it.

So now she strode across the grounds of Base Usido, her determination lending her a purposeful step, heading for Ryushi's hut. The endless activity around her held no interest; her thoughts were all trapped inside, whirling and fluttering like trapped fireflies in a jar. She felt nervous, and more than a little sick, but she would not allow herself to turn back now. Not now she'd made up her mind.

She remembered how she and Ryushi had talked on the way back from their meeting with Whist. She'd hardly even been paying attention to the words that passed between them; her traitorous mind kept on turning to his quirky smile, his elfin features, his clear, confident eyes. That had been two cycles ago, but she still remembered how she had felt as he talked morosely about having to turn down Whist's deal. He was plainly cut up about it, having his hopes raised like that, but he knew that he could never trust Whist, and to do so would be tantamount to giving himself up to Aurin. But while she had made the appropriate sympathetic comments, she had not been thinking at all about what he had been saying. Instead, she had been warring with her own feelings, debating the moment when she would finally declare herself to him. Selfish, but then love *was* selfish. And besides, he had done a good enough job of persuading himself that Whist's offer was too dangerous without her helping him out.

But even if he had decided otherwise, she would have gone with him. She was just thankful that he had seen sense and decided not to return.

And so now the moment was here. She walked towards the cluster of huts, her feet seeming to get more reluctant with every step, and thought about what she would say. She had every word ready, hanging at the back of her throat in preparation . . . for it had to be perfect, if she was to carry this through without faltering. She went, as if in a dream, along the paths between the black wychwood huts, seeking his one out. And when she found it, she paused for a long time before the door. It took the appearance of somebody further up the trail to spur her into action; after all, she couldn't be seen just standing aimlessly outside someone's home. She took a deep breath and knocked.

There was no reply.

A flood of relief washed through her, but it was followed quickly by a rolling mist of suspicion. She pushed gently on the door, and it creaked open.

"Ryushi?" she asked, stepping inside.

The hut was empty. His sword and pack were gone.

"Oh, you idiot," she said under her breath, closing her eyes and letting her head sink.

"You gotta admit," Whist said, "the guy did well for himself."

The province of Maar spread out before them, stretching to the horizon and beyond. Under the faint glare of the dark sun, it was beautiful. Fields – not square, like those of the Dominions, but elliptical, with a diamond-shaped central field for tessalation – stretched out across the flat land, sparkling softly with the fragile crystalline plants of Kirin Taq. There were orchards and vineyards, great strips of them; there were well-maintained roads winding between little clusters of buildings and farms; there was a smooth lake of the darkest blue, flashing shivers of dim light from its gently stirring surface. A trio of wyverns, flying in formation, scraped across the blue-purple sky, the red-armoured Riders on their backs bent low in their harnesses.

Ryushi took a step back, retreating into the shadow of the trees, watching the airborne beasts warily. They were standing on the provincial border, at the edge of a wychwood forest that fringed a low hill. The borders between the provinces were defined by features of geography rather than barriers with guards; after all, strife between the thanes was nonexistent under Aurin's rule. They were little more than caretakers of her land, and if any of them should get ideas above their station, they had a habit of disappearing. . .

It was an idyllic place, the province of Maar. But it was bought with the blood of Ryushi's father Banto, and the thane who ruled it was responsible for his murder. Ryushi looked over the land and saw only the spoils of Takami's betrayal.

Blink whuffed at Whist's feet, his head lying on his paws, his eyes lazily following the path of the distant wyvern patrol.

"Don't it strike you as strange, though?" Whist said, standing with his weight on one leg. "I mean, just that . . . just that *one single* incident has changed everything. He's a noble, with all this land. You and Kia are members of Parakka. And look where you are now.

You're following a guy you plainly don't trust in order to kill your own brother." He smiled wryly. "And all this 'cause Takami decided to betray your family. If not for that, it might all still be as it was. Makes you think, huh? How fragile everything is, or something."

"I never had you pegged for philosophy, Whist," Ryushi commented dryly. "I thought backstabbing was more your line."

Blink gave a warning growl in the back of his throat, but Whist just smiled. "Just remember, smart guy, I'm the only one who can get you to Takami. A deal's a deal, so why don't we just pretend to like each other for the moment?"

"Okay, I can do that," Ryushi replied. "So what's the next move, anyway?"

"First trick is to get across the province. We've been travelling along the borders the last couple of days; it's easy to stay out of sight that way. But Takami's stronghold is right in the centre of Maar, and both of us Dominion guys are gonna stand out in a land full of Kirins."

"I assume you've got a plan," Ryushi said.

"Natch," he said. "Follow me."

They made their way along the edge of the forest, keeping hidden among the thinning periphery of trees. They travelled in this manner for a short while, until they had moved around the curve of the hill and could see a little more of the landscape of Maar.

"Down there," Whist said.

Ryushi had seen the building several minutes beforehand, but he had not attached any special importance to it. Now that his attention was directed that way, however, he looked more closely. It was a strange shape, like two horseshoes back-to-back and joined in the centre, made of thick panels of weathered and beaten metal that looked faintly blue in the twilight. The body of the building was curved and rounded, tapering towards the four horns of the horseshoe-shapes, and a wide road ran through the centre of it, coming from the neighbouring province and heading away between the fields.

"What is it?"

"It's a land-train depot," Whist replied. "You've never seen one before?"

"Guess not," Ryushi said. "So what's it do?"

Whist absently ran a hand over his dog's back as he spoke. "You might have seen land-trains around in the Dominions, right?"

"From a distance," Ryushi said, remembering the battle at the Ley Warren.

"Well, anyway," came the reply, "they didn't have any of this stuff in Kirin Taq until Macaan started getting Machinists over to build them. They're great big heavy things, and it takes a lot of kick to make 'em go. So every so often they have to stop at depots to get the energy back up. See, land-trains are one of the only vehicles that you don't need a Pilot like Ty to drive; they've got engines. But you know what it's like; even the Machinists can't make engines that work without making them enormous. Plus they need drop-off points to unload and load cargo. So that's why they have those depots."

"We're gonna stow on a land-train?"

"Sure," Whist grinned. "If we get the right one, it'll take us all the way across the province. And right into Takami's stronghold."

"What, you think he won't have measures to stop that happening?" Ryushi said sceptically. "Otherwise anyone could just wander into his palace."

"Of course he does," Whist replied. "But I've worked for him, remember? There are ways and means. Unfortunately," he said, scratching his arm beneath his heavy glove, "it still don't mean it's gonna be *easy*, exactly." He looked at Ryushi, a glimmer in his eye. "But then it wouldn't be any fun, now would it?"

Ryushi didn't reply, his eyes fixed on the depot below. After a moment, Whist sighed at his lack of response, and then muttered: "Let's get going then," before leading the way down the hill, Blink padding after him.

Though the hill was quite exposed and devoid of cover, the lack of light and the sparseness of the nearby population worked for them. Even though Kirin eyes had long since adapted to the low level of brightness from the corona of the sun, most of the settlements had been built some way in from the provincial border, and the intruders would be little more than specks to the people in the nearest village as they ran low and swift down the hillside. Still, Ryushi kept his eyes out in case the Riders on wyvern-back might return.

The depot did not appear to be guarded on the outside. As they neared, they saw only the curved iron shell of the exterior, and the only sign of life was the faint huffing and clanking that came from within. The road was deserted in either direction, except for a distant group of pakpak riders that were heading into the province.

"I don't like this," he said. "It's too easy. There should be guards."

"Why waste the guards when a trespasser can't get *in*?" Whist strolled boldly up to the side of the depot, which towered many times his height, and rapped it with a knuckle. The sound fell dead. "Solid. A foot thick. Nothing's getting through there." He paused, then raised an eyebrow as he looked Ryushi over. "Well, actually, *you* could, if your little trick back on Os Dakar was anything to go by."

Ryushi shrugged. He remembered well the moment when he had been forced to unleash his power to annihilate the Keriags a few moments before their escape. "It wouldn't do any good, though. It'd make so much noise, they'd be bound to come and find me."

"And by then you'd be too weak to fight," Whist finished.

Ryushi looked at him strangely. He hadn't been about to reveal that particular facet of his power. "You know an awful lot about me and my family, Whist," he commented in a tone that suggested he found it unpleasant.

Whist beamed. "It's all one-sided. Very negative. Takami told me most of it; the rest I picked up from gossip in the stronghold. Correct me if I'm wrong," he winked, "but I think Tak's still sore you aced him in the Ley Warren."

"He's gonna be a lot sorer when I kill him," Ryushi said.

Whist made a face, conceding him the point. "Well, yeah, I s'pose so," he replied. "Anyway, do we wanna get in here or don't we?"

"Guess," Ryushi replied sarcastically.

"That's the spirit!" Whist said, full of spurious enthusiasm. "Now where'd that dog of mine get to?"

"Like you don't know," Ryushi said, as Blink nuzzled Whist's thigh, whining as if to say: *I'm here, look, it's me!*

"Oh, right," he said, dropping to one knee and rubbing Blink's face between his palms. "Think you can pull off some of your magic for us, big guy?"

Blink barked excitedly. Whist hushed him, and the dog calmed down a little; then he beckoned Ryushi over. "See," he said. "Once I found Blink could do it once, I started experimenting a little. Turns out he can wink all kinds of stuff with him when he goes. Put your arm round him and hug yourself as close as you can."

Ryushi hesitated for a second, reluctance on his face, and then did as he was instructed. Whist did the same, holding on to the body of the huge dog as if he were a barrel and they were trying to keep afloat. Up close, Blink smelt overpoweringly musty, and Ryushi wrinkled his nose.

"Are we gonna wink on to a land-train?" Ryushi asked. His experiences of being shifted between the worlds by Elani had left him a little wary of allowing himself to be transported by someone else. Especially a dog.

"'Fraid not," Whist replied apologetically. "He's got to be reasonably confident of where he's going, or he won't make the jump. He could wink himself half into the floor or something. But he's got kind of an instinct for short hops; and this *is* just a short hop. From *this* side of the wall . . ." he put his palm against the metal of the depot wall ". . . to *that* one. Now hold on."

The dog blinked, and Ryushi felt a jolt in his body that made all his muscles jump simultaneously, a split-second of nothingness, and then their surroundings flicked from the cool air of Kirin Taq to the grinding, roaring interior of the depot.

They disengaged themselves from the body of Blink, and Whist made a fuss of him while Ryushi's brain tried to catch up with his senses. They were on a narrow gantry, buried behind a bank of black, steaming machines. Imported Dominion glowstones provided a dim orange light, and the air smelt acrid, and felt strangely greasy in a way that Ryushi couldn't define. All around them was the deafening noise of gears clashing, pistons pumping and the hiss of hot steam; but at least they had not appeared in front of a guard, and they were in one piece.

"Where to now?" Ryushi asked, sliding his sword free.

"What, *I* should know?" Whist asked exasperatedly. "Let's just look around. It's not like we're gonna miss something as big as a land-train, now is it?"

"I thought you had a *plan*," Ryushi replied. "When I hear the word *plan*, I take it to mean more than just a vague idea of the direction we're meant to be going in."

"Yeah, but when I have a plan it *works*," Whist said, standing up again, his shoes clanking on the metal grilles beneath their feet. "You can moan at me after we've been caught. Until then, shut *up*; you're beginning to tick me off."

Ryushi swallowed back a retort. Arguing wouldn't do them any good here. Especially as Whist and Blink were his only way out of the depot at the moment.

"Okay, let's go," he said.

They crept through the bellowing guts of the depot, moving carefully along the maze of gantries that ran between the huge machines. They were not worried about the sound of their footsteps being heard over the din, but as they did not know the layout of the place, they were aware that they might run into guards at any moment; and if the alarm was raised, the game was up. So they peered warily around every corner, and jumped at every unexpected clank or jet of steam. Whist sent Blink ahead to scout out routes, his mind riding behind the dog's eyes as it slunk through the depot, sharing its vision. Occasionally, they saw the black form of a Guardsman wandering uninterestedly along a nearby gantry, and had to backtrack to go around him. Once, they were nearly surprised by a sentry who appeared from the top of a narrow set of stairs; but they managed to hide before he saw them. It was tense, but they were making steady progress, and the depot was not heavily guarded.

At one point, while they were taking a short rest in the shelter of a pair of huge, hissing pipes, Ryushi asked Whist what all the machinery was for.

"The fuel," he replied, having to shout to be heard over the racket of the pipes. "All this set-up is just for the fuel to make the land-trains run. You think it's easy to extract all that stuff from the earth, or to ship it to the depots? Nah, they just do it all here. But it's such a massive job, it's hardly worth it." He picked at a piece of metal flash on the grille at his feet. "If man was meant to drive, he wouldn't have been given spirit-stones, right? I think they keep these land-trains going more to keep the Pilot's Guild nervous, y'know? Like, 'we can do this without you,' or something. Besides, it's hard to get Pilots over in Kirin Taq. Since they made having spirit-stones an execution offence – except for the nobles and their armies and so on – the supply of Pilots sorta dried up."

"You *are* well-informed," Ryushi said, exaggeratedly impressed.

"I keep my ear to the ground," Whist replied, missing the irony in Ryushi's voice because of the noise that surrounded them.

Their encounters with the Guardsmen became more and more frequent as they headed towards what they thought was the centre of the building, where the two horseshoe-shapes joined up and a tunnel ran through them. Whist assured Ryushi that this was where the land-trains were resupplied, but he was not sure of the exact route to get to it. Ryushi guessed that they were not far off, though, because avoiding the sentries had by now become less of a nuisance and more of a full-time occupation. He wished Gerdi were here now. The green-haired Noman boy's ability to alter his appearance would have been invaluable. But this was *his* problem, and he could not allow anyone else to be endangered by it. And that included Calica.

"Alright! Am I not the *best*?" Whist suddenly said next to him. Ryushi blinked in momentary disorientation and then said: "What?"

"We're here," Whist grinned.

Ryushi glanced around. They were on a gantry like any other, still penned in by machinery. Blink was away somewhere out of sight.

"No, we're not," said Ryushi in puzzlement. "And where's *here*, anyway?"

"The land-train, you—" Whist began to snap, and then caught himself. "Oh, right. Sorry. Blink's found the land-train. It's just around the next corner."

Ryushi gave him an odd look. Riding behind Blink's eyes, Whist had forgotten where his real body was. Sometimes, his relationship with his dog was a little *too* close.

They turned a right-angle, and there they found Blink waiting for them, sitting on his haunches, his tongue lolling happily. Before them, there was a long railing that ran along the side of the gantry; and beyond that, there was the awesome spectacle of the land-train.

From where they stood, high up in the arch of the massive tunnel that ran through the centre of the depot, it crouched beneath them like a giant, fat spider. Eight enormous wheels on sprung axles supported the lozenge-shaped central body that hid between them, four on each side. The wheels were thick and bulky, adapted to protect the vehicle from shocks as it sped over the terrain, and each one was heavily rutted and grooved for grip. The body of the vehicle was smooth, with a rounded front and back end, and a curved strip of dark Dominion glass for the cockpit. A loading-ramp was just visible between the wheels, lowered from the vehicle's underbelly; large-bore pipes ran from the vast iron fuel tanks of the depot to intakes on the land-train's flanks.

"Come on," said Whist. "Just need to get close enough, and Blink'll get us in."

Tiny insects against the enormous labyrinth of gantries and ladders and stairs that sprawled over the sides of the tunnel, they began to make their way downward. As they descended through the many levels of grinding, roaring noise, the land-train seemed to rise higher and higher, until finally it dwarfed them entirely beneath its massive wheels and ironbound hide. They had a few more near-misses with sentries, but they were nothing worse than they had already gone through. After a short while, as they hurried along another metal walkway, Ryushi said what had been bothering him for some time.

"This is too easy," he remarked.

"What, because we haven't been caught yet? Are you *never* happy?" Whist cried over the din. "Look, they don't keep a heavy guard inside because nobody can get *in*. They guard the tunnel mouth at either end *very* carefully, if that makes you feel any better, but—"

"Hey!" came a cry from behind them, and they whirled to see two Guardsmen running towards them, their black armour sheening orange in the glowstone light, their halberds held with the force-muzzles levelled at the intruders.

"Ah, now you've jinxed us," Whist complained, and his gloved hand flashed out from his belt, two razor-edged discs spinning through the air from his outstretched palm faster than the eye could follow. The Guardsmen jerked as the discs hit; one was taken in the throat, in the narrow gap between his faceplate and his chest protector, while the other got the disc through the eyepiece. They toppled in a clatter of armour and were still.

Whist looked back at Ryushi. "Satisfied?"

Ryushi didn't rise to the goad. Instead, he said: "Are we close enough yet for your dog to get us in?"

"He thinks so," Whist replied immediately.

"Then let's hide those bodies and get on board," Ryushi said, his tone rigidly efficient and businesslike to mask his reaction to Whist's casual slaughter of the Guardsmen. He'd been forced to kill before, and he'd kill again, of that he was sure; but if he ever got so blasé about it that it ceased to affect him, he didn't think he could live with himself. Sometimes he thought he understood Ty's problem with the subject, even. Maybe his friend feared he would become like Whist was; a creature with no morals, for whom the killing of a man was merely the removal of an annoying obstacle.

But there was one man whose death would bring Ryushi no remorse, and it was that face that filled his mind as he and Whist set to work.

126

9

A Pantheon of Dim Ghosts

If Kia and the others had been footsore and tired before, then they were on the verge of dropping from exhaustion by the time they reached the Koth Taraan's settlement. They had been travelling for some time before they had even encountered the huge creatures, and the subsequent fight had drained them further. But when the strange truce had been called – and they still had no clear idea *why* the Koth Taraan had stopped attacking – they had been forced to follow their departing adversaries or be left behind. After going through everything that they had, Kia was not about to let the promise of a meeting get away from her; but the creatures did not seem to tire, and the wet ground sucked at their boots and made each step twice as hard as it should have been. They struggled to negotiate shallow bogs that the Koth Taraan swept effortlessly through; they fought to untangle themselves from the annoyingly adhesive vines that draped across their path; they clambered over the curling, stone-hard roots of the marsh trees.

In this manner, they continued for perhaps another tenth-cycle, their heads light and their limbs heavy but unable to stop for fear of losing their guides, who seemed almost oblivious to their presence. Gerdi collapsed at one point, but the barechested Hochi picked up the young Noman boy and carried him on his broad back; his oxlike endurance was standing him in good stead compared to the rest of them. Peliqua was flagging badly, too, but she never made even the slightest complaint. Despite her scatty manner, Peliqua was one of Parakka's most reliable members, and she had a core of steel.

And then suddenly they emerged at the shore of a vast, shallow lake of brackish, weed-choked water, and there was the settlement. It was built on the many islands that lay just above the murky surface, linked together by simple, flat bridges of some kind of artifically-made mud ceramic. The same substance had been used in the construction of their dwellings; tall, wide igloos of a light, sandy brown that were stacked together in clusters, built in mounds with each spherical facet merging into the next, like a pile of snowballs. Circular holes, twelve feet or so in diameter, pocked the surface of each cluster, and from within came a warm red-yellow glow. Torches on poles surrounded the islands, standing alone in the lake, throwing a hazy illumination through the marsh-mist. Overhead, the trees had grown close, and nothing of the sky could be seen. It was an enclosed world, an island of islands in the marsh; and as Kia saw it, she managed a weak smile of triumph.

Dwellings. Speech. The Koth Taraan were not mindless things; they were a *people*.

One of the creatures that had been guiding them – it *could* have been the one that spoke, but Kia wasn't sure – suddenly half-turned and looked at them, as if to see if they were still there. And then its voice rang in their heads again, seeming to emanate from within their skulls rather than entering through their ears.

((Stay here. Sleep. We will return))

Kia nodded. The creature did not seem to know what to make of that, so she affirmed her agreement vocally. With no further word, the Koth Taraan made their way across one of the bridges to the settlement, leaving the Parakkans to collapse in the wet mud in exhaustion.

"I'll watch out for us," said Hochi stolidly, pulling on a new shirt to replace his ripped one and settling himself in a cross-legged position with his hammer across his lap.

Soaked, mud-smeared and bone-tired, the others wearily dragged out their blankets, and fell asleep the moment they hit horizontal.

Even in the marsh, there were Glimmer plants growing in sparse clusters, little dots of light that speckled the darkness. When Jaan opened his eyes, the patch that he saw in amid the drooping leaves and vines told him that they had been out for a full cycle; the colour was almost exactly what it had been when they fell asleep. He rubbed the thick ropes of his hair muzzily, his palm running over the small ornaments and beads that resided there. Rummaging through his pack, he dug out a wineskin full of sugary juice. Taking a swig, he noted with a smile that Hochi had fallen asleep in his cross-legged position and was gently snoring. He put the skin back in his pack and got out of his blanket, stood up and stretched his aching spine, turned around and jumped half out of his senses.

A Koth Taraan was there, motionless, next to where the others were sleeping. It was standing in the neutral stance that the creatures seemed to adopt whenever they were still, with its massive forearms slightly crossed in front of it and its armoured back bent forward a little, as if it were leaning towards something just ahead. It was watching him with its wide, black eyes.

((You are different from the others)) came its voice inside his head, and strangely it carried with it the smudged impression of the colour purple, seeming to stain the message as it passed through Jaan's mind.

He didn't know what surprised him more; the appearance of the creature or the fact that it was *speaking* to him. He scrambled for a reply.

"Uhhh . . . how do you mean?"

((Kirins. Dominion-folk. But you are neither)) Again, the purple cloud of watercolour attended the words, but this time it was more distinct. Confusion.

"I'm a halfbreed," Jaan said, and even through his surprise a little bitterness leaked into his voice.

((But which culture do you choose?))

"Neither want me," Jaan replied, his yellow-irised eyes looking into the black of the Koth Taraan's. "So I choose my own."

((You are different from the others)) the creature repeated.

"No," Jaan said. "We're all the same. We just look different."

A warm flooding of reddish-yellow washed through his mind. Approval.

((Who are you?)) it said.

"I'm Jaan," he replied.

((Who are you?)) came the question again. This time, though he couldn't have said how, Jaan realized that the question was meant to encompass all of them.

"Parakka," he said.

The creature was silent for a few seconds. Then: *((Wake Parakka. You will come soon))* And with that pronouncement, it turned and lumbered away, back to the settlement.

Jaan stood where he was for a moment, watching the huge form as it departed with slow, deliberate steps. He didn't know what to make of the exchange that had just taken place, or of what the creature had intended to divine from it. Puzzled and a little shaken, he woke the others, beginning with Hochi so that the big man could avoid the ribbing he'd get from Gerdi about nodding off on watch. They grumbled as they forced themselves awake, but when Jaan told them what had happened they were fascinated, and there was a frantic round of suggestions as they tried to guess what his encounter had meant. They were still nowhere near a conclusion when Ty pointed out that the Koth Taraan were coming, and they gathered up the remainder of their soiled blankets and bedding and packed them away, then stood ready to meet the entourage, as proudly as they could manage considering that they were covered head-to-toe in dirt and grime.

There were five of them who approached across the mist-shrouded bridge. Jaan looked for the one who had talked to him before, but it was near-impossible to tell the creatures apart.

((Come with us)) said one of them; but which one, they could not have said.

They obeyed, accompanying the Koth Taraan on their unhurried return across the simple, unadorned bridge to the settlement. The curious stacks of spherical ceramic igloos had their highest points obscured by the mist – which had thickened as they had slept – but the lights of their circular entrances still shone, looking like hazy, disembodied suns in the white gloom.

They passed within the ring of torches that stood in the gently stirring swamp-water and on to the first island. Kia had originally thought that was the igloo-cluster that they were heading for, but they were led around that to one of the smaller satellite islands that formed a junction between three others, linked by the flat bridges, and on to another one near the centre of the lake. This one was the largest by far, with an enormous mountain of igloos, surrounded by a jumble of smaller heaps at its wide base. One of the glowing openings lay near ground level, and it was here that they were taken, stepping into the welcoming light.

Kia caught her breath. If she had ever had any doubts about her determination that the Koth Taraan were not just beasts, they were swept away as she stepped into the settlement. The interior of the large igloo that they had entered had an intricacy that belied the simple exterior. From the circular entrance, two sweeping ramps curved away on either side, meeting further up the igloo in a platform and crossing over again. Similar curved and sloping walkways wound their way up towards exits, high up the walls of the igloo. Kia's first impression was to think of the Snapper Run that she and Gerdi had endured on Os Dakar, but that was only partially accurate. The Snapper Run had been rough and chaotic in its construction, and held up by ugly pillars. The architecture of this place was perfectly symmetrical, and despite its many layers it was easy on the eye. Also, rather than pillars, the walkways were banked up with solid matter, so that the "floor" of the igloo seemed to slope diagonally up and away from them.

But the walkways and ramps in themselves were nothing. What pulled Kia up short was the decoration. Directly in front of them, between the two curving ramps on either side, was an enormous wooden sculpture, forty feet high or more, a smooth shape that twisted and dived inward on itself before shattering into a core of jagged spikes. Its surface was carved with a multitude of tiny black symbols on the creamy wood, thicker at some points and sparser at others, to draw the attention of the observer to certain parts of the shape. Higher up the cavern, the greenish swamp-water poured through an ornamental outlet and into a series of trenches which ran down the sloped interior, sometimes breaking up into terrifically intricate patterns, grids and spirals and other shapes that Kia's brain could barely grasp. She didn't understand the meaning of what she saw; it came from alien minds, incomprehensible to her. But what it said about the Koth Taraan as a people was far more important.

"Wow," Peliqua said, looking up at the sculpture. A moment later, she added: "I don't get it. What *is* it?"

Jaan punched her gently in the ribs to remind her about her lack of manners.

"Oh, right, sorry," she said, after a few moments' confusion as to why her brother had assaulted her.

They were led through several more chambers, each one populated by a few dozen Koth Taraan, engaged in unfathomable activities or resting in their neutral stance. Occasionally they saw one of the creatures intent on the creation of another sculpture, or on the construction of a new part of an igloo. These ones wore thick metal rings around the tips of their long claws, each ring bearing a different-shaped tool for their work; hooks, serrated edges, devices for smoothing texture, all controlled with a delicacy that seemed at odds with their vicious, unwieldy digits. The Parakkans watched in wonder the civilization that they had stumbled upon.

Eventually the Koth Taraan halted outside a semicircular entrance to a new chamber, from which fingers of swamp-mist – which had been absent inside the rest of the igloos – curled out teasingly.

((The Koth Macquai is inside)) said one of their escorts. *((If you try to harm the Koth Macquai, we will first kill you and then destroy one of your human villages for each of the limbs we tear from your bodies))*

The message was delivered with a thick black hue, emphasizing the threat. Jaan frowned. Why was it that they only got the colours sometimes, and at other times they didn't?

"We're here on a mission of *peace*," Kia said firmly, with admirable courage in the face of such creatures. "We don't want to hurt anyone."

The escorts stepped aside wordlessly, allowing them entrance to the chamber. Glancing warily at their huge hosts, they went inside.

The mist shrouded them immediately, yet strangely it was not cold as it had been outside but stiflingly warm. The floor of this chamber was covered with irregularly shaped pools of marshy water, a reddish glow from the bottom of each underlighting the gently swaying weeds. The mist seemed to emanate from the surface of these pools, lapping across the floor and rising in swirls and eddies.

They forged forward through the layers of obscuring warmth that filled the chamber, following Kia's lead as she picked her way between the pools along the rough, grainy floor. It was a small cavern by comparison to the others, for it took them only a short while before they reached the other side, and came into the presence of the Koth Macquai.

First the shadow of the creature had begun to form out of the mist, an indefinable blackness within the white, and then the curtains of vapour had seemed to tear aside and they saw it, standing in a carven alcove in the wall, an arch surrounded by a multitude of carvings and inscriptions. A pair of torches blazed on either side. The Koth Macquai was like its kin, the Koth Taraan, but its natural armour had branched out around it like a stag's antlers, curving into horny ridges and plates. Its shoulder armour had become almost grotesquely ornate; its back had sprouted fingers of hide like a combination of a headdress and rigid wings. Its elbows and knees bristled with a protrusion of thick, blunt spines. It was as if the armour had overgrown the creature inside it; for Kia, even in her awe, could not see how it could possibly move and fight as a normal Koth Taraan did.

Then she realized; it was not a freak of the race, nor a separate thing from the other Koth Taraan. It was merely *old*. Perhaps the creatures' armour continued growing throughout their lives. She wished that she had seen some of their young to back up her theory, but there had been none in evidence as they travelled through the cluster, or she hadn't recognized them if there had been.

The Koth Macquai raised its tiny head within the massive frame of its body and looked at them. Hochi dropped to one knee and bowed his head, and the others, seeing him, followed suit.

((We have no such customs here)) the voice came inside their head, like a warm autumn breeze. *((But I thank you for your display of respect. Please rise))*

They stood, facing once more the ancient alien being, and waited for it to speak again.

((Forgive the attitude of the elder Brethren)) the Koth Macquai said. *((They begrudge your presence. We are not fond of strangers))*

"I understand," Kia said.

((Yet you interest me)) the creature continued. *((Where is the root of this determination to speak with us, even after we proved hostile?))*

"Desperation," Kia admitted honestly. "We have little hope, and turning back empty-handed would do us no good."

((Please explain)) came the response, and so she did. She told the Koth Macquai all about Parakka and the Dominions, Aurin and the Keriags, the Integration and the sudden change in their fortunes which had led to time becoming suddenly short for them. She had no

reason to hide anything from it; they could not afford the luxury of dishonesty, and besides, she had a suspicion that the Koth Macquai would see through it anyway. She withheld only information that was unnecessary for the creature to know; locations of bases, numbers and so on. It was difficult to tell how much of what she was saying was information that the Koth Macquai already knew, but she went on anyway.

"If Parakka is wiped out," she concluded, "then the people of *both* worlds have no hope. Macaan's stranglehold gets tighter and tighter in the Dominions; it is already so tight here that this branch of Parakka could not have formed if we had not brought some of it with us from home. Soon, it will be over, unless we can develop some way to fight back."

((Your plight is not without merit)) said the creature, stirring its bulk slightly. *((But what do you want with us?))*

"We met a man who wanted to join Parakka. His name was Taacqan," Kia said. She waited for a reaction, but there was none that she could see. "He said he studied you, but I believe he *met* you, as we are doing now. He told us that you were a savage race of beasts, but I suspect he was trying to protect you. You value your solitude, I see that. But—"

((Where is Taacqan?)) the Koth Macquai interrupted.

"He died," Kia replied. "He was killed by Macaan's secret police for treason."

The others were silent. They had all unconsciously

138

retreated a little, aware that this was Kia's show; now they watched the creature to see how it would respond to her news.

((Taacqan was a friend to us)) it said at length. *((Like you, he would not be turned away. He brought us news from beyond our lands, and sought to learn all he could about our people. He had the mind of an ambassador and the heart of a scholar. He, like you, warned us about Macaan. But though many protested against a human in our midst, as many were intrigued and alarmed by the stories he brought to us. He started a change, a stirring among the younger and more impetuous of the Brethren))*

Kia expected it to go on, to elaborate; but the Koth Macquai seemed to falter, uncertain whether it should continue. Then it changed the subject instead, cheating her.

((The elder Brethren feared this)) it said suddenly, its words riding on a grey tide of despondency. *((That if we allowed one of you into our territory, more would follow))*

Again, a silence.

((Tell me what you ask of us))

"A year ago, one of our operatives managed to read the thoughts of Macaan. She told us that he has an overriding desire to conquer anything and everything; it's a reaction against his fear of death by the disease that killed his parents and his Queen." Kia paused for a moment, took a breath and continued. "I'm telling you this because I believe that your people will not be safe once Macaan has the Dominions under his power. Perhaps he hasn't come here before because his mind has been on the greater prizes, but he *will*, in the end."

((You come to warn us?))

"No," Kia said, her green eyes earnest. "I come to ask for your help. The power of Macaan's family is largely maintained by the Keriags. We have nothing that can fight them effectively. We need ... *something*. Something we can use against them. And we came here in the hope that you could help us in some way, because if we don't get that something soon, it's all gonna be over."

Mentally, she cursed her inability to find the right words to say to this creature. She was no diplomat; Calica had the talent for that, not her. She was only honest. And even though these creatures did not appear to stand on ceremony, she was not sure that it would be enough.

((Your intentions are vague at best)) the Koth Macquai observed.

"So are our plans," Kia said. "We have nothing to fight with, nothing that can bring the Keriags down. There are too many of them, and they are too strong. We have no defence. That is why we have to attack."

((It would seem)) the creature mused *((that your best course of action would be to determine the power that Aurin has over the Keriags, and destroy that power. That would solve your problems in one strike))*

"We've tried," Kia replied. "The Jachyra have rooted out every spy we've sent. We can't get close to her; and until we do, we can't learn about her. Her and her father are so surrounded in legends and falsehoods, we can't hope to learn the truth from out here." She paused, and then dared to ask: "Do *you* know anything of the Keriags?"

((We know something of them)) the Koth Macquai said slowly, the words tinged with the murky blue of distaste. It shifted its weight slightly amid the swirling heat of the mists and then raised its unwieldy bulk from its alcove. *((Come with me))* it said, and they moved away a little as it stepped down from where it had been resting, the horny protrusions of its body clacking against each other. Slowly, the huge creature lumbered past them, heading into the white murk, and the Parakkans followed uncertainly, at a distance. It seemed like only a short way before the Koth Macquai stopped in front of a wall, but the mists made it impossible to guage the size of the chamber, and Kia was completely disorientated. All that was forgotten, though, as her eyes fell on what the Koth Macquai was showing them.

It was a recording-wall. Kia had been told of them during her childhood by her Aunt Susa. They had once been common in the Dominions; remnants of past history, from before the time when paper was invented. Macaan had most of them destroyed soon after he came to power. But those had been merely carvings, etched into stone to depict events of great historical importance. This, on the other hand, was different. It was made of water.

The recording-wall was perhaps thirty feet high before it joined the curve of the outer sphere of the ceramic igloo, but from side to side its length was inestimable, disappearing into the haze in either direction. It was slightly sloped, with the top leaning back further than the bottom, and its surface was a maze of pictograms and icons, interspersed with pictures of things that Kia could not begin to guess at. The whole complex, intertwined network was composed of tiny, shallow trenches and sluices, and running along the top was a narrow stone trough of water which streamed down through the trenches into a gutter at floor level.

The detail was incredible. Junctions would suddenly pinch or expand to control the flow of water through a trench, thickening an outline with a gush or lending shading to a shape by gradiating less and less liquid to a series of lines. One pictogram would meld effortlessly into another without losing its own distinction. And the whole wall seemed to move, the tiny sparkle of the liquid making the figures shimmer in the mist, a pantheon of dim ghosts.

((Our history)) the Koth Macquai said. *((This is but a small part. There are many recording-walls. But they are purely an indulgence; we do not need them. We are an ancient folk, and our memory is eternal))*

Kia wondered what it meant by that; it was certainly a strange thing to say. But before she could ask, the Koth Macquai began to answer her previous question at last.

((The Koth Taraan and the Keriags shared a common ancestor once, a long time ago, before humanity began. Many ages passed, and our two races grew apart. Each recognized themselves in the other, and did not like what they saw. That is the beginning of many wars, Dominion child; and it was the beginning of ours, too)) It raised one huge claw, ridged and heavy, to indicate a section of the recording-wall where the pictures and pictograms seemed to take on an ugly, frenzied quality; and though they could not understand the language or decipher the meaning of the pictures, the Parakkans got the intended impression. *((Our war lasted for many of your lifetimes. But the Keriags were more numerous than we, for we have always been slow to breed as a race; and over time, they began to dominate. We retreated to the wetlands, which were unsuitable for the Keriags' biology. They were content to let us do so. Our people were beaten and chastened, but it was the price to be paid for giving in to our savage instincts. Our lesson had been learned. We will not war again on the Keriags, or any other race))*

"Not even for your own protection?" Hochi asked suddenly. "Not even to prevent Macaan invading your lands?"

((We will not make war simply to eliminate

something that may or may not become a threat to us. We fight only to protect our territory. For the elder Brethren to allow strangers to our settlement is rarer than you will ever know. Your lives were spared by the courage of this one)) Here it turned his black eyes on Ty. *((Your pacifism, even in the face of death, gave the Brethren reason to pause. It interested them, and me. So I let you live))*

"How could you have known when you weren't there?" Peliqua blurted.

((We have our ways, Kirin child, much as the Keriags do)) It shifted its gaze suddenly, placing it ponderously on Hochi. *((But there was something else that interested me. Your pendant))*

"You know what it *means*?" Hochi asked, his eyes alight with sudden hope.

A rainbow of colours flashed through their minds; the laughter of the Koth Taraan. *((Does that mean that you do not? How did you come about such an object?))*

So Hochi told it, his voice low with the pain of the memory, about the death of Tochaa in the Ley Warren, and how he had been given the pendant as the Kirin died.

"Now tell me, please . . . what does it mean?" he begged, taking it from his neck and holding it in the mud-smeared palm of his hand.

((It is a symbol from long ago, when the Kirin race was in its infancy. It is a piece of a language forgotten by humanity. That pendant is old, Dominion child,

very old)) The creature paused, the seconds dragging by unbearably for Hochi. *((It represents a phrase taken from part of an old Kirin folktale. They believed that Kirin Taq and the Dominions were once one world, and that they were torn apart in a cataclysm they called the Sundering. To be literal, the symbol means division with the eventual hope of unity))* The creature seemed to creak as it leaned closer, its alien eyes fixed on Hochi's.

((In your language, it translates as Broken Sky))

10

The Central Pivot

The keep of Takami-kos, Thane of Maar, stood alone in the midst of a grassy expanse of land, far removed from the nearest of the farming hamlets and towns that dotted the province. It was shaped like a snowflake, with its six symmetrical arms radiating outward from the central section. The arms were fat and rounded at the ends, displaying the usual Kirin disdain for corners, crafted of many huge bands of dull green metal pocked with high windows of Dominion glass. From the central section, a stubby tower thrust upwards, widening and then tapering at the top. It had none of the high spires of the Princess's palace, Fane Aracq; instead it was low and flat, hugging the ground jealously. And yet for all that, it could be seen for many miles around, across the level and unwrinkled farmland of Maar: an elegant green starfish, dim in the twilight.

A single road arrowed into the keep, a tributary of a main thoroughfare some distance away. Along it, a solitary land-train steamed and roared, its massive body jogging up and down slightly between its outsize wheels, a vast fin of dust rising from the trail behind it, silver beneath the Kirin Taq sun. A great hiss of pistons and brakes came from it as it began to decelerate, closing in on its destination. In the central section of the keep, between two of the stubby metal arms, a thick gate was clanking open to receive the new arrival. The land-train slowed further as it approached, until it was barely crawling by the time it slipped into the belly of the keep, and the gate clattered shut behind it.

No sooner had the great metal creature settled in a slowly dispersing skirt of its own steam than the workers in the vehicle bay began to attend to it. The land-train was late, and it was near the end of their shift, and they wanted to get the job done before the new batch of workers came on, or the unloading orders would get confused and heads would roll. Hurried eyes glanced at their Glimmer shards as they went about their work, scampering up and down the ramp that had lowered from the land-train's underbelly. Kirins ran this way and that while the maintenance crew set to work on checking over the metal body of the machine. The crew's green uniforms, stained with oil, were supplemented by thick wyvern-hide gloves and heavy masks of the same, with protective bibs that covered their upper chest and back. Occasionally, the land-train would emit a scalding jet of steam across them as they worked; but encased in their armour, they were safe, and simply wiped the condensation off their round lenses and carried on.

In all the chaos, nobody noticed two of the maintenance crew walking away from the vehicle. They *looked* like they knew what they were doing, and they strode confidently in the manner of those who were supposed to be where they were. Anonymous behind their masks, they crossed the vehicle bay and slipped away unseen, leaving the noise and hustle behind them.

They halted in a dirty antechamber, caked with grime, with dark pipes rumbling menacingly along the walls. Plain chests of wood were pushed up against the corners of the room, most lying open to reveal the clothes within. Some were the uniforms of the workers and maintenance crew; others were the simple, day-to-day clothes of the Maar people.

"Let's get before the next shift turns up," Whist said, pulling off his mask and shaking his multicoloured hair out. A moment later, Blink winked into existence next to him. They had been forced to leave him in the land-train while they crossed the vehicle bay, as the dog would draw too much attention; but now, seeing through Whist's eyes, Blink could confidently make the jump to his master's side. Ryushi looked at him warily. He'd had enough of that winking trick to last him a long time.

The journey across the province had been uncomfortable, but it could have been much worse. Once inside the vast cargo bay of the land-train, the stowaways had secreted themselves in the darkest corner that they could find and concealed themselves until the loading-ramp had been closed, plunging them into pitch darkness. Whist had thoughtfully brought a glowstone with him, stolen from the very keep that they were heading for, so they stretched and walked around between the tied-down stacks of crates and sacks. Whist assured him that there was no way into the cargo hold except via the loading ramp, and they would feel the land-train slowing to a stop long before anyone could open that. Once they had tired of investigating their surroundings, Whist entertained himself by telling Ryushi stories of his exploits on Os Dakar and what he had done in the year since his escape. Ryushi suspected most of what he said to be lies, but he was content to listen to pass the time, sitting cross-legged in the sickly orange light of the glowstone.

Whist was interrupted by the land-train's brakes beginning to grip, and the slight lurch as they began to decelerate.

Ryushi had known there would be some kind of checks carried out on the vehicle. Despite the difficulty of getting on to a land-train in the first place, he knew Takami wouldn't let any kind of transport inside the walls of his palace without it being thoroughly searched first. Whist had agreed with him, but told him not to worry; it was all in hand.

"They do a check at the last depot before the palace," he said, unhurriedly leading Ryushi back to their hiding-place with the loping, orange-tinged shadow of Blink at his heels. "Course, it helps if you know the routine. They check the outside first, then post guards on the exits and do the interior. That way, nothing gets out and slips past them." He ruffled the short, coarse hair on Blink's neck. "'Less you have a Flicker Dog with you."

In this way, they managed to evade the guards that combed the land-train. After waiting for the clanking of the exterior check to subside, they watched as the loading-ramp was opened in a cloud of steam, bringing a dim, grimy light from the depot into their hiding place. Holding on to Blink, they winked out of the cargo hold and took shelter in the shadow of one of the huge wheels of the land-train. The guards had lost interest in the vehicle now that they had scoured the metal skin for stowaways, and had taken up posts facing outward, watching for any intruders in the depot. Well-hidden in the darkness, the three interlopers stayed patient and motionless until the guards that were searching the interior left by the ramp, and the sentries that watched over it dispersed. The ramp closed, they winked back into the cargo hold, and so the check was passed.

Ryushi didn't trust Whist, didn't even like him. But he had to respect him. The boy was good; him and that dog of his.

Now, in the antechamber, they stripped off their protective suits and uniforms and stashed them away in a chest. It had been their good fortune that the land-train had been bringing a new consignment of gear for the depot workers, lashed together in hemp sacks. Ryushi thought it was perhaps a little *too* convenient, though. Maybe he wasn't giving them enough credit for their stealth so far, but he still could not shake the unwavering certainty that this was a trap, and that he was being allowed into Takami's keep with just enough obstacles to make the whole thing look realistic.

Maybe I'm paranoid, he thought. He glanced at Whist. *Probably not.*

It didn't matter. His honour forced his hand to vengeance, no matter what the risk to himself. His father's spirit demanded it.

"Nobody wears these things outside of the depot," Whist informed him, pulling off his wyvern-hide gloves, which he had slipped on over his own metal one. "We'll do better just trying to get by unseen. If we're spotted, don't worry; the keep folk know me and Blink, and as long as they don't recognize you, there'll be no problem. Not that they ought to; I mean, most of them have never laid eyes on you before. And there's plenty of Dominion-folk around the keep, which Aurin lets your brother—"

Ryushi looked up sharply. Whist coughed.

"—lets *Takami* have around," he continued. "So our skin thing shouldn't be an issue. Shall we just go, huh?"

They crept out of the antechamber into the corridors of the keep. There were few people out and about; the Glimmer shards that were occasionally set into a wall-bracket shone faintly blue in the light of the torches, and Whist informed Ryushi that Takami's court was usually in session at this kind of time. That meant that most people were in the upper levels of the central section, a few floors above them. The arms of the keep were living quarters and kitchens, armouries and so on; that was where they wanted to go.

"Takami's bedchamber," Whist said. "You'll never get him alone anywhere else. You can bolt the door from inside, and by the time anyone gets to him he'll be dead, and we can escape with Blink." He grinned, talking quietly. "It'll be like he was killed by a ghost."

"No," Ryushi said. "I want everyone to know who killed him."

"Okay, okay, it's your show," Whist said. "Just remember what I get when it's through."

"We'll talk about that afterwards," Ryushi replied, mentally adding: *if I'm still alive by then.*

For a moment, he thought about refusing to go along with Whist's idea. If Whist *was* setting a trap, it was best to be as unpredictable as possible, so as to lessen any chance of walking directly into the loop of the snare. But Whist had unwittingly hit on exactly the plan that Ryushi had been formulating during the journey across Maar; and really, Ryushi didn't have any other alternatives that he could see working.

Are you really gonna trust this guy? a voice in his head queried him in disbelief.

I've got my stones, he thought to himself. *I'll be alright. Whist's got nothing he can pull on me that I can't handle with these.*

Maybe not Whist, but what about Takami? Or the Jachyra? continued his argumentative other.

I've beaten them both before, he replied. *I have to take the chance. No matter how much he's shown himself to be a liar in the past, I have to take the chance that he's telling the truth. It's the only way I can make Takami pay.*

They passed through the corridors of Takami's keep, trying to keep out of sight, avoiding contact with other people as much as possible. Sometimes they were able to hide as the sound of approaching footsteps warned them of danger; more often, they found themselves in a blank corridor with nowhere to turn as other keep-folk walked by them, and were forced to keep going and trust to luck. Each time, Ryushi felt his heart suddenly begin to thump in his ears; but he was not recognized, and some of them even nodded at Whist in a friendly fashion.

The interior of the place was more opulent than the smooth, metal exterior. It was decorated in shades of primarily dark green, white and blue. Ornaments were placed on window-sills, and crystalline plants stood in pots and beds against the walls. The theme of the keep seemed to revolve around a form of oddly kinked ceramic tile, which were placed in such a way that they overlapped each other like scales; and these, in various colours, were in evidence in almost every room and corridor, on sloping roofs, fountains and sills, lending contrast to the white stone of the interior walls. The now-familiar Kirin adherence to smooth lines was in effect once again, and as they progressed further from the central section towards the living quarters, the dwindling amount of people they saw allowed Ryushi time grudgingly to admire what his brother's treachery had brought him.

Then they passed into a wide chamber, and all thoughts of admiration went sour in his belly.

It was a mural, and though Ryushi was no judge of art, he could see that it was a very accomplished piece. It covered one wall, thousands of tiny, flat stones in different colours picking out the shapes depicted within. His disbelieving eyes ranged over it from end to end, scanning every detail, each new sight bringing with it a fresh stab of horror.

It was the sacking of Osaka Stud.

Ryushi felt sick. There were the King's war-wyverns, sweeping through the air as the Artillerists on their backs unleashed deadly force-bolts into the ruined buidings below. There was the twisted, smoking wreck of the stables, where Ty had so nearly died and where dozens of their father's wyverns had been massacred. There were Kia, Elani and himself, fleeing in the distance on the back of the bull wyvern. And there was Takami, the central pivot around which the rest of the picture swirled, his nodachi sword held high above his head, about to strike down Banto, who was kneeling in the picture as he never had in real life.

Takami was *proud* of it.

Ryushi felt anger suffuse every pore of his body. He was trembling with fury, his skin reddening under the rush of hatred that followed in its wake. Takami was *gloating* about what he'd done. He had actually commissioned a mural to commemorate the moment when he sold his honour for riches and power, the day when he'd rounded up his whole family and had them executed. Certain details had been changed: he was no longer hiding behind a silver mask, for one thing, as he had been when Ryushi witnessed him slaying their father. But the rest of the scene, apart from his father's kneeling, had been faithfully represented.

He was *proud* of it, Ryushi repeated to himself in horrified amazement. Actually *proud* of it. What kind of creature was he, that their kind father Banto had raised, that they had once called brother? What kind of soulless viper? What kind of *evil*?

He turned away, squeezing his eyes shut hard.

"Pretty messed up, huh?" Whist said tactfully. Blink whuffed softly in agreement.

"Show me where he sleeps," Ryushi said through gritted teeth.

"You look riled, kid," Whist said with a grin. "Come on, then. Not far now."

They went on through the corridors for a short while. Ryushi was becoming emboldened about his chances now, for they had been passed several times by a Kirin servant or retainer and once by a Dominion maid, and he had not been recognized yet. His hair was longer, he supposed, and he wore different clothes now. There would be no accurate pictures of him, only a vague description. Seventeen winters, a lean Dominion boy with blond hair . . . it might be applied to dozens of people within the keep. The only danger lay in crossing paths with someone who knew him, but Takami had seen to it that most of them had gone back to the earth. Occasionally, people glanced at the weapons that he and Whist carried openly; but it was mere curiosity, for all nobles and their retainers were allowed to possess weapons in a thane's house. They knew well what Aurin and the Jachyra would do if they were ever foolish enough to use them.

The mural. It kept flashing into Ryushi's head, appearing in every corner of his mind, filling his thoughts. He tried to bottle his rage, for his fierce expression was hardly helping them stay anonymous, but he did not have Kia's gift for suppressing her anger. Instead, his hands gripped into fists, he followed Whist until he was brought to a stop outside a small, carven door in an alcove, nondescript and positioned to be out of the way.

"This isn't it, surely," Ryushi said, looking over the wychwood frame.

"What, the thane's bedroom? *Please*. This is just the vapour-room."

"Why are we—" Ryushi began, but Whist cut him off with a hiss.

"You think Takami's bedroom isn't going to be *guarded*? Are you *dumb*?" He sighed, and Blink looked at him quizzically. "Sometimes I think I'm the only one making any effort."

"Then why don't *you* kill him?" Ryushi said sarcastically.

"Somehow, I don't think you'd let me even if I tried," Whist replied blandly. "And besides, what reward would I get then? I don't care whether Takami lives or dies, as long as I get my deal."

"If Takami lives, then I won't be around to have a deal *with*," Ryushi said irritably.

"I know," Whist replied. "Why else d'you think I'm doing all your work for you? Now shut up and get inside."

"You go first," Ryushi said.

Whist hesitated a moment. "Still don't trust me, huh? Okay, fine." He pushed open the door to the vapour-room and stalked in, his dog slinking behind him. Ryushi followed warily.

The room was small and bare, its only features being a large, cast-iron brazier in the centre of the room and a multitude of ornamentally-wrought grilles around the upper edge of the walls. The brazier was full of fresh coals, cold and unused.

Ryushi shut the door behind them with a soft click, keeping his eyes on Whist.

"These grilles go to all the master bedrooms," Whist said, motioning with his gloved hand. "They put water mixed with all kinds o' herbs on the coals, and it filters through to the rooms."

"What kind of herbs?"

"Sometimes just things to make the room smell nice,"

157

Whist said, shrugging. "Sometimes aphrodisiacs, if they're in that kinda mood. Sometimes narcotics. You can shut off different grilles so only some of the rooms get the benefit. 'S very clever, really."

"What about poison gas? Couldn't you just take out the whole of the Maar nobles with the right ingredient thrown on the coals?"

"You got a sick mind, you know that?" Whist commented, cocking an eyebrow at him. "Anyway, they thought of it. See that door? Machinist lock on it. When the brazier's on to heat the coals, the door stays shut. Some kinda sensor. It's supposed to be a measure to make sure someone watches the brazier at all times when it's on, so no one gets too much of whatever they're using; but it also means that the guys who get paid to do this have to sit around and breathe whatever they're pumping through the system. I mean, they get masks and stuff, but nothing's a hundred per cent, y'know? You should see the state of some of those guys after a heavy narc session." He shook his head in mock-disgust. "Anyway, point is, you try and gas someone, you gas *yourself* too. Or you're locked in long enough for the bodies to be discovered and you to get caught and executed. They don't miss much here."

Ryushi looked up at the grilles, bored with the explanation now. "And one of these leads to Takami's bedchamber," Ryushi stated. His tone was sceptical enough to get a response out of Whist.

"Hey, don't go thinkin' it was *easy* clearing a route

from here to your bro – to Takami's bedchamber," he protested. Blink raised his ears. "Those ventilation ducts are so loaded with traps, you wouldn't get halfway before you got caught out by *something*. Took me two cycles to disarm every little trick between here and there; I'd like a bit of appreciation, huh?"

"You'll get your appreciation when Takami's dead and we're outta here," Ryushi said. "Now which one is it? And you know that you'll be going first, don't you?"

"Figures," Whist grumbled. He clambered up and pulled loose a grate. It came away easily in his hands, evidence that it had been previously worked on, unlike the others that were set deep in stone.

"You put a lot of preparation into this," Ryushi observed.

"Like I said," he grunted, hauling himself into the shaft. "When I have a plan, it *works*. What I didn't mention was all the cursed legwork that goes into making it turn out that way. Blink, you stay here and follow when we get through."

Blink hunkered down, his head on his forepaws, and scratched his haunch absently with a hind leg.

The vent was narrow and restrictive, barely wider than their shoulders. It was too tight to kneel, so they lay on their bellies with their arms forward and crawled on their elbows, thighs and hips. The interior was mercifully made of smooth metal, so it did not chafe as badly as it might have; but even so, Ryushi found their going slow and uncomfortable. He cast his mind back to the days when he and Kia used to explore the mountain caves back home, often squeezing through tunnels that were barely wider than these ducts. It calmed him slightly.

At first, he could see little but the soles of Whist's boots, his trousers and the three silver ovals of his spirit-stones in his painted back. But as they progressed, he began to see evidence of the traps Whist had spoken of. Here, a curved spring-blade in the floor of the duct had to be gently pushed down so they could wriggle past it; had it not already been sprung, it would have slashed across the belly or throat of an intruder. A little further on, a dry click made him jump, and something jerked near Whist's shoulder. "Poison darts," he said unconcernedly. "Course, a poison dart mechanism with all the darts removed don't make much of a threat."

By the time they reached the grille at the end of the duct, Ryushi wholeheartedly believed what Whist had said. He would not have got even halfway to Takami's bedroom before something killed him.

In the bedchamber beyond the grille, it was pitch dark. Even the windows were covered, with only the faintest line of the grey light from outside showing where they were. They could see nothing.

Whist pushed the grille out of its setting and passed it back to Ryushi. "Bring that with you when you come through; we'll need to replace it, so he doesn't think anything's amiss when he comes in." With that, he wormed his glowstone out of his pocket and unwrapped it. The pale orange glow drove back the darkness a little, sending long, wavering shadows lunging out of the furniture in the room. Whist clambered around and made the short drop down into the room; Ryushi followed him, his eyes alert.

From what he could see, the room was opulent without being garish. Small, low tables stood about, with bowls full of delicate white ornamental pebbles on them, their colour turned apricot by the light of the glowstone. He could almost make out the edge of a fine bed, somewhere in the centre. Wardrobes stood all around, but thankfully no mirrors that he could see.

Whist was quietly replacing the grille, when Ryushi suddenly whirled at a movement from the edge of the light, his sword ringing free of his scabbard.

"Just Blink," Whist said, without turning around. "You'd better hope the guards outside didn't hear that."

The dog padded over to his master. Ryushi looked around the room. It was so dark, he couldn't even locate where the main door was. For a time, he stayed tense, his sword held ready before him; then, when there was no indication that the noise had been heard, he relaxed a little.

"Thick doors," Whist said, talking at normal conversational volume. "They can't hear anything. Don't worry about it."

Ryushi suddenly shifted the edge of his sword, swinging it round so it hovered a centimetre from Whist's throat. Blink growled, his hackles raising and his shoulders bunching. Whist looked at him calmly.

"I will never trust you," Ryushi said. "If I kill Takami, then I'll fulfil our deal. But I'll never trust you. And if this is an ambush—"

"Oh, get real," Whist said impatiently, pushing his sword aside with his armoured glove. "Enough with the posturing. You've got enough spirit-stones in your spine to blow half this keep to pieces. Put your sword away. I'm not stupid enough to try and betray you here."

Ryushi hesitated, then sheathed his blade again. He was sweating with the tension. Making a bargain with a person such as this had left his nerves frayed.

Whist squatted down next to Blink and stroked his back roughly, calming him down. The dog reluctantly quieted, the threatening rumble in his chest gradually dying. And then Whist looked up again, a mocking smile on his lips.

"Unless, of course," he added, "the reward was suitably worthwhile."

"*No!*" Ryushi cried, sensing what was coming and lunging at him, but the room was suddenly plunged into darkness as Blink disappeared along with Whist and the glowstone he held.

"*Whist! I'll kill you!*" he shouted in anger at the emptiness, stumbling backwards and banging the backs of his knees against a low table with a crash. He was blind, and without a glowstone. Panic welled within him.

Betrayed. Get out. Escape.

He could not possibly suppose that Takami did not

know of his presence now. He was trapped here, in the dark. And now, from the endless black all around him, he could hear the sound of a door creaking gently open; a thin door, like that of a wardrobe. And a soft footfall, from another side of the room.

He couldn't fight them here. It was time to make his own exit.

Gritting his teeth, he called upon the power of the Flow, stored in his spirit-stones, willing it forth into his hands to unleash upon something, anything, to make an escape route for himself. Maybe he could hold enough back this time so that he would not drain himself totally. He'd done it before, he could—

But nothing was happening. His stones were not responding. Like a dry-retch, the sensation and feeling were right, but there was nothing coming out. He could feel the energy, still stocked up in the batteries along his spine; but he could not *release* it.

The stones! he thought in panic. *The ornamental pebbles! They're* Damper *stones, like they used on Kia in Os Dakar.*

That was when he realized the full extent of the trap he had been let into. Robbed of power and blind, he could not hope to beat whoever or whatever prowled around in the sea of inky darkness. Perhaps they were Kirins, for Kirin eyes could make the most of a tiny scrap of available light in much the same way as cats could. Perhaps they were Jachyra, for who knew what they could do?

He held his sword out before him and prayed it was the former, his ears straining for a sound, any sound.

The only thing he heard was the *whoosh* of a blowpipe and felt the sting on his cheek as the dart bit; and after that there was nothing.

11

Our Memory is Eternal

Outside the settlement of the Koth Taraan, the Parakkans sat around the flickering phoenix of a newly emerging fire, watching it lapping tentatively between the damp nest of sticks that were piled up around it. Ty had been trying for some time to get the mist-soaked wood to catch, but to no avail. In the end, Gerdi had offered him a small dose of clear liquid that he carried in a small flask, hidden in one of his many pockets. It had flamed up eagerly, and the combination of that and some tinder that Kia had miraculously managed to keep dry in her pack got the fire going at last.

"What *is* that stuff, anyway?" Hochi asked, from where he had been watching nearby. Gerdi started, not realizing he had been there.

"Err . . . it's medicinal, that's all," he replied with a nervous grin.

"Medicinal?" Hochi cried. "I know what *that* means. Give me that flask; you're too young."

"No way, fat guy," Gerdi said, leaping to his feet. "You'll just drink it all yourself!"

"I said give it to me!" Hochi shouted, chasing after

the young Noman boy as he disappeared from the mud banks of the marsh and into the trees. Kia and Ty listened to Hochi crash after him for a while, until the sounds faded.

"I'm not sure I think much of their hospitality," Kia said after a moment, glancing back at the Koth Taraan's settlement, out in the murky lake. They were still clad in the wet clothes that they had set out in, and covered in smears of mud. It was useless trying to wash it off in the brackish swamp-water of the lake; that only gave them clean skin for new spatters and patches to appear on.

"They're suspicious, that's all," Ty said. "It's not like they've had much contact with strangers, is it?"

"Even so, though," Kia said, poking idly at the fledgling fire with a spare stick, "it's kinda rude that they won't even let us stay inside, where it's warm."

After their audience with the Koth Macquai, they had been returned to the tender care of their escorts, who had told them in no uncertain terms that they would have to remain outside the settlement until someone came to fetch them. The Koth Macquai had promised to think on what they had said; but how long it would be before they got a reply, they had no idea.

"You're judging them by our standards, Kia," Ty said. "They probably don't even know what *rude* is. They're just wary; they don't want us near them until they decide whether they trust us or not." He paused. "And besides, they don't know whether we're really dangerous. Would *you* let a bunch of Keriags stay in Base Usido, no matter how well guarded they were?"

She smiled. "I guess not." Then she added: "But I wouldn't make them sit on a mud-bank for hours, either."

"No, you'd just put them in a cage with manacles attached to every available joint," Ty replied.

She shuffled round the edge of the fire and nestled up to Ty, and together they sat watching the fire.

"You think they'll help us out?" he said.

She sighed. "I don't know, Ty. I can't see that we've given them much reason to. We've got no leverage, nothing to offer them really. I just wanted to be doing *something*, y'know? Something that might make a bit of a difference, something that'll . . . I dunno, give Parakka a *chance*." She frowned. "You think I'm just clinging to a false hope or something?"

"Stop picking yourself to pieces," he told her. "It's the best idea anyone's had so far to deal with Aurin. And look, you were *right* about the Koth Taraan. I mean, this is a whole undiscovered culture we've found. That's gotta be worth something."

"Maybe they were undiscovered for a reason," Kia said. "Maybe they wanted to keep it that way."

"Yeah, well," Ty replied. "Things are tough all over.

And you and me both know that nobody can hide for ever."

Kia made a faint noise of agreement.

Jaan wandered the marshes, careful not to stray too far from the settlement in case he got lost. He was used to his own company. He had been born with an unfortunate set of features that showed his halfbreed blood clearly, and he had been largely shunned because of it. He had got over the unfairness of it all long ago; some halfbreeds looked so close to purebreeds that they could live perfectly normal lives if their parentage was not known, and it was just his bad luck that he was such an equal mix of Kirin and Dominion stock that he was clearly neither. Yellow irises, coffee-coloured skin, broad, blocky features; there was no way he could hide it from the world. He had simply had to learn to numb himself.

He hadn't known his father, but he suspected that he had been of the desert-folk in the south of the Dominions. Their mother had found brief solace in the arms of a man like that after Peliqua's father had died of whiplash fever – a Kirin ailment characterized by bright white welts that appeared across the back and chest of the sufferer. She had never spoken of him, but Peliqua had been old enough to remember vague details. The Dominion man disappeared soon after, taking his secrets with him. Perhaps he had been a Resonant; how else could he have turned up in Kirin

Taq? It didn't matter. It did mean, of course, that Peliqua and Jaan were technically only half-siblings, but Peliqua refused to call him anything but a brother. To her, his parentage didn't matter.

Unfortunately, the world was sadly lacking in people to share that opinion. As if the prejudice between Kirin and Dominion folk was not bad enough, Jaan had been forced to contend with it from both sides. It was this, he suspected, that led him to join Parakka when the chance arose. It was an organization composed of both Kirin and Dominion-folk, and professed to allow no discrimination between them. In general, this was true, although there were still odd individuals who had difficulty shedding their old mistrusts and hatreds that had been hammered into them since birth. But Jaan thought it ironic, really; the catalyst for Kirins and Dominion-folk working in harmony was that Parakka were so desperately outnumbered that they couldn't *afford* to discriminate.

What a state of affairs, he thought to himself, brushing aside a vine and plodding through the mushy, damp grass between the trees. *And now there's the Koth Taraan, who've done their best to stay out of it. Sensible decision. Why involve yourself in something so* stupid?

((Your minds are alien to us)) came a voice in his head, accompanied by an indigo shower of puzzlement. *((We cannot see them as we can our own))*

Jaan looked around, and there was one of them, standing less than a metre away from him. For such huge creatures, they moved stealthily and hid themselves well in the wetland terrain.

"I thought you'd turn up," he said. It was the same one that had talked to him before. He didn't know how he knew; maybe it was something in the shade of the colours that crossed his mind when it spoke.

((How did you know?))

"Just a feeling."

The creature turned its head to one side a little, studying him with its wide eyes of endless black. It was fully twice his height, dwarfing Jaan in its presence; yet Jaan felt strangely unafraid as he stood before it, the wetland mists curling around their feet.

He brushed back an errant rope of thick hair from his face and met its gaze. "What did you mean before, when you said you can see your own minds?"

((Each individual shares the thoughts of the Brethren. We are open to each other))

"Like the Keriags?"

A dark rill of displeasure skated over the surface of his mind. *((We are not like the Keriags. The Keriags have no minds of their own. Their queen is the hive-mind, and the drones are merely her eyes and claws))*

"Sorry," Jaan said, sensing he had insulted the other. A light blue, cleansing wave of forgiveness was his reward. He took a step back and sat down at the twisted base of an old and warped tree, resting on the wet grass. The Koth Taraan settled its huge frame, reverting to its neutral stance.

"Why did you talk to me, out of everyone?" he asked at length.

((Your situation is not dissimilar to our own)) came the reply.

Jaan hesitated. "I . . . don't understand."

((You are neither Kirin nor Dominion stock. You are not accepted by either. Yet you live alongside both. And you maintain your own personal, private culture, without feeling the need to be one or the other)) There was a pause, broken by the howling of some marsh-beast in the murky distance and the incessant drip of water. *((The Koth Taraan have kept themselves segregated for hundreds of years. We are afraid of losing what we have. Our identity. The culture of our people))*

Jaan was faintly disturbed by the creature's stark bluntness, but he listened as it went on.

((The Koth Macquai and the elder Brethren believe that this is the way it should stay. They fear that contact with the Kirin folk will result in our culture being crushed under them))

"They're probably right," Jaan said. "At least at the moment." He found it strange that he should feel so at ease in a conversation with a creature so utterly alien to him, especially as communication had never been his strong point. But he was fascinated by the colours that doused the Koth Taraan's speech, and the directness of its words, both figuratively and literally; after all, they were certainly not passing through the medium of his ears on the way to his brain.

((The younger Brethren among us believe that this is what will happen if we do not make contact. Your Kia-Brethren's words were what we had feared for some time. This King Macaan will eventually find us, or his child, or her children after her. If we are unprepared, we will be beaten, and our histories lost for ever)) It turned its glittering eyes up to the thick, dark foliage above them. *((Taacqan was a great teacher to us. The elder ones distrusted him, but we who are younger listened to what he had to say. He told us how Macaan had destroyed and suppressed the histories of the Dominions and Kirin Taq. He fears the knowledge that history brings with it. He rules through ignorance))* The creature looked back at Jaan. *((You have seen our recording-walls. But we do not need them. Our memory is eternal. Macaan could not make us ignorant by destroying them. For Macaan to erase our history, he would have to destroy the Koth Macquai. We cannot allow that))*

Our memory is eternal? The Koth Macquai had mentioned that earlier. Jaan was about to ask about it, when the implication of the creature's last words made him sit up straighter. "Are you saying you'll help us?"

((We cannot. Not without the Koth Macquai's permission))

"But does he know about all that you've said?"

A rainbow of silent laughter. *((Of course. Just as each*

172

of us knows about the conversation we are now having.
We are not Keriags. We are individuals. Each of us has
their own thoughts and opinions. But we cannot keep
them secret from our Brethren, in the way you humans
can))

"Yeah, well *that's* a talent that's not all it's cracked up
to be," Jaan muttered, vaguely bitter. Secrets and
withheld information were half the reason they were in
this situation in the first place. Then, at that moment, a
thought occurred to him.

"The Koth Taraan and the Keriags used to be the
same breed, didn't they?" he said. He knew that the
Koth Taraan did not like to be reminded of the fact, but
it was suddenly necessary to reiterate it.

((You have been told as much)) A soft swipe of
unhappy blue, annoyed black and puzzled purple rode
on the back of its words.

"Then can you *talk* to them?"

((We have no wish to)) came the carefully considered
reply.

"Does that mean you *can*?" Jaan asked, excited.

((Perhaps)) it said after a time. *((It has been lifetimes*
since we have tried))

"Then couldn't you—?" he began, but for the first
time the Koth Taraan interrupted him, barging in on
his speech with its thoughts, sheathed in the iron grey of
firm insistence.

((We will not. Do not pursue that line of thinking,
human child. It will lead you nowhere))

Jaan fell quiet, but he was not chastened. That particular piece of information was a victory beyond anything he had expected to come from this conversation. Securing their cooperation was a step that could be handled later. But if the Koth Taraan could *talk* to the Keriags . . . what if the Keriags *themselves* could tell them what Aurin's power was over them? What if—?

The creature suddenly raised itself again, its massive plates of armour seeming to expand as it did so. *((The decision has been made))* it said suddenly. *((The Koth Macquai has reached a decision. Return to the others. You will be informed))*

Jaan got to his feet, rubbing uselessly at the wet patches on his legs. "Can't you tell me?"

((No)) came the simple reply. Then it almost seemed to soften, and leaned a little closer to the halfbreed boy. *((What is your name, human child?))*

"Jaan," he said. "What's yours?"

((The Koth Taraan do not have names))

"But we humans need them," he said with a faint smile. "It's a side-effect of this individual isolation thing you were talking about. I need to call you something."

((What would you have me be called among humans?)) A faint sparkle of intrigue and amusement.

"Iriqi," Jaan said, without hesitation.

((Iriqi)) it repeated. *((Then that is what you may call me))* With that, it turned and lumbered away into the

wetlands, heading back towards the settlement. Jaan watched it go with his yellow eyes, still unable to fathom the mind of the creature that had seemed to take such an interest in him. After a short time, he suddenly remembered what Iriqi had said, and started quickly back for the camp.

The decision had been made. What was it to be?

"You named it after our *dog*?" Peliqua cried in disbelief. Gerdi was howling with laughter next to her, thumping the muddy ground with his fist and holding his ribs with his other hand.

"What was I supposed to do?" Jaan protested. "I've got a ten-foot-high creature standing in front of me asking me to give it a name. I didn't exactly have time to come up with something appropriate. I just said the first thing that popped into my head."

"But your *dog*?" Gerdi screamed through his tears, still having seizures in the mud. Hochi regarded him much as he would regard a smear of half-eaten bread on the the floor of his hut.

"No, perhaps he was right to call it that," Peliqua said thoughtfully, reverting to her usual habit of swinging everything to a positive angle. "It's a fitting tribute. We loved our old dog, before its time came."

"Yeah, I'm sure the Koth Taraan will be *so* impressed when they find out," Gerdi put in, but his words were mangled by his hysterical laughter and nobody could make much sense of them.

"Can we drop it, okay? It's done now. I shouldn't have bothered telling you," Jaan said sullenly, pulling his hood up over the thick nest of his hair and lapsing back into silence.

"Okay guys, enough," Kia said, from the other side of the campfire. "Here they come." She motioned towards the small procession of Koth Taraan that were approaching across the flat bridge between the settlement and the mud bank on the edge of the lake. She was not much in the mood for laughing. Gerdi didn't seem to appreciate how important the Koth Macquai's decision was. Even though the information Jaan had gleaned from Iriqi had added a fresh sheen of hope across things, it would still all be for nothing if the Koth Macquai refused to help them. A simple yes or no answer, but it could be the catalyst that saved or doomed Parakka.

She found herself barely able to breathe as she stood up. Ty took her hand and squeezed it reassuringly. Even that did little good. They all waited, still caked in mud and looking more like vagabonds than diplomats, as the three Koth Taraan came to a halt at the end of the bridge, in front of them. Gerdi was still biting his lip and chuckling, but he had positioned himself well out of Hochi's way, so there was nothing the big man could do to shut him up.

((The Koth Macquai has reached a decision)) they were informed. The short pause was strung taut with anticipation. *((It has been deemed that this issue is too*

delicate to commit ourselves to, even tentatively, without knowing more about yourselves. Therefore, one of you is invited to submit yourself to a test to prove your worth to us))

"I'll do it," said Kia, without even waiting to hear what it was. The creatures turned their eyes upon her.

((Then come with us now. Alone. The test begins at once))

12

Strike and Counterstrike

A long tunnel. There's an archway ahead, leading into a huge room, filled with the hushed whispers of a hundred people. Steady strides carry him past the finely-crafted panelling on the walls, beneath the green, fluted tiling of the ceiling. His footsteps are accompanied by the tramp of two Guardsmen, walking by each elbow, propelling him onward, inexorably, towards the archway.

And then Ryushi walked out into the Great Hall of his brother Takami's keep.

It was like a small amphitheatre in design. A large, central floor area of white and blue tiles had a raised dais and an ornate seat like a throne at its head. Around its oval perimeter, a smooth wall of white rose to a height of perhaps twenty feet; and above that were three tiers of seats, carved from fine wood and plush with cushions, upon which sat the members of Takami's court. Ryushi looked around them fearlessly as he entered, meeting their gazes. They were almost exclusively Kirin, and they watched him with a mixture of curiosity, sympathy and disdain in their white eyes.

The Guardsmen had stopped at the archway and

taken up position there, so he was left to walk out into the hall alone, his boots tapping hollow as he came. He had no weapons, but nor was he chained. A Damper Collar was affixed around his neck, the single stone of frosty white set into the thin, strong metal at his throat. He made his way a short distance across the echoing room, his head held high, determined not to give the onlookers the satisfaction of seeing him shamed; and there he stopped, waiting expectantly.

Two swords stood point down in the centre of the room, supported by a metal bracket; his own, and the longer blade of the nodachi used by his brother. Beyond them, sitting on the chair that was so nearly a throne, was Takami, clad in his elegant green armour, a cruel smile twisting his face. He was framed against a hanging tapestry, draped across the wall behind him, bearing a stylized depiction of a wyvern. Had Ryushi been in a mind to notice, he might have thought that it seemed curiously out of place here, incongruous amid the rest of the fine décor. It didn't hang quite right, either; almost as if it had been put up in some haste. But he was focused only on his brother, and in the silence that filled the room, he glared at Takami with naked hate in his eyes.

"Ryushi, Ryushi," Takami sighed. "When will you ever learn?" He got to his feet, and his next appeal was addressed half to Ryushi and half to the surrounding court, playing up to his audience. "Don't you remember last time we met, you tried to give me a lecture on *real life*, brother? It seems you know less than you think you do; for here we are again, and this time you've brought yourself right into my hands."

"I also seem to remember that last time we met, I beat you soundly," Ryushi said. If Takami wanted this to be in public, he'd *make* it public. "And I would have killed you there, had not one of Macaan's little helpers been there to drag you out of trouble."

Ryushi had expected Takami to show at least a flicker of anger at the reminder of his humiliation, but he shrugged it off with an insouciant smile. "Ah, but you're bringing up the past; and what really matters is the here and now. You see, *I'm* a thane here. I have money, I have power, I want for nothing. While *you* are still grubbing around in the dirt, putting your life in peril for the sake of a misplaced sense of honour. Are you still sure you made the right choice? Has this last year been as easy for you as it has for me? I doubt it, little brother. Really I do."

"Well, no, it's not been easy," Ryushi said, his voice loud enough to carry around the room. "But then, perhaps, I've been doing something more constructive than getting fat from Aurin's teats and commissioning murals to celebrate murdering my defenceless family."

A shocked outcry arose from the upper galleries; not at the second slight, but at the first. To insult the Princess was a death sentence. Ryushi didn't care. Treason was a way of life to him now; he'd incurred the death sentence many times over.

"I see that mixing with the dirt and beetles has coarsened your vocabulary," Takami said, strolling down the steps of the dais. "That's one more reason to end your pitiful life."

"You need reasons now?" Ryushi asked. "You didn't need a reason to execute women and children back at Osaka Stud, did you? Or to kill your own father because you dared not face him in a fair fight."

"*Please*, little brother," Takami said. "Look at where you are. You're hardly in a position to make effective taunts. But as to a *fair fight*. . ." He strolled over to where the two swords stood in the bracket. "Well, that is exactly what I'm offering you. You see, I do owe you for beating me back in the Ley Warren, and as you've so graciously allowed yourself to be tricked into coming to my keep, it is now time to even the score."

"Take this Damper Collar off me and we'll see a fair fight," Ryushi said.

"Unlikely," Takami said. "However, I will make you this concession." He motioned at another archway, and a page crossed the room towards him. He knelt down on one knee, keeping his eyes fixed on his brother, and allowed a Damper Collar to be fixed to his own neck. For a wild moment, Ryushi pictured seizing his blade and striking him down right then; without his powers, he was weaponless. But it was madness. Takami undoubtedly had several Guardsmen with their halberds trained on him, ready to unleash their deadly force-bolts. And besides, such a victory would have no honour, and would sully his father's memory. He could beat Takami again, he told himself. Fairly.

But somehow, he doubted it would really be that easy.

When Takami was sure the Collar was secure, he stood back up again. Slowly, he drew his nodachi from the free-standing bracket, savouring the sound of metal sliding over metal as it came. The crowd above, minor nobles and other dignitaries or people seeking to curry favour within the thane's court, were utterly silent. Only the faint muttering of the torches that lit the room brightly could be heard as Takami stepped back and Ryushi reached forward to take his own blade. The page scooped up the bracket and scampered off, back into the shadow of the archway; and then there was only Takami and Ryushi in the arena of the Great Hall, their eyes locked together, each waiting for the other to make the first strike, *daring* them.

"When I kill you," Ryushi said suddenly, "what then?"

Takami laughed tersely. "*If* you kill me," he repeated, smirking, "you'll still be executed. But at least you'll have the satisfaction of watching me die first. Isn't that enough for you?"

"Plenty," Ryushi said; and a moment later he swung his sword up and low, hoping to take Takami's knuckles off his sword-hand. It was an awkward angle to block from, but Takami rose to the challenge, shifting his blade to repel the strike with a harsh clash of steel. The gallery gasped as Takami responded by dropping into a leg sweep, his armour hampering his movement not one bit; but Ryushi jumped over the scything arc of his heel and brought his sword down in a two-handed smash. Takami had been ready, though; he knocked the blade aside as he rose and brought the elbow of his free arm viciously up into Ryushi's jaw. The clack of his teeth jarring together echoed around the arena, and he staggered back a way, allowing Takami time to compose himself.

"As you see," Takami said, "I haven't spent the last year letting my fighting skills get stagnant."

Ryushi spat blood, staining his lips a deep red. "You know, I'm curious," he said. He wanted Takami to talk for a moment, to allow him to shake off the effects of the last blow. "What was really the deal with you and Whist?"

"I imagine it was very much different to what he told you," Takami observed, closing in and circling again. "My Guardsmen found him, half-starved near Os Dakar. After he told me what he knew – and we had a lot of false starts that I had to persuade him out of; you know, he's terrible for lying—"

"Really?" Ryushi said sarcastically.

Takami made a small, tight smile in response. "Anyway, when they told me you were dead, I never believed them. I mean, no body? You just disappeared off the veldt outside the Ley Warren? Very impressive, but hardly conclusive. So I held on to Whist in my dungeons for a while. I knew he'd turn out to be useful one day. Then, when I heard you'd been sighted alive, I knew it was time to bring him out. A simple trade; his freedom, if he would deliver you to me. And if he tried to run, I had Aurin's permission to set the Jachyra on him. That kept him on a leash, well enough." He paused. "Of course, we had to make it all convincing. I made sure everyone knew who he was, and would pretend he was a familiar member of the keep. I allowed you to get into the land-train depot and past the checkpoint. And we set up a false bedroom, disarmed the traps in the ventilation ducts, and led you into it."

"That's a lot of detail. Congratulations," Ryushi said, never taking his eyes off his brother.

"We knew you'd be suspicious from the start, especially as it was Whist we were sending. But who else would you believe could get you into my keep? Certainly not—"

He cried out as Ryushi suddenly flicked the point of his sword-blade up. His heavier nodachi was not fast enough to block it, but he managed to pull his head back quickly enough so that instead of cutting into his throat, it sliced a short, stinging line up his chin. The gallery thundered in anger, but Ryushi only smiled.

"You lose concentration when you boast, Takami. Arrogance is a weakness in combat. By the way, how's your shoulder healing up?"

Takami's eyes filled with anger as he touched his chin with his armoured glove and saw the blood on his fingertips; the reminder of the injury he had sustained last time they met was just salt in the wound.

"You'll pay dearly for that," he promised.

"I'm bored of your threats, Takami," Ryushi said, his tone full of disdain. "Let's get this over with, shall we? Father's spirit is impatient for his vengeance, and frankly, I'm sick of looking at you."

"Very well, little brother," Takami replied, his voice grating. "We will finish this now, once and for all."

Their swords met, parrying high, low, sweeping in short arcs of death as the wielders danced and weaved between them. The air sang with the punching chimes of their combat, flurries of blows exchanged, strike and counterstrike, feint and dodge. Both of them had been trained since early childhood towards mastery of their weapons; and while neither had the experience to make them truly great fighters, they were still swift and deadly. Both fought with a viciousness that sometimes slipped just beyond its reins, making them occasionally overswing or lunge too hard – for neither had Kia's iron self-control – but the two were evenly matched, and the combat was frighteningly close. Those in the galleries held their breath as the brothers matched swords again and again, but neither could find the crucial advantage that they needed to land the fatal strike on the other.

Eventually they broke apart, panting, their backs heaving as they leaned low over their weapons, facing the other.

"You can't beat me," Ryushi said with a fierce grin, and what was more, he believed it. The anger and adrenalin surging around his body made him feel indestructible, and as he stood with his sweat-soaked fringe dripping into his eyes, he knew without a doubt that he would kill Takami, here and now, and whatever happened after would not matter any more. His honour would be satisfied.

"Oh, but little brother," Takami replied. "I haven't even *begun* to fight yet."

They launched back into each other, leaping together and clashing in mid-air; but this time, as their swords hit, Ryushi felt an unexpected force behind his brother's blow. His sword recoiled hard, bruising his hands and almost making him drop it. He landed and rolled as Takami sent a backhand swipe at his neck. The blade passed harmlessly over his head, and he flipped to his feet again; but he was unable to conceal the sudden worry on his face.

So strong . . . where is it coming from?

But Takami was already attacking again, his nodachi blurring into a slash at his ribs. Ryushi stepped aside easily and glanced it away, but even that small contact made his sword jump in his hands. The metal of the hilt was getting uncomfortably warm, too. He had thought it was the heat from his palms, but now he realized it could not be. His sword was getting hotter.

Another blow from Takami; and this one he barely fended off, even with his whole weight behind the parry. There was a glint in Takami's eyes, an evil triumph on his face; and as the swords parted, just for the briefest of seconds, there was a flicker of green fire that puffed out in the air between them.

Takami was using his spirit-stones. His Damper Collar was a dud. Subtly, underhandedly, so his audience could not see, he was cheating. Ryushi should have known he would never submit to a truly fair fight; where was the sense in risking defeat when he could simply execute his brother and be done with it? No, he was exacting retribution; his reputation had been damaged by his defeat at the Ley Warren, and he had to redress the balance. To his court, he had heroically offered his brother a chance for an honourable death; but really, he had known what he had been doing all along. The chance he offered was very slim indeed.

But it's still a chance. A lucky strike could end this.

Kill him. For Father.

When next Takami's blade came down, Ryushi's parry was a fake. Keeping his wrist loose, he put no strength into the block, but instead twisted out of the way behind it. Takami's nodachi smashed through his guard much further than Takami had intended, but found only empty air on the other side; Ryushi's blade, capitalizing on the recoil, was already swinging back towards his brother. Takami saw the danger, spinning out of the way, as the bright slash of the sword cut through the torchlight. The combination was enacted faster than the eye could follow, and they seemed to part in slow motion, both suddenly stepping back and away from each other.

For a long second, there was nothing.

Then Takami's howl of pain and anger rose up to fill the Great Hall, and his armoured hand pressed against the side of his head as if it could contain the flow of blood there, running out between his fingers, staining the green metal black. On the floor between them, in a steadily growing puddle of its own blood, was Takami's left ear. The gallery was hushed in horror as they watched him stumble backwards, his eyes wide in disbelief at the evidence of his own mutilation.

"Cut the theatrics," Ryushi said. "If you're gonna cheat, finish me now. But don't pretend you can kill me with honour, my erstwhile brother, because honour is something you'll never have again."

That final goad was all it took. Takami roared, his sword erupting into ochre flame, and he threw himself at his brother, one side of his face stained dark with blood. The first strike was wild, but Ryushi was unable to hit back under the sheer force of his brother's fury. His previous elation had died; he knew now that there was no way to win without his spirit-stones. All he had left was the hope that he could make Takami regret ever giving him the chance to fight for his life.

The second blow, accompanied by a searing arc of fire, swooped past Ryushi's head with a savagery that took him off-guard. He tried to get a counterstrike in, but it was hurried and weak, and Takami's defences turned it aside.

"*Die!*" Takami cried, and then his nodachi was coming down in a double-handed swipe, and though Ryushi knew he could parry it in time he saw what was coming. The two blades met in an explosion of flame, and Ryushi's blade snapped in half under the terrible force. He fell back, his arms numb, his fingers falling open under the shock and the hilt falling free. Hitting the ground heavily, he tried to roll, but his angle was bad and he landed awkwardly, unprepared for the next strike. Not that it would matter now, of course, because—

And then something flashed between them, leaping over Ryushi and crashing into his brother, almost too fast to follow. Then another, and another; and suddenly the gallery was in uproar, shouting and stamping as Ryushi dazedly raised his head and looked. . .

"He is *mine*! He is *mine*!" Takami was screaming, and Ryushi's eyes widened as he saw the scene before him. "*I'll kill you all!*"

+++ **That would be unwise, Takami-kos. Most unwise** +++

Takami was pinned under three Jachyra, hunched over him like ghouls. The central one he recognized from the assemblage of its metal features; it was the same one that he had faced in the Ley Warren a year ago. It had its finger-claws pressed up against Takami's throat, while its companions controlled his thrashing arms.

+++ **I would kill you before you could summon your power, Takami-kos** +++ Tatterdemalion said through a screen of static. +++ **Princess Aurin is displeased with you, my thane. Very displeased** +++

"Let me go! He took my *ear*! You can't have him!"

+++ **But we can** +++ came the implacable reply. +++ **And you will not prevent us. Your status as a thane of my Princess has already been called into question today. Such an act might well result in you becoming an ex-thane** +++

The way the Jachyra phrased the sentence, along with the stories Ryushi had already heard about those who displeased Aurin, left him in no doubt as to what being an ex-thane meant.

He felt sudden, rough hands on his shoulders and arms, and a moment later he was being dragged up by more of the Jachyra. They surrounded him with their repulsive, musty oil-and-rags smell and their mechanical wheeps and crackles as they held him between them, their disjointed and unnatural bodies arranged around him as a guard, their retractable finger-blades never more than an inch away. If he tried to escape, they would shred him. He remembered what had happened to the defectors on the beach at Mon Tetsaa and swallowed.

Behind Takami's chair of office, the tapestry that had hung there had been torn to pieces, revealing a tall mirror, three times the height of a man and perhaps half that distance in width. Takami had been covering it to hide what he was doing from Aurin's secret police; did that mean that it was not *him* that had planned Ryushi's capture, but Aurin after all?

He had no time to consider the question. Ryushi was dragged roughly towards the mirror, his head swimming in a mixture of elation and terror. He had escaped death once again; but was he heading into something worse?

With his arms held fast, he could not obey his instinct to throw his hands in front of his face as he was pulled towards the hard, cold face of the mirror; but the impact he expected never came, and the last thing he heard before disappearing into his own reflection was Takami's shriek of frustration as he departed.

13

Your Father Nonetheless

Kia stood alone in the slowly churning mist, her skin and clothes soaked from the hot, damp air, fronds of hair plastered to her forehead, cheeks and neck. The hard, uneven floor at her feet was her only point of stable reference in the shifting netherworld that surrounded her, and though the logical side of her mind told itself it knew exactly where she was, it was difficult to convince herself that the emptiness on all sides did not go on for ever.

It was the room of mists, where they had previously met the Koth Macquai. But that time there had been all of them together, and she had had Ty by her side to draw strength from. Now she had no one; the others had been forbidden to enter the settlement with her, and she had been left by her silent escort at the mouth of the ceramic blister that contained the recording-wall that they had admired earlier. She had no idea what she was supposed to be doing, or what the test was that she had agreed to take. Butterflies that felt more like bats thrashed around in her stomach, and she felt cold despite the heat as her nervous mind flitted over the possibilities of the ordeal she might have to face.

But it didn't matter. There had never really been any question about her agreeing. She had to, and she knew it.

Enough. She began to walk forward slowly again. The red, steaming pools of weed-laden water slowly formed at her feet, and she stepped carefully around them. *((Human child))* came the voice, suddenly. *((This way))*

Though the voice had no source that Kia could follow, it was pursued by a strong impression of the location of the Koth Macquai in the room. She blinked in surprise, then automatically turned towards where she had been told to go and plunged onward through the mist.

The Koth Macquai was there, its huge form describing the outline of a thick, branching tree as it hunkered at the edge of a particularly small pool, only six feet from one irregular side to the other. The antler-like protrusions on its joints and back rattled as it stood taller, acknowledging Kia's arrival. She dropped to one knee and bowed briefly, knowing that the creature did not stand on ceremony but doing it anyway.

((Rise, I ask you)) the Koth Macquai said, faint amusement and indulgence colouring its words. *((Your kind owe no fealty to me))*

Kia didn't comment on that as she got back to her feet, but instead said: "What sort of test would you have me do?"

((You are a brave and reckless one, to take a test without knowing what it entails)) the Koth Macquai stated.

"No," she said. "I just don't have a choice."

((You always have a choice, human child. It is only the limitations you impose on yourself that restrict you))

"Well, those limitations are restricting me pretty good right now," she said, with half a smile. "Tell me about the test. Will I have to fight?"

A sparkling smudge of many colours spread across her mind as the Koth Macquai laughed. *((It is merely a test of character. No physical harm can come to you. We seek only to divine the true motivation behind your proposal, and to know what kind of person it is that brings us such an offer))*

Kia was faintly relieved; after the exhausting journey here and the poor sleep she'd had since, she was in no state for anything physical. "How will you do that? With questions?"

((Questions can be answered falsely)) came the reply, the wide, dark eyes studying her closely. *((The pool. You must immerse yourself in the pool. We will do the rest))*

Kia was hesitant. "The pool?" she asked, looking doubtfully at the murky, steaming water and the gently waving reeds and leaves beneath its surface. The red light that suffused the cavern glowed at its bottom, but the water was too cloudy to see where it came from.

((Do not worry. We have used the pools for many of our generations. They will teach you things. Insights that even you yourself may not be aware of. Premonitions. Dreams. Hopes and fears. The pool strips you to nothing, human child, and leaves only that which cannot be washed away: the truth))

"The truth," Kia repeated. "I can handle that."

((We shall see. Are you ready, human child?))

Kia took a breath. For a moment, her will faltered; but she set it rigidly again, allowing herself no pity. She must do this, she told herself.

"Ready," she said firmly.

The Koth Macquai settled again, compacting its huge weight down on its haunches so its massive claws hung over the lip of the pool and dipped into the water. The chipped sabres that were its digits were heavily adorned with the curious rings that Kia had seen the artisans of the race wearing, except they carried not tools but simple symbols and pictograms. She watched, fascinated, as a small, sharp white glow began to suffuse the deeper red of the room. In the midst of the Koth Macquai's thin, unprotected chest, an oval of flesh was burning bright, a light from something within its body. It was mesmerizing, the resonance of a million frozen moments, its radiance carrying with it much more than mere light, but also sound . . . and *memory*.

((Climb into the pool)) the Koth Macquai ordered.

Kia lowered herself until she was sitting on the

edge of the pool, with her legs dangling in the water. It was warm as it soaked through her clothes and boots. Well, no matter, they were already wet. With that as her final thought, she slipped into the water, and as her head plunged beneath the surface she felt a sudden, breathless lift in her chest and she was gone.

It was sunny again. The best time of the day, when the morning sun had just crested the eastern mountains and was blasting heat down into the valley. The kitchen had three tall windows that caught the light full on, and on summer days like this one it transformed the room into a haven of cosy, sluggish heat as they breakfasted. They were sitting on benches at a table of smoothed wood, with melting honeycomb and cream in pitchers next to pancakes and scones and glasses of berry water. The floor and walls were of plain, varnished planks, but rugs and pictures kept the room lively, and a stove sat comfortably at one end. Outside, the noises of the workers that had been up with the dawn could be faintly heard, as they busied themselves with the hardest jobs before the ascending heat made them unbearable.

Osaka Stud. It was the best and only place in the world to Kia.

She glanced at Ryushi, who was sitting next to her on the bench. He was eating with characteristic abandon, his face smeared in honey. He stuck his tongue out at her as he caught her gaze, and she punched his thigh underneath the table.

"Don't start, you two," said their mother from where she stood at the stove. Kia gave her twin a poisonous glance and turned away.

Across the table, Calica and Aurin were sitting next to each other, wearing the same immaculate smocks. Both of them had their hair in pigtails, and Kia could tell by the angle of their shoulders that they held hands beneath the tabletop. They were watching her with a combined, unwavering stare, cold and reptilian.

Kia frowned. She had always thought of Aurin as being older than the rest of them, somehow; but here she was, in the flesh, with no more than six winters under her belt. She didn't like playing with either the Princess or her creepy friend. What were they doing here, anyway? This was *her* kitchen, not theirs. She began to get angry. Why were they always muscling in on her? They weren't family. Cuckoos in the nest, that's what they were; and Mother was taken in by them. But Kia knew, alright. She saw through them. They were just there to take what was hers. Well, she wasn't going to let them.

The door to the hallway opened then, and Takami came in. He was as she had always remembered him; towering over them, tall and thin and frighteningly old and mature. He sat down on the bench next to the twin entity of Calica and Aurin, and didn't say anything, just glared disapprovingly at everyone and everything until Kia got bored of watching him.

Instead, she turned her attention to Mother. She was doing something on the stove, but Kia couldn't see what. That was no surprise; everything her mother did was done in secret. Kia spooned another mound of cream and honey into her mouth, her huge green eyes fixed on their mother's back, and suddenly she felt a terrible desire to see the face of the person at the stove, the *real* face. But when she tried to speak and get her attention, she found that she couldn't, and in the end she gave up trying.

"Father's home," Mother said, without looking up from the stove or turning around.

All of them turned to the door expectantly; but as it swung open, Kia felt an awful wrench somewhere inside her, and time seemed suddenly to decelerate hard. The sun slipped behind a thick cloud and the room darkened. Walking in, as if through syrup, was a lean, dark shadow. Dreamlike, it left streamers of itself behind as it moved, wisps and after-images; and it radiated a chill that had nothing to do with temperature.

She watched in horror as it darted across the room, touching her mother on the shoulder with one crooked finger, and with a sigh she slumped to the ground, dead. Aurin and Calica's eyes followed it dispassionately as it lunged past them to touch Takami in a similar way, and Kia squealed as he seemed to shrivel and gnarl in front of her, becoming twisted and rotten, his eyes bright and cruel like an owl's.

"You're not my father!" she shrieked at the shadow.

"*Not your first father, no*," it replied in a rasping voice. "*But your father nonetheless*."

And with that, it reached across the table and grabbed Ryushi by the wrist, picking up his small body effortlessly and carrying him out of the door. Ryushi did not scream or struggle, showing no sign of resistance as he was dragged away from her; but she cried out at the sudden loss, scrambling to her feet and chasing out of the door and into the twilight. For Osaka Stud was gone now, and they ran under the cold eye of the Kirin Taq sun.

She spied the shadow, impossibly fast, streaking away from her with her brother lying calmly in the crook of its arm. She felt a stab of pain, as if someone had thrust a knife in her back and held it there, twisting gradually more and more as the distance between them increased. Desperate to end or at least reduce the agony, she ran after, her tiny feet carrying her across the stony ground, but she could not catch up with him. And then, suddenly, the ground betrayed her, and what had been flat earth suddenly terminated in a clifftop. She wheeled her arms, balancing herself as she skidded to a halt, and then a voice behind her made. . .

. . .her spin and there was Takami, not bent and foul as he had been before but tall and strong, his silver mask on his face, fashioned in the effigy of a spirit howling in despair and agony. She was no longer a child, but back to her natural age, with her bo staff gripped tightly in her hands and her red hair whipping about her face in the salty sea wind. They stood on a pinnacle, a straight finger of rock that thrust out of the raging ocean beneath them. Lowering clouds lashed them with rain, and a howling gale cut around them. Takami was in his green armour, the armour he had worn when he had murdered their father, and he held his nodachi out before him, the long edge crawling with tiny rivulets of water.

With a cry, they struck together, her staff meeting his blade hard. His metal visage was impassive as he sliced at her, making him faceless and anonymous, like Macaan's Guardsmen. She fought him away, her feet steady on the tiny platform of stone that they battled on. There was no urgency in the combat, no excitement or fear; it was as if they were enacting a puppet-play. Each stroke was planned; each stab, each parry, the blade and the staff meeting time and time again as if they were predestined to do so. And the outcome was equally as inevitable. Kia felt hardly even in control of herself as she knocked aside a clumsy strike and hammered the end of her weapon brutally into Takami's armoured shin. His foot slipped back on the wet rock, his sword went wild; and Kia planted her boot in his stomach and shoved.

With a shriek, he stumbled backwards and lost his

footing, and at that moment Kia felt control of her body return to her. His mask fell free somehow, his nodachi falling after it into the thrashing sea below; and for the longest of seconds Takami hung on the edge of falling, his arms wheeling, his eyes fixed on hers in an expression of supplication. He was missing an ear.

"Sister! *Please!*" he cried, unable to regain his balance.

Please? Here was the man that had murdered their father, that had killed their family, that had exiled her and Ryushi from the sanctuary of Osaka Stud . . . and he asked her to save his life? When she knew that he was capable of the worst treachery, and that if he lived, he would only continue to hunt them down? When, if their situations were reversed, he would let her fall without a second thought?

Takami pitched backwards, his balance finally lost.

Her arm shot out through the rain and grabbed his, pulling him back from the brink, clasping hard on his gloved. . .

. . .hand in hand with her father, her palm sleepily in his cracked and calloused fingers, dozing in the soporific warmth of a blazing fire. It has been a hard day of work and play, and though she hasn't slept in her father's lap for years, she finds herself drowsing now on the big, old armchair that he had brought back from his travels one day. Her mother is talking nearby, and though she hears what is being said, it doesn't register in her sleep-fogged mind.

"Look at her, Banto. Fifteen winters old and she still looks like a little girl when she curls up on your lap."

She can feel Banto's smile in his voice. "It does my heart good to see them so happy. Exhausted, but happy. It is my fear that it cannot last much longer. Soon the time will come for Takami to learn about—"

"Banto!" her mother whispers urgently. "She could still hear!"

A pause. "Kia?" her father says, and she can feel the depth of his voice through his broad chest. "Kia?"

She stirs, making a noise of dreamy gibberish. She is asleep, right enough.

"She'll not know a thing," Banto says.

"She could be faking it."

"I'd know."

A sigh from her mother. "I suppose we must leave tomorrow."

For some reason, that sentence evokes a dread in Kia such as she has never felt before. She wants to wake up, wants to scream *No! Don't go!* But she can't.

"I'm sure it'll be okay. It's not as if she's ever been wrong before, is it?"

Her mother shifts uncomfortably in her chair. "This one feels wrong, though."

"You always say that."

"I know. And one time I'll be right." A short laugh. "It's just nerves, I know. These recruitment missions always set me on edge. You never know, you just never. . . I mean, one day Macaan's going to get wise to us, and set us a trap. It could be this one."

"It could," Banto replies. "But we have the best operatives. The best intelligence."

No, don't listen to him, Mother! If you go, you'll never come back to me! If you go, I'll never see you again!

Her mother relaxes. "I suppose so. And like you say, it's not as if Calica's ever been wrong before, is it?"

Calica? Calica!

She opens her eyes and gets up calmly, and as she walks out of the room her parents appear not to notice her. As if sleepwalking, she pushes open the door and heads for the stairs. A single glowstone at the top shines orange light down the steps; she puts one hand on the banister and heads for it. Upstairs is where they are sleeping.

Upstairs is where she will kill Calica.

She sent my mother to die.

At the top there's a bedroom that she's never seen before, much bigger than the rest of them. There are two sleeping-pallets here, each wide enough for two. She can't see well in the darkness, but she knows exactly where she's going. She walks softly over to the bed where Calica's orange-gold hair is visible, framing her sleeping, six-winter face. Without hesitation, she slips her hands around the child's throat and squeezes.

Instantly the world around her becomes a screeching,

scratching mass as Aurin leaps on her, tearing at her, protecting her sibling. She cries out and stumbles back, but Aurin bears her to the floor, and Calica now with her, two frenzied children that thrash and bite and flail and—

Suddenly they stop. Kia opens her eyes. They are watching her again with the cold, reptilian eyes. Aurin is holding out a dagger with a long, curved blade, offering it to her. Numbly, she takes it. Aurin points slowly to the other bed. Kia gets up and walks over to it, and there in the bed is the shadow, the one that stole her brother and killed her mother and replaced her father. The two children watch from the floor as she raises the knife above the sleeping victim.

"Don't, Kia," says a voice at her shoulder, and it's Ty. She turns to look at him, and there he is, gazing earnestly at her, the Pilot's apprentice she once knew, shy and sensitive.

"I have to," she says.

"If you try and kill him, I will die too."

"No," she says, shaking her head. "No, I'll make sure you don't."

And with that, she suddenly plunges the dagger into the face of the shadow in the bed, and the screech it makes as she stabs it again and again seems to go on for ever, ending in a high-pitched. . .

. . .whine of blood in her ears, her lungs aching, and she broke the surface of the pool, gasping for air. The steam and mist around her dulled the sounds of her struggle as she grabbed hold of the edge of the pool and pulled herself out. Fronds of weed lay limply against her neck, falling free as she hauled herself on to the hard, uneven floor of the room in a cascade of water and then lay there, breathing hard, forming a pool of her own.

((Rest, human child)) came the voice of the Koth Macquai, as it slowly raised its claws out of the pool and the white glow in its chest died. *((Taacqan before you suffered much the same fatigue))*

"I . . . failed," Kia panted bitterly.

((In this test, there is no failure. The truth is always a victory))

"Then . . ." she gasped, "what happens . . . now?"

((Now you go back to your lands))

She coughed and raised herself a little, looking into the black eyes of the Koth Macquai as it regarded her impassively. "Your decision. When will we know?"

((The decision has already been made. You have neither the best interests of the Koth Taraan nor of Parakka at heart when you ask us to join you. You seek only to destroy the shadow that dominates your life; the welfare of my Brethren is unimportant to you in comparison. We will not help you))

Kia sagged, slumping back to the floor, the weight of disappointment bearing her down again.

((But do not despair, human child)) it continued, a powdery blue cloud of sympathy engulfing her. *((Your*

ordeal revealed that you, at least, believe what you say about the threat Macaan poses to us. This corroborates what Taacqan told us some time ago. A proportion of the younger Brethren have made known that they would have us send a representative with you, to observe and judge the truth of this for the Koth Taraan))

"Iriqi," Kia said distantly.

((Iriqi)) the Koth Macquai agreed.

14

As Inevitable as Time

Ryushi opened his eyes and wished he hadn't. The hunger was still there, waiting to spring on him the moment his conscious mind was aware enough to recognize it. His stomach had shrunk considerably, but it did little good now. It felt like it was trying to eat itself for want of anything better to digest.

He lay on the hard creamstone floor of his cell, feeling a headache begin to rise at the back of his skull. It was better than lying on the smooth, curved bench that jutted out of the gently rounded wall; since his captors had allowed him no bedding, the only advantage that sleeping there might provide was that he might fall off and break his neck, sparing him whatever was in store for him later.

There was no chance of him getting back to sleep now; his body had already started its insistent clamour for food. He sat up, feeling a wave of lightheadedness clutch at him as he did so, and gave his Damper Collar an experimental tug in case it had somehow loosened in the night. The cell around him was clean and immaculate, a slightly yellowish white. He estimated that he had been here for three cycles by now, but there was no way of telling without a Glimmer shard. It was featureless but for a thin trench against the far wall, flowing with water for his ablutions, and the three tiny oval wind-holes in the elliptical door. These were only big enough for him to fit three fingers through, and looked out on an equally blank and featureless corridor. A single torch burned in a locked and shielded alcove bracket, and was replaced periodically. Occasionally a young Kirin boy brought him a thimble-sized bowl of rice and some water, flanked by two Guardsmen with their deadly halberds trained on him. That was the only sign of life he had seen.

He was a prisoner in Aurin's palace, Fane Aracq. And he had a nasty suspicion that they were softening him up for something.

Clambering over to the bench, he sat down and rested his face in his hands. He had been so close, *so* close. An inch to the left, and he could have ended it then. Takami would be dead. His honour would be satisfied. So Takami had lost an ear; so what? Ryushi derived a little satisfaction from that, but not enough. Because he'd never get a chance to finish the job now, and so in the end, Takami would get away with it. He felt miserable; and worse, he felt that he had let everyone down. He'd failed to kill Takami, and now he was in Aurin's hands. She had, at last, a genuine Parakkan to play with. One who knew a lot about the operation of the organization. One who would know where they were based.

And she would find out what he knew. He remembered stories Ty had told him, the pain etched on his face, about what Macaan had done to him after he had been captured at Osaka Stud. He did not relish the thought of experiencing that at first-hand. But it was as inevitable as time, and there was nothing he could do to stop it.

Suicide? The thought had crossed and recrossed his mind, each passing leaving deeper footprints. But no, that was no option. It was something his honour would not allow him to do. He had got himself into this situation because even the tiniest chance at avenging his father's death had to be taken. While he was still alive, a chance might arise again. It was terrifically unlikely, but it *might*. And so, even at the risk of betraying Parakka, he had to endure. Besides, anything he might use to end his own life had been removed from his person, and he doubted he had the willpower to smash his skull against the wall.

Footsteps. He looked up at the cell door. Not the boy and the Guardsmen, this time. The footfalls were more frequent and varied.

The time had come.

The mask of a Guardsman filled the wind-holes in the cell door. "Get on your knees, prisoner, for the Princess," he barked.

Ryushi smiled weakly. "Tell your Princess that if I get on my knees I may not have the strength to get up again," he replied, his voice full of scorn.

There was the sliding of a bolt and the door was pushed open angrily. Two Guardsmen came in, dragging him roughly up from the bench and shoving him to his knees. He did not have the strength to resist physically, but he could still defy them.

"You could cut off my feet and then I'd *have* to kneel," he said. "But I still wouldn't mean it."

The blow around the back of his head made his vision whirl. He squeezed his eyes shut to steady himself. When he opened them again, the Princess Aurin stood before him, flanked by one of her Jachyra and another aide.

"Get out, you two," she said to the guards with a hint of disgust in her tone. They obeyed, bowing as they left and closing the door behind them, sliding the bolt home after.

Ryushi stayed where he was, looking at her. She was breathtakingly beautiful, as the reports had said, thin and willowy with porcelain features and pale skin. Her hair was blacker than onyx in comparison, and her narrow frame was draped in an elegant gown of cobalt blue and white, with three turquoise stones on a pair of silver chains strung across her collarbone. For a few moments, there was silence as each appraised the other. Then Ryushi got up, struggling to his feet. The aide on Aurin's left made to push him back down again, but Aurin stopped him.

"There's no need for all this unpleasantness about kneeling and bowing, Corm. It's really only for the benefit of my subjects, yes?" She turned her steady gaze on Ryushi. "And you don't seem to think of yourself as such."

"You're very observant, Princess," he said, sitting down on the smooth creamstone bench again. He glanced at her other companion, the Jachyra. The same one he had fought in the Ley Warren, and who had come to his rescue in Takami's court. This one appeared to be Aurin's favourite.

"Forgive me," she said, following his eyes. "This is Tatterdemalion, Chief of the Jachyra. And this is Corm, a representative of the Machinists' Guild."

That was no surprise to Ryushi. The Machinists he had met that worked for Parakka were all instantly recognizable by their Augmentations, and this one was no different. The long black coat and high, rigid collar that covered the lower half of his face probably hid most of them, but the evidence of machine-flesh fusion was visible elsewhere on his body too. One hand had been replaced by a mechanical claw, with two strong pincers for his fingers and an opposing one for his thumb. Clustered around the wrist were all manner of minuiscule tools, ratchets, minute metal tendons and other devices. Judging by the bulge of his shoulder, the whole arm had been done as well. His face was spare and gaunt, with one cheek replaced by a dull, bronze-coloured plate. A circular band ran around his hairless head, covering and replacing both eyes and one ear with grotesque mechanical substitutes that chipped and chittered as they operated.

"My name is Ryushi, son of Banto and a traitor to the throne," Ryushi told them, as if they needed to know. "I'd offer you a seat, but as you can see…" he trailed off, indicating the bare room.

"*The* Ryushi," Aurin said, spuriously impressed. "It is my privilege to meet you, after all I've heard. I have to admit I was a little disappointed when I heard of your death during the Integration, but I should have known this day would come sometime. People like you have a habit of coming back from the grave, yes?"

"Only because you guys never bury us deep enough," Ryushi offered as a rejoinder.

"Yes, well, that's a failing of my father's, perhaps. But not of mine," she said casually, with a cold smile. "First, though, I believe you have something for me."

"What's that?"

"I'm sure you've figured it out by now."

"I assume you want information about Parakka, then?" He gave her a shrug. "I don't know exactly what you expect. I've been in the organization just over a year; that's not long enough for them to tell me anything sensitive."

"Oh, I'm sure you're just being modest," Aurin said chidingly. "After all, Tatterdemalion himself saw you recruiting for Parakka at Mon Tetsaa."

The Jachyra's eyepiece whirred out fractionally, focusing on Ryushi. He was crouched in his customary coiled stance, watching for the slightest movement from the prisoner. Ryushi had no doubt he would be cut down before he got half the distance to the Princess's sleek throat.

"I do the recruiting, that's true," he said slowly. "Most people who've heard of Parakka have heard of me and Kia. So we go to collect them, to put them at ease, let them meet some of the people they've been told about; and then we pass them on to the real recruiters, the ones who are part of the central organization." He gave her a sympathetic look. "You've not made much of a catch, I'm afraid. I don't know anything. Like when your father caught Ty." He paused, and then smiled. "You royal types really aren't very good at this, are you?"

"Enough lies," she snapped, the colour rising in her cheeks. She wasn't used to being mocked. "I have subjects that can rip the answers out of your mind, if necessary." Her voice quietened. "It will be far more unpleasant than simply telling me now. The location of Parakka's base."

"Chita, on the Iron Coast," he replied instantly.

"Another lie!" she hissed.

"On Tetsu Mountain? Jii Lan in the western provinces? Deepwater? Even if I told you, you wouldn't believe me, Princess. What can I—"

She slapped him, hard, across the face; and with her touch came something else, an undercurrent of force that brushed his soul and made him quail at the contact, a power cold and dark and brooding. . .

He forced down the sudden fear and looked up defiantly into the Princess's eyes, which flashed with haughty anger.

"You're very easy to wind up, Princess," he said, his voice low. "I'd expect a little more restraint from the ruler of Kirin Taq."

She laid a hand on Corm's arm to stay him; he looked as if he would lunge at the prisoner at any moment. Tatterdemalion merely watched Ryushi, his mechanical features incapable of expression. Ryushi's face smarted, but he could sense that he had won a victory. He didn't care about the pain his disrespect would bring him eventually. He needled her out of spite.

+++ **My lady** +++ Tatterdemalion spoke up suddenly. +++ **Will you have us bring the Scour?** +++

Aurin glared at Ryushi hotly. "Well?" she demanded. "It is your choice. Spare yourself the pain."

"You think you can do something worse to me than slaughtering my family?" Ryushi said, and suddenly burst into hysterical, desperate laughter, a mixture of fear and amusement. "Really, please try. I'd be interested to see it."

Aurin's chest heaved in indignation, but this time she controlled the angry flush of her pale cheeks. "You will regret the request you have just made," she said, and with that Corm knocked on the cell door and it swung open. Aurin stalked out, followed by her aides. The Guardsmen were nowhere in sight. For a moment,

Ryushi thought that they had actually left him to walk free.

Then the Scour stepped into the doorway, and the blood drained from his face.

It wore a loose, black cloak, belted at the waist, which swirled around its feet as it came. Its hands were held together in front of it, buried in its long sleeves. But its chalk-white face was unhooded, and there were no features there. Shallow indentations or slight lumps indicated where eyes, nose and mouth should have been, but the Scour possessed only a smooth skull of naked flesh, uninterrupted by the features by which humans recognized each other. There was something inexpressibly horrible about their absence. But not as horrible as the paralysis which suddenly gripped Ryushi, pinning his heart to his ribs and making his arms go limp. Strange, then, that he still had breath to scream as the Scour clamped its fingers around his face and began to tear and shred at his memories. . .

"Are you alright, Princess?" Corm enquired in a high, nasal voice.

"Of course I am," she snapped, striding along the corridors of Fane Aracq, heading back to her chambers. Tatterdemalion dogged their heels. Ryushi's howls were fading behind them, but they still caught a faint shriek from time to time.

"I hope that hurts as much as it sounds like," Aurin muttered bitterly.

Corm frowned. This kind of pettiness was unusual, and did not become the Princess.

+ + + **You seem angry, my lady** + + + Tatterdemalion observed.

"That's because I *am*," she replied sharply.

+ + + **Why?** + + + the Jachyra enquired. Corm had noticed before that Aurin and Tatterdemalion did not adhere to the rules of conduct that should exist between ruler and subject, but such forthright interrogation still made him flinch inwardly.

Aurin pulled up short in the middle of the corridor, turned on the creature as if to shout, and then seemed to deflate a little. "I don't know. Why am I like this? His taunts are laughably ineffective. Yet they affect *me*." She paused. "Perhaps he has been trained by a wordsmith to add barbs to his tongue, yes? I will be more careful." She turned and resumed her walk.

The Machinist watched her back with his mechanical eyes as she headed once more for her chambers. He had been an aide to the Princess for five years now, since she was thirteen winters by the calendar of his Dominion homeland. And now she had come of age, grown into womanhood; and he feared for her. She had been brought up as a Princess, accustomed to being obeyed by everyone, with a power at her hands that was enough to make even the bravest man nervous. Children played with her because they were forced to, and because they were afraid of her. She had missed the tough lessons that children inflict on each other to harden their skins for the tribulations they will face later in life. Nobody had dared to insult her or go against her whims.

But a girl who was used to her own way was not about to sit back and let everyone else do things for her. And now, with her father gone and her coming of age, she had involved herself more and more in matters that were previously left to her underlings, things that she was painfully ill-prepared for. The incident with Ryushi was only one example. He had tried to ask Tatterdemalion to explain this to her, to warn her against herself, but it was useless; a creature like that had only a very slippery grip on the finer emotions. Most of them had been numbed and deadened by the cruel experience of being Converted.

"Corm," she said suddenly, making him jump. "The Machinists' Guild. Where do they stand?"

She already knew the answer to that, but Corm replied anyway. It was another facet of her immature personality; she needed constant reassurance that her plans were not straying.

"The Master Machinist issued a communiqué a few cycles ago, stating that all was well, Princess. The Guild is pleased with the trade that your father's subjugation of the Dominions has brought. War makes profit, both in the building of war machines and in repairing damaged items."

"But. . .?" Aurin prompted, eager to hear again any sign of dissent against her father.

Corm frowned for a moment. He understood the reasons behind his Princess's coldness where her father was concerned, but there were times when her disrespectful attitude – at least when out of his earshot – gave him cause for concern.

"But now that the war is over," he continued, "and the Dominions are under his control, there are fears in the Guild that the profit will dry up somewhat. This in itself is not a catastrophe, but the unrest it has provoked has fuelled the cause of those who are wary of your father. They believe he will not be content with trading and paying for the Guild's services when he can invade the Citadel and turn the Machinists into little more than slaves. For precedent, they cite both the subjugation of the Keriags and the more recent Integration, when the King was not content with his power over the Dominions until it was totally in his grip."

"They may rise against him, you think?" Aurin asked, sounding almost hopeful.

"There are not enough of the dissenters yet. However, there had been a steady trickle of Guild members who had left the Citadel and taken up with Parakka, before they relocated to Kirin Taq. We believe that some of the dissenting Machinists are now using their Guild privilege to cross over at the Ley Warrens and join the reformed organization over here."

"Interesting," she mused, and then they were at her chambers. She led them into her largest room, where her great mirror was fused with the creamstone wall, and where white glowstones lit up the graceful curves of the windowsills, benches and tables. Like herself, the room's appearance was elegant and understated, with only a few ornaments of exquisite beauty breaking the simplicity.

"Sit down, please," she said to Corm. She had learned long ago that it was not worth making the offer to Tatterdemalion; he didn't even sleep, let alone sit. Corm thanked her and sat on a wicker mat, his Augmented eyes following her above the high ridge of his stiff collar. She walked over to one of the wind-holes, looking out, as she often did, over the provinces beneath her. After a time, she turned away with an expression of faint disgust.

"Tatterdemalion," she said. The Jachyra raised itself a little from its crouch and looked at her attentively. "What news from the Jachyra?"

+++ **The search for the Parakkan base continues apace, my lady** +++ he said, the last words almost inaudible under a sudden squeal of feedback. +++ **We hoped to acquire Whist from Takami-kos, in case he had gleaned any clues from his time with Ryushi; but the boy was gone, and we were unable to catch him** +++

"Takami," Aurin said distastefully. "I admit, it was a stroke of genius to use Whist to lure the boy here, even though it was my idea to use Takami as bait. But if we had not had spies in his court to warn you, and Takami's lust for revenge had got the better of him. . ." She turned aside for a moment. "Losing an ear is less than he deserves. But I will leave him be for now." She looked sharply back at Tatterdemalion. "What else?"

+++ **Now that Parakka know that their presence has been revealed, they have abandoned their secrecy where Resonants are concerned. Previously, they did not dare shift to the Dominions because they would alert us if they did. Now they have nothing to lose by that, and Resonant activity has increased dramatically** +++

"Can we use it to pinpoint their location?" Aurin asked halfheartedly.

+++ **Parakka have always travelled far away from any sensitive locations before shifting, my lady, so as not to lead us to them. And some, particularly the little girl, are very good at covering their tracks** +++

"They're throwing out branches again," Aurin said. "Spores of their organization, in case we wipe them out here. Gathering information about what is happening in the Dominions, yes?"

+++ **It would seem probable** +++

"You have not told my father?"

+++ **The Jachyra are ever loyal to you. And the King relies on us for information of that kind. We shall not tell him, if you so desire** +++

Corm glanced between the two of them and felt the ever-present worry about his Princess gnaw at his insides once more. These dangerous power games she played were one day going to trip her up. Her father had indoctrinated the Guardsmen to be loyal to him, and he was their first concern, even those who served and protected the Princess. He had given the Keriags to his daughter in one of his many attempts to buy her love; but his gift was also a curse that she openly resented him for. So she had spent her time winning the Jachyra over to her side, knowing that they were the linchpin of her father's information network. Her job was not a hard one; after all, the Jachyra hated Macaan more than Parakka did.

It was a strange thing, that Macaan's most trusted force were also his bitterest enemies. But though they kept it carefully secret from him, each and every Jachyra desired his death more than anything. For he was the one who captured them; he was the one who had them Converted, turned from humans to the nightmarish scarecrows of rag and metal that they were. For the Jachyra were Resonants, heavily Augmented by the Machinists' Guild under Macaan's orders, made into lightning-fast killing machines to carry out his bidding. It was a curious side-effect of the process that the Jachyra lost their ability to shift between worlds at will; but they gained instead the power to use mirrors as portals. It had been suggested that the loss of half their human body meant they could only half-shift, into the world of reflections, and so they were forced to travel in that way; but nobody knew for sure.

If the Jachyra were ever to rise against Macaan, they would be a fearful enemy. But Macaan was too wary to create such a force without some means of controlling them. For the Jachyra, like Macaan's other top aides, were implanted with special stones beneath their rags, stones that were linked to the indigo trigger-stone set in Macaan's forehead. With a thought, Macaan could end what was left of their lives; and while this would be no great loss to many of them, still there was enough humanity inside them to keep them in line at the threat.

"And what do you think of the fears of the Machinists, Tatterdemalion?" Aurin asked. "Are they justified?"

+++ **Possibly, my lady. Though perhaps your father will remain content with possession of both Kirin Taq and the Dominions** +++

"I doubt it," she replied.

+++ **As do I, my lady** +++ Tatterdemalion said.

She turned away from the wind-hole and walked slowly across the room, talking as she went. "So *now* what?" she repeated. "What will he do now? You know he won't be able to stop *here*."

Tatterdemalion's reply was uneasy, even through the wheeps and distortion of his voice. +++ **Perhaps the Unclaimed Lands. There are stretches of the Dominions as yet unexplored. Your father still has no firm grip on the nomadic tribes of the steppes or the desert folk. And there is always Deepwater, and whatever lies beyond** +++

"But it's all worthless!" Aurin cried suddenly. "And what good is it? What will he do with it? Give it to me? *I* don't want it! I don't even want *this*!" She swept a slender arm out towards the wind-hole and the lands beyond.

Tatterdemalion did not respond for a time; when he did, it was to change the subject. +++ **The Scour is one of the best, my lady. The prisoner should not be long in giving up his secrets** +++

"How long?" she asked.

+++ **Ten cycles, if we intend to leave him the power of reason after we are done. Perhaps less, if we do not** +++

"That's too long. If the Parakkans are sending Resonants about, we have to stop them before they can take root in the Dominions, yes?"

"Perhaps if you told your father, he could deal with it?" Corm suggested, but was silenced by a blazing glare from the Princess.

"*I* will deal with it. I will see the prisoner. Soon, in a few cycles' time. Let the Scour soften him up. Perhaps I can get out of him what we need."

+++ **My lady, that could be unwise** +++ Tatterdemalion ventured.

"At least let us use an interrogator, Princess," Corm pleaded.

"No. I will do it," she said, and the tone of finality in her voice told them that her will was firmly set in the foundations of stubbornness. She turned back to the window and rested her thin fingers on the sill. "Go now, both of you. I will send for you later."

+++ **My lady** +++

"Princess."

And then they were gone, the Jachyra through the mirror and Corm through the door, closing it softly behind him. Aurin stood alone and looked out over a land she cared nothing about, and listened to the silence for a time.

15

A Gesture of Support

"He's gone? What do you *mean* he's gone?"

"He's gone, that's all. He left to go off with Whist on some stupid point of honour to kill your brother," Calica replied.

"Why didn't you *stop* him?" Kia cried in disbelief.

"I *tried*," Calica shouted back. "Maybe if his sister hadn't been away on some fool mission to nowhere then *she* might have been able to."

"Don't try and blame this on *me*! You're the only one he listens to any more anyway!"

"And whose fault is that?"

"You're saying it's *mine*?"

"Of course it's *yours*! It wasn't me that cut him off from you. That was all your own work. If I—"

"*Please!*" the Convener roared, silencing them both. The longhouse hushed, and the mutterings from the blackness outside the bright circle of wavering light faded. The firepit cracked noisily. Seated on their wicker mats around it, Kia and Calica glared at each other. Baki smirked at them, his ash-grey face creasing smugly.

"Enough of these petty arguments," the Convener

spoke at last, his voice echoing through the room. "Why Ryushi went does not matter. The fact that he is gone and has not returned is sufficient. We have more pressing concerns at the moment; we cannot waste time speculating on what he may or may not be doing."

"Waste *time*?" Kia cried, but she was cut off by another voice.

"Your pardon, Convener, but what Ryushi is doing at the moment is of the very utmost importance."

It was Anaaca who spoke, a trim, middle-aged Kirin with long, free-falling red hair that contrasted sharply with her dark skin. She was the centre of Parakka's information network; a spy by trade and now a teacher of spies for the organization. She was regarded with some suspicion by the rest of the Council, but she was an invaluable resource and she knew it. Her narrow, cream-on-white eyes surveyed the Council before she continued.

"As you know, we have been trying for a long while now to get people into Fane Aracq for the purposes of gathering information on Aurin. It has proved so far impossible. However, we do have the next best thing; a spy in the court of almost every thane in Kirin Taq. Not necessarily in a position of any importance, but there nonetheless." She paused, smoothing her hair back over her head with both hands. "I have a page-boy in Takami-kos's court whose message reached me only today. The court is in uproar. Ryushi was captured there during an attempt to assassinate the thane, after which

Takami-kos challenged him to single combat. The fight was stopped by Aurin's Jachyra. They took Ryushi with them, presumably to Fane Aracq."

"He's been *taken*?" Kia said, blanching.

"Your brother's recklessness has put us all in danger," she said, without a taint of emotion in her voice. "He knows far too much about Parakka. Aurin will force his secrets out of him eventually. She may already have done so."

"Then what do you suggest, Anaaca?" the Convener asked, his eyes flickering to Kia as if expecting her to interrupt. She didn't, surprisingly; but only because Calica got there first.

"We get him out!" she said firmly. "We have to! For his sake and for ours." There was a mutter of agreement from those shadows seated outside the circle of firelight; they had not forgotten Ryushi's part in the destruction of the Ley Warren.

"We must get to him, that much is true," Anaaca said softly. "To divine how much he has told them, if anything. Get him out, if possible. If not, kill him."

"Kill him and I'll leave your *head* on his tomb!" Kia shouted at her.

Anaaca sighed. "I doubt that, girl. But all that is moot right now. First we have to get to him. A direct assault on Fane Aracq would be useless. Spies would take too long. We need—"

"You need *me*," came a voice from the darkness, and into the firelight stepped Gerdi, his impish face grave beneath the green shock of his hair. Kia subsided a little, settling back down.

"The Council recognizes Gerdi," said the Convener. "Speak."

"Look, spying's not my strong point and straight combat's hardly my brew," Gerdi said, looking at Anaaca. "And I'm no assassin, either. But I'm a Noman kid. I've got stealth in my blood. I can get into and out of anywhere, and you guys know it. Let me go, on my own. I'll bring him back somehow."

"He's just a child!" Baki protested, characteristically obstructive.

"I could be older than you think," said Gerdi in a dry, phlegmy voice; except that it wasn't Gerdi there any more, but an old and bent Kirin, tottering on a stout staff of warped wood. Those in the Council that did not know of Gerdi's talent exclaimed out loud in surprise, but those outside the firelight murmured in puzzlement. Only the Council had seen Gerdi change, for he could only influence the perceptions of so many people at one time. With the power of his Noman spirit-stones, he could make others see him as anything he chose; but the ability only worked on those he was able to direct it at, and though he was improving every day, he was still not strong enough to make a whole room full of people succumb to his illusion.

"You know he can do it!" Kia said. "I'll go with him."

"And me," Calica volunteered.

"No, you won't," Gerdi said, his voice for once devoid

of humour. "I'm gonna have a hard enough time as it is without you guys tagging along. If I go, I go alone." He addressed the whole of the Council. "I'm the best chance he's got. Let me do it."

"Those who agree?" the Convener asked. The decision was unanimous; even Baki put his hands flat in front of him in a gesture of support.

"Alright, you guys have got some sense," said Gerdi. "I'll see you when I get back." And with that, he walked out of the firelight and back into the shadows.

"Stay where you are, Kia," the Convener ordered, as she made to rise and follow. "He will do better without your interference. You can't help your brother, except by leaving the boy to do his job."

She hesitated a moment in indecision, her distress evident on her face, then got to her feet and plunged into the darkness after him.

"Uncle Hochi?" Elani asked, more to let him know she was there than out of any real doubt as to his identity. It was hard to mistake Hochi, even in the dim Kirin Taq light and with his back turned. He was at the edge of the artificial clearing at the top lip of the valley where Base Usido resided, a narrow strip of land where the forest had been pushed back to allow the sentries on the huge mechanical lift nearby a chance to see and react to an attack from out of the forest. Shadowy metal skeletons stood about, bits of half-constructed machines and items waiting to be loaded on to the lift.

Hochi looked over his shoulder in alarm from where he was leaning against a thick stack of girders. "What are you doing out here? It's dangerous!"

"Gerdi told me where you'd gone," she replied. "He said you two had an argument and you went to cool off."

"And the lift sentries let you come up the canyon wall alone? They should know better. *You* should know better."

Elani's eyes fell to the ground. "You want me to go?" she asked, her voice hardly audible.

Hochi hesitated for a moment, then sighed and heaved himself down on to the grass. "Come and sit with me, Elani."

Her face shifted from doe-eyed sadness to sparkling joy in a single jump, and she scampered over to where he sat and threw herself down alongside him, nestling between him and the girders that rose at his flank.

"Whatcha looking at?" she asked eagerly.

Hochi pointed a meaty finger out into the forest. Sparks of light danced there, very distant, popping in and out of sight in the black depths of the forest.

"Oh," said Elani, her elation muted a little.

"The Banes are getting closer," Hochi said. "There's more and more of them every day. They're drawn by our spirit-stones."

"Why?" she asked.

"Nobody knows," he said simply.

"We'll be okay," said Elani, toying with her dress, the

hem of which had become muddied. "It's happened loadsa times before. We can handle a few Snagglebacks and Snappers."

"I hope so," he replied. "You know that a young Kirin boy called Paani was actually *bitten* by a Bane yesterday?"

"I thought Banes didn't attack people," Elani said. "They just scavenge off dead bodies."

"Exactly. The boy just dropped into a coma. He doesn't respond to anything. Where the Bane that bit him went, we don't know either." He looked down at his hands. "These are bad days for us."

There was a pause for a time. "Are things alright with you and Gerdi?" she asked.

Hochi frowned, his bushy brows gathering like thunderheads over his small eyes. "That fool boy. He wants to get himself killed. No one's got into Fane Aracq before, let alone got out again."

"Kia says that might not be true; Aurin would have covered it up if it had happened, just like all the other things she—"

"Oh, of course, Kia *would* say that," Hochi grumped. "She doesn't care about Gerdi. She's only worried about her brother."

"And what about you, Uncle Hochi? Do you care about Ryushi?"

"Obviously I do," Hochi said, sounding a little uneasy at admitting such a thing. "He's Banto's son, for one."

"Don't you owe it to Banto to look after—"

"Curse it, girl!" he snapped. "Letting Gerdi get killed is not going to help Ryushi one bit!"

Elani fell silent, looking at her lap. She knew how Hochi felt about the Noman boy. Despite their antagonistic relationship, the boy was practically a son to him.

"I can't stop him, anyway," Hochi said, his voice diminishing in volume. "He's always gone his own way."

"Kia wanted to go with him," she commented, picking out a strand of her fine black hair and chewing on it absently.

"She's upset about Ryushi," Hochi said. "She knows she couldn't do any good, but she wants to do something. Gerdi will slip away from her if necessary, but I'm sure she'll see sense before that."

"I'm surprised Calica didn't want to go too."

"What's she got to do with anything?" Hochi asked, looking down at the little girl who sat in his shadow.

Elani blinked back at him in surprise. "Don't you know? Calica and Ryushi are in love."

"Mauni's Eyes, Elani!" Hochi exclaimed. "You can't just go around saying things like that!"

"Why not?" she shrugged. "It's true. Just look at them."

"I haven't noticed anything like that," Hochi said firmly. "It's just your imagination."

"If you say so, Uncle Hochi. Not that you *would*

notice, anyway, with all the mooning you've been doing over that pendant of yours."

"You know how important this pendant is to me, Elani," he replied gravely.

"Yeah, I know," she replied, wrapping her arms round her knees and looking up at the curling corona of light that was the Kirin Taq sun. Unlike Gar Jenna, Base Usido had no need for canopies to protect itself from being seen by aerial reconnaissance. There were wild wyverns here, and worse things that plied the skies above the shattered landscape. The Princess's wyvern patrols were few and far between in this dangerous place, and those that went in were as likely as not to never come out again. The Parakkans had lost many mounts and riders before establishing the safest routes to fly, avoiding the feeding-areas and brood sites of the winged Rift beasts; and they had lost more men and women in their difficult task of domesticating the wild wyverns than nested near Base Usido. Wyverns, unlike most creatures, were found in both Kirin Taq and the Dominions; it had been suggested that breeding pairs had been brought over by Resonants far back in history, but nobody knew for sure. Like everything since the Integration, it had been a hard and costly struggle; and now that it seemed to be finally paying off, it looked like they would have to run again.

"I had. . ." Hochi began suddenly, and then stopped.

Elani nudged his leg. "What?" she prompted.

"I had hoped for an answer," he said downheartedly.

233

"An answer for what? From the pendant, you mean?" she asked.

"Broken Sky," he said, confusion and frustration written on his face. "What does *that* signify? All this time I spent trying to puzzle over what Tochaa meant when he gave me this thing –" here he touched the small silver medallion that rested beneath his shirt – "and when I'm told what it is, it raises more questions than solutions."

"Why don't you ask Iriqi?" Elani suggested. "He might know."

"He's gone off somewhere with Jaan. The Council are voting whether to let him into Base Usido or not." He frowned. "*Division with the eventual hope of unity*," he said, repeating the Koth Macquai's words to him. "What does it mean? Tochaa asked me to bring Parakka to his people, and I've tried to *do* that; I've worked myself to the bone over this last year to help make Parakka a force in Kirin Taq. But this? I don't know. How can I know what he meant?"

"You can't," Elani replied. "You just have to make your best guess."

Her sudden switches from childishness to maturity did not faze Hochi in the least any more, but still he found that he could not be satisfied with her answer. "If the Sundering that the Kirins speak of is the division," he mused. "Maybe the bringing together of the worlds is the unity? But Macaan's already *done* that with the Integration. It doesn't make any *sense*."

"Uncle Hochi, I'm worried about you," Elani said. "You've got to stop thinking about it. Remember what the philosopher Muachi said? Sometimes answers are like sleep; the harder you look for them, the better they hide."

"I wish I *could* stop, Elani," Hochi said, a great sigh making his back swell. "I wish I could."

Calica rode the great enclosed plain outside Base Usido, her thoughts studded by the rhythm of her pakpak's feet on the grass. She knew about the increase in Bane activity, and the threat it posed to the settlement, but it was not enough to stop her. She had to get out and alone for a while, to organize herself. Away from the constant industry of the Base, and the endless calls on her attention. Just herself, and the wind rushing past her as the pakpak sped across the great expanses of blank grass between the soaring cliffs that hemmed her in.

The Council meeting had gone on to other things after Kia had left, but she had scarcely been able to bring herself to concentrate on them. Her thoughts had been full of Ryushi, and the danger he was in. She had wanted to run with Kia, to see what she could do, full of the vain hope that she could possibly help in some way; but she had restrained herself. She tried to tell herself that the decision was nothing to do with pride; because any reaction on her part would have revealed to all who were watching how deeply she felt for him. It didn't work.

And so had passed the rest of the time in the lone circle of light. The decision to let Iriqi into the settlement had been made, and a messenger sent to Hochi to tell him to find the creature and its perpetual companion Jaan. Reports were made on some of the forays into Dominion territories, mostly involving Elani. There was little that they had learned that was not already known by other channels; Macaan had subjugated the greater part of the Dominions, crushing utterly any resistance against him, and was using his now-stable foothold to implement the same kind of measures that were used in Kirin Taq to ensure that the downtrodden people never got up again. But it was early days yet, and hope still existed that the operation would bear greater fruit.

She had been unable to focus on the meeting. On top of all her confusion and worry about Ryushi, there was something else on her mind. Ever since she had first touched Macaan's earring, way back before the Integration, she had been having sporadic dreams of the Princess. There was no theme or linking subject to them; they were as random as her dreams usually were. But they all had the common bond of featuring Princess Aurin somewhere, and when she awoke she was often convinced they had been real for a time. She told herself that this was a side-effect of entering Macaan's memories, for the cruel King had a fierce and hopeless love for his daughter that was powerful enough to invade her own mind. But as time passed, the dreams had increased in both frequency and potency, and now she was not sure any more. She could not help remembering the familiarity she had felt when she had first seen the grown Aurin in Macaan's memory, something more than just recognition. It troubled her.

Recently, the dreams visited her almost every other night.

"Calica!"

At first, she thought she had imagined her name being called. It was a faint sound, and seemed to come from a long distance away, flitting past her ears.

"Calica!"

This time she did hear it, and she turned her face into the swirling stream of her orange-gold hair to look behind her. There, catching up with her fast on a pakpak of her own, was Kia.

*

There had been plenty for Kia to think about on the return journey from the Unclaimed Lands. At first, she had only been obsessed with how she had failed the test, let them all down, that her character was not strong enough for the Koth Taraan to trust. But her self-blame only lasted for so long, and it soon gave way to other thoughts. Ty had worried about her, for she had barely spoken since she had emerged from the settlement and given them the news that they were returning, empty-handed but for a single one of the Koth Taraan. She had hardly noticed. She had been intent on picking apart the events that she had seen in her dream-visions while in

the pool, on analysing the things the Koth Macquai had
dredged out of her.

*Insights that even you yourself may not be aware of.
Premonitions. Dreams. Hopes and fears. The pool strips you
to nothing, human child, and leaves only that which cannot
be washed away: the truth.*

The surreal events that she had been part of during
the test had begun to take on a semblance of meaning as
she fought to put them together. The most difficult
thing was being honest with herself, allowing herself to
believe the answers that she came up with. But as she
began to accept the things that she had seen, she became
more and more convinced that they carried with them
a truth free of all self-deception.

Takami's truth was the easiest. She had faced him on
a pinnacle of rock and beaten him, but all that had
seemed automatic and predetermined. She only gained
the power of choice when it came to the simple decision;
let him die, or let him live. She remembered how all the
evil he had committed had flashed through her mind at
that moment, and yet still she reached out for his hand.

Why had he been missing an ear?

She hated him. That was unavoidable. But she had
sometimes wondered, in the same way her twin had,
why her hate for him was not as strong as Ryushi's. Why
her fury was reserved for Macaan and his troops.

But in her vision, Takami had been corrupted by the
shadow. It wasn't his fault. And in the most hidden
depths of her heart, Kia believed their brother could be

saved. He had killed their father, but he was just a pawn. Macaan was the real evil. Macaan, the shadow.

Did she really believe that? On the surface, no. It was Takami's choice to betray them, Takami's initiative to sacrifice his family for his own gain. But somehow, down in a place where logic and reason were powerless, she did believe. She held in that darkness a tiny flame of hope that would not allow her to despise her brother utterly; and much as she wanted to put that flame out, she could do nothing about it.

Then there were other signs, clear indications of emotions that she would not have previously admitted to herself. The shadow had stolen Ryushi away from her, and it had hurt her terribly; just as the conflict that they had been thrown into was tearing them apart now. The shadow had killed her mother, just as in real life she had died for Parakka, fighting against Macaan.

Macaan. Macaan. It all came back to him. He was the root, the cause, the wellspring of all the strife that Kia had endured since being ripped out of her home and cast adrift in an unfamiliar world. He had said he was her father, and he was right. Because of him, she had been reborn; the carefree, happy girl that had lived on Osaka Stud had become a warrior, an outlaw, even a leader. When Macaan's troops had destroyed her home, the old Kia had been destroyed with it. A new Kia had emerged, one better equipped to deal with the tribulations of her new environment. But she had lost so much in the transition. . .

The Koth Macquai had been right. Her interests were purely selfish. She had wanted to get the Koth Taraan on their side so Parakka could survive and eventually win, but underlying it was all one single ambition: to see Macaan dead. If she could somehow plug the fountain of discord that he represented, her ruined life might return to what it was. Maybe she could find real peace again, her and Ty. Maybe.

But there had been someone else in her visions. Calica. And Kia needed to have words with her about that. About the truth.

Calica reined in her pakpak and Kia brought her mount to a halt alongside. She waited a moment for Kia to catch her breath after the exhilaration of the ride, studying her with naked suspicion in her eyes. Kia shook out her hair over her face and retied it into a ponytail, then met Calica's gaze as if only just noticing she was there.

"Well?" Calica asked. She was not giving any ground; Kia was the one that had been cold to her for over a year now, and if the girl was here for a reconciliation, she was not interested.

"I need to talk with you," Kia said, glancing around across the plains in a habitual check for approaching Rift beasts.

"I'm not going anywhere. Talk."

Kia frowned slightly at Calica's hostile tone. She should have expected it, really, but it still made her own tone turn aggressive in response.

"I told you and the Council about the test I had to take for the Koth Taraan," she said. "What I didn't say was that some of it concerned you."

"Oh?" Calica queried.

"I wanted to clear some things up, y'know? Make sense of the visions I had, what they meant and so on."

"I'll help you if I can," Calica replied, her words dripping with distaste. There was a moment's pause.

"So what's the connection between you and Aurin?" Kia asked, and Calica was not quick enough to keep the surprise off her face. "I see that there *is* one," she commented flatly.

"There's no connection," Calica protested. "What are you talking about?"

"I saw you twice in the visions. Each time you were with Aurin, dressed the same or holding hands or something. More like twins than me and Ryushi are."

"That's not much of a stretch," Calica shot back acidly. "You're hardly even like brother and sister any more."

"Don't change the subject."

"Well, what do you want me to say?" she cried, and her pakpak crabstepped nervously at the tension in her voice. She roughly pulled it back into line. "You had a dream. So what? You think because you dreamed something that it's real? You think just 'cause some creature tells you that you'll experience insights and truth that you actually *will*? You're looking too hard, you wanted this Koth Taraan thing too much. You wanted too much to be *right*. You're not being objective, Kia. That's—"

"My mother *died* because of you!" Kia shouted suddenly. "Is that objective enough for you?"

The speech froze in Calica's throat, her mouth half-open. Shock and sorrow battled in her eyes, but she was unable to tear them from Kia's steady green stare. A cold fire burned there, frost and steel. Calica's lip trembled for a moment as she fought to find words in her lungs, but her body betrayed her and she could not make a noise.

"I heard them talking about it," Kia said, her voice like a wolf slinking up on its prey. "The day before they left. I was asleep then, but somewhere in my mind I must have been awake, because the visions took me back and let me listen. You sent her to her death. There was an ambush, a trap set, and you didn't warn them."

"I didn't *know*!" she choked, finally forcing her tongue over the dam of her shock. "It was a little village west of Tusami City. It should have been simple; just a meeting with a few farmers who wanted to know more. I don't know what happened. Maybe one of their own sold them out. But there were Jachyra waiting for them when they got there. How Banto got away . . . I don't know that either. Your mother, though. . ." she trailed off. "She never got out."

"They trusted you. It was your information. Your fault."

"I couldn't have *known*!"

"My mother's blood is on your hands," Kia said. "And in case you need reminding, she was *Ryushi's* mother also." She wheeled her pakpak, the sudden upswell of emotion making her want to get away from Calica before it overtook her completely. "If he makes it back from Fane Aracq, I'll be sure he knows just who was responsible."

"Kia!" Calica cried, turning her own beast to follow as Kia sped away. "Kia , no!"

But her protest was cut off by a sound, a sudden wail that split the valley and chilled her blood. The alarm siren. A glance around the cliffs confirmed that all the lifts were being hastily drawn down, that all the Parakkans outside of the protection of Base Usido were rapidly making for sanctuary. She urged her pakpak forward and it sprang to her command, racing after Kia, back towards the settlement.

Base Usido was under attack.

16
Far From Over

Awareness was becoming an increasingly unwelcome state of mind for Ryushi, but it had a nasty way of forcing itself upon him from time to time, reminding him that outside the sweet peace of sleep and unconsciousness there was a world of pain waiting for him. It had been eight cycles now, perhaps, though he really had no idea any more. He had been starved for that long, given only the barest of subsistence rations. He had been visited by the Scour many times. His head simultaneously ached and felt numb, like a cramp in his brain. His joints throbbed, his stomach felt full of knives, and it hurt to move his eyes too much.

He felt like he wanted to die.

But this time, when consciousness roughly mugged him and dragged him back into reality once more, he found that he was not alone in his cell. Curled up on the floor as he was, his eyes opened to see a long white boot in front of him. He did not need to look up to see who it belonged to. Instead, he gritted his teeth and pushed himself into a sitting position. He wasn't yet so weak that he couldn't straighten his back to face his enemies.

Aurin sat on the smooth creamstone bench that protruded from the wall of the cell, her slender legs draped in a simple white-and-jade dress, her hands folded in her lap. She looked immaculate in contrast to his dishevelled appearance, and her narrow, curved eyes watched him closely as he arranged himself. How long had she been there, watching him sleep? He felt somehow violated, that he had been so defenceless before her.

"I took your bench; I hope you don't mind," she said. "You didn't seem to be using it."

Ryushi ran a hand muzzily through the short, fat tentacles of his hair and looked at her blandly. "My cell is your cell, Princess," he said.

A tiny smile tugged at the edge of her mouth. "How true. I'm told you put up quite a fight against the Scour."

"If I ask you for some water first, would you be offended?" he asked sarcastically.

"Of course not. You must think me an ungracious host." She called for a guard, and a pitcher of water was brought in for him. He took a drink, and the water was painfully unsatisfying in his stomach. He looked wearily up at the Princess.

"I'll die before you get what you want," he said. "There's nothing in my mind for your leech to find, Princess. I told you, I am not as much a part of Parakka as you think."

"Then why do you torture yourself so?" Aurin asked,

leaning back a little, the looped braids at the side of her head swaying with the movement. "Stop fighting the Scour. Once we've established what you don't know, it will be over."

"And then you'll kill me," Ryushi said with a grim smile. "Sorry, but I'm not keen to hasten that particular outcome. You tell your Scour I've got a lot of fight in me yet."

"Yes, I can tell," said Aurin sarcastically, running a critical eye over his sunken face and weary body.

Ryushi felt his shoulders begin to sag forward, and pulled himself back straight again. He was more weakened by lack of food than he had first thought. "You're very brave, Princess," he said, more to distract her from his plight than out of any real desire to talk. "After all, you've no bodyguards here now. What if I should attack you? You could be dead before the guard gets through the cell door."

Aurin laughed lightly. "I think you'll find I'm perfectly capable of defending myself, yes?" She raised a hand, and it seemed to seethe with a dark green and black radiance, like a heat-haze around her skin. Ryushi felt himself go cold as he recognized the power he had felt when Aurin had slapped him in anger. She met his eyes and said: "I can kill you with a touch. And without your spirit-stones to help you, you are little more than another peasant warrior. Do not be foolish." She closed her hand, and the shimmering disappeared.

"So," Ryushi said, fighting to ignore the all-consuming ache in his body. "To what do I owe the honour of this royal visit?"

"Must you keep up this scornful politeness, Ryushi?" Aurin said with a sigh. "It is becoming tiresome."

"Would you prefer I insulted you outright?" he asked. "Forgive me, Princess, but this is as civil as I get towards those who starve and torture me."

Aurin waved a hand, dismissing the point. "Let us talk of other things, then."

"What did you have in mind?"

"I want to know about you," she said. When he gave her a curious look, she added: "Call it an attempt to understand the mind of my enemy."

"A trade, then," Ryushi said, taking another sip of water from the pitcher. "A question for a question." He met her dark eyes. "It's only fair."

"I could simply Scour the answers out of you," she said.

Ryushi shrugged. "It's your choice, of course."

She did not reply for a moment. Then she laughed to herself and said: "Very well, Ryushi. A question for a question."

"You know, of course, that I won't answer anything you might ask me about—"

"Oh, no. This is of a purely personal nature."

Ryushi coughed, a little noise that rapidly grew into a loud hacking. When it had subsided, he glanced wryly at the Princess and said: "Anything you learn about me will have a very short-lived value."

Aurin ignored the comment. "Tell me, then. What is the attraction of Parakka to the people? What was the attraction for you?"

"You really need to ask?" Ryushi said; but by the expression on her face at his words, he saw she genuinely meant it. "Okay. I guess I have nothing to lose by honesty, so I hope you're ready to listen to the truth." She leaned a little closer, indicating that he had her full attention.

"Parakka is an attraction because it's an alternative to you," he said, watching her face for a reaction but seeing that she kept her thoughts well hidden. "Your ancestors had ruled Kirin Taq for generations, keeping the land in relative peace and order, before your father decided that being a custodian of the land and its people was not good enough for him. A King should do well by his people; Macaan didn't want that. He simply crushed them. Ruling by fear takes all the effort out of being a King, because nobody dares stand up to you; but once you start, you can't ever stop. Because people hate to be afraid, and under the fear there is always that hate. You're like your father. You rule by fear. And if you ever stop, the people will rise up against you in revenge for what you've done to them." He paused, taking a drink of water. Aurin did not say a word. He took it as a sign to continue.

"Parakka is about freedom. It's about elected leaders,

and each person having a voice with which to influence the whole organization. It's where a person makes their own choices and gains their own position based on their merits, not on age, race, sex or birthright. It's where a farmer and a Machinist are equal, and nobody is turned away until they have proven themselves unable to adapt to our credos. It's not perfect by a long way, but we make it work." He looked deep into Aurin's eyes. "Can you understand what something like that means to a person? To suddenly have a measure of freedom again, instead of feeling like cattle to be herded by your Guardsmen and your Keriags, under threat of death from your whims and edicts? To have a choice, however small, in the shaping of their future and their *children's* future?" He held her gaze for a moment, seeing nothing there, and then broke off. "You don't, do you? To you, a person is not a person. It's a subject, a pawn, to be used or disposed of with no more thought than a stick. You've put yourself so far above the common folk for so long, that they're as insignificant as ants to you."

There was a silence then, during which Aurin appeared to study him closely. "Are you trying to anger me again?" she said at last, though her voice sounded as far from anger as it was possible to be.

"That's two questions, Princess. It's my turn."

She settled back on the bench. "Ask, then."

"How do you feel when you command a whole village to be executed?" he said levelly. "To have the

Keriags overrun it, and have them butcher the men, women and children with their *gaer bolga*? Do you ever put yourself in their place, think how they must feel as they see their families slaughtered before them, the pain as they meet their end?"

"I think you have already answered your own question, yes?" she replied. "They're as insignificant as ants. You have already made up your mind about me, it seems."

"Forgive me, Princess, but you hardly deserve any sympathy from me," Ryushi said. "Still, that's beside the point. What I think doesn't matter. I want you to tell me how *you* feel. Is it really nothing at all? Or do all those deaths weigh on your conscience at night?"

"At night?" she said with a faint laugh. "Your Dominion habits have not left you yet, I see."

"You're avoiding the question."

"I don't wish to answer it."

Ryushi shrugged again. "Then the game is over. Goodbye, Princess. You can send your Scour if you want any more information from me." He lay back down on the floor, turning his back on her, and pillowed his head with the crook of his elbow. After a few moments, he closed his eyes. Several minutes later, his breathing deepened as his exhausted body drifted irresistibly back towards sleep.

She sat there watching him, for a long while, her head full of uncomfortable thoughts. Later, when she knocked on the door to be released, she ordered a page-boy to fetch bedding and a good meal for the prisoner.

Getting into the palace was easy for Gerdi. It was Festide; the nobles had gathered, and a great market was going on inside. The tall, white, oval gates of the tradesmen's entrance were always open, and a constant stream of traffic poured in and out of it, bringing wares to sell or livestock for the kitchens. Disguised as a Kirin, he walked beneath the huge creamstone arches and into Fane Aracq, tagging himself on to a caravan and following them in. In the crowded market hall, with a little make-up, concealing clothes, and just a touch of his spirit-stone magic to perfect the illusion, he passed himself off as a Kirin quite well. It was only a tiny use of his power, but he had to maintain it for many people at once, and it exhausted him. A necessary drain, though, for his Dominion eyes would make him stand out a mile and probably get him arrested.

After that, it got a little trickier. Fane Aracq was divided into many sections, and getting from one to another was an extremely difficult process. The first major problem was getting out of the market hall and into the corridors of the palace. There was only one access route, and it was for palace personnel only, not farmers or traders. Anyone entering or exiting the antechamber at the end of the short corridor that ran off the market hall was checked visually, and each guard had a private password known only to themselves and the Gatekeeper. It was not as simple as walking in wearing a Guardsman's uniform – not that he would have fitted in one anyway. All Guardsmen had to remove their helmets, and the Gatekeeper had a pin-sharp memory for faces and knew exactly who was supposed to be there and who was not. He was a tall, dark-haired Dominion man with pale skin and a pinched face, who dressed in robes of black silk. It seemed that Dominion-folk in the nobility's employ were tolerated; after all, some of the nobles like Takami were from the Dominions themselves.

Gerdi had learned of these primary security measures by posing as an ignorant Kirin cereal-thresher, and walking up the hall after a couple of Guardsmen. After observing the checks that were carried out on them in the small, arched antechamber inside the gate, he made up some blather about how he was here to see his cousin. The Gatekeeper asked him for his password. He had none, and was firmly told to leave. He was lucky; they believed that his character was really muddled enough to walk into Fane Aracq and think he could get into its heart, and they suspected nothing more.

That first run had been tiring. Having to maintain his illusion for so many eyes at once – for there were other guards besides the Gatekeeper – drained him quickly. Next he tried something simpler – posing as a Guardsman when one of the palace folk left to travel by pakpak to a nearby town. He hailed the rider down, a cook-boy, under the pretence of searching for a spy, and then tried to extract the boy's password as proof that he was allowed in the palace. The boy was initially intimidated by the tall, black-armoured figure that Gerdi presented him with, but when Gerdi got on to the subject of passwords he became immediately suspicious, and Gerdi ended up changing his story and telling the boy that it was a security test to be sure that nobody would give up their password to a stranger. Bemused and uncertain, the boy left with a worried expression on his face, and Gerdi was still at a loss as to how to get into the palace. All other entrances, like the land-train depot and the entrance for nobility, were guarded even more fiercely than the tradesmen's one. And all the while, he thought of Ryushi, trapped in there, maybe being tortured at the orders of the Princess. . .

In the end, he took a gamble, and it paid off.

A way back up the road that the land-trains ploughed along was a large inn, used as a rest-stop for the traders and farmers. It was also where some of the Guardsmen went on their time off. Gerdi spent several cycles hanging about that place before he managed to get into a conversation with a suitable Guardsman, for they were not frequent visitors, and they were suspicious of those who tried to befriend them. It was vaguely disconcerting to meet a Guardsman out of his black carapace of armour; somehow, he had never really thought of them as being human underneath. But this was a Dominion man, blond-haired and a little gruff, and Gerdi almost enjoyed his rough anecdotes and heavy humour. Once they got talking, he was careful not even to approach the subject of passwords or the palace; he merely concentrated on memorizing every detail of his face, his speech, his mannerisms, and learning everything he could about the man. What he found was that the Guardsman was on a ten-cycle leave, and was going away to see his parents in Dacqii. Perfect.

While he and the Guardsman talked, Gerdi spun a fabric of lies about his own past, all the while trying to maintain the faint illusion that kept the make-up on his face and hands looking good enough to fool onlookers. He was wearing a cowled cloak and they sat in a dim, sheltered corner; but even so, he soon had to make his excuses and leave, for his stones were being drained almost dry by their constant usage.

After resting once more, and armed with his new knowledge, he tried the Gatekeeper again. He still had no password. But he did have a plan.

There had been quite a commotion when the Guardsman that Gerdi had been talking to at the inn came stumbling into the antechamber, his helmet missing, clutching a bleeding wound on his forehead.

"Let me through!" he said, in his bluff and rugged voice. "I need a healer!"

"Jutar!" one of Guardsmen on sentry duty cried. "What happened? I thought you—"

"My pakpak threw me," Jutar replied, followed by a string of epithets directed at the animal. "You know how I hate those things."

"Aye, and it makes me wonder why you choose to ride one after—"

"I was bringing it as a present for Mother's birthday," he interrupted. That was easy for them to swallow; they knew how Jutar doted on his mother, and it *was* her birthday soon. "Now let me pass, I need to have this looked at."

"Your password," said the Gatekeeper, standing up in his sheltered booth at the side of the antechamber. Each person who passed through had to whisper it to the sallow man before they could proceed.

"For Cetra's sake," said one of the other Guardsmen. "You know who he is. Let him pass."

"Your password," the Gatekeeper demanded again.

"Fridia? Kenia? Reto?" Jutar said, waving his hands as he listed off the names of members of his family. "I can't think! I can't remember! My head is hurting! Let me through!"

"His wits have been muddled by the blow to his head," one of the Guardsmen, obviously not a friend of Jutar's, pointed out with no small amount of glee.

"I need a healer!" Jutar cried again, his legs buckling suddenly. He staggered forward, and only just managed to bear himself up again.

"Use your eyes, man!" the first Guardsman shouted at the Gatekeeper. "He needs to—"

"You may pass, Jutar," said the Gatekeeper, waving him away with sudden disinterest.

"Do you want someone to go with you?" another of

the Guardsmen enquired as Jutar stumbled past them and out of the antechamber.

"And have you leave your posts?" he said as he was leaving. "No. Stay and guard the Princess's palace. What would she say if you let an intruder get past you?"

The Gatekeeper looked sharply after him as he left, but Gerdi hadn't been able to resist his last cheeky comment. His plan had worked, and he was in. But it was far from over.

17

A Species Indigenous

In the isolated world of the Rifts, chaos had erupted. All over the valley, the Parakkan troops swarmed from their outposts back towards the relative safety of Base Usido, running for their lives. The air resounded and echoed with the shrieking *yip! yip!* of the Snagglebacks, a strangled sound half-bird and half-dog which stabbed at them from the depths of the foliage. On the ridges of the valley walls, the trees were bright with the luminescence of Banes as they flowed sinuously between the trunks, writhing and coiling as they led the other Rift-beasts towards their prey. The great mechanical haulage-lifts had long been lowered down the sheer cliffs, but everyone knew this would not slow the creatures by much. They had faced attacks like this before several times now; it was part and parcel of living in the Rifts. They knew that their only hope of survival was to get behind the Base defences.

Kia and Calica were racing across the plains as the noisy mass burst out of the treeline and came boiling over the edge of the cliff. The Snappers scuttled head-first down the rock walls as if they were spindly yellow spiders, their ridged tails curling behind them for balance. Kia felt a shiver of repulsion as she remembered the overlapping jaws and milk-white eyes of the creatures that had terrorized them on Os Dakar. Meanwhile, the Snagglebacks took a slower route down, their immensely powerful fingers crunching into the stone to provide them with handholds as they descended. The Banes swirled around them, shadowing them like eager lapdogs.

Kia's eyes hardened as she saw them beginning to pour down into the valley. They had appeared on both sides at almost the same time, and suddenly the rim of the cliffs was alive with a churning, thrashing mass of creatures that tumbled and crawled down towards the plain like a foaming tide. In their haste, the occasional creature was swept off the edge by the weight of numbers behind it and sent flailing to its death, hundreds of feet below.

"Looks like the whole of the Rifts have come out to play," Calica said from behind her. "*Ride!*"

They spurred their pakpaks to fresh vigour, and their mounts responded to the urgency in their riders. Ahead of them, the spiked outer wall of Base Usido rose out of the plain, a vast, jagged semicircle against the cliffs. And from behind it, with a screech, three enormous wyverns suddenly tore upwards, their vast double-paired wings spreading as the momentum of their skyward leap began to dwindle. Kia's eyes ran over their thick, squat bodies, the white plates of bony armour that covered their black hides, the long necks and twin tails; and then they dipped in their flight and began to streak across the plains towards her and Calica, the riders on their backs hunched low. They were carrying force-cannons, mounted on specially modified harnesses, and Parakkan Artillerists rode shotgun to operate them.

Kia and Calica instinctively ducked as the creatures flew low over them, pushing a blast of wind in their wake which buffeted their faces as they passed. They turned around to look over their shoulders as the wyverns wheeled into a shallow turn, and the Artillerists let fly with their force-bolts, blasting pulses of invisible energy into the attacking creatures, blowing them off the cliffs as they scuttled or crawled down them.

"Kia! The gates!" Calica yelled, and somehow Kia heard her. She looked ahead, already knowing what had to be happening. The huge metal gates were being closed. The Base security dared not wait any longer. They were being locked out. Even at this distance, she could hear the screech of the mechanism as the two halves of the gate began to slide together on its heavy rollers. She gauged how fast they were going and how far they had to go to reach the Base.

No dice. They'd never make it.

She exchanged a glance with Calica, who was riding alongside her. It conveyed nothing. They had been too long at odds to share the kind of communication she had with Ryushi. So she turned back to the gate, gripped the reins of the pakpak hard in one hand, kept it steady on its course towards the Base, and closed her eyes.

"There's still two riders out there!" one of the Base security cried, squinting through a Kirin spyglass with his cream-on-white eyes from his vantage point atop the perimeter wall.

"The Snappers are reaching the valley floor! There's nothing we can do!" shouted another Kirin, his superior, from ground level.

"It's Kia and Calica! We can't leave them outside!"

"We've got no choice. If the Snappers get to the gate before it closes, all these defences won't be worth a thing!"

"We can stop the gates. They'll make it!"

From where he stood at the lever to drive the grinding, clanking gate mechanism, another Kirin shouted to the ranking security member on ground level over the din. "Do we keep closing or not?"

"Keep closing!" came the reply, as he waved his hand to indicate he should continue. "We can't risk it. They'll have to take their—"

He was drowned out by a great rumbling and tearing of earth, and he staggered back a step as the ground between the two closing halves of the gate suddenly spasmed and retched out an arm, an enormous, thick forelimb composed of the dirt and stone of the plains. It slammed down, its fat, unwieldy fingers digging in as if something was climbing up from beneath, and then it pulled itself out. Slow, massive, the golem broke the surface of the ground and hefted its huge body upright, a creature knitted from the very soil it came from. As the fissure it had risen out of closed beneath it, it planted its spatulate feet wide, and braced its hands and shoulders against the closing gates of Base Usido, then opened its ragged mouth in a roar as it took the immense strain. The gates shrieked and ground to a halt, propped apart by the golem's arms. It swept the shallow pits of its blind eyes over the assembled security men.

"THE GATE STAYS OPEN," it said in a deep rumble, the rattle of stones in its throat rendering the words only barely decipherable.

To that, the Base security had no reply.

Peliqua arrived at the main gate at almost the same time as Calica and Kia came through it, riding full pelt on their pakpaks, ducking beneath the legs of the behemoth that held the gates open for them. Calica had the reins of Kia's mount in her hand, leading it for her while her concentration was fixed on maintaining the golem. No sooner were they through than the golem collapsed in a shower of dirt, the security personnel set the machinery in operation again and the gates powered onward, pushing the debris of the discarded golem aside as they rumbled closed. Kia's green eyes flicked open as Calica pulled both their mounts to a halt, and they jumped from their saddles to the grass.

"Thanks," she said to Calica, her voice a little dull from the weariness that she had sustained from maintaining the golem.

"You'd have been too slow otherwise," Calica said. "I led your pakpak. You kept the gates open. We're even."

"This changes nothing, you realize," Kia said.

"I know."

Peliqua ran up to them, her red braided hair curling in the torchlight around her grey-skinned shoulders as she stopped.

"Oh! Oh! Are you two alright?" she asked.

"I will be when I find out who it was who tried to close that gate on us," Kia said, her eyes ranging the assembled security personnel, who were all racing to secure the perimeter of the Base against the approaching swarm. As if to emphasize her point, the gates slammed shut behind her.

"There's no time for that now," Calica said. "We were cutting it close anyway; it was a judgement call, and whoever did it was overcautious."

"I'll give them overcautious," Kia growled. "I'll—"

"*Drop* it, Kia," Calica said firmly.

"What are you talking about?" Peliqua put in, then changed her mind with her customary flightiness. "Oh, it doesn't matter. Have either of you seen Jaan?"

"Jaan? He's with that Koth Taraan thing, surely," Calica replied, glancing around as if impatient to be somewhere else.

"Yes, but *where*? He was outside the compound last I heard. I'm so worried!"

Calica looked back at her. "We sent Hochi to tell him that Iriqi would be allowed into the compound with him. Hochi will know."

Peliqua's face broke into a sudden smile. "Thanks, Calica. I'll go find him." With that, she sprinted off towards the clusters of huts where their living-quarters were.

"I'm going to check the clifftop defences," Calica said. "You coming?"

Kia met her eyes blandly, then they flickered away. Running across the settlement towards them was Ty. "I've got my own concerns," she said.

For a moment, they just gazed at each other, the long history of their antagonism and the aftertaste of their recent conflict running between them. Then Calica turned away and ran after Peliqua, towards where Base Usido backed up against the cliffside. Kia watched her go for a moment, then turned and went her own way. Each of them had their priorities to follow in a crisis, she reflected, as Ty came up to her with words of relief and greeting. Except that one of hers was even now languishing in Aurin's grip.

On the plain, the battle continued in earnest. The Rift-beasts darted between the force-bolts that pounded them from the Parakkan wyverns, heading towards the rough semicircle of Base Usido. They were suffering heavy losses, for the airborne defenders had multiplied fourfold by now and they had no way to strike back at the winged creatures or their riders; but they went on, heedless, driven by the Banes towards the island of prey that was the Parakkan stronghold. The thin, wiry forms of the Snappers jostled with the massive shoulders and corded muscle of the Snagglebacks as they stampeded across the blue grass, grey under the cold eye of the Kirin Taq sun.

"What are they doing?" Ty asked. "This is suicide for them. I don't know about the Snagglebacks, but Snappers are brighter than this."

Kia tilted her head in agreement, her face shadowed in the twilight. The Snappers that she had fought on Os Dakar had been a devious and cunning breed, and Ty had spent a lot longer there than she had. "It's the Banes," she said at last. "They're doing this. They've got some sort of plan."

"Plan?" Ty asked, incredulous. "They can't *plan*."

"No?" she replied. "Did you notice that they started coming down opposite sides of the plain at almost exactly the same time? From two points that were a mile or more apart? Don't you remember when they destroyed that outpost of one of the collectives to the East, when they pulled an ambush on them? That takes forward planning. No one knows *what* Banes are capable of. Hardly anyone has seen them in action."

They waited on the defensive ledge that ran below the lip of the perimeter wall, where warriors could stand to repel anything that somehow managed to scale the forest of bladed spikes. The ragged attackers were almost upon them now, the air full of the Snagglebacks' *yip! yip!* cry, and though there seemed to be no apparent way for the creatures to get inside the compound, they were running full pelt at it as if they could batter through by sheer weight of numbers.

They couldn't, Kia thought. *Could they?*

All eyes were turned outward. The camp was in a state of frantic preparation. That was why nobody was in the medical hut to look after the patients, whose unconscious forms were wrapped in blankets underneath the orange glowstone radiance. And that was why nobody noticed when a young Kirin boy called Paani suddenly opened his eyes, awakening from his coma without the slightest evidence of disorientation, and got out of his bed. He stood up, wearing only his long undergarments of coarse wool, his chin-length red hair falling uncombed around the ashen skin of his face; and then he walked to the door of the hut and opened it.

The boy knew more of the Banes than Kia could hope to guess at. As he walked through the camp, people running past him and shouting in all directions, nobody gave him more than a second glance. If the fact that he was half-dressed seemed unusual, it was not enough to stop anyone to ask him why; if he did not walk with his usual light skip but with a fast, purposeful tread today, then it was a difference so slight that only his mother or his friends might notice. But his veins ran with fire now, scorched with energy, and the brain that drove his body had a new occupant.

The Banes were creatures of pure Flow – the rushing energy that ran beneath the earth in torrents called ley lines. The ley lines behaved in many ways like the rivers they were often likened to. They branched and divided, curved and twisted; they had small tributary channels which leaked out into the surrounding ground. The Rifts, due to its heavily sunken and broken terrain, ran very close to one particularly strong example of these, the planet's arteries. And the excess energy that bled out of the earth formed the Banes; congealed clots of the very essence of the planet. Their arcane nature granted them a kind of strange intelligence, but it also cursed them with a hunger, so that they were drawn like moths to flame when the Flow was in use. Mostly they sated themselves on the recently dead, the release of life-energy as their essences rejoined the Flow from which they had come. But with the arrival of the Dominion-folk, they had found a new source of energy: spirit-stones, gorged with Flow. And all collected here, at Base Usido.

The Parakkans thought that the Snagglebacks and Snappers followed the Banes for some reason. They were wrong. The creatures were pack animals, and the Banes simply possessed their leaders, and led the rest like a herd. Once it had bitten, a Bane could dissipate itself into the bloodstream of its victim, the particles of the Flow that composed its body taking over the weaker ions that ran through its prey's veins. By manipulating the electric impulses in the brain in a similar way, a Bane could gain control of its victim's body. As it had with Paani.

Now the young Kirin boy walked through the milling defenders towards the main gate. Everyone's eyes were turned outward, watching the approaching stampede, wondering why they were running to impale themselves on the vicious spikes of the perimeter wall. Only one man stood to guard the mechanism that operated the main gate. Paani strode confidently up to him, meeting his puzzled gaze with a friendly smile.

"Hey, kid, you shouldn't be—" the guard began, but Paani clamped a hand on his forearm and there was a short crack of Flow energy. The guard's joints buckled and he slumped to the ground, his life extinguished. The boy stepped over the limp corpse, to where a long, slightly rusted metal lever was buried in a mass of huge cogs and gears. Paani did not have the strength to pull it alone, but he gripped the handle anyway. The Bane in control of his body dumped adrenalin into his system, a sudden surge that boosted the strength in his muscles tenfold. He pulled the lever.

The Banes' previous attacks on Base Usido had been tests, probing the defences, working out the best way in. They had been small affairs, conducted while the main gathering of Rift-beasts was being carried out. This was the real thing.

The lever moved.

The Bane left Paani's body in a fizz of tiny lights as the boy's heart gave out under the massive overdose of adrenalin he had received.

The gates began to open.

Ty felt a flood of ice spread through his chest as he heard the grinding and clanking of the gates start up. His eyes were still on the approaching mass of Snappers, Snagglebacks and Banes, but his ears gave him in a split-second a premonition of what was about to happen.

Plan? They can't plan!

He heard his own words of a few moments ago, echoing hollowly. They could plan, alright. Parakka had underestimated them. And that was going to cost them dear.

"Close the *gate*!" someone shouted, an edge of panic to their voice.

Ty saw a pair of men leap down from the ledge on the inside of the wall, half scrambling and half sliding down the ladders in an attempt to get to the mechanism in time. Two other security men on the ground floor were doing the same, running across the short stretch of grass as the two metal halves of the gate withdrew to their fullest extent.

But it was hopeless. The Banes' timing had been impeccable. They had allowed no margin for mistakes. At almost the exact second that the gates finally came to a rest, the stampede hit Base Usido, and the attackers exploded into the settlement. They caught up with one of the guards a hand's breadth away from the lever, sweeping him into their ranks and tearing him apart; the others that had made the run to mend the breach suffered the same end. The Parakkans' one chance at sealing the gates and keeping the enemy out was buried under the heaving mass of bodies as they surged into the Base, and the carnage began.

"Get down there! Keep them out!" Kia cried over the sickening crunch and slice as hundreds of their attackers, propelled by the weight of numbers behind them, threw themselves on the jagged spikes of the perimeter walls.

But some of the enemy were already clambering up the ladders to the wide ledge while the rest of them dispersed across the compound, and the defenders turned their attention inward to deal with the new threat. A wyvern screeched overhead, the Artillerist on its back sowing force-bolts into the horde, the blast of its wings blowing Kia's hair about as she stood with her bo staff ready. Ty stood by her side with his hooking-flail spinning.

It was a Snaggleback that finally gained the ledge in front of them, reaching around one sentry's careless sword-swing to grab his arm and fling him bodily to the ground below. It pulled itself up to their level and began loping across towards them, as they prepared to receive its charge.

The Snagglebacks were a species indigenous to the Rifts, where their vicious nature and hardy constitution made them the ideal predator for the environment. If they could have been said to resemble anything, it would be a huge, hairless ape. Their skin was a grey-brown hide sewn thick with veins that bulged over limbs and a torso crammed with muscle; their hands and feet were massively strong. They had no eyes, only the wide nostrils of a snout; but it was their jaws that were the most disturbing thing about their appearance. When not in use, they were sheathed in the flesh of their cheeks and chin, only the tips of their crooked, long teeth visible between their lips. But when they opened their mouths to feed or bite or make their shrieking *yip! yip!* cry, their jaws pushed outwards, their lips skinning back all the way along them to reveal the stringy flesh of their gums and the roots of their fangs.

Now Kia and Ty faced one of them as it ran along the ledge towards them, its bunched muscles pistoning as it came. Kia lashed at its head with her staff, cracking it around the skull and making it skid to a halt, checking its headlong charge. Ty used the moment of disorientation to send his hooking-flail slicing out, the three bladed balls carving three different paths of blood along its back. It made a strange, low mewling sound of pain, then swung one heavy arm at Ty; but he was too quick, and had pulled himself away. The ledge was wide, but not so wide that a creature as big and cumbersome as the Snaggleback could fight comfortably on it, so Kia took advantage of the clumsy overswing and levered her staff behind its knee, shoving it further off-balance and buckling its legs. It tipped over the edge with a shriek and fell into the stampede below, knocking some of its kindred to the ground where they were trampled.

"Go for the lever!" Ty cried over the tumult, but it was useless. Everybody was engaged in the fighting. There was no way anybody could close the gate while the creatures were still pouring through it; and no way to stop the creatures except by closing the gate. A no-win situation. Unless. . .

He turned suddenly to Kia, his eyes alight with inspiration. "Kia! Use the earth! Seal the gate!"

It took a moment for his words to sink in, but then her own face changed into a grim expression of agreement.

"I'll watch you," he said, laying a hand on her shoulder as a pair of Snappers that had fought their way along the ledge came scuttling towards him, their lean, yellowish bodies and overlapping fangs picked out in the torchlight of the camp.

She closed her eyes, trusting him totally. Gripping her fist, she called out the Flow. Her spirit-stones began to sear as they released their energy, pouring into the ground, agitating the soil, meshing the particles, knitting them under her will, until…

The ground at the entrance of Base Usido began to churn for the second time that day, but this time it was no golem that came forth. It was a wall of earth and rock, as solid as any metal barrier could be, that burst out from beneath the enemy's feet and shot upward, flinging them away. In a moment, the gap that the gate had left was filled with the thick earthen barricade, flattened at the top into a narrow platform. The creatures on the outside pulled up short, some of them being crushed into the unyielding surface and slumping to the ground; but the pause was only momentary, for the barricade did not have spikes like the perimeter wall did, and they began clambering up it.

Kia began to falter. The golem, and now the wall of earth she had raised, had tired her out; she did not have the strength to repel the creatures that were scaling her wall.

"Get to the breach and hold it!" Ty yelled, his hooking-flail smashing through the skull of a Snapper, sending it flailing over the wall and on to the spikes on the outward side. Most of the troops, seeing the chance that had been presented to them, had already run to do just that, and the fighting atop Kia's barricade became savage as the defenders fought to repel the invaders and keep them from getting any more of their number in. Others concentrated on driving away those creatures that sought to get up to the ledge and attack from behind those who protected the wall; but the enemy's numbers were thinning rapidly now as they split up and ran through the Base, in search of easier prey.

Outside, the stampede had stopped. Kia noticed this as she returned to herself, having no need to maintain her barricade any more now that it was set and hardened. The creatures were no longer throwing themselves on the spikes, but concentrating on trying to clamber over the corpses of their dead to get inside through the heavily guarded gate. The wyvern-riders and Artillerists swooped over them again and again, each force-bolt blast pulverizing more and more of the enemy as they ran about in the open.

Kia managed a weak smile amid a lull in the fray. They had sealed the breach, and they were holding the enemy out on this side. Just.

But what of those that had got inside?

18

Trickery And Wordplay

If asked, Aurin would have been unable to say how she knew when her father was in his sanctum. Similarly, Macaan could not determine exactly how he knew when his daughter would be calling, and made sure he was there. The process operated on a kind of instinctive level; or perhaps it was something to do with the mirrors themselves, for their glass had been impregnated with fine grains of powdered spirit-stone residue, and who could say what subtle side-effects that would have?

So it was that when Aurin stood before the huge mirror in her chambers and willed it, her reflection faded into the reflection of her father, standing in his sanctum, surrounded by flashing blue ripples from the glowstone-bowls of water that flanked him. He looked the same as he always did, flawlessly handsome and straight-backed, his piercing eyes of the lightest blue gazing steadily from beneath his cascade of pure white hair and the small indigo stone in the centre of his forehead. He wore a long cloak of white over a black velvet robe, belted with an ornate gold clasp.

"Daughter," he said, his voice quiet yet crystal clear. "How goes it in Kirin Taq?"

"The same as always, father," she replied curtly. "Little changes in this realm with the passing of the cycles, yes? A small incident here and there. I have dealt with them."

"Good. Things are settling here in the Dominions. Perhaps soon you will be able to come over and join me for a time."

Aurin's face turned to false sorrow. "I'm afraid that I will be too tied up with the affairs of court to leave Kirin Taq for a while. It will soon be Festide, and the nobles of my provinces will want me here. Who else would they grovel to otherwise?"

A hint of amusement passed over the King. "You should be thankful for the mundane. It seems that our fears of Parakka resurrecting itself were unfounded."

"Did you ever really take them seriously, father?" Aurin asked. "Parakka are dead and gone. Worrying about them is a waste of time."

The conversation faltered. Aurin gazed at her father coolly, her silence more eloquent than speech. Macaan seemed about to say something, took a breath to give the words voice . . . and then changed his mind. Still Aurin stood like a statue. They were not father and daughter; just strangers trying to fake their roles. Perhaps she seemed cold to him only because she was unwilling to play out the deception. Well, let him struggle for sentences if he wished. His child had been reared in the care of nannies while an absent father conquered lands to thrust into the arms of his little girl. It was his choice to maintain the fiction, and his fault that he did not know his part well enough.

"I will be in contact again soon," he said at last, indicating that he had given up attempting to bridge the impassable chasm to his daughter for now. "I am going away for a short time, to survey the southern deserts here. There is still a little . . . resistance there."

"Till then," she said, and the reflection wavered and shifted back to her own.

She had no compunction about lying to her father. It only galled her that she had to lie at all. Not that lying bothered her much; it was just that it seemed to be beneath her. A Princess should not have to lie. She watched herself in the mirror for a time, flattering her vanity, until the sound of hasty footsteps outside her door brought her around.

"Come in, Corm," she said loudly, and the Machinist stepped through the smooth, arched doorway, his eyes a frenzy of tiny clicks and chatters as they adjusted to the different light in the room. Even with the high collar of his greatcoat hiding his lower face, Aurin could tell that he was agitated.

"Speak," she said. She had tried to discourage her closest retainers from sticking to protocol, but it had never taken with Corm. She knew he would stand there in silence indefinitely until she bade him to report whatever was troubling him.

"Princess, I have just spoken with the jailor," he said, his voice even higher and sharper than usual. "He tells me that the Scour has been called off the prisoner, that it was a direct command from you. Surely he is mistaken, Princess?"

"Really? And why is that?"

"Because it would be—" Corm began, then swiftly and wisely checked himself. "Because such an act would make no sense," he finished.

Aurin turned his back on him, looking out of one of the wind-holes with her hands linked loosely behind her. "There was no mistake. I did order that we stop using the Scour."

"But Princess!" Corm protested. "It . . . just. . . *Why*?"

"The Scour is too rough a method to get what we want from him," she said. "We might find the location of Parakka, but we'd lose a lot of precious information in the meantime, yes?" She looked at him over her shoulder, her narrow eyes blinking laconically. "You know what happens to people if we Scour too hard. Some die before they have the chance to give up what we need. Ryushi is our only link to Parakka at the moment; if he dies, we lose everything. We have to be careful."

"But you said yourself that finding Parakka was of the utmost urgency," Corm said, visibly fighting to keep the frustration out of his voice.

"And I have changed my mind," she said implacably. "I have spoken with the prisoner several times now. I am learning from him, Corm. He tells me things about the attitude of the people I rule over that I have been unaware of. He tells me about the low folk, and what they think of me. He talks to me about the common people's lives, and how they are affected by what we do, and—"

"These are *lies*, Princess!" Corm cried. "He is taking you in with lies and trying to prolong his own miserable life."

Aurin turned back to the window, a dark and menacing glint in her eyes. "You forget yourself, Corm. Don't ever interrupt me again."

"I . . . apologize, Princess," he said, bowing his hairless head; but the way he flexed the metal grips of his Augmented hand showed that he was just as angry as he was chastened.

"The point is this," she said. "It is to my advantage to fully realize the potential for rebellion in my kingdom. That way I am better equipped to deal with it, yes? Having the Scour tear out the location of Parakka's base may well kill him, but it is much more likely to scar him enough so that he would scarcely be capable of continuing to educate me."

Corm was silent. Her explanation sounded rehearsed; she'd obviously justified it over and over to herself. But who was she trying to convince? After all, she'd never felt she had to explain her actions to an underling before.

"My Princess, may I speak freely?" he said at length.

Aurin waved a hand to indicate that he should proceed.

"Please understand that what I say comes only

from concern for yourself, and that I am more than willing to accept any punishment you see fit to deal me if I should offend you by saying it," he explained. "But your attachment to this prisoner is a most unwise development, Princess. You are not trained or experienced enough to deal with him, and he has snared you with his trickery and wordplay. He has duped you into calling off the Scour, and I understand that you have also abandoned the starvation tactic. He is less a prisoner now and more of a guest. You may think this is your idea, Princess, but I assure you it is—"

"Don't treat me like a child, Corm!" she snapped, her posture suddenly alive with indignation. "I am not some little girl to be deceived by the words of a stranger. I have come of age, I am a woman now! The prisoner does not have the wit for your *trickery and wordplay*; it is *I* who is manipulating *him*! Each privilege I allow him makes him trust me further. And with each breath, he gives away more and more about the attitudes and priorities of Parakka. The more we know of the enemy, the easier they will be to predict, yes? A few cycles will make no difference to us; Parakka are scarcely a force we need to fear with the Keriags on our side. When I have learned all I can from him, then you may Scour him until his brain melts if you wish; but until then, do *not* presume to treat me like a fledgling."

Her words rang around the chamber, dying quickly into a throbbing silence. Corm's head was bowed inside his tall collar, the bald dome of his skull pale in the white glowstone-light.

"Besides," she said, a little calmer but still acid-tongued, "what do you think is going to happen, Corm? I'm hardly going to let him escape, and he's not likely to persuade me into giving up my throne, now is he? Where's the harm that you can see? I'm listening and learning. He isn't *brainwashing* me, as you seem to think, yes?"

"Forgive me, Princess," he said; and this time he sounded like he meant it.

"You're forgiven," she snapped. "Get out."

He bowed further, this time from the waist, and retreated hastily through the archway, closing the ivory door behind him. The moment he was out of her sight, he dropped his façade of an apology, and his face set hard in the island of flesh between the brassy metal of his cheek and the mechanical band around his eyes and ear. He walked away down the cornerless, creamstone innards of Fane Aracq, frustration lending speed to his heavy steps.

What did she think she was doing? *What?* Before, when Macaan was here, a whim as dangerous as this would never have been tolerated; he was the only one who could check her. But she was too used to her own way, and in her flush of independence she was indulging herself far too much. She was too stubborn to listen to reason.

Treat her like a fledgling? How ironic, that she could

not be dealt with like a child but that she could act like one.

Ryushi paced his cell. His strength had largely returned to him over the last few days, and the aches and pains in his body had gone. He had a hard cushion on the bench to sleep on now, and he had been furnished with regular meals that, while not exactly fine fare, were nourishing enough.

What he could not fathom was why.

Having nothing else to do and no human contact other than Aurin's visits and the page-boy's food deliveries, he spent his time thinking. Thinking of what had gone wrong, thinking of how stupid and foolish he'd been, thinking of his sister, of Calica . . . and of Aurin.

She plagued his mind now, and no matter how much he tried to steer it towards something else, it always returned to her. Her image superceded any other in his head. He couldn't understand her. It was by her orders that his torture had stopped, she had made that clear enough by hints and asides in their conversations; but she would never tell him why she had done it.

She fascinated him. She was so easy to anger, and she would leave the cell each time in a high rage at a barbed comment or an observation that he made; yet each time she would return a little later and the sparring would begin again. Some of the time she seemed almost unaware that he was a prisoner at her behest, and spoke to him like an equal, expecting him to do the same. He invariably disappointed her. It was a bizarre situation; she knew that Ryushi was part of an organization dedicated to her downfall, yet sometimes she treated him almost as a friend. There was always the haughtiness, the temper, the condescension bubbling just under the surface, breaking out at the slightest provocation, but she was *trying*.

Why?

They talked of many things, of events in Kirin Taq, of the circumstances of her father's conquest and the opinions of the varying sides, of the lives and trades of villagers in the various provinces in comparison to those of the Dominions. They speculated on the mystery of the Deliverers, and talked about the Machinists, and sometimes even exchanged stories about childhood. Usually Aurin was reluctant to speak on matters of any personal importance, but when she refused, Ryushi would always clam up like he had the first time. Then she would storm away, and come back a little later ready to talk about it. And despite the fact that he had not wholly abandoned his snide tone with her, she would often reward him for a particularly lengthy conversation. He would be given a meal from her kitchens instead of prison food, or given a cup of wine; once he was escorted out of his cell and allowed to bathe while his clothes were washed.

"You aren't afraid of me, are you?" she asked once. It wasn't a question, it was an observation.

"How could I be afraid of you? What can you do to me that's worse than you've done already?" he had replied.

"It wasn't me that had your family killed," she said, her voice going cold.

"But how many of me are out there?" he had asked, his eyes flat and grey. "How many who *have* had their families killed by your order?" He had paused then, and sighed. "The whos and wherefores of responsibility don't matter. You, Takami, Macaan; you're all part of the same thing. And you'll all pay the same price."

He had seen her react then in a way she had never done before; she looked shocked, and hurt, as if someone she trusted had suddenly turned and plunged a knife into her belly. Then she had got up and silently left.

Aurin was an enigma. Why did she obsess him so? At first, it had been because he had finally come face to face with his enemy, an enemy that so few people had ever seen and less had survived to speak of. Aurin, like Macaan, had been simply faceless forces up until now, the anonymous power behind the Guardsmen, Keriags and Jachyra that they fought. But now, he had a face to link it with.

And it *was* a beautiful face. She was staggeringly attractive. Perhaps this, too, contributed to the way he felt about her. There was no denying that she had a physical magnetism that was far and above anything he had felt before; but she was his sworn enemy, and he knew that beneath the surface lurked a mind that was much less beautiful.

Now, though, he told himself that it was curiosity that made him think of her almost constantly. Why, why, why? What was her scheme? Why was she acting so irrationally; or was it just that he could not see the plan she was carrying out, that she was being too devious for him to follow?

He had been pacing for a long time when the bolt drew back and Aurin was allowed in, banishing the guard out of earshot. He was surprised to find that he greeted her with a smile. . .

19
Flesh and Bone and Blood

"**H**ochi!" Peliqua cried as she shoved open what remained of the door to his hut.

Her arrival was greeted by a shriek from Elani, and accompanied by the sound of Hochi's hammer smashing into one of the Snappers that had been unwise enough to look around as she came through the door, breaking its bones like twigs. Fast as an eyeblink, Peliqua pulled free the weighted chain at her waist and sent it snaking out towards one of the two remaining creatures that had the big man and the Resonant backed into a corner.

It curled around the spindly wrist of one, arresting its arm in mid-strike; she pulled hard, yanking it off-balance and dragging it away from the couple, leaving Hochi to concentrate on the remaining attacker. As it stumbled towards her, she lashed the other end of the chain across the creature's face, smashing its jaw with a brutal crack and bringing a well of blood spewing from its mouth. Stunned, it was not fast enough to react as she ran one foot up on a stool and flipped over it, bringing the chain of her manriki-gusari looping around its neck. As she landed, she spun and pulled the chain taut, breaking the Snapper's neck over her shoulder, then flicked her weapon free and went to help Hochi.

The big man scarcely needed it. Heartened by the arrival of his companion, he had begun hefting his great warhammer in wide arcs, switching from a defensive stance to one of aggression. The Snapper was fast, but it was fighting in a confined space and there was nowhere to dodge the heavy swings. At the same time Peliqua finished off her opponent, Hochi's adversary finally ran out of luck and was caught square in the chest, sending its spindly, broken body crashing against the wall of the hut, where it lay still.

"Mauni's Eyes, Peliqua, you know when to make an entrance," Hochi said, crouching to hug the frightened Elani in one beefy arm.

"Really? You know I wanted to be in the theatre once, 'cause my mother said that to me and *she* thought I had talent, but of course we didn't have theatres any more 'cause of Macaan so I guess I . . . um. . ." she trailed off as she realized, by Hochi's expression, that this really wasn't the time. "Where's Jaan?" she said, trying a new tack.

"I don't know," he said. "I gave him and Iriqi the message from the Council, and they said they'd follow along later."

Elani looked at Peliqua with wide, teary eyes. "Do you think they're still *out* there?" she whispered, but Hochi cut in before the Kirin girl could reply.

"I'm sure they got in. They were up at the back gate of Base Usido, on the cliffs past the defences. That's where they'll be, I imagine. They'd have got inside when the alarm was raised."

"Okay, I'm gonna go see," she said, then suddenly shifted from an expression of dire concern to a cheery beam. "Holler if you need any more help."

"I'm gonna get Elani somewhere safe," Hochi said grimly. "You take care, okay?"

"You too. See ya, Elani."

Elani waved a goodbye, and then Peliqua darted back through the ruined doorway and into the camp again.

Outside, it was chaos. Somewhere beyond the perimeter wall, the giant beetle-like mukhili had been released from their caves and were rampaging through the ranks of the enemy, guided by desert-folk in howdahs. The mukhili had been invaluable during the battle at the Ley Warren during the Integration; coming from the southern deserts of the Dominions, they were massive mobile fortresses that the people of the region had learned to harness for war. Transported with the rest of the army after the Ley Warren exploded, they were kept in the caves that honeycombed the floor of the plains; but now they had been brought into the battle, and were sowing havoc.

Inside the walls, it was even more hectic. Banes swirled between the leaping Snappers and the hulking Snagglebacks as they fought with the Parakkans. A cohort of riders, on pakpaks and horses both, had raided the stables for mounts and come out fighting, using both weapons and spirit-stones in an attempt to drive away the Rift-beasts from the living-quarters.

Everywhere there were little islands of conflict; a woman locked in single combat with a Snaggleback twice her weight; a group of Kirin children of about Gerdi's age that leaped and scampered among the roofs of the huts, shooting poison-tipped arrows at the creatures that ran below them; a cluster of Banes feeding on what was left after a group of Dominion-folk had been cornered and killed by a group of Snappers. But Peliqua could not stop to help without entangling herself in the constant combat, and she had other concerns right at this moment. Where was her brother?

She was forced to stop and fight twice before she reached the foot of the wide, flat section of cliff that Base Usido backed up against. It was as she had suspected; while all the lifts outside the Base had been lowered to the plain floor to prevent any of the creatures somehow using the mechanisms to get down the cliff wall, all the lifts within the perimeter had been *raised* the moment that they got word of the breach, to stop the reverse happening. They had taken as many of the children that they could, along with anyone else who was incapable of fighting, and brought them to the sanctuary of high ground, where they would hopefully be safe behind the clifftop defences. Peliqua didn't doubt that any creature who tried scaling the cliffs would get an unfriendly reception at the top.

Looking around to be sure that none of the creatures were nearby, she darted into a small hut of weathered iron that stood next to the huge cogs and pulleys set into the stone of the cliffs. Inside, among the several layers of Machinist instrumentation that ran around the small room at waist-and-eye height, there was a small speaker grille. She pressed the button next to it and put her mouth close.

"This is Peliqua. Is anyone up there?"

There was no reply.

"Is anyone—" she began, but she was cut off as another voice came through, crackly and faint, its nuances mangled by the crude technology that worked it.

"Peliqua, this is Bicio. We're holding out up here, but only just. We need reinforcements."

"Is my brother up there? Jaan? A halfbreed boy, probably with that great big Koth Taraan?"

"Listen, girl, I haven't seen them and I don't have time to go look for them. You want them, come up here and find them yourself."

"Send me a lift down," she replied. "The smallest one."

"You make sure it's only you that comes up," Bicio said sternly, and cut the connection.

Peliqua released the button and ran outside again. A Snapper scampered between two huts to her right, but it was intent on something else and did not see her. She double-checked in case anything was trying to sneak up on her, and then looked up at the cliff, where a narrow metal cage – big enough for two people at most – was clanking down towards her. She scanned around, and found a spot behind a hut where she could hide until it arrived; standing out in the open like she was, trouble was bound to find her. She watched the lift descend and settle with a grinding thump and a hiss of steam.

As she prepared to cross the open ground between her and the lift, she hoped that fortune would be with her. It wasn't. The moment she broke cover and ran, a Snaggleback that had been ambling across the blood-soaked grass nearby sensed the movement, its nostrils flaring, and began to bound towards her, screeching its *yip! yip!* cry.

She saw it coming out of the corner of her eye as she scrambled into the cage, yanking the lever upwards to start its ascent as she shut the door behind her with her other hand. For one terrible moment, the cage didn't move; then the mechanism kicked in, and it started to climb. She pressed her back to the cliff side of the cage and held her breath, watching the Snaggleback charge towards her. It had a lot of ground to cover, but the lift was slow, too cursed *slow*! As it neared, her transfixed eyes skittered over its thick, taut bunches of muscle, its protruding jaws, and the forest of stiff, spiny hairs on its back that gave its species their nickname. Snappers she could handle, but one of these? And on her own? She doubted it.

Go faster! she urged the unheeding metal, as it lifted her higher. But would it be high enough?

The Snaggleback pounded over the grass, becoming gradually smaller beneath her. She must be thirty feet up by now, at least. Surely well out of its reach?

Wrong again. It took one long stride and then launched itself upwards and towards her, its grotesque jaws wide, its cheeks and lips skinned back across its skull. Peliqua cried out in fear and shock as it crashed into the cage, making it shudder and almost ripping it from its moorings and sending them both plummeting. It tried to get a handhold, failed, and slid off the dented metal bars, falling away; but then one strong hand shot out, grabbing the bottom of the cage just by Peliqua's booted feet, its fingers punching through the mesh. The lift shuddered and groaned, unable to take the immense weight of the beast.

But then a second Snaggleback appeared, attracted by the struggle, racing across the ground and leaping up for the cage. Peliqua screamed; but right at that moment, the mechanism of the lift lurched and pulled her upwards a few feet. The Snaggleback fell short, grabbing on to the back of its hanging companion. The lift screeched, beginning to pull free of its securing-bolts; but the mesh in the floor gave way first. The Snaggleback's tenuous hold was suddenly foiled as the metal under its fingertips bent downwards, unable to support the weight of two creatures. With a shrieking *yip!* it fell free, its companion with it, and the two of them smashed heavily into the rocky ground at the base of the cliffs and remained there.

Peliqua breathed an oath in relief as the cage began to ascend again, carefully arranging herself so that she was not standing near the hole in the cage floor. The lift limped up the cliff face, carrying her to the top, and when she got out she had never been so glad to feel solid earth beneath her feet.

On the cliff top, things were only a little better than down below.

When Base Usido had first been constructed, it had been necessary to build it up against the cliffs that surrounded the huge, sunken plain because they had not had enough materials to build an encircling wall for the whole base. Building against the cliffs meant they did not have to worry about being attacked from behind, and they could concentrate on defending one area from the Rift-beasts that roamed the plains while they erected a semicircular perimeter wall. However, as time went on and more resources became available, it became obvious that this had been a mistake. There were many creatures that could scale down the cliffs at Base Usido's back easily, and they could get inside the walls that way.

So it was decided that the top of the cliffs would be guarded, too, in an attempt to prevent this happening. Lifts were built to haul materials up and down the cliff face. The forest of haaka and wychwood was cut back, and another semicircular wall was constructed, forming a small island of safety at the top of the cliffs where weapons and stores were stockpiled. It was there to guard Base Usido's back; but as Peliqua stepped out of the lift, she saw that it was only barely managing to do that.

The hordes were battering at the walls, oblivious of the force-cannon blasts that ripped into them from the turret-mounted weapons. Their dead had blunted the spikes, sheathing their edges in flesh and bone and blood, and now the Parakkans fought like demons to keep the creatures from clambering over and into the compound. The air was dense with screeches, cries, and the repetitive *whumph* of force-bolts. All around them, the Banes swirled madly, curling among the carnage and feeding on the dead, writhing away if anyone came near. She spotted Calica in the thick of it, and made her way towards the wall, through the clusters of frightened children and the elderly that sheltered here. It was safer for them here than below, where the creatures had already broken through and were rampaging across the Base.

Climbing up the iron rungs of a ladder, she hurried along the narrow ledge where the defenders lashed and sliced to keep the creatures down. Calica was hacking wildly with her katana, her face and chest and arms sprayed in blood and dirt, streaked through with sweat. She looked exhausted, and her usual precision and skill with her weapon had been abandoned through tiredness for clumsy strikes.

"Calica!" Peliqua said. "Take a break!" She stepped in to cover for her, and Calica gratefully took a step back, panting, while the Kirin girl brought her manriki-gusari to bear on the invaders, dislodging handholds, smashing into foreheads, entangling and killing.

"Where's Jaan?" Calica shouted over the noise, when she had taken a few breaths.

"Isn't he here?" Peliqua shouted back, not taking her eyes from the battle.

"Haven't seen him. Or the Koth Taraan."

"You think they're still out there?"

"If they are, they'll be safe enough. Banes don't go for anything without a spirit-stone."

"They went for that little boy, Paani," Peliqua argued.

Calica hesitated. "They were out by the caves. Maybe they'll be okay."

Peliqua felt a terrible helplessness overwhelm her. Maybe? *Maybe* they'll be okay? Maybe wasn't good enough. But if they were out there and she was in here, there was nothing she could do. She had always been there to look after him, to cajole him when he got down, to defend him when other children mocked his halfbreed features. Now he was alone, except for a creature that wasn't even human.

What chance did he have without her? she thought, and blinked back tears as she fought on.

Jaan pressed himself hard against the cold, dank stone and tried not to breathe, his yellow eyes fixed on the glowing white of the Bane as it slipped through the air further up the tunnel, its snakelike body curling in the still darkness, leaving tiny streamers of light behind it as it went. Its wide mouth opened and closed as it turned, as if it could taste Jaan's presence; but then it coiled upon itself and headed back up the tunnel, away from where they hid.

He stayed still for a long while, listening to the scuff and scrape of the Snappers and Snagglebacks that roamed the caves in search of him. The Snappers, like him, did not need more than a glimmer of light to see by, while the Snagglebacks had no eyes at all; and they were hunting for him now, led here by a Bane.

((Your home is a dangerous place to live)) Iriqi commented silently, the words tinged with an ironic blue.

"It's not like we had much of a choice," Jaan whispered back to the hulking form that stood next to him, sheltered from sight by an alcove in the rock. "And if that Bane hadn't seen us, we'd never have been in danger at all."

((Why?))

"They say the Banes only go for spirit-stones. They don't usually attack the living. It's the Snagglebacks and Snappers who—"

((But we don't have any spirit-stones)) Iriqi interrupted.

"That's what puzzles me." He drew back into the

alcove, and slid down the wall to the ground, dwarfed by the huge, armoured frame of his companion.

((It senses the Communion)) the Koth Taraan stated.

Jaan looked up at it, the tiniest glimmer of illumination dancing across the moist planes of its eyes. "And you're gonna tell me what that is, right?"

((The link that the Koth Taraan share. Each of us are connected to each other, but no link is stronger than with the Koth Macquai. It holds the Communion in its breast))

"That glowing light Kia mentioned?" he queried, remembering the few times that Kia had spoken on their way back from the Unclaimed Lands.

((It is passed on by each Koth Macquai on their death to their successor. It holds the memories of the deceased, and therefore the memories of all the Brethren. And they hold the memories of those that they succeeded, and so on. It has been so for thousands of generations. Our memory is eternal))

Jaan nodded to himself. At last he understood what Iriqi meant when he said that same phrase, back at the Koth Taraan's settlement. That was why the only way to entirely erase the Koth Taraan would be to kill them and destroy the Communion. That was why the younger Brethren feared Macaan, and wanted to help Parakka. In hiding, they had been trying to preserve their species and their culture. Now they wanted to do the same by attacking.

"You think the Bane's after you?"

((It senses something it has not sensed before. A power it does not recognize. It wants to feed))

"How do you *know* that?"

((I have many wiser Brethren to advise me))

Jaan shook his head, the tangled ropes of his hair clinking with the ornaments that were sewn there. He could never fully accept the fact that Iriqi shared a link with every other member of his species, and was in constant contact at all times. It was a human thing, to think of someone as an individual. As such, he tended to forget that everything he told the Koth Taraan was instantly relayed to each of his Brethren.

And he had talked to Iriqi about some deeply personal things during the time they had spent together; as one alien to another, they shared something of a rapport. When talking to a creature neither Dominion-born or Kirin, Jaan did not find himself being self-conscious about his halfbreed face. It was only by contrast that he realized how withdrawn he was with his other friends, how his silence was a product of his own shame. No matter how much he protested against it, and despite his sister's best efforts, he was ashamed to be a halfbreed. It had been drilled into him since he was born, through the taunts of the children in their hometown, through the looks of disgust on elder folk's faces as he passed. Even with a friend such as Gerdi, who harboured none of their prejudice, who had never heeded Aurin's propaganda; even with him, he felt inferior. He couldn't help it.

But not with Iriqi. Iriqi was too far removed from either race to provoke the shame that he always kept just beneath the surface of his skin. And Jaan liked that. It put him at ease; and that was a state of mind that he had not been in for a very long time.

((We should go)) Iriqi said. *((The Rift-beasts are getting closer))*

Jaan listened, and realized that it was true. The snuffles and scratches from all around them were louder now, coming through the walls or echoing down the long, narrow tunnels.

"We should try and make our way round to the entrance," Jaan whispered. Then, as it suddenly occurred to him, he asked: "You remember the way?"

((Our memory is eternal)) the Koth Taraan said in a faint pink cloud of amusement.

"Yeah, that's what I thought," Jaan muttered, and they headed off through the tunnels.

The Koth Taraan were a surprisingly stealthy people, for all their huge size and cumbersome bulk. Despite the fact that Iriqi filled up the tunnel as he lumbered along, he made hardly any noise. Jaan supposed that, as a race, they were used to hiding – something that they shared with Parakka – but it still defied belief that a creature so heavy could have a tread so light.

They crept through the thick, underground darkness, surrounded by ghostly scratches and scrapes, which sounded frighteningly close at times and at others would be distant and barely audible.

The rock twisted sound so that Jaan's ears were unreliable; and his eyes were scarcely better, for even with his Kirin low-light vision it was difficult to make out more than a vague impression of the shape of the tunnel they followed. He hoped that his pursuers were having the same problem, but he doubted it. What did darkness matter to creatures like the Banes, which produced their own light, or Snagglebacks, which had no eyes?

They had gone scarcely fifty metres when something moved across the lighter dark of a tunnel junction ahead, and paused suddenly. Jaan froze; by its size, it could only be a Snaggleback. Behind him, Iriqi became similarly motionless.

((If it comes for us, get behind me)) the Koth Taraan said silently in grave, iron-shod colours.

But there was really no question that it would. By whatever sense the Snagglebacks hunted by, whether it was scent or vibration, hearing or something else, they were right in its path. Jaan felt his stomach sink as it turned its silhouetted head towards them, and its jaws slid out of the sheath of its lips; and then it loosed the distinctive cry of its race, sounding the alarm, that the prey had been found.

Jaan looked past Iriqi, down the tunnel the other way, but he already knew what he would see. It was a long and featureless tube of rock that they had travelled down, with no side-arteries in which to lose themselves, no escape route. And besides, there were already shapes moving at the far limit of his vision, galloping towards them.

"There's at least two coming up behind us," he said urgently. "You take them, Iriqi, and I'll –" he clashed his forearms together, and the long blades of his dagnas sprang out of their hollow wooden tubes – "take this one."

((Agreed. Be careful)) A purple-blue wash of concern.

Jaan didn't reply, his eyes fixed on the Snaggleback as it crept towards them, not yet charging but slinking insidiously closer. Iriqi turned around, rotating his hulking form with a quiet shuffling noise, and they stood back-to-back in the tunnel, the halfbreed boy and the Koth Taraan.

"Come on!" Jaan challenged, and the creature responded instantly, accelerating and pounding towards him on all fours. The others followed suit, tearing up the tunnel towards their prey.

The one that had spotted them reached the pair first, hurtling into them with suicidal abandon. Snagglebacks were not clever fighters; they relied on brute force to overwhelm their prey. But despite the closeness of the tunnel, Jaan still had space to jump out of the way as it approached, slashing down at it as it passed and slicing deeply into the rippling expanse of its ribs. Screeching a high *yip!*, it slammed into the armoured hide of Iriqi's back, scarcely even rocking the Koth Taraan. Jaan heard something break inside it, but he could not afford the leisure of hesitation to see if it had been finished off. He plunged his right dagna deep into the nape of its neck; it spasmed once, violently, and then went limp.

But its approach had masked another problem: there were two more shapes coming down Jaan's side of the corridor, two more that he hadn't seen. And there was the Bane, suddenly appearing from around the corner of a tunnel, curling and twisting as it followed them, casting its ethereal light.

The two on Jaan's side and the two approaching Iriqi converged at almost the same moment, a savage mass of fangs and nails. At least one of them was a Snapper, but Jaan could barely see, and he was too preoccupied with the cut and parry of survival to take the time to care. Somewhere behind him, he heard a nauseating crack as Iriqi smashed one of his opponents against the tunnel wall with his outsize claws. A late parry left him with shallow score-marks down the coffee-coloured skin of his arm. He was vaguely aware of the Bane, hanging back, waiting to feed after its companions had finished off the prey. But they were finding Iriqi a harder opponent than they thought; for Jaan heard the shriek of a Snapper as it was crushed by the Koth Taraan's immense strength, even as he fought off the grasping claws of the Snaggleback, and. . .

Suddenly he was aware of a bright movement, and the Bane darted past him and wrapped around the narrow part of Iriqi's arm, between the huge shoulder plate and his massive forearm.

"Iriqi!" Jaan cried, but he could do nothing more.

The Bane bit deep, its body dissipating as it flowed into the wound, entering the Koth Taraan's body, seizing its mind.

And then the darkness was pounded by a terrible screech, a noise such as Jaan had never heard before, which sanded his nerves and made his body shudder. Even his opponents paused and drew back, as the corridor was suddenly filled with a million tiny tadpoles of light, skittering away from the Koth Taraan's body and fading into nowhere. Jaan stood, uncertain, watching the huge creature as it turned around to face them. What had happened to it? Was it hurt? Would it—?

((Get behind me, human child)) it said again, and this time its words were soaked in black anger. Jaan did so, slipping around its huge leg; but the remaining Snapper and Snaggleback seemed less than eager to continue the fight now, and they turned and ran, disappearing up the corridor.

"What happened?" he asked in wonderment. "What happened to the Bane?"

((Later)) came the reply. *((Let us go back to Base Usido))*

"But it's—"

((I do not think the Base will be under attack for much longer))

The effect was instant and simultaneous. The defenders did not know what they were seeing, but the reaction of the beseiging hordes told them it had to be good. All across the battlefield, even inside the walls of Base Usido where the invaders still ran amok, sparkling fountains of light suddenly burst forth, swirling upwards like the dust devils in the southern deserts of the Dominions, miniature tornadoes of luminescence that dissolved into hundreds upon thousands of tiny wriggles of light and then disappeared. The light seemed to be coming from the creatures themselves, the Snagglebacks and Snappers – only certain ones, perhaps one in twenty-five or more, but it was as if something had flowed out of their bodies. At the same time, the Banes that flitted across the battlefield lifted their voices as one in an unearthly screech and exploded in a shower of light.

And though none of the Parakkans knew what had happened, one thing had become certain. The tide had turned. The enemy were already beaten.

The assault was over.

From high in the sky over the Fin Jaarek mountain range, the Rifts were a dark, heavily forested smear, stretching for vast miles in a long strip between the feet of the mountains and the plains to the west. It was dangerous to fly over, because of the many wild wyverns and other airborne beasts that made the shattered lands their home. But the Princess Aurin had stepped up patrols recently, tripling their frequency and spreading them out over a wider area, and even the Rifts now were to be flown over whenever it was judged safe to do so. Not that there was much point; no Riders dared go low enough to see anything in the dim Kirin Taq light, and the trees obscured almost everything. It would only be possible to find something in the maze of the Rifts if they were skimming the treetops and flew directly over it, and that was hardly likely.

But there *was* a patrol that particular cycle, three Riders on wyvern-back, their red armour dull in the glow of the eclipsed sun, winging silently through the sky. They were skimming the edge of the Rifts, following the feet of the mountains around, making no more than a cursory check of the black expanse beneath them. They had not been told what to look for, for Aurin was keeping the news of Parakka's re-emergence as secret as she could to prevent word leaking back to her father; but they knew, by the sudden increase in patrols, that something was happening in Kirin Taq. Something big.

And it was only really a case of bad fortune for Parakka. The Riders happened to be flying through that still night sky when the eruption of light from the dissipating Banes lit up a small section of the forest beneath them like a flare. One pointed, and they wheeled around, watching the blazing white, memorizing its position before diving down towards it. It had faded before they reached it.

They did not see the sudden change in the battle. Nor did they see the Snagglebacks and Snappers routed, turning and fleeing back into the forests or panicking on the plains where they were crushed by the enormous mukhili. They did not see the Parakkans turning their attention inward to purge the invaders that had got inside the wall. But they heard the erratic *whumph* of the force-cannons, and they heard the shrieking of the wyverns as they mopped up the last of the enemy that could not escape, and so they passed silently overhead and turned their mounts towards Fane Aracq, where the Princess would be very interested to hear their news. . .

20

A Sign of Weakness

Corm strode through the bone-smooth corridors of Fane Aracq, his mechanical eyes clicking and chattering as they peered out from above the rim of his high, stiff collar. His black greatcoat flapped around his feet as he walked, his face set hard. It was time for their regular three-cycle report to the Princess. Usually, it was a routine, even a pleasure. Today, he did not know how he was going to handle it.

The prisoner had been allowed out. He was permitted to exercise in the courtyard, under escort. He was permitted to practise with weapons, albeit with a heavy guard. These were not the sort of privileges extended to a prisoner who was soon to be executed.

He hoped he had himself under control, but he was not confident that the outrage he felt at the Princess's actions would not leak into his voice and manner when he spoke to her. What next? Would she remove his Damper Collar? Would she give him the run of the palace? What did Aurin think she was *doing*?

Up here, nearer the Princess's chambers, the smokeless wychwood torches had been replaced by white glowstones in the corridors. It was a gesture of

306

excessive opulence, for the white stones were rare and much-prized because their light showed colours true, instead of the orange hue from common glowstones. Corm barely noticed the change as he walked, his mind fixed only on what he must say and how he had to say it. Minutes later, he arrived at Aurin's chambers.

Tatterdemalion was already there, crouching by the massive wall-mirror, a scrawny, misshapen mass of rags, belts and metal. Aurin, by contrast, looked a picture of perfection, sleek and elegant as she stood in wait for Corm's arrival. He entered with as much composure as he could, bowed and then awaited her command.

"Greetings once again to you both," she said. "What developments in my realm?" The question was asked with the barest minimum of interest, even less than she usually mustered. She seemed preoccupied. After a moment, she looked up at the Machinist. "Corm?"

"Things are as ever, my Princess. I have nothing to report. But I do have a question, if I may."

"Is it about the prisoner?" she asked sharply.

"Yes," he replied.

"Then guard your tongue carefully this time, Corm," she warned. "What is it?"

Corm hesitated a moment before speaking, wondering if it was entirely wise to risk her wrath when today it seemed so easily aroused. "I have been informed that the prisoner has been allowed certain extra privileges, my Princess. . ." he began.

"We've been over this ground, yes?" she interrupted. "I have told you the reason behind my generosity to him."

She *was* touchy. "I am not presuming to question your plan, my Princess," Corm said hastily in his thin, reedy voice. "I merely wish to know if you still intend to execute the prisoner after the location of the Parakkan base is revealed."

"Of course," she said. "What *else* would I do with him? Set him free?" She paused, thinking. "Perhaps I would keep him for a short while, the better to use him to understand the minds of my enemy. But there will come a time when his usefulness expires, yes?"

"I understand, my Princess."

"And what of the stirrings in the Machinist Citadel?" she asked, changing the subject.

"No change," he replied. "At the moment, your father keeps trade up with the Guild, and until he ceases to do so things are unlikely to shift drastically."

"Tatterdemalion?" she prompted, turning to the silent creature.

+++ The Jachyra are loyal to you, as always +++

"And do *you* have anything to report?" she asked, turning away from them and pacing across the room, her thigh-high white boots clicking on the creamstone floor as they moved beneath her long dress.

+++ A minor incident in Taitai, my lady. Two members of the ruling council were found to be sympathizers with the recent uprising in Kitika. They

308

disapproved of your methods of crushing the rebellion. We have watched them for a time. Last cycle they began making treasonous statements to the villagers in the support of Parakka. We took them; we await your decision on their fate +++ The Jachyra's report faded off into a static hum, and his telescopic eye whirred, adjusting focus, as he watched the Princess.

She did not reply with her usual speed. In fact, she spent a long minute in silence, looking out of one of the wind-holes at the velvety-blue sky.

"Princess? Are you alright?" Corm asked. She jumped infinitesimally in surprise, suddenly realizing where she was again.

"I'm sorry. What?" she said, turning around and leaning against the sill, her long index and middle finger resting in the bridge of her small nose in thought.

+++ The sympathizers in Taitai +++ Tatterdemalion said, then added: +++ They *are* Councillors, my lady +++

"Do they have families?" she asked.

+++ They do +++ came the crackling reply. +++ Shall we execute them also? +++

Aurin looked up, and a tired shadow seemed to cross her pretty features. "Scourge them, yes? Just the Councillors, not their families. Ten times each, in the public square of Taitai. Make sure everyone knows why, and that everyone is clear that a repeat occurrence will result in the village being burnt to the ground. With everyone inside."

"Princess!" Corm exclaimed, before his better judgement could stop him.

"You have a better suggestion?" Aurin said quietly, unmistakable menace in her voice.

"It's just ... Parakkan sympathizers are always punished by death. At *least*," the Machinist said. "Their families almost always suffer with them, to discourage traitors. It has worked so far, Princess. If we become lax, people will see it as a sign of weakness and—"

"I don't care," she interrupted dismissively. "I am heartsick of killing. And the policy of execution *hasn't* worked so far, Corm, because we still have to do it. I am not suggesting we change; but for this particular instance, I choose to have mercy on them. I will not hear any argument. And if you *dare* suggest that this is the prisoner's doing, I will have you scourged with them."

Corm bowed his head and was silent, but he seethed inside. The very fact that she had been thinking of his next comment proved to him that he was right.

"Unless there is anything else, you may go. Both of you," she said, her tone ending the audience more finally than her words did. They both made their parting gestures of respect and left.

When she was alone again, she sat down on a cushioned bench of creamstone, moulded out of the wall, and poured herself a glass of Dominion summerleaf wine. She swirled it thoughtfully as she looked at herself in the huge mirror that seemed to grow seamlessly out of the wall. She knew what Corm thought; it was written plainly on his half-Augmented face, despite his attempts to hide it. What rankled was that he was right, and she knew it. It *was* Ryushi that was affecting her this way. Over the span of their visits, he had urged her to think of the people that she ruled over when she made decisions, to put herself in their place, to empathize with them; and gradually, unstoppably, it had begun to seep through.

She felt guilty. She felt guilty, because she had begun to imagine the sinking feeling, the terrible cold that the traitors in Kitika must have felt as her pronouncement of death was passed on to them, the horror as they were told that their families would be sent into slavery in the mines for generations to come. It made her sad, but it also made her ashamed. It was she that had done that to them, and even though they were just lowly villagers, their emotions, their *humanity* was no less than hers.

She had never thought about it before. Never. And now she was being forced to. Because try as she might, she could not seem to stay away from the Dominion boy in her prison; and while she kept on visiting him, under the paper-thin pretense of extracting information, he kept on making her think about it. And now she couldn't stop.

What was *wrong* with her?

She got up, leaving the untouched glass of wine, and walked through the corridors of her palace, taking a route that had recently become well-known to her. On the way, she ignored the small bows of fealty that the

Guardsmen and retainers made as she passed, and avoided contact with any of the nobles who might want to take up her time with idle talk. She headed for the cells, and when she got there, she dismissed the Guardsman on watch and told him to wait further up the corridor.

Slipping the key in the lock, she opened the cell door and stepped inside.

Ryushi looked up from the bench as she entered, raising his face from the pillow where it had rested a moment before. He blinked blearily at her, his short, thick tentacles of blond hair falling about his elfin face, then smiled a greeting and raised his tired body into a sitting position.

"I woke you? I'm sorry," she said.

"S'okay," Ryushi replied, rubbing one eye with the heel of his palm. "The exercise yard pretty much burned me out. Been cooped up so long I was getting out of shape, and I pushed myself a little hard." He let his hands fall to his lap and looked at her. "I have you to thank for that?" he asked, though he already knew the answer.

She smiled an affirmative, standing where she was.

"You want to sit down?" he offered, indicating the bench next to him. It seemed absurd, that he should be offering the hospitality of his prison cell to the one who put him there; but she declined anyway.

"I won't stay long," she said. "You're tired, yes?"

Ryushi's eyelids were already drooping. He nodded wearily.

"I just came to tell you," she said. "Tatterdemalion found some defectors in Taitai. I . . . spared them."

His face came suddenly alive, momentarily seeming to shed the drowsiness that fogged it. "You did? That's . . . that's great."

She was a little taken aback. She had expected a sarcastic comment, some sort of snide remark about how she was *so* generous to let them live when it was her that was choking their freedom of choice in the first place. Instead, he seemed genuine, if a little surprised.

"Well . . . I just came to tell you, that's all," she said, suddenly awkward. This was no way for a Princess to act, she told herself; but at the same time, she felt strangely good about it, childishly happy. "I'll go now, yes?"

"You could stay if you wanted. I'm not tired," Ryushi said, his eyes already beginning to droop again.

She laughed lightly. "Go to sleep. I will see you again soon." She went to let herself out, hearing him nestle back on to the sleeping-bench behind her. Opening the ivory cell door, she almost walked into Corm, who peered at her with his Augmented eyes, his face half-covered by his collar.

"What is it, Corm?" she snapped, surprise making her short-tempered.

"I have just received word, Princess. Three Riders have come in with some very interesting information. You should hear it."

She frowned, disappointed that her elation had been

soured by Corm's disapproval before she had a chance to savour it. "Very well. I will see them in the audience chamber. Go and bring them there."

Corm bowed, a slight movement of his bald head, and then stalked away past the waiting Guardsman sentry. Aurin stood where she was for a moment, the cell door still ajar next to her. On impulse, she looked back through the oval spy-holes, and saw Ryushi lying on his side, his ribs rising and falling with the slow breath of sleep. For a moment, she didn't move. Then she pushed the door open, very quietly, her heart beginning to flutter in her chest. Ryushi did not stir.

Softly, like a girl who had been sent into a Master's house on a dare, she took two quick steps towards him and gently leaned down to kiss the lobe of his ear. It was a fleeting touch, the soft pressure and moistness of her lips; and then she left in haste, closing the door behind her and locking it.

Ryushi lay listening to her footsteps recede for a long time before he opened his eyes.

Gerdi slept. Curled up like a foetus in a thin, threadbare woollen blanket, he was oblivious to the twenty-foot drop that waited a few inches away from the curve of his spine. He was not aware of the dim light that barely touched him from the single orange glowstone in the room, obscured behind a bookcase; nor of the slightly dry and musty odour of the old library. He was exhausted, stone-drained. He had to sleep, and sleep he did.

The library was ideal. Its poor lighting and the stiffness of the door betrayed how little it was used, and the tall bookcases that rose high above him provided perfect hiding places. He had scaled one that was pushed up against the wall, furthest from the light, and clambered on top of it. On the thick ledge of wood he had wearily made his bed. Even if someone came looking, the step-ladder in the corner was only high enough so that a tall man could barely reach the top shelf. Someone could take a book from right under Gerdi and not see him.

He was safe, or as safe as he could be in the heart of Fane Aracq.

Five cycles now he had spent in the halls of Aurin's palace. Five cycles of constant watchfulness, alertness, fear. It wore him down. His nerves were shredded. His mind was clogged with remembering different mannerisms, faces and speech patterns, and who to use on which people. But now, finally, he was nearing his goal. He knew at last where they were keeping Ryushi.

The last few cycles had all followed a similar pattern. Keeping to sparsely-walked areas of the palace, he would use whatever guise he had adopted to get into conversation with somebody else of a higher rank than he, and then make his way further into the palace. The chaotic exterior betrayed an ingeniously planned system of corridors where certain areas and sections could be restricted simply by putting a few Guards on a few entrances. A whole slice of the palace would be for visiting nobility only, and the encircling corridors for their retainers; while another cluster of rooms might be for highborn ladies, and no men allowed. It was a labyrinth of sections within sections within sections, and at the heart of it, he imagined, would be the Princess's chambers. Thankfully, the password system did not operate inside the main section of the palace. He was able to pass by the checks by adopting the faces of those people with authorization, after studying them for a while beforehand to get the nuances of their actions right. It was all done so as not to arouse suspicion, and so far he had succeeded. There had been tricky situations when he had almost walked into the real-life version of the person he was impersonating, and one interesting conversation with an ex-lover of another.

But it would all be for nothing if Jutar came back early from leave and anyone asked him about his head wound.

Then, finally, he had hit pay dirt. A sentry who recognized the Guard Captain he was impersonating hailed him as he was looking for a new victim to copy.

"Going to the prison section, Mujio?"

Gerdi had halted, frowning. The corridor had been only a random choice, but now he pointed down it, and said with the exaggerated sarcasm that was Mujio's mode of speech: "You mean the prisons are down here? I've had so little cause to visit them, I'd never have guessed."

The sentry laughed at his jest, but he'd confirmed the underlying question. The prison section was indeed down that way, and he went far enough along the smooth, white corridor to confirm that before doubling back and finding the library where he now slept. It was important to be at full strength when he went to rescue Ryushi. If Ryushi was still there at all, he reminded himself.

21
Simply a Circle

When she came back to him, perhaps a half-cycle later, he was awake again. He had thought that he would never drop off, so turbulent was his mind after the Princess's last visit; but the wolves of sleep had stalked him stealthily, and they were too great in number to avoid for long. Even his sleep was no refuge, though; his dreams continued to sort and shuffle through the dilemmas that had been presented to him, visiting him with visions and possibilities until he was no longer sure what had happened and what hadn't.

The Princess had *kissed* him. All this time, he had been wondering what she had up her sleeve, what she was doing, why she spent hours talking with him about nothing. He had thought it might be a trick at first, but that had been only the most likely of many possible reasons. He had even thought that she might be lonely, that she talked to him because he was the only one who did not treat her like a Princess, or pussyfoot around her in fear of her wrath; but he had dismissed that as ridiculous. She was the enemy, the daughter of Macaan, strong-willed and stubborn, and not prone to those kind of weaknesses.

But this . . . the idea that she might be in *love* with him had never crossed his mind until now.

It wasn't his fault. After all, he had spent much of his childhood under their father's strict training regime, and most of his time on the Stud had been spent with his twin. While there were many boys tending the wyverns, there were only few girls, and none of them could really measure up to the lighthearted tomboyishness of Kia. Then, of course, when Osaka Stud was destroyed, he had been forced to devote himself to Parakka, and had no time for any other, more frivolous interests. Naïvety had been pretty much his defining characteristic for a long time, and the ways of the opposite sex were no exception.

The enemy, the daughter of the one who had been partly responsible for the murder of his family, was falling in love with Ryushi. And the hornet's nest of confusion it had stirred up within him was not something that could easily be quieted.

His chest was taut with anticipation as he heard the key turn in the lock, and when she stepped through, it was as if he saw her anew for the first time. Her long, slender neck; the delicate curve of her collarbone; the gentle slope of her nose; her narrow, dark eyes. His breathing shallowed out as she came in, and he stared at her; and she, as if sensing the change, paused for a moment.

"Are you alright?" she said, and the spell was dislodged enough for Ryushi to speak.

"I'm okay," he replied, from where he sat on the edge

of his bench. It was then that he noticed the air of sadness around the Princess, a sorrowful quality to her expression. "Are you?"

"Of course," she answered dismissively, closing the door behind her. "Why wouldn't I be?"

"You tell me."

She turned back to him, a sudden archness in her voice. "Nothing is wrong."

He shrugged. "Okay then. Will you sit?"

"No," she said distractedly. "No, I think not."

She stood there, looking around the bare creamstone walls of the cell. It was obvious she had something to say, but did not know how to say it. It was—

"Your necklace," Ryushi heard himself begin, interrupting even his own thoughts. "You wear many different clothes, but they're always matched to your necklace, and I've never seen you without it. Why is that, Aurin?"

He had wondered about it for some time, but he had never asked the question until now. He had not intended to put it so directly. It just came out to fill the awkward void in the conversation. But so preoccupied was he with wondering where the question had come from, that he did not notice the sudden softening of Aurin's features, the almost visible melting inside her. Without realizing it, he had called her by her name instead of her title for the first time.

She broke into a little smile. "You're very forthright today," she observed.

"I'm interested, is all," Ryushi replied.

"My heartstone," she said, forsaking her previous inclination and sitting down on the bench next to him. She toyed with the three turquoise stones that lay against her collarbone, a larger one flanked by two smaller siblings, suspended between two thin silver chains.

"Your heartstone," he repeated flatly.

"Oh yes," she said. "I suppose I thought it was a simple gift, once. But then, I doubt it. I knew what I was doing. I knew the price. My father would go to any lengths to bribe affection out of me, but I don't think even he expected I would take him up on the chance to have the Keriags."

"The Keriags?" Ryushi asked, suddenly very interested. At that moment, a mercenary thought leaped to the forefront of his mind; if Aurin trusted him, had he not accomplished what dozens of Parakka spies had not been able to achieve? To get close to the Princess? And wasn't it his duty to his friends to exploit that?

But Aurin went on, conversationally, blithely unconcerned with what she was telling him. "The Keriags. See this big central stone here? My heartstone. Every Keriag Queen has a different stone implanted in their bodies, yes? If I take this off, within a cycle, every one of them will die. And so will the whole Keriag race."

Ryushi was dumbstruck. "I don't. . ." he began, then couldn't finish. The enormity of what she had just said, and the casual way she said it, choked off the sentence.

"It's quite simple," she said, brushing back one of the coils of her black hair over her bare shoulder. "A heartstone is cut from a much bigger gem, and many smaller offspring stones are taken at the time of its carving. In the same way that spirit-stones are attuned to the substance they affect, so the heartstone is attuned to its wearer's body. Their *aura*, I suppose you'd say. If it is removed from the beat of my heart for longer than a cycle or so, it cracks. And so do the offspring stones, which reside in the bodies of the Keriag Queens. And that kills them, yes?"

"But how did they . . . how did they *get* there?"

"My father. The Keriags have to come out to collect water for their fungus-gardens. He poisoned the water, and hence the gardens. Within cycles, the whole hive was incapacitated, and that was when he took the Queen and had her implanted. The Keriags share a hive-mind, and that includes the various Queens. Once one was done, the others could not voluntarily allow her to die; it would be like a man cutting off his own arm. So they, too, had to submit to the implants."

Ryushi was reeling. "And . . . you mentioned a price."

She nodded. "It's as you said; if you rule by fear, you can't ever stop. How can I take it off now? The Keriags would know the moment I did; and a cycle is plenty of time for them to swarm. They would home in on the heartstone and find me, and either make me put it back on or kill me."

"Couldn't you just take it off and leave it here, and go

with the Jachyra through the mirrors to hide elsewhere? They'd never find you in time then."

"I *could*," she said. "That possibility is what keeps the Keriags in line; that is why they obey me. But how can I do that? I would keep the breath in my body; but I would lose my *life*. Without the Keriags, I could not rule. I would have to forsake everything I have, yes? I care nothing for the lands I have been given; but how could I go from this –" here she made a motion that encompassed everything beyond the walls of the cell – "to poverty? And who knows what my father would do if he ever found me?"

"What about him? Couldn't you . . . use the Keriags against him?" Ryushi ventured, hardly even daring to hope.

Aurin laughed, high and clear. "You think he would have got to where he is if he didn't think of things like that? No, Father was clever. He knew, if he gave me the Keriags, I could use them against him if ever I felt the inclination; and there are many more Keriags than Guardsmen. He might profess that he loves me, but he is not stupid. No, this heartstone is linked to the trigger-stone in his forehead; just like the Jachyra and his top-ranking aides have implanted stones that can kill them if they get out of line. If he dies, the heartstone will react as if I had taken it off. Within a cycle, the Keriags will die. Nothing can stop that, and the Keriags know it. They will not raise weapons against him. They would not even try and capture him; they dare not risk that he might take his own life before they could stop him." She gave a shallow sigh. "He knows I'd never turn against him. . ." Looking into Ryushi's horror-stricken eyes, she shrugged. "So really, I have no power at all. It is simply a circle, keeping both myself and the Keriags in check."

"Can't you reverse it somehow?"

Aurin smiled pityingly. "There are ways. A Deliverer could do it. Presumably my father intends to deactivate his trigger-stone when he gets old, to pass on the legacy of the Keriags to me after his death. But how could I set the Keriags free now? It comes back again to what you said; ruling by fear. If I reversed what my father had done, the Keriags would turn against me and kill me in revenge for their slavery. Nothing could stop that."

Ryushi looked down at his feet. Now he saw the trap that Aurin had stepped into; gaining the great strength of the Keriag race, in return for being tied inextricably into their fate. To have the dilemma of sacrificing everything for her freedom from the heartstone, or holding on to all the privileges that royalty offered her in return for staying in that trap. But then, it was plain that she did not *want* what Ryushi would call freedom. That was the gulf between them. She was happy to keep the power and the price, rather than forsake her royal life and its privileges. Macaan had banked on that, on her fear of poverty after a life of riches, and that was why she would never give it up.

Ryushi had been staring at the floor for a time; now he looked up at the Princess, and he was shocked to see a tear sliding down one porcelain cheek. He met the watery pools of her eyes as she spoke again, her voice full of sorrow.

"We have found the Parakkan base, Ryushi. Spies are being sent to confirm it, and on their return, all my forces will mobilize. In thirty cycles, maybe less, it will all be over."

Ryushi felt ice slide through his veins.

"I'm sorry," she said, and then leaned over and kissed him, lightly, on the lips. He told himself after she left that it was shock at her pronouncement that had led him to let her do it; but that was only a partial truth. He had wanted her to, despite everything.

It was about a cycle later when the door of his cell opened, and Ryushi looked up, an odd eagerness in his eyes; but the gaze turned to puzzlement as he saw a tall, grizzled man walk in instead of Aurin. The man turned and told the sentry to wait further up the corridor, and instructed that nobody else was to be admitted.

"Not even the Princess?" the sentry asked, his surprise muffled by the voice-grilles of his face-visor.

"As if the Princess would let you stop her," he said, the words thick with scorn. "Of course it doesn't apply to the Princess." But then, Gerdi thought to himself, it was hardly likely that the Princess Aurin would be along personally to visit her prisoners, now was it?

The door was closed and locked, and Ryushi was on his feet, asking what this was all about, when the tall man turned round and he was suddenly no longer a man at all, but a boy, small and green-haired and wearing a wry grin on his face.

"You," he said, wagging a finger, "are a hard man to find."

"Gerdi!" Ryushi whispered in amazement. "I don't believe it!"

"Yeah, well," the Noman boy said modestly. "Believe it, 'cause they sent the best."

Ryushi impulsively reached out and hugged him, and Gerdi squirmed in his grip, embarrassed by the display of affection. "You came all the way in here—"

"—to get you, yeah, yeah. Only 'cause your sister would have killed me if I hadn't. Or that Calica chick; now *she's* been going spare while you've been away. What've you been up to there, huh?"

Ryushi looked up at the door, letting his jibe pass. "Listen, you've got to get out of here. Someone could come."

"Alright," he said. "Now here's the plan. We—"

"Gerdi," Ryushi said, holding up his hand. "Gerdi, wait. I can't go with you."

Gerdi blinked, then decided that he hadn't heard what he had just thought he had, and carried on talking. "Anyway, we go out into the corridor, and I pretend that I'm taking you to—"

"You're not *listening*," Ryushi hissed. "I can't go with you."

Gerdi narrowed his eyes. "You'd better have one

giant-sized reason for what you've just said, 'cause let me tell you I have had a *bad* time of it recently."

"I've got *two* giant-sized reasons," came the reply. "One: Aurin's found Base Usido, and in less than thirty cycles from now she'll hit it with the full force of her armies. She's just waiting for confirmation from her spies, then she'll mobilize. And two: I know how she controls the Keriags. What I don't know is what I can do about it."

Gerdi and he hunkered down together. "Talk fast, Ryushi," said the Noman boy. "I need a lot of explaining done real quick."

So Ryushi told him about Aurin's heartstone, and how it was linked to the Keriag Queens, and how it would crack if it was taken away from her heartbeat for more than a cycle. And he told her about how Macaan had put down the Keriags before, and about how Aurin told him they had discovered the Parakkan Base, and about—

"*What?*" Gerdi almost shouted, but caught himself at the last moment and dropped his voice to a loud hiss. "Don't even think about it, Ryushi. It's Princess Aurin we're talking about here! You can't—"

"I didn't say *I* was in love with *her*," Ryushi said, the embarrassed heat in his face gathering as he spoke. "I think that *she* loves *me*."

"Tell me you don't return the compliment," Gerdi said, his eyes narrowed suspiciously.

Ryushi paused, caught for a moment, then decided

not to answer. "Look, that's not important at the moment," he said. "We've tried for ages to get spies on the inside of this place, people close to Aurin who could find this stuff out! I mean, about the Keriags . . . I just *asked* her and she *told* me."

Gerdi looked at him, his impish face frozen in disbelief.

"I've been thinking," Ryushi said. "Ever since Aurin told me about the Base, a cycle or so ago. I can *get* that heartstone. But *you* need to figure out how to stop it killing the Keriags, and how to stop the Keriags killing her."

"What for? Let 'em both die. Unless you *are* sweet on Aurin?" He said this last in a scornful, half-mocking tone.

"I am *not* gonna be part of the indiscriminate murder of an entire *species*," Ryushi hissed. "And besides, how much damage do you think the Keriags can do in a single cycle? If we destroy the heartstone, you can be sure they'll take us with them."

"Nice and small task you've just lumped on me, then," Gerdi said sulkily.

"You got a better idea?"

"Yes! I get you out of here and then we evacuate Base Usido!"

"And then we're right back where we started! Except we're even worse off; we'll have nothing to build with, no equipment, nothing. We might as well just stay where we are and be massacred."

Gerdi was silent, gazing levelly at his friend in the torchlight.

"Look, there's something else as well. Aurin's been telling me about these dreams she has. The person she describes in them is *Calica*; but Aurin's never met her, and she doesn't know her."

Gerdi's eyes lit up. "Wait, wait. Kia said something about that, after her trial with the Koth Taraan."

"Her what?"

"I'll tell you later. But she kept on seeing Aurin and Calica together, and she didn't know why. And *Calica* was talking, too; she said she hadn't been sleeping well lately. Might be 'cause she's been having dreams. . ." He paused, then looked up at him. "Is that the best connection you've got?"

"Best and only."

"Good enough for me. Whatcha wanna do?"

Ryushi broke into a smile. "Okay. Now you know about the heartstone and what it does, you can work out how to get around it. I'll stay here. When the time comes, I'll be in the right place to snatch it, or whatever. Now Parakka have got to do something, and do it *now*. I think that taking out the Keriags is the only way they can win."

"You'd take the Princess's heartstone? Listen, if you say you're gonna do it, you'd better *do* it."

"I'll do it," he replied. "All you've got to do is guarantee me that if you make a move, and I snatch that necklace, you have a way to deactivate it or get rid of it or *something*. Within a cycle or less."

"Got it," Gerdi said. "You know, Kia's gonna turn me inside out when she finds out about this. If Calica doesn't get me first."

"That's tough," Ryushi replied. "The way I figure it, there's only one way you can go. And that's this way. Attack is the only option; hit the palace by surprise. We can't run any more."

"You make me this promise, before I go," Gerdi said, turning suddenly grave. "You're close to the Princess, right? Maybe you're closer to her than you say. Well, promise me this. Whatever it takes, *whatever* it takes, you remember who your friends are. And if that means tearing that thing off her neck and stamping on it, then you do that. If the whole of the Keriag race goes down and Princess Aurin with it, that's fine by me. But don't even *think* about putting her in front of us if it comes to the choice."

Ryushi was taken aback by the change in the usually jovial Gerdi. "I . . . I . . ."

"*Promise* me," he said, and for a moment it was Banto crouching there again, speaking those words, reminding him of a promise he made a lifetime ago to his dead father: to protect Elani, whatever the cost. The only thing he had left of the man was that promise, and he realized then that if he did not agree to what Gerdi said, then he was breaking it. And nothing was strong enough to make him do that.

He didn't know if it was Gerdi or his own mind that had conjured the image, but as they stood up

330

from where they had been squatting, he bowed his head.

"You've got my promise," he said.

"Great," said Gerdi, suddenly smiling. "Now, the perk." He rummaged in his pocket and drew out a small key. "Thought they'd have to keep your powers down somehow, so I got this. I bet you're real sick of your Damper Collar by now, right?"

Outside, under the black, hollow eye of the Kirin Taq sun, the sky was clear, belying the storm to come.

22

A Cancer in the Web

Deep in the Rifts, the residents of Base Usido were counting the cost of their victory.

The Snagglebacks and Snappers, following the disappearance of the Banes that controlled their pack leaders, had suddenly found themselves without direction. Most of the leaders were killed by the shock of having the Banes leave their bodies; those few that were not became disorientated and confused. Whatever communication went on between the leaders and their packs faltered, and the creatures dissolved into panic and disorder. The Parakkans, seeing their chance, leaped on the routed army and drove them away, pushing them back across the plains where they scaled the cliffs and scattered into the forest. Those creatures that had got inside the perimeter wall were similarly robbed of purpose and organization, and the troops had wiped them out with relative ease after that.

But the Base had been crippled. Huts had been destroyed, vital machinery wrecked by the Snagglebacks' powerful fists. The small hatchery that they had maintained was beyond repair. Some of the grain silos were ruptured, and the grain would spoil. At least the small vehicles that they had left had remained undamaged. But the dead ... the dead numbered perhaps a quarter of the Base's population. Broken bodies lay on the bluish grass, twisted and torn, their eyes staring after their departed essences. Men, women and children; Kirin and Dominion-folk alike.

"Funny," said Calica, as she sat on the remains of a log fence next to Hochi and surveyed the clean-up effort. "All this time, we were worried about Aurin finding the Base. And it turns out to be the land itself that got us. I guess we underestimated the danger of building a Base in the Rifts."

"It was that, or nothing," Hochi said grimly, bowing his bald head. "If not for Aurin's tyranny, we wouldn't *have* to hide. This was the only place we could build in secret without her finding us."

"So now what?" Calica said, brushing her orange-gold hair back over her shoulder. A moment later, she answered her own question. "We rebuild, I suppose. Start again. Make sure we do sweeps for Bane more regularly. Work out a way to keep them out."

"I suppose," Hochi agreed without enthusiasm, his small eyes dark under his heavy brow, ranging over the destruction around him. He was weary of war, tired of the killing. He had seen too much to feel horror at the death that surrounded them; so had Calica. But he was tired, *so* tired, of struggling against a seemingly impossible enemy only to face setback after setback. "The fight goes on," he said to nobody, and the words seemed to have no force behind them.

Calica turned her olive eyes to the ground. She knew how he felt. Sometimes it felt like they were living a fool's dream, thinking that they could change anything. The power of Macaan and Aurin was too great; what could a motley group of idealists ever do against such an implacable enemy? So they could turn around a few people, make them see the Parakkan point of view instead of Macaan's indoctrination. So what? What did it really matter? They weren't achieving anything unless they could follow their talk up with action. And how could they do that now? Every time they looked like they were making progress, they were cut down again.

Sometimes she felt like just throwing it all in. But there was only one thing stopping her; and that was the fact that there was no other choice. She couldn't live as a happy citizen of an empire that had killed her parents and orphaned her. So the only alternative was to oppose that empire, and hope to bring it down.

But it was so heartbreakingly *hard*.

She looked up as Elani, Jaan and Iriqi approached from across the blood-darkened grass. It was an odd sight, to see the two Parakkans followed by the hulking creature, over twice their size. Neither of the young humans took much notice of the carnage around them.

Calica felt a sudden stab of sorrow; their innocence and childhood had been just another casualty of the war that had enveloped their lives. If Iriqi felt something, she could not read it on its alien features.

They walked up and joined Calica and Hochi, the slight wind stirring their hair, carrying the smell of oily smoke and dirty blood.

"Shouldn't you be helping with the clean-up?" Calica asked Elani.

"Shouldn't you?" Elani countered. Calica shrugged as the girl hopped up next to her. It seemed that the lowering of spirits was universal in Base Usido, and the usual pulling-together attitude of the Parakkans had faltered.

"How are you finding humankind, Iriqi?" she asked the Koth Taraan, her voice heavy with irony.

((We are distressed by what has occurred here. The younger Brethren believe it is similar to what will happen to our home if Macaan is not checked. The Koth Macquai has been given cause to think again about his policy of non-involvement))

"Nothing like a demonstration to really bring a point home, is there?" Calica said, but she sounded too weary to make the effort at sarcasm.

((I am sorry for your loss)) Iriqi said, and a powder-blue cloud of plaintive sorrow glowed in their minds.

"How do you *do* that?" Elani asked, looking quizzically at the hulking creature.

"It's their way of expressing themselves," Jaan said in its place. "They don't have any features, or a mouth, so they project their emotions instead." He patted Iriqi's armoured foreleg in a companionable way. "Iriqi's only young. It hasn't quite mastered the art of restraint yet, so whatever it's feeling comes out when it talks. The older Koth Taraan can hold back their colours so as not to give themselves away to strangers like us."

Calica blinked. She didn't think she'd ever heard Jaan speak for that length of time before. Iriqi, obviously deciding that the answer had already been given well enough, did not say anything. It just gazed at them with its huge, black eyes.

"What happened to the Banes?" Hochi asked Iriqi suddenly. "It *was* you, wasn't it?"

((The Bane that Jaan and I met in the caves sensed the Communion that binds the Koth Taraan together. Like us, it can see the links that are invisible to human eyes. It did not understand what it sensed, because it had never encountered one of us before. But it desired it. It tried to enter my body, in the same way that they enter human bodies))

"Yeah, we know that *now*," Calica said, thinking of the little boy, Paani, who had opened the gate and let the hordes inside.

The Koth Taraan shifted and settled into its neutral stance. *((As it entered me, every one of my Brethren turned their attention to expelling it. The Communion will not abide a cancer in the web. The reaction was immediate and instinctive. But the Bane, too, are linked as we are; and the backlash from the destruction of the one who tried to possess me travelled to the rest of the Bane and annihilated them))*

"The Bane are gone, then?" Calica asked, faint hope in her voice.

((Dispersed)) Iriqi said. *((They cannot be destroyed entirely. They will reform, in time))*

Calica's shoulders slumped. "Then we can look forward to a repeat performance of today."

"You think *that's* bad," said a voice from behind them. "Wait'll you hear *this*."

"Gerdi?" Hochi cried, turning around. There, on the other side of the log fence that they had been sitting on, the green-haired Noman boy grinned at them.

"In the flesh," he said, but his breath was suddenly robbed as Hochi swung off the fence and gathered him up in a bear hug.

"Mauni's Eyes, Gerdi, I thought you wouldn't be coming back!" he said, his face a picture of joy.

"Not . . . sure . . . I wanna . . . *be* back," Gerdi gasped, struggling in the crushing circle of Hochi's massive arms. He half-suspected that the big man was hugging him a little too hard on purpose, for putting him through all that worry. "Let me *go* already!"

"Where's Ryushi?" Calica asked, desperate worry on her face. "Is he okay?"

Gerdi prised himself out of Hochi's arms and then

looked around the assembled faces. "Someone get Kia. She's gonna want to hear this."

Gerdi would not speak until they were all assembled, and he did not want them to be distracted, so he arranged for them to meet in the ruined shell of the wyvern hatchery. The furnaces were quiet now, and the heat had dispersed through the great tear in the roof, the result of an explosion where a Snaggleback had smashed a fuel pod. Most of the eggs were undamaged, but they lay cold in their metal cradles, never to hatch now. It was deserted inside, and the ring of their boots on the floor grilles echoed through the massive chamber. The few glowstones that had not been shattered in the explosion threw their faint orange cast across the faces of those who gathered there, small figures in the near-dark.

"Get on with it, Gerdi," Kia snapped. "We don't need the theatrics. You could have just told us outside."

"You're lucky I'm here to tell you at all," Gerdi replied. "I've got a lot to say, and I don't want someone trying to rope you into corpse-mopping duty while I'm doing it, okay? Now shut up and listen." If his customary good humour seemed to have run a little dry of late, then nobody could blame him; he had been having a hard time of it recently, and there was little that even he could laugh about.

So they fell silent, and he began to speak. He told them that Ryushi was well, and that he remained a prisoner in Fane Aracq. He told them that he seemed to

338

be in no immediate danger, and how he had managed to prise delicate information out of Aurin; but he did not say anything of his suspicions about Ryushi's feelings for the Princess or of her feelings for him. He glanced guiltily at Calica as he glossed over that part, but she was too taut with concern for Ryushi to notice.

He told them that Aurin knew where the Base was, and that she was readying her forces to wipe out Parakka once and for all. He told them also that Aurin's heartstone was the key to her control of the Keriags, but that it could not be removed without the death of the entire Keriag race and, most probably, Aurin herself. And he told them of Ryushi's resolution to stay, and his plan, and how he had charged Gerdi with finding a way to stop the murderous effects of the heartstone.

"The idiot!" Kia cried, raging. "What does he care about the Keriags, or Aurin? He should just steal it from her and let them all die; then Parakka might have a chance! Without the Keriags, Aurin's power in Kirin Taq would collapse. There'd be a revolution within a few cycles!"

"It's hardly that simple," said Hochi. "He can't exactly just walk up to her and take it." He looked at Gerdi and sighed heavily. "This news could not have come at a worse time. Our Base is poorly defended, our manpower is down; and now we are told that Aurin is soon to be on her way and that our only chance of winning is to attack her."

"I seem to remember a similar tactic a year ago," Calica said. "It didn't work then. It won't work now."

"What if she's *lying*?" Elani piped up suddenly, cutting them all dead. "You know, like Aurin's feeding him false information or something. Maybe they *let* Gerdi in so we'd panic and run and then we'd—"

"Hey, nobody *lets* me in anywhere!" Gerdi huffed, indignant. "If you knew *half* of what I had to go through to get to Ryushi, you wouldn't be so—"

"She does have a point, Gerdi," Jaan said softly. "Did she actually tell him the location, or just that she'd found it?"

Gerdi ruffled his hair with one hand, the green turned yellow in the orange light. "I don't know. I didn't exactly have time to chat with him about the particulars."

"The heartstone could be a bluff, too," Calica pointed out, her olive eyes steady.

"It could *all* be a bluff," Gerdi said. "But Ryushi doesn't think so, and right now he's the only thing we've got to rely on. Now we can argue whether Aurin was telling the truth or not all night, but what it comes down to is that we've gotta have some faith in him. 'Cause if what he says is true, then we've got one chance to get ourselves out of this or we're all dead."

There was a few moments of silence following his pronouncement. The assembled band of Parakkans looked at each other in the flat light, and listened to the metallic emptiness of the hatchery.

340

"Why didn't you go to the Council with this?" Kia asked.

"The Council will take too long. I'm not here to debate with anyone, anyway. I'm just telling you what I know."

"What are we gonna do?" Elani asked.

"Well, that depends." Gerdi flicked his eyes to Calica. "Ryushi said you had something to do with it."

"With what?" Calica asked, taken aback.

"The heartstone. Aurin's been having dreams about you. Kia says she kept seeing you and Aurin together in her vision. Have you been dreaming about Aurin?"

The question was bluntly put, and Calica had no other answer but the truth. "Yes," she said.

"So what's the connection between you and Aurin?" Gerdi demanded.

"There *is* no connection! We've never met!" Calica cried. "Except when I touched Macaan's mind, that time. That was when it started."

Calica's comment sent their minds back to the time just before the Integration, back in the sunlight of the Dominions. It seemed so long ago now for those who were present when Calica used her power of psychometry on Macaan's earring to divine the mind and plans of the person who wore it. She had also come across previously unguessed aspects of the King's life, such as his fierce and unrequited love for his daughter and his fear of the death that had carried off his queen and his parents.

((You do have a connection)) Iriqi said suddenly.

Jaan looked up at the great creature. "Does she?" he asked in surprise.

((I do not know the nature of the link. But they are connected. A single shared bond hangs between them))

"You can *see* that?" Elani asked, fascinated.

((Not as you see. But it is there, human child))

"How can I have a . . . a *connection* with her?" Calica cried. "What have we got in common?"

Elani scratched the back of her ear. "You're Splitlings, aren't you?" By the tone of her voice, it was less of a question, more of an obvious statement.

"Don't be stupid!" Calica replied, a look approaching panic on her face.

Elani looked at her pityingly, adopting once more a voice belonging to someone much older than she was. "Reports say she's about the same age as you. She was most likely born in Kirin Taq; you were born in the Dominions. Remember, back on Os Dakar, I told you about the greatest philosophers of Kirin Taq and the Dominions? Baan Ju and Muachi? How they were Splitlings, each one balancing the other in the cosmic order just like Kirin Taq balances our homeland?" She paused, and then smiled. "I think you've just found your Splitling."

"That's a lie!" Calica almost shouted, her hair whipping around her face as she looked from her to Iriqi and back again.

"You had contact with her through Macaan's

memories when you touched the King's earring. Even though you didn't realize it, you found your bond. And subconsciously, you've been keeping it alive ever since. Through your dreams."

"And what I saw in the vision. . ." Kia said, caught up in the thrust of communal deduction. "The Koth Taraan said that the trial could bring up insights I didn't know I had, or premonitions. It was telling me about Calica and Aurin! That's why they were always together!"

Was *that* the reason behind Kia's lasting dislike of Calica? She had thought it was jealousy, that she was taking up the attentions of her twin, but had she *known*, somehow, deep down, that—

"Shut *up*!" Calica cried, turning on her. "Stop making decisions about me! What, you're gonna listen to a nine-winter kid who thinks she's solved the mysteries of the universe? And something that isn't even the same *species* as us? All this stuff about Splitlings is just a bunch of Resonant myth! I'm nothing to do with Aurin and I never will be! It was her family that killed my *parents*!"

She shoved Kia aside and stormed away from them, her hurried steps clacking through the still air of the hatchery until she stepped through the small, dim rectangle of the workers' entrance and was gone.

"She's in denial," Elani said confidently, putting a finger on her lips.

"Forget that for a minute," Kia said, suddenly

seeming energized by the idea that had come to her. "You've been coming up with all kinds of theories about stuff like Splitlings, haven't you?"

"You wanna hear some, Cousin Kia?" Elani asked, beaming.

"I wanna know if a Splitling can fool a heartstone." Dead silence.

"Replace Aurin with Calica?" Hochi said after the implications of what she had just said had been given adequate time to sink in.

"Get the heartstone off the Princess," Kia said. "Put it on Calica." She clicked her fingers, the loud snap dissolving into the recesses of the dim chamber. "We have the Keriags. And it's no more Macaan. The *worst* that can happen is we destroy the heartstone and the Keriags die."

"You're *that* sure Iriqi's right?" Elani asked.

"Listen: when I saw Takami in those visions, he was missing an ear. I didn't know why then; now I've been hearing reports and rumours from the spies that Ryushi cut it off during their duel. What I saw in the Koth Macquai's pool was genuine. If it was right about Takami, it'll be right about Calica and Aurin."

"I'm not sure slavery is exactly part of Parakka's ethic," Gerdi commented, remembering what Ryushi had said. "Or mass genocide, for that matter."

Kia shot him a scathing look, then grabbed Elani by the shoulders. "*Would it work?*" she demanded.

Elani looked confused for a moment. "Well, yeah,

sure, I guess it *might*. Heartstones don't care about the pace of the heartbeat, 'cause that would go faster and slower with exercise and sleep and stuff. They're tuned in to the person's aura."

"Do Aurin and Calica share the same *aura*, then?" Kia asked in exasperation, her green eyes urgent.

"Well, you gotta look at it like this," said the little girl, pulling away from Kia's grip – which was beginning to hurt a little – and moving back a step. "See, twins like you and Ryushi share a lot of physical stuff that's the same, but you're *totally* different in, like, spiritual ways. Personality and attitude and so on. So you have different auras. Splitlings are the other way around. Physically, they have nothing in common except the time of their birth, 'cause that's when the bond forms. But their aura, their core being, is the same." She shrugged. "I got most of this from the old writings that we saved from other Resonants. Maybe Aurin's what Calica would have been if their positions were reversed, if their situations were different. Certainly explains why Ryushi's in love with both of them."

"*What?*" Kia and Gerdi chorused together.

Elani gave the Noman boy a sad smile. "Oh, come *on*, Gerdi. You gave *so* much away. And apart from that, how else would Ryushi find out all that stuff? You never explained that, did you? And as for *Calica*, you'd have to have less eyes than a Snaggleback not to see that one." She paused. "Though I'm not sure if Ryushi knows it himself yet," she mused thoughtfully.

Gerdi's jaw dropped. Elani had always displayed the ability to come up with some staggering insights that people three times her age would have been hard-pressed to manage, but she had nailed him so convincingly this time that he was beginning to think she was nothing short of psychic.

"He is *not* in love with Calica!" Kia cried, even though she had suspected it for some time. "And he is *certainly* not in love with Aurin." She turned on Gerdi, anger written on her face. "*Is* he, Gerdi?"

Gerdi swallowed, his eyes moving nervously over her features, before breaking into a sheepish grin. "Errr . . . I was kinda holding that one back," he admitted.

"He *told* you?"

"He didn't *say*, but I got my suspicions."

"Oh, that's just *great*!"

"Isn't it, though?"

"Shut up!"

Gerdi shrugged. "If you can't *handle* it. . ."

"Stop this, all of you!" Hochi roared suddenly, raising his huge hands to quiet them. They all looked at him, his enormous belly and bald head limned in orange light. When he had their attention, he went on.

"Now I don't have much in the way of words, and I don't have the smarts that some of you have—"

"You got *that* right," said Gerdi; but Hochi had anticipated a clever comment from the boy, and sent a pre-emptive strike his way. Gerdi had barely finished his sentence and was preparing to dodge when a cuff struck him off-guard and sent him flying into the darkness.

"But I know what's important, and that's what counts here," Hochi continued. "Now Aurin *may* have been lying, but there's one thing we can say is looking pretty likely. And that is that we have Aurin's Splitling here with us. Ryushi is relying on us to get him out of there, don't let's forget that. He had in mind an attack on Fane Aracq. In the confusion, he would get the heartstone. Right, Gerdi?"

"Right," Gerdi replied, getting up and rubbing the back of his head; but the string of mumbled insults that followed his agreement were a little too quiet to be heard.

"Now think about it. Kia, you say he should snatch the heartstone and be done with it. That's no good. He would be killed before he could escape, and the heartstone returned to Aurin. So we need an attack, an attack strong enough to break into Fane Aracq."

"The Keriags," Kia said. "But we can't get the stone without the Keriags, and we can't get the *Keriags* without the stone."

"Maybe we can," said Jaan. He was looking at his huge companion.

((You are suggesting that we communicate with the Keriags)) Iriqi said, a pale shiver of distaste riding shotgun.

"You can't communicate with the Keriags!" Kia said.

((The Keriags are intelligent beings. They can communicate)) the Koth Taraan said, shifting uneasily. It turned its huge, black eyes on Jaan. *((You will ask me to do this thing, won't you?))*

"You have to, Iriqi," said Jaan. "For all of us. It's our only chance."

"Will the Koth Macquai allow you to?" Kia asked.

((It leaves the decision to me. It is my choice))

"Will you?" Jaan pleaded. "I know how you all feel about the Keriags, but—"

"Whoa, hang on here," said Gerdi, waving his hands. "You're actually suggesting going to *talk* with the Keriags?"

"To cut a deal," Hochi said in his deep bass voice. "They help us storm Fane Aracq and get the stone. We free them from their slavery."

Gerdi slowly covered his face with his hand. "I don't believe I'm hearing this," he said, the words muffled by his palm.

23

Blind Trust Alone

"Err . . . so explain again why I got volunteered for this when I got one of the long straws," Peliqua said in puzzlement, lying on her stomach on a small hillock of dark blue grass.

"Just lucky, I guess," Kia replied. "Now keep it quiet, or you'll get heard."

In the dimness of Kirin Taq, they lay peering over the rim of their hiding place. All around them, tiny flowers bloomed, their translucent, crystalline petals trapping the feeble light from the black sun overhead and reflecting it endlessly inward. Glimmer plants shone green, pinpricks of light that clustered in bunches against the darker hills all around.

Before them was a Ley Warren, rising out of the land to scratch the sky, its irregular earthen towers like huge, misshapen fingers. It was not unlike the structure south of Tusami City in the Dominions; unsupported walkways crisscrossed between the tall towers, and the base of the structure was a mass of ramps and tunnels for the Keriags and the Guardsmen to get in and out. It was an enormous termitary, stretching towards the clouds, and crawling with the black, insectile forms of the Keriags.

The Ley Warrens. When they had first appeared in the Dominions over a year ago, they had been a mystery. They had turned out to be the linchpin of Macaan's Integration; huge Keriag warrens surrounding Ley Boosters, the machines that created a bridge between Kirin Taq and the Dominions. The Ley Warrens existed in both worlds at once, passing-places for Macaan's men, guarded fiercely by the Keriags.

Kia watched the creatures for a time. She didn't need a spyglass to remind herself what they looked like. Humanoid torsos, slung low between six chitinous, spiderlike legs that angled upwards from their ribs and then bent back down at the knee-joint. Their bodies covered in horny spikes of armour; their eyes small and black beneath their jutting eye-ridges. And each carrying a *gaer bolga*, a short spear with backward-facing serrations to rip and tear at an enemy's flesh as it was pulled out.

Hard to believe that they were distant relatives of the Koth Taraan. The onyx eyes, the armour . . . but that was where the similarity ended.

She hoped that this was going to work; because they were taking an awful chance with their plan. Would Iriqi even be able to communicate with a Keriag? Would it respond? And what then? What did they have to offer the Keriags as assurance except theories and possibilities? Would the Keriags be willing to gamble with the extinction of their species for a chance to be free? And even if they *were* freed, what then? Would they rampage across the faces of both worlds, destroying everything they came across?

They had no other choice, so she put it out of her mind. It was the only thing she could do.

"Oh! Oh! Kia!" Peliqua said excitedly, nudging her. "Here it comes."

It had taken them a short while to study the patrol routes of this particular Ley Warren. Nestled as it was in a natural basin in the hills, it was easier to approach than the one on the plains south of Tusami City, so the inhabitants had compensated with a tight net of sentries that combed the landscape around the main structure. These comprised both Keriag and Guardsman patrols.

Kia and Peliqua weren't interested in the Guardsmen. It was the Keriags that they were waiting for. And now, as Peliqua pointed, Kia saw that their patience had at last been rewarded. A single Keriag was coming, rounding the shoulder of a nearby hill, each of its six legs moving independently of the others as it stalked along.

Kia swallowed, and exchanged a glance with Peliqua.

"Let's do it," she said, and with that they suddenly scrambled to their feet and ran. The Keriag snapped its head around instantly, fixing them with its cold, cruel eyes. There was a moment's pause, and then it came for them.

Kia and Peliqua sprinted to where their pakpaks waited silently nearby, the sudden thrill of the chase firing their bodies. They swung up on to the waiting mounts and spurred them just as the Keriag skittered over the ridge of the hillock. They couldn't outrun a Keriag; but a pakpak could.

"*Go!*" Kia cried as she spurred her mount, and her pakpak took off with such a burst of acceleration that she was forced back in her saddle by the wind drag. Peliqua was close behind her, her red braids blowing around her face.

The Keriag was not far behind. The pakpaks were faster in a straight run, but the terrain was hilly and the Keriag's six legs carried it effortlessly over the uneven ground. Kia and Peliqua bolted down the hillock and into a shallow trench between two rocky hills, and the Keriag followed, moving with sure treads where the pakpaks skidded.

The hive-mind of the Keriag Queen in the Warren would know of them already. Probably other Keriags were already heading towards them from other directions to intercept them. The fact that they did not have far to ride did nothing to alleviate Peliqua's worry, as she saw the terrible black insect-thing come down the trench after her. One trip, one wrong foot, and it would all be over.

The rock walls suddenly gave way, receding back into the blue grass of the hills, and their narrow path opened into a stony clearing, a flat spot of neutral ground between three neighbouring hills. Kia broke left as she reached the clearing; Peliqua swung right, and then both wheeled around. The Keriag burst through after them . . . and stopped, utterly motionless and still.

((Greetings to you, Keriag))

Iriqi was there, in the centre of the clearing. Aside from Kia and Peliqua, there were also Jaan and Ty. Their weapons were drawn, but they were making no move to attack and were staying at a distance from the creature. All of them watched the Keriag, as if any of them could divine what it was thinking. The black of its eyes were fixed on the black of the Koth Taraan's.

((I am of the race of the Koth Taraan. We seek an audience with your Queen)) Iriqi was unable to keep the slight taint of disgust from the hue of the words.

Still the Keriag made no response. It stayed, motionless and poised, relaying what it saw back to the hive-mind and waiting to be told what to do. Kia looked nervously around the hills that surrounded the gravel clearing; other Keriags were beginning to arrive now, summoned by the plight of the first. The plan had been to get the attention of the Keriags without the Guardsmen noticing anything untoward; but they were getting an uncomfortable amount of attention right now. Were the Keriags just stalling them until they could get their warriors into place?

((Respond if you understand me, Keriag. We shared the same ancestor, once)) The Koth Taraan looked suddenly at Jaan, and then back to the Keriag. *((Our differences are superficial at best. We have not grown so far apart that we cannot share communication))*

Peliqua could not help a twinge of sadness, even in their present situation, as she caught that glance towards her brother. The smallest of moments, it spoke volumes about what was between them now, the creature and the halfbreed. Had that been why Iriqi had agreed to talk to the Keriags for them? Because of what Jaan had taught him, about how prejudices against race and species can be overcome? About how even a halfbreed, despised by both the races he was born from, has the same heart and soul as other people, even other *species*?

She knew that it had, and it pained her. For all of the protection, all of the self-esteem she had tried to give her brother, it had taken a creature that was not even human to give him the companionship he needed, and help strip away the shame and disgust that he felt for himself.

"Kia!" she said. "There's more of them coming. If we don't get out of here soon, I think we might be in a bit of trouble."

Kia sat up on her pakpak and looked around. The Keriags lined the three ridges above the clearing now, silhouetted against the velvet purple sky, their *gaer bolga* held low between their long, spindly legs. She felt prickly sweat begin to gather on her scalp. It would soon be time to make the call. If she left it too late, they might not get out alive. But if they fought now, they would lose any chance of talking to the Keriags; and that would mean the eventual destruction of Parakka. She set her jaw and watched the lone Keriag, and willed it to respond.

((We have a proposal)) said Iriqi. *((We can free you*

from the heartstone. All of you. But we need your help in return))

There was a long silence. Then, in a voice like a thousand rats scratching at a metal door, the Keriag hive-mind replied.

<<<*Follow us*>>>

The Keriags had many different ways into and out of the Ley Warren, and the Guardsmen knew less than half of them. The labyrinthine tunnels were too complicated to be mapped by the human mind, and too numerous to be counted. They had underground paths that came out over a mile away from this particular Warren, and it was down these that the Parakkans were led. Their pakpaks had been left on the surface, and they had brought glowstones with them to fend off the utter darkness within those parts of the Warren that were not travelled by Guardsmen. But the light hardly lessened the terror that they felt as they trod the earthen corridors of the Keriags, surrounded by the skittering of hard, clawed feet and the hum of the Flow from the nearby Ley Booster.

Kia's throat was tight and she hardly dared to swallow. She had Ty's hand clutched tightly in hers, her eyes darting this way and that as the light of Ty's glowstone slid over a black carapace or a leg, reflecting a shine both dull and moist. They were utterly, totally in the power of the Keriags now. There would be no way to fight out of this one, no miracle escape or last-minute rescue. They were deep in the heart of the enemy's territory, and all around them was an escort of creatures that could tear them apart in moments. Even Iriqi. The Koth Taraan was hardly helping matters, either; she was unable to get the icy black-blue of mortal fear out of her head, and she suspected this was a spill-over from Iriqi's own emotions.

But at least they were being granted an audience. That was something. However, that only posed new problems for her. For what she had to say was not something the Keriag Queen would want to hear. If Calica had come with them, maybe she could have handled it; but she had been forced to stay at Base Usido and try to coordinate some kind of response to the threat of Aurin's armies. So it was up to her, again. She had failed last time; why did they think that now would be any different?

She took a shuddering, nervous breath; Ty glanced at her and squeezed her hand, letting her know that he was there. She turned her thoughts to the offer she was to make the Keriag Queen. The Keriags were to help them besiege Fane Aracq; and in the meantime, her twin on the inside would steal the heartstone. The moment the heartstone was removed, the Keriags would know of it. They would then storm the palace, Ryushi would place the heartstone on Calica, and order would be restored. They could then work out how to deactivate the heartstone at their leisure, and Aurin's power would be shattered. For without the

Keriags, she did not have enough of a force to hold Kirin Taq.

There were a hundred things that could go wrong. First, Calica's agreement to cooperate had been very reluctant; but that was a minor thing. Kia trusted that she would come through. She knew it was Ryushi's life at stake. She would do it for him. Secondly, they had no guarantee that the heartstone would be fooled by Aurin's Splitling. If it was not, then disaster would ensue. Thirdly, it was uncertain whether Ryushi could get the stone at all; that was going on blind trust alone. *Fourthly*, would the Keriags be happy about switching the stone to Calica? After all, they had no reason to trust her. If Calica chose to abuse her power, then they had simply swapped one mistress for another.

And was it wise to let the Keriags free at all? She didn't think so. She wanted them kept, so they could be used against Macaan in the Dominions. With the force of the Keriags at their command, they could wipe their homeland free of the stain of the tyrant King. But Calica was being terrifically stubborn about it; she refused even to consider Kia's point of view on the matter. Granted, it was selfish and unethical to use the Keriags as their slaves, but it would only be for a short time, and it was an action that had to be weighed against the thousands of lives they would save by using the insect-creatures against Macaan's troops and freeing the land. Did Calica's decision have something to do with the

357

antagonism between she and Kia? *Probably*, she thought bitterly. With this thing about being Aurin's Splitling, and the rumours that had reached her about Ryushi's feelings for the Princess, she was most likely doing it out of pique against the world.

She just had to rely on Ryushi. And hope that he was not really in love with Aurin, that Gerdi was mistaken somehow.

Now she felt sick. Why did everything have to revolve on such a tenuous thread? It was always the same; relying on the flimsiest of chances, hoping against hope that things would turn out alright. Well, this time she had a backup plan. For if the Queen did not agree to help her out, then she would threaten. Even in the heart of the Keriag lair, she would threaten.

Ryushi had made a promise to Gerdi. And in all the years they had been brother and sister, he had never broken a promise. If the Queen did not agree to Kia's offer, Parakka were going to attack the palace anyway. And Ryushi would destroy the heartstone. Somehow, in some way, he would do it or die trying. He had the power, now that Gerdi had fixed his Damper Collar. He could destroy a whole floor of the palace, if he needed to. And if he failed, someone else would try, and someone else, until eventually. . .

Now that Parakka knew about the heartstone, the Keriags were vulnerable. They could either join Parakka in an attempt to free themselves, or die with the Princess. Even if they took Parakka down with them, they would still die. That was the choice she would put to them. It was all bluff and uncertainty, but bluff and uncertainty were all she had right now. She would make out that they were far more confident than they really were, and hope that the Keriag Queen would not oppose them.

For if she did, then they really had no hope at all.

The darkness, the scratches and scrapes seemed endless. They were moving in a bubble of their own light, able to see only what the edges of that bubble brushed against; a tunnel wall, a retreating leg of a Keriag, other things less identifiable. All around them, uncomfortably close, were their escorts. It was terrifying to be so near to the creatures that they had fought with on Os Dakar and in the Ley Warren south of Tusami City, and the fear did not seem to recede but to increase as they were led deeper and deeper into trackless darkness. The air smelt dry and close, and seemed to press in on them hard from every side.

Eventually, the bare tunnels began to become more varied, and they caught glimpses of side-caverns at which small Keriags busied themselves around fat white grubs the size of humans, who thrust their blind heads out of holes in the earthen wall where they appeared to live, and clamoured to be fed. They passed through one of the gardens that Ryushi and Elani had seen on their last foray into a Ley Warren, huge puffballs of multicoloured fungus that rustled and swayed in the light of white glowstones.

The presence of glowstones meant that they were getting near the routes that humans trod, and Kia found herself getting uneasy. But *white* glowstones? Hadn't Ryushi mentioned the same thing in the other Warren? Perhaps the special light helped the fungus to grow. Maybe the Keriags had mined the stones themselves; they were certainly too expensive to obtain by other means.

They started to take an upsloping tunnel from the gardens, and then were suddenly turned off it and down a steep decline . . . and then, without warning, they were brought to a halt.

Darkness all around them, beyond the bubble of light. But they could sense, by the echoes of the tiniest of sounds, that they were in a cavern. A huge cavern. There were no tunnel walls visible now. Their Keriag escort retreated out of the range of their glowstones. And then there they were, alone, an island of reality in a void of infinite black nothingness, and only the whispers and scratches of the Keriags to indicate that there was anything outside their island at all.

And then there was a movement. Vast. And something enormous leaned forward from the darkness, so that the orange light shone in shaky lines across its jet-black carapace. Kia felt her stomach coil.

The Keriag Queen was nothing like her servants in appearance. Where they were thin, fast and deadly, she was monstrous and cumbersome, a huge thing with thousands of thick, millipede-like legs around the base of her body. She was protected by a pocked shell of chitin, with no visible break in her length, a dome of armour that surrounded her completely. Of her other organs, only her mouth was visible, a wide gash beneath the front lip of her armour, set on the underside of her body. She was like a whale that had adapted itself to the land, massive and blunt; and around her many legs and over her back raced many hundreds of the smaller Keriags, picking her clean, attending to her, washing her.

Nobody could speak.

The Keriag Queen shifted her immense weight, the movement like a miniature earthquake.

<<<*Koth Taraan. Old Brethren. Keriags waited. You have come*>>>

The speech was audible only to Iriqi, and he found it strangely welcoming.

((*We have come*)) he replied.

<<<*Then speak*>>> she said, and so it began.

Back at Base Usido, all was preparation. Calica strode among the chaos, directing a man here, giving orders there, overseeing the frantic operation that was underway. She knew that whatever they did would not be enough; it was just a question of maximizing their chances of survival for as long as possible.

It had long since been decided that evacuation was not an option. It was just impossible to get out of the Rifts at such short notice, due to the geography of the place. They would have to leave everything behind, and that would put them in an untenable position, leaving them defenceless for Aurin to hunt down. Besides, there was no place else to hide. And with the Snappers and Snagglebacks stirred up and roaming around, she didn't give much for the survival ratio of the Parakkans if they tried to move out *en masse*.

Standing and fighting. Well, if there was no other choice, then that was what they had to do. Most of the corpses of the previous attack had not been properly seen to yet, and they were beginning to smell bad; but they had to be ignored for the moment, while defences were prepared. She'd give them a few more cycles before the risk of disease would demand that they were disposed of.

Many of the fighters in the camp had already left, making their way through the hazardous forest to a rendezvous point on the northwest edge. From there they would receive word as to whether Kia's mission was successful or not; but if they heard nothing at all, they would go on regardless, to make a final, hopeless stab at Fane Aracq in the hope that Ryushi could pull off something from the inside. If all went to plan, the Keriag Queen would send her troops – or at least a messenger – to the rendezvous point. Meanwhile, Kia and the others would return to take up the defence of Base Usido, for they could not possibly travel as fast as the Keriags from the Ley Warren, fast enough to rendezvous with the Parakkan forces in time. Calica herself was leaving in less than a cycle with Hochi and

Gerdi to join the front line, to be the bearer of the heartstone if they were successful.

All they could do at Base Usido was hold out and hope that Aurin's troops did not reach them before Fane Aracq had fallen and the army had returned. If Ryushi's information was reliable, and all went to plan, then there would be just enough time. Their one chance was to get the first strike in, while Aurin was unaware that they knew. And after that . . . well, none of them could say. They could only survive. It was all that was left to them.

"I have bad news," said a flat voice by her shoulder, and she knew, somehow, that Anaaca was about to tell her something relevant to her thoughts.

"Aurin has sent her troops earlier than expected?" Calica asked, turning around.

Anaaca's expression was bland. "Nearly right." The spymistress watched her lazily for a moment, like a basking crocodile, before speaking again. "Takami is on the move. He's mobilized the forces of the province of Maar, and he's headed this way."

"Are you certain?"

"My spy in his court is sure. He has been in a rage for many cycles, since Ryushi took his ear. We can surmise that Aurin has told her thanes about the location of our Base, but she was waiting for her own spies to get here and confirm it. Rather like us, Takami has decided to jump the gun."

"Why?"

"Kia. Or so the nobles say. Ryushi is safe in Fane

Aracq, so he wants to strike at the next best thing, the thing that will hurt him most. He thinks Kia is here."

"She will be, if she isn't killed by the Keriags first." Calica shifted her weight to her other leg. "Do you really think Takami would risk his position as a thane in the name of revenge? That he is really that angry to have lost all reason?"

Anaaca examined her nails, painted a sharp red against the grey of her skin to match her hair. "Since his mutilation, he refuses to appear in court, and will allow nobody but his closest servants to see his face. Several retainers have been executed for offences that deserved little more than a reprimand."

Calica nodded thoughtfully. "How long before he gets here?"

"They're coming in on an awkward route, and it's not the shortest way either. Plus they'll be transporting weaponry and so on. Three cycles, probably."

"That'll be almost the same time as we hit Fane Aracq."

"Indeed."

Calica's eyes became focused on the middle distance, as if she was looking at something far away. "Then we can only hope our forces can fend him off until we return to help them."

"If we return at all."

She blinked, refocusing. "Thank you, Anaaca. You've been invaluable."

"I know," she replied, and with that she left.

Calica closed her eyes and rested her bunched fist on her mouth. It was an expression of deep thought and deeper sorrow. Things had gone from bad to worse, and she was one of those who was forced to deal with it. But she couldn't concentrate, she couldn't take it all, not with Ryushi imprisoned in their enemy's keep.

And not if the rumours were true. Not if the boy she loved felt the same for another woman. Aurin. Her Splitling.

She had missed her chance. Through pride, she had left it too late to declare her passion. And now just maybe she'd lost him for good.

She felt tears gathering behind her closed lids, but she drew in a sharp breath and swallowed them back, wiping her eyes. No. No weakness. Too many people were relying on her now.

Endure. Survive. Win. And that's all.

It was a mantra that she repeated to herself, over and over, as she walked away.

24

A Matter of Shades

The wyvern scythed through the purple sky, its forewings steering the airflow past its larger hindwings as it soared on the wind. On its back, a Rider lay in his harness, suited in his full-body armour of dark red. His face was a blank visor, with two dark eyepieces that scanned the ground far beneath him. Long black braids – the signature hairstyle of the King's Riders – streamed out from the crest of his helmet as he flew from Fane Aracq, the chaotic mass of white spikes and bubbles, parapets and cupolas becoming smaller with distance. It was his shift on patrol, here at the point where six provinces met, and so he led his two wingmen, beginning a long spiral across the lands, his flight path radiating outward from the central point – the palace – and swinging wider and wider.

All was peace below him. The dark carpet of Kirin Taq spread out in a chequerboard of fields and roads under the black sun. Here and there, clusters of torchlight indicated the location of towns or villages. Strips of Glimmer plants kept their ceaseless marking of time, faint smudges of red.

The Rider spiralled further away from the palace in

a long, slow arc, his wingmen keeping abreast. His thoughts were not really on his patrol, but on other things; the upcoming assault, for one. Aurin had tried to keep it secret, but she couldn't hide the massing of troops that was being carried out at strategic points around Fane Aracq and the thanes' keeps. Something was going to happen, something *major*. It was only a matter of time.

He was curving south over the province of Dacqii when he noticed something odd. Far below him, against the deep blue-black of the twilit fields, there was movement. Actually, it looked almost as if the fields themselves were moving, undulating like the sea on a choppy day. He waved a gloved hand at his wingmen, indicating that he was about to descend, and then angled his wyvern towards the oddity. As he got closer, he frowned: what *was* it that he was seeing? The definition was too hard to hold on to, but it *looked* like. . .

His white Kirin eyes widened in horror behind his mask.

The Keriags were swarming.

It was a dark cloud, spreading across the fields like ink, their black bodies almost invisible in the dim light. Thousands upon thousands of them, a stick-forest of ratcheting legs and jagged spears, eating up the ground beneath them as they moved with inhuman speed across the province. Heading towards the palace.

The sudden *whoomph* of a concussion-bolt made him flinch involuntarily, and the screech of one of his wingmen's wyverns sliced through his ears as it plummeted towards the all-consuming mass below, its Rider pawing the air desperately as he fell. He banked his own creature steeply as the sky suddenly came alive with force-cannon fire, fear flooding his veins. As if from nowhere, a fleet of wyverns had suddenly come up from beneath them, where they had been flying low to the ground, skimming the fields. Now, as his other wingman took a direct hit only a few metres away from him, he dug his fingers into the nerve-points on his wyvern – where the base of the neck met the shoulders of the forewings – and urged it forward hard. It complied with a screech, tearing away from the hail of force-bolts, dodging and swerving between the rippling trails of air distortion that they left behind them.

Parakka. Parakka were here, and there had been no warning. He had to get back to the palace, had to raise the alarm, had to—

He heard the report of the force-bolt as it launched even above all the others, as if by some kind of sixth sense that told him it carried his death with it. Blasted out of the sky, his wyvern dropped like a stone, trailing smoke and vapour behind it as it made its final descent.

The Keriags had been sighted leagues away from Fane Aracq on many occasions by the time they came into sight of the palace and the alarm went up. But still there had been no warning. Some that witnessed the swarm, villagers and townsfolk primarily, had learned through many hard lessons not to interfere in the Princess's business, and kept their heads down. Others would not have tried to warn the palace even if they could. Most ran home, locked their doors and bit their lips, hoping the swarm was not a harbinger of something awful. Any of the Princess's men that witnessed the horde suffered the same fate as the patrol Riders; outposts were overrun, vehicles were destroyed, Guardsmen were slain. But all of this was irrelevant, really, for there was nothing short of a wyvern that could have possibly outrun the advancing force by far enough to make any difference. The Keriags were immensely fast, and they did not tire. In the end, the palace had only the slimmest of warnings – little over a half-hour in Dominion time – before the Keriags reached them.

The Keriags had poured from tunnels that the Princess had no idea existed, deep in the hills of Dacqii. The Keriags' subterranean network spanned a much greater area than anyone but they were aware of, and they still had their secrets, even in slavery. Aurin had sophisticated Machinist devices to warn her of any insurrection in the Ley Warrens; but she had never imagined that the Keriags could have managed to tunnel so close to Fane Aracq.

With them had come the Parakkans. Aurin was unaware of the damage that their forces had suffered at the hands of the Bane, and was similarly in the dark about how little machinery, vehicles and equipment they had. What she did not expect was a slimmed-down, mobile force of troops on pakpaks and wyverns, comprising of little over a half of Parakka's fighting strength. They had been a small enough army to make their way through the sparsely populated Dacqii hills without being seen, and now formed the rearguard of the Keriag assault.

Nobody was ready for it. Nobody was prepared for an attack of such speed, during the moment when Fane Aracq was most vulnerable, when many of its troops were assembling elsewhere for the push into the Rifts. Nobody could have imagined it would be the Keriags.

The Queens had been waiting, waiting for a long time. Waiting for the Koth Taraan to arrive. Ever since Macaan had first tricked them, had exploited their hive-mind link with each other, they had suffered their bondage in silence. Because they knew that, elsewhere, there were more of their kin. Those that Macaan did not know about, those who had hidden for centuries. The Old Brethren. The Koth Taraan.

The Keriags did not possess the eternal memory of the Koth Taraan. They did not hold on to the past, nor did they have anything like the Communion with which to pass on knowledge from one Queen to another. Their minds were always on the present, on the relentless industry of their colonies, seeing through thousands of different eyes at the same time. And whereas the Koth Taraan had cultivated emotion, even into creating expressive art, the Keriags had found it a hindrance to the efficient running of their colonies. Their emotions, except for the most rudimentary, had been allowed to wither and die, leaving them with only the most basic and primal of responses to interfere with their multi-minded reasoning.

But they remembered the Koth Taraan. It was not in a Keriag's nature to forget one of its own, even one separated by generations and centuries. The Koth Taraan and the Keriags had once been one and the same, before they had taken divergent paths and warred. The Koth Taraan had nurtured their grudges ever since, fearing and hating their distant brothers. The Keriags had forgotten why they fought a long time ago. To the Keriags, the Koth Taraan were still part of the hive, the great and ancient hive from which they all came.

And they had been waiting all this time. Waiting for their kin to come and free them from Macaan's yoke. After all, why wouldn't they? Wouldn't the Keriags do the same for them? Was that not kin? If a part of the hive was attacked, the whole hive went to its defence. That was the way the Keriags thought, the only way they knew *how* to think, and they could only assume that everything else thought the same way.

But they had waited, and waited, and the Koth Taraan had not come to their aid.

Until now.

The emissaries of Parakka had been taken aback by

how instantly the Keriag Queen agreed with the plan put to them by Kia, through Iriqi. But if they had known the Keriag mind, it would not have surprised them. Trust was not a matter of shades of grey for a Keriag; it was absolute and total. A Keriag could not conceive of one of its kin, even one as distant as the Old Brethren, lying to it or falsifying anything. If the Koth Taraan said it could be done, it could be done. That there was a margin for error did not matter to them. Their kin believed it would work, so they did too.

The day of their emancipation had come.

Deep inside Fane Aracq, Ryushi heard the wailing of a Machinist wind-siren and knew that it was time to act. The alarm was sounding. Parakka were here.

Now it was up to him to deliver on his promise.

Since Gerdi had left him, Aurin had visited him several more times, to steal a secret kiss or to beg his forgiveness for the imminent destruction of Parakka. But as they talked, as she cried, as they kissed, there was one thing that lurked always in his mind. He had to betray her, and it ate at his insides.

But he had made a promise, and he was compelled to keep it; and so he began preparations. He had been patient like never before. When the Princess was not with him, he spent every waking hour flexing his abilities, reaching out with his power and then drawing back just before he lost control. He had never been in an environment where there were so few distractions before, and if he allowed himself to lapse into thought he inevitably came back to his feelings about betraying Aurin; the pain of that was not something he relished dwelling on, so he did not allow himself to think at all. The combination of solitude and denial did wonders for his concentration.

So he practised, and practised, and practised. Gerdi had undone his Damper Collar so that he could put it on or take it off as necessary, and he always had a warning of anyone approaching his cell by the echoing footsteps in the corridor, giving him time to snap on the metal collar with the ice-white Damper Stone at his throat, leaving the tiny snap-catch loose. But visits were few and far between, and so he spent hours at a stretch just sitting on the creamstone floor of his cell, his brow furrowed in concentration, reaching out with his power, focusing, drawing back, and then reaching out further. If he overstepped himself just once, his spirit-stones would release the energy inside him, and the game would be up. He might destroy a section of the palace, but he would drain himself in doing so, and he would not be able to defend himself when they came to kill him.

Control. He had always been unable to rein in his power once it was unleashed. Like him, it was reckless. He had been getting better over time, but the progress was painfully slow.

Now everything relied on him keeping his head. If he lost control this time, then everything they had planned would be for nothing. Thousands of lives would be on his conscience.

The pressure was unbearable. But when the wind-siren started up, he knew that all the practice, all the preparation, everything had come down to this. This one moment, this infinitesimal pivot on which the fate of a world revolved.

On such small things are kingdoms built and destroyed, he thought; and then he stood up, closed his eyes, bowed his head and clenched his fist.

It was time.

He undid his Damper Collar. All Damper Stones gave off a charge that crippled the use of spirit-stones within their area of effect. When only a single Damper Stone was in effect, the aura was generally only enough to affect the person wearing it with any degree of efficiency; for it to have even a minor influence on another person's spirit-stones, the wearer would have to be practically hugging him or her. However, the auras of Damper Stones were cumulative, in the same way as spirit-stones; that was, the more that were placed together, the more powerful they were and the greater their area of effect. When his energy had been sapped in Takami's bedchamber, there had been many piled together. With the single stone on his collar, he only had to hold it away from him and he was out of its range.

Freed, he felt the first surge of the Flow from his stones and checked it ruthlessly. Starting again, he let the energy trickle out, a warming glow that spread into his chest. Like a sheepdog driving a herd, he fought to keep the energy together, and reined it in when it sought to break out of his control. Slowly, he opened another floodgate inside, only the tiniest crack, giving the trapped energy an outlet, directing it along his arms and into his hands, shutting off the Flow from his stones so that all that was left were two small, throbbing pockets of energy that burned beneath the skin of his palm.

Then, with steps so measured and careful that he might have been balancing plates on his shoulders, he walked across the cell and placed his hand on the door. In his mind, the wind-siren was silent. The feel of the cell floor through his boots was gone. All there was was the lock, and the power in his hand. He placed his left palm on it, sweat inching its way down from his hairline.

It all comes down to this, he thought.

Now!

The surge of power was short and brutal, and he viciously shut it off a moment after it got loose. The lock blew outwards, its ivory substance smashing into splinters beneath his palm, and the door shuddered under the force.

He opened his eyes. The lock was destroyed. His second pocket of power waited in his right hand.

"*Yeah!*" he cried in exultation, throwing open the cell door and leaping out into the corridor. The Guardsman sentry – who had been stunned by the blast so close to him – raised his halberd to fire, but he was too slow.

Ryushi stepped inside the range of his weapon, pressed his right palm to the Guardsman's metal chest and loosed the energy stored there. An explosion of concussion blasted his hair flat, and blew the Guardsman heavily into the curved creamstone wall of the corridor. The sentry collapsed, his halberd falling free.

"Yeah! Yeah, yeah, *yeah*!" Ryushi muttered to himself. "I got it at *last*!" He looked up and down the empty corridor, feeling the energy still stored in his spirit-stone battery, and smiled to himself.

"Phase Two," he said, and took hold of the Guardsman's wrists, dragging him into the cell, before returning to pick up the halberd and closing the door behind him.

The Keriags hit the palace with the fury of a tornado. The hastily assembled array of vehicles and war-machines that had sallied out of the bowels of Fane Aracq met the onslaught with crushing wheels and thumping salvos of force-cannon fire. Turrets and cupolas swivelled on the palace walls, hissing steam as they aligned and fired, blasting concussion bolts into the endless horde, scattering the black bodies of the Keriags. Parakkan wyverns engaged the Princess's Riders, screeching and swooping and wheeling as the Artillerists that rode shotgun traded fire. Keriags splintered and cracked beneath the great tracked wheels of Aurin's war-machines, while others swarmed up and over their metal bodies, hacking at them with their *gaer bolga*.

The battle was strangely weighted. On Aurin's side, there were precious few foot-troops – for she knew better than to send them out against Keriags – but plenty of immense, impenetrable vehicles that rumbled slowly around the battlefield, things of steam and weathered iron powered by their Pilots. On the side of Parakka, only those troops that could move fast enough to keep up with the Keriags had been brought: a fleet of wyverns and a group of pakpaks that were arriving at the rear. Aurin's forces were powerful but slow and few in number. Parakka's were fast and numerous, but they lacked the strength to do any real damage to the Princess's war-machines.

Hochi, Gerdi and Calica hung back on a single wyvern, soaring high in the twilight above the battle. Hochi was in the front of the harness, lying low against the creature's massive neck, his thick fingers steering them with the confidence of years of experience. They watched the fight below, their eyes flickering anxiously over the mayhem, and hoped that it was not all for nothing.

The Keriags were allowing themselves to be held back. They pushed up against the soaring palace walls, but they did not attempt to scale them. From what Calica had seen of the Keriags, even smooth, curved walls with no obvious grip would be little problem to the insectoid creatures. The war-machines could cut swathes through the ranks of black chitin, but they could not prevent the horde from swarming round them and up to the palace. The Keriags could storm Fane Aracq and gut it in less than a quarter-cycle. But they did not. They were waiting for the signal from the Queens. They would sense when the heartstone had been removed, by the reaction in the offspring stones set deep inside them. That would be the moment when they attacked. Until then, all they had to do was sow confusion, even at the expense of their own lives. But then, what was a Keriag but a single part of a whole, subservient to the needs of its hive? Their lives meant nothing, if the hive survived.

"Ryushi better know what he's doing in there," Gerdi commented, his eyes on the cloudlike palace that rose like a mountain amid the ocean of combatants.

"And what if he *gets* the stone?" Calica said sharply. She had been snappish ever since they had left Base Usido. "What if this stupid Splitling idea doesn't work? If Elani's wrong?"

"We can put the stone back on Aurin," Hochi said over his shoulder. "That'll stop the Keriags turning on us. However, that does mean that—"

"Ryushi doesn't *know* about our idea! He doesn't know to keep Aurin nearby in case it goes wrong! What if he kills her?"

"Oh, I doubt that," said Gerdi, then realized who he was talking to and shut up.

Calica's shoulders tightened in a physical reaction to the reminder Gerdi had just dealt her. More quietly she said: "What I mean is, there's still so much that can go wrong."

Gerdi turned his face into the wind and frowned. "No. He promised me that he'd look out for his friends first, before anything. If he takes that stone, he won't put it back on her. Even if the Keriags die, and she dies with them. 'Cause if he gives the stone back, then she's still got the Keriags, and we're all dead anyway."

"But what if—" Calica began.

"He *won't*, okay?" Gerdi said. "He promised me." Then, quieter, to himself: "He *promised* me."

"What are they *doing*?" Aurin cried, looking out of one of the oval wind-holes of her chambers.

+++ **My lady, we should leave** +++ Tatterdemalion buzzed from where he crouched by the enormous, ornate wall-mirror.

"Leave? Leave *where*?" she raged. "Where can I go? Running will solve nothing. Without the Keriags, I have no *power*. No, I must stay, at least until I know what has caused this sudden turn."

"The Parakkans are behind it, Princess," said Corm, standing by the door, the pale skin of his bald head made ghostly by the white glowstone nearby. "All the more reason why we should leave now, while we can."

"No! We cannot weaken!" she shouted, her voice shrill with fear and anger. "The Keriags know that my death would mean their death. They know that my heartstone, if removed, will kill them all. That is the circle we are trapped in, yes?"

+++ **It seems the Keriags intend to break that circle** +++ Tatterdemalion observed.

"They must have a plan," Corm said, his Augmented eyes chattering as they moved from the Princess to the Jachyra and back again. "Isn't it a little coincidental that the Parakkans thought to pre-empt our strike on their headquarters? Perhaps the prisoner got a message away somehow. I would—"

"Impossible!" Aurin snapped. "And should you suggest again that any of this is *my* fault, Corm, I will have you executed! I know what you think of the way I have handled the prisoner! Didn't we find the hideout, *without* using the Scour?"

"Then why is he still *alive*?" Corm hissed.

+++ **This arguing is pointless** +++ Tatterdemalion said, his mechanical voice cutting through their words. +++ **We must act instead** +++

"What if running is what they *want* us to do, yes?" Aurin said, looking back out of the wind-hole. "What if we would just be falling into their trap?" She suddenly turned and fixed her gaze on Tatterdemalion. "What about the Keriags in the Dominions? Do they act in the same way? Does my *father* know of this?"

+++ **The Keriags in the Dominions seem unaffected by this uprising** +++ Tatterdemalion crackled. +++ **Though I have no doubt that they are aware of it. They** are biding their time. The King is away on his survey of the southern deserts, and out of contact by normal means. He relies on my Jachyra to keep him in touch with events +++

"Good. Then he can find out about this little . . . *incident* after it's over, yes?"

+++ **Understood, my lady** +++

She looked back out of the wind-hole at the raging battle below.

"Fetch me the prisoner," she said suddenly. "Corm, no arguments, do it now."

Corm hesitated for the slightest of moments, then bowed and left, his footsteps dying as the door closed behind him.

"What are they *doing*?" she whispered to herself again, her fingers running absently over the three turquoise stones that hung cold against her collarbone.

Ryushi swallowed, the acid taste of fear stinging the back of his mouth. He felt like he was not really there, that he was watching everything through a spyglass and that the events occurring around him were merely a play before his eyes, powerless to physically affect him. The corridors of Fane Aracq, and the people that hurried past him, were rendered in a greyer palette than the naked eye when seen through the eyepieces of a Guardsman's helmet. The black carapace of armour surrounded him, weighing heavily on his shoulders and legs and head, pressing and pinching uncomfortably in some places, so loose that it chafed in others. It was a bad fit, and there was a dent in the chest where he had loosed his power on the previous occupant, but it would have to do.

He headed for Aurin's chambers, his halberd clutched in both hands, jogging along as fast as he dared in the cumbersome armour. He was not used to the weight, and he did not trust himself not to trip if he ran too fast. Nobody stopped to give him more than a glance; the interior of Fane Aracq was in turmoil. Nobles shouted at each other in panic, retainers scurried back and forth to try and secure escape for their masters, Guardsmen hurried to different posts. The noise and chaos washed around the black metal of his armour, and muffled by his helmet, the boy inside was untouched.

Gerdi had supplied him with general directions to where he thought the Princess's chambers were, but it soon became obvious that they were painfully insufficient in the maze of corridors. In despair of ever finding Aurin on his own, he took a risk. Grabbing a Guardsman who was hurrying the other way, he hollered at him urgently.

"The Princess! Quick, where are the Princess's chambers? I have an important message for the Princess!"

"Two levels up, and keep going in this direction," the Guardsman replied, equally urgently.

"My thanks!" Ryushi said, slapping him on the

shoulder in a rough, companionable way, and hurried off.

"You'll need clearance!" the Guardsman shouted after him.

Ryushi raised one hand in acknowledgement, but he did not slow. He supposed that, in a place as big as this, it would not seem suspicious for the occasional person to ask directions; and in the confusion, the man would probably have not thought about it anyway before he made his reply.

He had just found the smooth, moulded creamstone steps that led up to the next level when he stopped, a judder of panic running through his body. There, descending the curved steps, was Corm, the loyal Machinist that Aurin kept as her aide. Could his mechanical eyes see through Ryushi's improvised disguise? Would he recognize the Damper Collar at his Guardsman's utility belt for what it was? Conscious that his pause would make him look suspicious, he hurried onward, up the stairs. The chittering goggles of Corm's eyes seemed to bore into him as he approached, but then the moment was gone, and they passed each other on the wide stairwell. Ryushi jogged on, his heart pounding in his chest as if it would smash his ribs to splinters, his breathing loud in his ears inside his helmet.

Keep focused. Do what you have to. Everything relies on you.

The thought helped to drive him onward, to keep putting one foot in front of the other in the face of his mounting terror. He ascended another level and then ran out into a new corridor.

This one was different. At first, he was puzzled as to what the change was; but a moment later he realized. There were no torches here, no smokeless wychwood. White glowstones were set in the walls, making the light brighter and subtly different, without the yellow-orange tint of flame.

White glowstones? He was on the right track. It had to be close now.

Following the corridor along, his heart lost some of its buoyancy as he saw what was at the end of it. Three Guardsmen, standing before an ivory, carven door. This must be one of the security points that Gerdi had told him about. He had been lucky so far, in that most of them had been abandoned to stop them hindering the Guardsmen in defence of the palace. After all, it would be impossible to stop and check each person in the chaos, and it would make moving from one section of the palace to another an incredibly slow process. But the most important of them were still maintained, and this was one. The Princess's chambers lay within, of that he was sure.

He walked steadily down the long, tubelike corridor towards them, and the sentries looked up at him, expecting him to state his business. But inside his armour, the quiet hum of his spirit-stones was building.

"Nothing's happening!" Calica cried, looking over Gerdi's shoulder at the battle below. "Why don't they attack?"

Gerdi followed her gaze. From their vantage point, high up on wyvern-back, the battlefield was an endless, swarming mass of black – the Keriags' numbers seemed inexhaustible – through which the occasional hulking shape of a war-machine lumbered, sowing concussion-bolts to all sides. Some of the war-machines had been taken out, either by a choice shot from one of the dogfighting wyverns, or because their tracks and wheels were so choked with the tough bodies of the crushed Keriags that they could not move any longer. The Princess's fleet of Riders still attacked from the purple skies, and the palace guns were still fully operational, their heavy *whoomph* audible even at this distance. But still the Keriags would not assault Fane Aracq, instead staying outside the walls, where they were being slowly but steadily massacred.

"Ryushi hasn't got the necklace yet," said Gerdi. "Gotta give him time."

"We don't *have* time! Right now Takami's probably already at Base Usido. Every minute we waste here means—"

"Hey, I *know* what it means, alright?" Gerdi snapped over his shoulder. "We've got to give him *time*!"

25

The Twisting, Stabbing Stain

The forces of Maar hit Base Usido like a sledgehammer.

Reports had been that the army had entered the Rifts two cycles beforehand, but after that the scouts had lost them. Parakka no longer had the manpower to send troops into the Rifts to harass the army on their way; for without sufficient skill and numbers, they would most likely be killed by the angry beasts that roamed the near forests, still smarting from their recent defeat. The few wyverns they had left they dared not use to keep an eye on the army in case Takami's own wyverns spotted them and shot them down. All they could do was dig in and wait, and hope that the hostile terrain of the Rifts would keep Takami's army out as efficiently as it kept the Parakkans in.

The first strike came out of nowhere. Skimming dangerously low over the treetops of the Rifts, a fleet of twelve wyverns heralded the arrival of Takami, and the end of that frail hope. They came from the west, not from the north-east like the rest of the army, plunging down the cliff faces into the huge, flat valley where Base Usido lay and screaming across the twilight plains. Their Riders arced them into a wide turn, the green-armoured Artillerists on their backs spraying the settlement with concussion bolts as they banked. Huts exploded into splinters, sending a deadly rain of spikes that thudded into everything and everyone nearby. The cliff-face lifts that linked the main body of the base to the clifftop defences took a pounding; huge chunks of rubble and heavy, snaking metal cables crashed down on to the structures below. Force-bolts raked the wyvern hatchery, reducing its already damaged shell to a mass of crumpled metal. People ran shouting and screaming, women hurrying their children indoors, fighters running to the defence of their base, all amid the shattering bolts of force that rained down on them like meteors, destroying everything they hit.

Their first pass complete, the wyverns turned, their bellies skimming the cliff face as they banked to race back along the plain, ready to turn and fire again.

That was when the counterstrike hit. Two wyverns were blasted from the sky, their bodies pulverized, before any of the Riders realized what was happening. Before they had located where the attack was coming from, three more were sent spinning to the ground, their force-cannons imploding with a flat *whoomph* on impact.

They had expected a few wyverns, at most. Instead, what they saw was mukhili. Three of them, the gargantuan beetle-like creatures from the southern deserts of the Dominions, lumbering out from the caves at the base of the cliffs. And strapped to each of their immense carapaces were not just one but four force-cannons, each one mounted on a pivot and firing independently of the others, setting up a close mesh of near-constant fire. The dark-skinned desert-folk that rode in howdahs on their backs whooped and jeered as the Parakkan Artillerists zeroed in on another wyvern, three bolts from the same mukhili hitting it simultaneously and annihilating it.

And then the Parakkan wyverns joined the fray, those few that had been left behind in defence of the Base, launching themselves from their hiding places on the surrounding cliffs and soaring down towards the intruders. Takami's wyverns were caught in a sudden crossfire, and two more of them fell before they retreated back to where they had come from, their numbers decimated by two-thirds.

But their assault had been planned to coincide with the arrival of the ground forces, and their timing was good. No sooner had the noise of the first attack died down than the forest around Base Usido's clifftop defences erupted in a hail of force-cannon fire, as the first of the foot troops arrived. The air warped and swelled around the invisible bolts of energy as they flew back and forth, smashing trees or denting the spiked outer wall. The Guardsmen's halberds were less powerful than the force-cannons operated by Parakkan Artillerists, but they were far more numerous, and each blast punched the wall with enough force to bend it inwards. Enough hits and it would fall.

"They're staying back in the trees!" Jaan shouted in Peliqua's ear over the noise. They were standing just inside the perimeter, surrounded by the yells and hollering of the Artillerists and the other fighters as they ran to and fro, co-ordinating attacks and carrying orders. High above them, the turret-mounted force-cannons hissed and spat steam as they swivelled, recoiling violently with each devastating blast.

"They don't want to risk a full-on attack!" Peliqua shouted back.

((Perhaps the trek through the Rifts has decimated them more than they wish to let on)) Iriqi observed through a bright fog of mingled hope and alarm. The Koth Taraan, like its companions, could not help in the defence of the wall, as it possessed no weapon that could reach the enemy; instead, they waited anxiously, ready to react to a breach or to be called elsewhere in the Base.

"If they had waited for the whole of Aurin's army, they could have swept through the Rifts with no problem at all," Peliqua said. "It's this horrible, horrible place. You need the strength of numbers, or few enough people so you can be stealthy. But Takami's awful mad, and he wants to get in first. Oh! I wonder how Kia feels about all this?"

"All I'm hoping is that they had to leave most of their heavy equipment behind," said Jaan gravely. He talked a lot more nowadays, since his friendship with the Koth

Taraan had brought him out of his shell a little. "See, the Rifts are hard to get *out* of at short notice – that's why we couldn't evacuate everyone – but they're just as hard to get *into*," he said, explaining for Iriqi's benefit. "With the way the ground drops sheer in some places, you can't get war-machines up or down the cliffs without a lot of manpower and machinery to help you out. And if you don't know the Rifts like we do, it can be made twice as hard." He paused, his yellow eyes feral. "That's why Aurin was taking so long to assemble her people. Takami's haste might be our best chance for survival."

On the lower plain, the Guardsmen were arriving, abseiling down the vast cliffs, hundreds of tiny threads supporting minuscule soldiers against the immensity of the rock. Bereft of their air support, they were proving to be easy targets for the Artillerists on the backs of the mukhili, who picked them off as they descended; but they had the advantage of numbers, and their descent was fast, and they were artfully spread so as not to allow the cannons to take out more than one at a time. Soon the base of the cliffs were thick with Guardsmen, and the mukhili had to concentrate on defending themselves rather than attacking the abseiling troops.

At that moment, both sides threw in another card from their hands. The wyverns that had been repulsed in the first strike reappeared, this time bringing with them more of Takami's fleet, swooping low over the valley to deliver a few cursory blasts at the mukhili before sending another shattering salvo into the Base, smashing buildings and people alike with their concussion bolts. And at the same time, the gates of Base Usido opened and out poured what was left of the Parakkan troops, riding on horse or pakpak, charging across the plains towards the enemy. With them came cricktracks – converted for war with crude force-cannons and blades – and an assortment of other haulage vehicles, each one brimming with troops.

Last came the giant construction machine nicknamed the Mule, a huge crane that ran on two massive, triangular sets of treads. Its arm was a towering thing of weather-beaten iron, riding on a flat, squarish base, with a massive hook at its tip. It had been one of the first machines that had been made during the erection of Base Usido, and the one that had borne most of the brunt of the heavy loads that followed: the building of the hatchery and the stables, the assembly of the perimeter walls, lifting of force-cannons and so on. But now it had a new use, as an engine of war; its flat body was the perfect platform for force-weapons, and warriors crowded on its back with shoulder-mounted cannons as it rumbled out of the gates of Base Usido. At the helm, hidden behind thick iron plating, one boy's knuckles gripped the control levers tightly, his spirit-stones burning with energy, forcing life into the veins of the awesome machine. Ty, the Pilot.

Kia was there, too, riding on the back of the Mule, crouched low with one hand gripping the handle of the

Pilot's hatch for support, the other holding her bo staff close. She cried out in exultation as they thundered into the fray, the old hate back in her eyes again, the cold fire that burned at the thought of killing those who served Macaan. Her thirst for revenge was an unknown quantity, and nobody – least of all Kia herself – knew the depths that her well of rage went to. But here, in the heat of impending battle, it was clear that there was a way to go yet before it ran dry.

The two fronts collided, their disorderly advance troops pouring into each other with unstoppable momentum. The sound of concussion-bolts and the dull rumble of thousands of armoured feet was drowned out by the clash of hand-to-hand combat as the fighters joined weapons savagely. Parakkans slid off the backs of the slow-moving construction machines, throwing themselves into battle; and within minutes the two sides had met and merged into one great mass, and the plains were alive with combat.

Kia had meant to stay on the back of the Mule with the others that remained to guard it, their bows thudding and cannons thumping as they fired from the raised platform. She had meant to stay near Ty, to help keep away the Guardsmen that tried to clamber on to the slow-moving metal beast. But the battle fired her blood with iceburn, and she lost all thought of tactics or strategy in the rush. Screaming her hate, she flung herself headlong into the fight, her staff cracking down on the shoulder of a Guardsman as she leaped down from the back of the Mule, and lost herself in the twisting, stabbing stain that spread across the blue grass of the plains.

Back at the clifftop defences, the fortunes of Parakka were ailing. The stalemate was rapidly coming to an end now, and only one conclusion was likely. The towering metal wall of spikes that circumscribed the compound had buckled and broken in several places, great plates of iron torn from their rivets and hanging inward under the hammering barrage of force-bolts from the Guardsmen that hid in the treeline. The near edge of the forest was a shattered mess of splinters now, a thick haze of sawdust hanging in the air amid the fallen boughs of the haaka trees, and the bodies of Guardsmen lay scattered all around. Five of them had fallen to every one Parakkan, but they had been relentless, their armoured forms darting from cover to cover as they kept up their ceaseless assault. And it was paying off at last. The wall was about to break.

"Get ready for it!" somebody shouted above the noise.

But there was one thing to give them hope. Takami had been forced to sacrifice many troops during his assault. It would have been unnecessary to use that many men had he managed to get even *one* mobile force-cannon to the Base, of a size such as the ones that defended Fane Aracq. But, as Jaan had hoped, Takami had been unable to get his heavy machinery across the terrain of the Rifts with the limited resources of his

393

relatively small army, and so he had been forced to rely on this costly use of men to gradually batter down the walls of Base Usido with their smaller force-cannon halberds.

Takami had many soldiers, and they were well armoured and well equipped; but he had been forced to strip his army down to the bare essentials on his journey across the Rifts, and had endured many attacks on the way by the rampaging Rift-beasts. Parakka were in with a chance, more of a chance than any of them had dared to believe.

Unless Takami had something else up his sleeve.

At that moment, the wall came down. A final, concerted blast ripped out from the dark treeline, and a great section of the perimeter wall groaned and toppled inward, tearing away from its neighbours and buckling them backwards in the process. The defenders that manned the ledge that ran around the inside of the wall howled in alarm as they fell, some to be crushed underneath the falling plate of metal, some to scramble to safety.

Jaan felt the sinking nausea of the inevitable conflict in his belly, even before he heard the wind-siren suddenly screech out from the forest. The signal for attack. All around him, Parakkans were rushing towards the breach to plug it, but the Guardsmen were already breaking from cover, surging through the rain of concussion bolts towards the gap they had created. He swallowed bile, and looked to his right, his yellow eyes meeting the cream-on-white of his sister's.

"Ready?" she asked, all flightiness gone from her.

He nodded slowly; and then, as one, the Kirin girl and the halfbreed ran into the combat, followed by the awesome bulk of the Koth Taraan.

Jaan clashed his forearms together as the throng of black-armoured Guardsmen rose up to meet them, his dagnas slicing out of their wooden tubes in response. Next to him, Peliqua's manriki-gusari snaked around her like something alive, the deadly lead weights at each end spinning in a twilight blur. She glanced at her brother once; but if she had had any doubts before about his ability to handle himself, she lost them then. She was his elder sister, and she had always set herself up as his protector, shielding him from the prejudices and troubles that his halfbreed blood brought him; but now she saw that he needed no protection from her any more. She had not been there to save him in the caves during the Bane attack, and he had come through that just fine.

But she was still his sister, and they were still a team; and as they entered the battle, their movements were so fluidly synchronized that they seemed to share the same mind. Her chain lashed around the wrist of a Guardsman, yanking him forward and into the driving path of Jaan's dagnas, while the other end spun over her brother's head as he ducked, smashing brutally into the faceplate of another Guardsman who was aiming a swipe at him. A moment later, Jaan was parrying for her while she loosed her chain from the dead Guardsman's wrist and wrapped it around the second Guardsman's throat, cracking his neck. The two moved as one, sweat flying free from their faces as they tackled the invaders, trying to hold them out.

But they would not be held out.

The Guardsmen's superior armour and weight lent them the advantage in the press of the breach, and they were steadily applying their efforts to forcing the Parakkans back from the gap, pushing their way in as they hacked and sliced with the bladed edges of their halberds. Nobody saw what their real intention was at first; everybody's mind was on the fight that surrounded them. But when the Guardsmen had pushed far enough inside, the Parakkans saw suddenly the mistake they had made. They weren't trying to power their way inside; they were only trying to secure the sides of the breach so they could get up the inside of the wall. The black-armoured figures poured in, clambering up the ladders to where the force-cannon turrets were, overpowering the few guards that had been left there. And before the Parakkans could stop them, they had loosed their halberds on the Artillerists that powered the cannons, compact blasts of force that pulverized the operators and left them limp and dead.

But worse was yet to come. The sudden silencing of the Parakkan guns heralded a second wave of Guardsmen who had been hanging far back in the forest. Now with nothing to fear from the wall defences, they boldly ran across the shattered and cratered battlefield and began to blast at the edges of the breach, concentrating their fire on the seams of the wall. In moments, another section of the wall leaned inwards and then collapsed, and this time it brought its neighbour down with it. The breach had been torn open too wide to plug now, and the Guardsmen swarmed in with redoubled fury.

The fray resounded with the shrieks of the wounded and the trampled, the hum and release of spirit-stones and the muted thumps of the Guardsmen's halberds as they loosed their concussion-bolts. Through it all, Iriqi stood by Jaan and Peliqua, its outsize claws rending and swatting the enemy like they were toys, tearing through armour and limbs with equal ease. The Koth Taraan rose like a blood-spattered mountain in the midst of the combat. Force-bolts only rocked it, but did no real damage. The blades of the halberds were ineffective. It was as the rock it resembled; immovable, unstoppable.

And then Peliqua's eyes fell on what was happening in the rear ranks of the Guardsmen, and she cried out in warning; but there was nothing anyone could do now to prevent what was about to occur. For amid the beetle-black of the Guardsmen were the green-armoured figures of Artillerists, Takami's Artillerists this time, and they were ascending the ladders with heavy escorts to where the vacant force-cannon turrets waited. She realized then what was about to happen, and grabbed Jaan's upper arm.

"Get back! We've gotta get out of here!"

Jaan responded immediately, trusting her without question. They began to fall back as fast as they could, Peliqua shouting her warning to anyone who would listen, Iriqi moving with them. Some heeded her, joining the fighting retreat towards the clifftop. Most stood their ground.

That was when the force-cannons began firing again.

Takami's Artillerists had taken over the steam-driven swivel turrets, and now the great guns pointed not outwards but inwards, directed down at the Parakkan forces. Suddenly, the tables were turned, and it was not the Guardsmen who faced the barrage of force-bolts but the defenders. Inevitably, some of the front ranks of black-armoured fighters were caught in the ensuing destruction; but mostly the semi-invisible ripples crashed over their heads and into the Parakkans, throwing them violently through the air or smashing them where they stood. The onslaught was more than the beleaguered fighters could take, and the last of their resistance crumbled under the shattering force of the assault. The defence dissolved into a rout, as the Parakkans ran for their lives.

But they were on the top edge of a cliff, with a drop of several hundred feet behind them. There was nowhere to go.

"Come on! Get in!" Peliqua yelled, ushering a young, wounded Kirin man into the lift with her. There were ten in the metal cage of the lift now, including Iriqi, who

398

took up the space of four. Already she could feel the groaning of the protesting supports, and she glanced doubtfully at the huge Koth Taraan and hoped that the lift would take its weight. She pulled the barrier closed behind the wounded man, sandwiching him inside the close press of the lift, and then yanked the lever downwards to descend.

Only those that had heeded Peliqua's warning – and others who had seen what she had seen and reacted in time – had got the head-start necessary to get to the lifts on the cliff edge. The retreating Parakkans were being hacked down nearby, caught between the halberds of the Guardsmen and the blasts of the force-cannons. Peliqua could feel the shock of each impact stirring her red braids against her ash-grey skin. But now she looked down at the terrible damage that Takami's first strike – the wyvern assault – had wreaked on the cables, chains, winches and pulleys that ran all the way up the cliff face, and she hoped that the lift she had chosen was one that would work. Already, the other lifts were full; and some were not moving at all, or had halted a little way down, marooning their occupants.

The second's delay that she knew would occur between her pulling the lever and the lift starting to move seemed endless, stretching out for longer than a second could possibly last. . .

And then, with a lurch, the lift jolted and began to grind its way down the sheer cliff towards the ground below, mercifully carrying the sights and sounds of the massacre above them further and further away as they descended.

Kia rammed her staff hard into the ground, and the earth rose up in a thick ripple that spread out in a semicircle from where she stood, bulging beneath the feet of the Guardsmen that faced her and throwing them to the ground. The less battle-weary of the Parakkans took ruthless advantage, jumping on their fallen opponents and running them through, while their exhausted or wounded companions used the respite to pull back from the front ranks. Next to them, the immense presence of the Mule rumbled onward, driving the enemy before it, cracking the bones of the dead under its treads.

The Parakkan troops on the plain, unaware that their Base had already been invaded, were faring better than their companions who guarded the clifftop defences. Takami's troops had been unable to get any machinery or even any pakpaks down on to the plains, for the Parakkans had brought all the cargo lifts to the valley floor and guarded them heavily as soon as they knew of Takami's imminent arrival. In contrast, the Parakkans had both an abundance of pakpaks and a good many vehicles, crude though they were. Despite being outnumbered, they held the upper hand, and exploited it without remorse.

Many of the troops had rallied around the twin foci

of Kia and Ty, and were forming a tight offensive knot that the enemy were finding hard to keep back. Kia's battle savagery was legendary among Parakkans since the Integration, and now she found herself once more a leader as she threw herself body and soul into the fight. Her shouted orders were followed eagerly, for she had trained herself well in tactics, and despite her inner fury she kept her reason on a tight rein. If she had been able to see herself, she might have thought how similar she had become to Calica now: both of them tacticians and leaders, forged by war; both of them orphaned by Macaan; both of them with a fierce love for Ryushi, though the nature of it was different. Had circumstances been otherwise, they should have been friends and allies instead of rivals. But the last link was not there, the bond that might have hung between them, and in its place was a bitter enmity.

With her was Ty, whose selfless sacrifice during that same battle had earned him the respect of his contemporaries. The crane arm of the Mule served as a beacon to the troops, stabbing high out of the fray, and the rumbling presence of the mobile fortress of grease and iron was the point from which Kia launched her many attacks. Elsewhere, the lumbering mukhili cut swathes into Takami's forces, the batteries of force-cannons on their backs sending pulses of concussion into the Guardsmen, while their vast mandibles swept up clusters of the hapless enemy and bit them in two.

It seemed that the Guardsmen had no defence against

the strength of Parakka's most formidable weapons. But it was a false sense of security. For in the sky, the last of the Parakkan wyverns was dropping in a ragged spiral, its bones shattered; and the three remaining Riders in Takami's fleet turned their red-visored faces to the battle below, and saw what was happening there. They signalled to each other, unnoticed above the combatants, and then they acted.

The gunners on the backs of the mukhili had forgotten about shooting down the wyverns overhead since the ground engagement had begun. The Parakkan riders had been keeping Takami's wyverns occupied, dogfighting beneath the twilit eye of the Kirin Taq sun. But now the Parakkans were gone, and the victors were free to fire at whatever they chose. But it was not the mukhili that the Riders flew towards, with the Artillerists in the harnesses behind them sighting their cannons with deadly aim. It was the Mule. They saw how the troops clustered around it, using it as an impenetrable island from which to stage their forays; and they intended to take it out.

Kia heard the shriek of one of the wyverns as it powered downwards, a thin challenge above the chaos of the combat, and she took a step back from the fight, brushed her red hair away from her forehead and looked up. Her pupils shrank in terror as she saw—

The three force-bolts tore into the Mule simultaneously, rending through the metal and blasting it into ragged leaves of shrapnel that peppered the surrounding Parakkans with deadly flying blades. One of the huge, triangular tracks was blown free of the main body, tipping over sideways and crushing those below it. The crane arm had half of its supports destroyed; and like a tree chopped by a woodcutter, it toppled sideways with a monolithic howl of tortured iron and fell on to the fray below, killing Guardsmen and Parakkan alike. The flat body of the Mule also took a direct hit, cracking it in half, the shockwave sending those on its back writhing through the air.

In the space of a few seconds, what had been the largest construction machine in the Parakkan force had been reduced to a broken, derelict cripple, slumped at an angle amid the blood and smashed bodies of those it had fallen on.

"*Ty!*" Kia screamed, all battle-fury gone now, dissipating in the face of the clawed grip of terror that seized her. Ignoring the fight around her – which had continued without a pause – she pushed her way back through the troops that had adopted her as a leader. She did not notice their expectant glances, or the way that they looked to her to provide a new game-plan now that the Mule was defunct. She was focused on only one thing: Ty.

I'll not lose you again, she swore.

She reached the immense form of the shattered thing, shoved her bo staff into the crossbelts on her back and began to climb. The dented and makeshift surface of the Mule's outer armour provided easy handholds for her, and she clambered up to the struts of the undamaged tracks with the thoughtless skill of the mountain-born, one who had been climbing since she could walk. From there she pulled herself up to the flat roof, which now listed at a treacherous downwards angle, and slid down the decline towards the Pilot's hatch, skirting the edge of the jagged rent of twisted metal where the Mule's body had split in half. Around the broken vehicle, the battle continued to rage, the Guardsmen being steadily beaten away. Her heart was thumping against her ribs as she grasped the handle of the Pilot's hatch, and her breathing came hard.

This happened before, she thought, the words flashing through her head with diamond clarity. *First we're forced into an attack against Fane Aracq, just like the Ley Warren last time. And now Ty's down and I'm here to pull him out, just like in the Bear Claw. Is this what war is? Is history just gonna repeat itself until there's nobody left to record it any more? Is there any point to it at all?*

But what if this time the results are different? What if this time we win at Fane Aracq? What if Ty—?

She twisted the handle and pulled the hatch open, dread flooding through her. The cockpit had been built for one, and it was close and dark, with a faded orange glowstone lighting the banks of brass levers and palm-studs and steam-releases. Ty was there, his shoulders limp, his head back and his mouth open, his unruly black hair falling down his neck.

"*Ty!*" she cried, reaching in and shaking him. He jolted, and a long groan escaped his lips, but his eyes did not open. A broad smile of desperate relief spread across Kia's face at the sound he made, but it did not last long. He could be badly hurt, and she could not afford to leave him here. Not her Ty. She withdrew herself, kneeling up and looking around. A tall, broad-shouldered Kirin man with a white mohawk was getting to his feet on the ground nearby, stunned but unharmed amid the wreckage of the Mule. It took her only a moment to recognize him.

"Aaris! I need some help here!" she shouted.

The Kirin looked around, saw her, and seemed to shake off his daze. He clambered up the slope of the Mule's body to reach her, and between them they managed to manhandle Ty out of the cockpit and down to the ground.

"Find me a pakpak," she ordered harshly, all courtesy lost in the concern for her loved one. Aaris understood, though, and he was quick to comply. Kia ran her hands over Ty, checking him for broken bones, her face taut with worry; but he appeared unharmed apart from a lump at the base of his skull where he had hit his head. She patted his cheek, talking to him, trying to wake him, and was rewarded with a slight lifting of his lids. The pupils beneath were unfocused and ranged wildly around, but he was at least partially awake. She smiled again, her battle-bloodied features shining from within at the sight.

"Don't you ever leave me," she said, the words hardly audible over the noise of the nearby combat and the sounds of the mukhili's cannon batteries obliterating the last of Takami's wyverns.

And then Aaris was there, pushing back through the throng of Parakkans, leading an alarmed pakpak by its reins. Between them, Kia and Aaris helped Ty into the saddle, and she swung herself up behind him. The pakpak lowed in protest, accustomed to only one rider at a time, but Kia ignored it. This was war; everyone had to carry more than their share of the burden.

Kia's eyes met Aaris's, still holding the reins, and between the Dominion girl and the Kirin there passed an unspoken thanks; then Kia spurred her mount, heading back through the fields of the fallen towards Base Usido, and Aaris picked up a double-bladed axe and returned to the fray.

26

Daggers in a Spray

Aurin and Tatterdemalion looked up at the door together, suddenly alert.

"What was that?" Aurin demanded, her colour high.

The dull crack in the corridor outside had been heard by both of them, sounding like several sledgehammers hitting the creamstone wall in unison. A force-cannon bolt? But had it been fired from one of the Parakkan wyverns that swooped around the spires of Fane Aracq, or had it come from inside?

+++ **I will investigate, my lady** +++

"No," she said, taking a step away from the door. "Stay here. I may need you."

+++ **As you wish** +++ the Jachyra replied, stepping closer to her, a ragged scarecrow of a bodyguard.

"Could someone have got into the palace?" she asked.

+++ **There would not have been time to—** +++ Tatterdemalion began to reply, but his buzzing voice was shredded by a sudden shock of concussion as the door blew inwards, sprinkling sharp chips of ivory and stone in amid the clatter as it fell to the floor. Aurin shrieked as she fell, borne down by her Chief of Jachyra as he pounced on her, protecting her with his body.

A Guardsman was there, the black, beetle-like figure standing amid the settling cloud of dust, his halberd discarded, the raw hum of Flow energy resonating from his body.

"Aurin! It's time to end this!" Ryushi roared through the speaking-grille of his mask.

Tatterdemalion moved like a blur, springing sideways off the prone form of the Princess and changing direction as he hit the floor, leaping forward at Ryushi, his retractable finger-claws flicking out with a sharp ring. But Ryushi was ready for him, and he threw out his hand, five rippling shards of energy shooting out like daggers in a spray. Two of them caught the Jachyra in mid-air, tossing him one way and then the other in rapid succession before sending him crashing in a sprawl to the floor at the base of the great wall-mirror.

"Ryushi! What are you *doing*?" Aurin cried, from where she lay.

But Tatterdemalion was already back on his feet, his scrawny, disproportionate body weaving insidiously, searching for an opening where he could strike again. Ryushi watched him intently through the eyepieces of his mask. He desperately wanted to get out of the restrictive Guardsman armour, to fight freely, but there had simply been no time. He had to keep the Jachyra away from him, but he dared not risk too much of his power in one blast in case it ran out of control.

+++ **It seems Corm was right about this one** +++

Tatterdemalion crackled, ending in a trailing squeal of feedback.

"No! Ryushi, how *could* you?" Aurin shrieked, getting to her feet, tears of anger and betrayal starting to her eyes.

Ryushi felt his throat tighten involuntarily at the sound of the grief in her voice, but he dared not look at her. Tatterdemalion was prowling towards him like a wildcat, waiting for him to make the next move. The creature was quick; he might be able to dodge anything Ryushi threw at him, now that he was ready for it. And if he did, Ryushi wouldn't have time for a follow-up strike before the Jachyra reached him.

In that moment, it came to him. He remembered with sudden clarity his first encounter with a Jachyra, back at Osaka Stud, when it had been after Elani. And how it had reacted when. . .

He dug the toe of his boot under a small chunk of rubble, one of many that were scattered around the chamber in the wake of his explosive entrance. Tatterdemalion saw the movement, his telescopic eye whirring as he looked down at Ryushi's foot. And then Ryushi kicked it, scooping it up with his foot and flinging it with as much force as he could.

The Jachyra sidestepped it neatly, almost casually, as it flew by. But it had not been Tatterdemalion that Ryushi was aiming for. It was the wall-mirror behind him; and being the size it was, it was a target that was hard to miss. The chunk of rubble hit the edge of the mirror and shattered it, sending a wide, black spider-web of cracks across a quarter of its surface with a terse crunch. Tatterdemalion made an odd *wheep* of alarm, turning back to look over his shoulder as an instinctive reaction, to check that his escape route was still viable.

And Ryushi struck.

There had been no time to prepare the blow. It came directly from the batteries of his spirit-stones, channelled through his fists; one fast moment of release and then he clamped off the floodgates. A short, heavy double-punch of concentrated power, streaking an invisible line, forcing the slower air aside like water. It smashed into Tatterdemalion, blasting him backwards, his disjointed limbs flailing. He was thrown with sickening force into the mirror, cracking it further along its length, and then crumpled to the floor in a ragged, limp heap of belts and claws and scraps of cloth.

"*Stop* it!" Aurin screamed at him, and the elation of his victory suddenly faded. He pulled off his helmet, throwing it aside, and turned to her with his blond tentacles of hair falling free around his face. She was crying, her beauty marred by the flush of her tears. "What are you *doing*? Is this how much it all meant to you? That you come to try and *kill* me, yes?"

"It's the heartstone I want," Ryushi said, keeping his voice rigid because the sight of her in such distress was making his insides twist around on themselves.

"That *is* killing me!" she cried. "Don't you see?"

"I won't let them get to you," Ryushi said gravely.

"You can't stop them! The Keriags! They'll tear me to pieces!"

"There's. . ." Ryushi began. His throat tightened again suddenly, but he swallowed and started again. "There's thousands of lives at stake, Aurin. Thousands. I can't let you win." For a moment they faced each other across the once-beautiful room that was now scattered with rubble. "Give up the heartstone, Aurin. It's a curse that binds you to your father's will. You're not a tyrant by nature. You're not this callous and cruel because you want to be. You just don't know any *better*. You can free yourself if you—"

"Don't patronize me!" she shrieked. "I am the daughter of a line of kings that has ruled this land for generations! Who are you to tell me how I should and shouldn't be? To force your peasant views on a Princess? I *loved* you, Ryushi, despite everything that you were." She lowered her head, and when she raised it again, her eyes were suddenly dark. "But now I have to kill you."

She raised her slim hands, and they seethed and boiled with the green and black radiance that he had felt before, the terrible, unknown power that she wielded. His heart lurched at the sight, his body remembering the time when her angry touch had once brushed him with that power and made him tremble. A shadow seemed to wrap itself around her now, her beautiful features turned icy and merciless.

"It doesn't have to be like this, Aurin," Ryushi said, feeling the power charge up in his own stones. "Give me the heartstone. You can get away. The Keriags won't follow you; not if I have the stone."

"Lose everything? For you, yes? Because you think your Parakkan ideals are the way the world should be, you want me to give up *everything* and *everyone* I've ever *known*?" She laughed bitterly, advancing towards him with slow, deliberate steps. "Did you really imagine I would agree to your generous proposition, Ryushi? You *are* naïve."

"Aurin, I don't want to fight you."

"But Ryushi, *I* want to fight *you*. You've betrayed me, peasant. You hurt me."

"You knew what I was when you met me. You knew where my loyalties lay. I had no choice."

"And because of what you have done, nor now do I," Aurin said.

"Don't make me—" he began, but Aurin cut him off with a sharp laugh.

"Make you what? Use your power? Please try, Ryushi; you'll find it an educating experience."

And as she said it, she kept advancing, so close now that she might almost touch him; and he thought of his promise and unleashed the Flow.

It was like throwing water at a wall. Her defences were staggering. Such *power* she held, such complex weaves of bluff and decoy and raw impenetrable energy. The concussion blasted across the room, scattering the rubble anew and stirring the curled form of the Jachyra

412

in the corner; but not a hair on Aurin's head was touched by the force.

She stood before him, a soft, mocking smile on her perfect lips, gazing at him in cruel amusement. Open-mouthed, speechless, he staggered back a step; for in assaulting the fortress of her power, he had finally determined the nature of it. Entropy. Chaos. The lack of pattern or organization. With her ability, she could turn order into disorder, make the bonds and structures that hold an object together collapse and decay and disintegrate. Her powers of destruction made his and Kia's seem pale and feeble in comparison, and the sheer *magnitude* of her energy awed him.

He could not beat her. He could not hope to.

"Now you see," she said, standing before him, her voice a whisper. "The world is a cruel place, Ryushi, and those with the highest ideals are not always the victors. But soon that won't worry you any more."

"I loved you, Aurin," Ryushi said suddenly. "And I still do. You have to know that, before I die."

Aurin's eyes welled with tears again, the raw fury in them softened suddenly. She kissed him then, and the kiss had all the tenderness and passion of a final parting. She embraced him, her slender arms wrapping around his body, the power in her held back just beneath her skin; and he returned the embrace and the kiss, his hand sliding up her back towards her hair as if for a last touch of her dark coils before the end.

And then he pulled away from her, and there was a

sharp *click*, and the Damper Collar was around her throat.

"*No!*" she shrieked, her eyes full of horror as she realized that he had tricked her. As he had embraced her, he had taken the Collar from his belt and snapped it on her from behind. It was a crude job, trapping most of her hair beneath the tight band of metal, but it didn't matter. The lock was in place, the white Damper stone rested next to her skin, and her power was suddenly rendered impotent.

"Princess!" came a cry from the ruined doorway, and Ryushi gathered Aurin's neck in the crook of his arm and roughly pulled her away as Corm appeared. "Princess, what is—"

He fell silent as he saw what had occurred. Tatterdemalion, crumpled in a corner next to the shattered mirror but now beginning to move slightly as he regained consciousness; the room in turmoil, ornaments shattered and splinters of creamstone everywhere; and the prisoner, dressed in the uniform of a Guardsman, with his arm around the Princess's neck. Her eyes were pleading, panicky; she was genuinely in fear of her life, as she had never been before. His Augmented eyes spotted the edge of a Damper Collar on her throat. With that one glance, he understood everything, reconstructed exactly what had happened.

For a moment, he did not speak, just stood impassive behind the high wall of his collar, his metal claw-arm flexing and unflexing with a tiny whirr. Then: "Let her go."

"Take a step closer, and I'll kill her. Look around you. You can see what my power does. You know I can do it," Ryushi said, his voice devoid of emotion.

"The Damper stone; you're too close," Corm said. "Your own stones will be affected."

"You sure? That's a chance you want to take?"

Corm hesitated. "Let her go *now*," he repeated, a waver of near-panic in his voice as his flimsy façade of control began to crumble.

Ryushi reached around her, his hand clamping around the largest of the turquoise stones that hung against Aurin's slender collarbone, and tore her necklace from her, the silver chain snapping free against her nape. Aurin gave a shriek of such pain and animal terror that Ryushi shuddered; but he gritted his teeth, and held her head brutally still, and she subsided into sobbing. He raised the heartstone high above his head, showing it to Corm.

"It's over," he said.

The effect was instantaneous. As one, every Keriag on the battlefield halted where it was, their black, blank eyes turned towards Fane Aracq. Even those in the path of the mighty war-machines – the few that were still operational – froze in the same manner, standing still as the immense tracks rumbled up to them and crushed them under the treads. But for these sounds, and the

415

erratic *whumph* of the force-cannons from the palace and the wyverns flying overhead, everything went dead. The click and shuffle and clash of spear, the background sound of the whole battle stopped. And just for one brief moment, it was like time had frozen, and only machines and flying beasts were exempt from its grip.

A sea of alien eyes, surrounding the whole palace, all focused on one spot. The chamber of Aurin.

They exploded forward in one gargantuan concerted surge, swarming past the war-machines and spreading up the white creamstone walls like a black blight, the hooked ends of their spiderlike legs carrying them effortlessly up the sheer surface. It was as if an invisible barrier had held them back until now, physically preventing them from touching the palace; but now it had fallen, and they attacked with a vigour and savagery that was terrifying to behold. Up the walls they went, and over, scampering down into the courtyards beyond. The sound of force-cannon fire struck up anew as the Guardsmen within made a vain attempt to defend their palace, but the weight of numbers that the Keriags possessed was overwhelming. Careless of their own safety, they tore into the palace, pouring over the walls on all sides, hacking through gates, scaling walls, clambering through wind-holes. No place was safe from the Keriags; Fane Aracq had not been built to withstand such creatures as they. And as they ripped through the lower levels of the palace, their viciousness laid testament to the fact that they had been unable to purge *all* emotions from their race; for they fought with a fury that left no stone unturned, and no living being in its wake. They fought for revenge.

"Mauni's Eyes!" Hochi breathed, from where he steered the wyvern high up in the cool night sky. The spectacle, when viewed from above, was even more extraordinary. The chaotic and beautiful architecture of Fane Aracq, the asymmetry of the spikes and spires and curves, domes and blisters, was being subsumed in the squirming black of the Keriags. The sheer number of the insectile race made him feel humbled and afraid. What if the Keriags did turn on them after they were freed? What if Kia was right in her protests? Wouldn't they be an enemy with even less mercy than Macaan? Should Calica really give them back their freedom?

"He did it," Gerdi said in the harness behind him, his hands tightening where he held Hochi's belt for stability. "Whaddya know? He really *did* it!" He whooped suddenly, raising one hand in salute. "I told you he'd pull it off!"

But Calica, in the hindmost seat, couldn't smile. Somewhere down there, she knew, Ryushi was still in great danger. And if he survived, then it would be her turn. To be the bearer of the heartstone. It was a responsibility that terrified her. A responsibility, of course, which depended on the plan that they had formulated actually *working*.

Seeing the onslaught of the Keriags below, she wasn't sure that she even *wanted* it to work. So what if the heartstone was not fooled into thinking she was Aurin? The Keriags would die, perhaps Aurin would be killed, and Macaan's forces would be terribly weakened. Parakka's greatest threat would be eliminated, and the woman who had reportedly stolen the heart of the one who was supposed to be hers would be no more. Hardly a tragedy from her point of view.

And yet she had to try, for now her course was set. To refuse the heartstone would mean she was responsible for the genocide of an entire species. And she would never have Ryushi then, much less be able to live with herself.

But deep in a selfish part of her, she hoped and hoped that the heartstone would not accept her. Because if it did, that meant she *was* Aurin's Splitling. Aurin was what Calica could have been if things had gone a different way for her. And she did not like the suggestions that possibility made about herself.

"Let my Princess *go*!" Corm shouted, his voice high and shrill. In Ryushi's hard grip, Aurin trembled and sobbed, her composure lost with her power, a spoilt and frightened girl once more. Ryushi loathed himself at that moment, hated himself for having to hurt a woman like this, especially *this* one. Instead, he flicked his glance over to where Tatterdemalion was getting up from the floor, cradling a broken limb across his emaciated chest.

"Don't come near," Ryushi warned the Jachyra. "I'll kill her if you do." He wondered, would he really be able to, if it came to it? Would his spirit-stones respond? Would the Damper stone stifle his power, or his own reluctance? He didn't know.

Tatterdemalion observed him hatefully, the expression somehow coming across through the metal features of the creature. +++ **The Keriags will kill us all when they arrive** +++ he said, his voice more loaded with static than ever.

"Not with me here," Ryushi replied, sounding more confident than he was. He had faith that the Parakkans would have told the rampaging Keriags who they were trying to save, but he was not certain that the Keriags would recognize him. The sound of their frantic invasion was all around them.

"Ryushi, let me *go*!" Aurin sobbed. "You've got the stone, yes? You've beaten me, you've *won*! Don't let me die, Ryushi!"

"They won't kill you," he insisted, sounding unsure now. "You'll be . . . alright with me."

"You can't keep her," Corm said, and the suddenly calm and level tone in his voice made Ryushi pay attention. He had guessed a long while ago what had been going on between the Princess and the prisoner, and he was better equipped to understand it than a Jachyra. Now it had all come to a bad end, as he knew it would. But at least he could try and save his Princess.

"I don't want—"

"Parakkan, you *do*," said Corm. "You want to keep her with you. You don't want to let her go. But you know that the rest of Kirin Taq will demand blood, even if the Keriags do not kill her first. No matter how much you want to, you cannot stop that; and even if you put your life in front of hers, retribution *will* be exacted." He paused, seeing the cold knowledge force itself on to Ryushi's face. "You must let her go, or see her die. Or give her back the heartstone. But you cannot keep her now."

"*Please*," she begged. "Let me go!"

"And where will you go?" Ryushi demanded. "To your father? What if we meet again like this, repeat this ordeal? You think I can risk that?"

"No! No, not to my father! Do you think I can face him now? Do you think I dare risk what he will *do* to me in return for losing one of his kingdoms?" She turned in his arms, and he loosed his grip so that she could, but his hand still held tight to her shoulder, ready to unleash the fatal power if either of her aides tried to attack. Now he looked into her eyes, tear-reddened but undiminished in their perfection, and she spoke low and raggedly. "You have ruined me, Ryushi. Let me go. I will leave this life you have shattered behind me, and find a new one."

"You'll not survive. Too many people know of you," Ryushi said. He was being deliberately obstructive; he could not face the choice that Corm had shown him.

"But only a few have *seen* me, and they are dying as we speak. The world knows me only by reputation, not by sight."

There was a silence in the room, but all around the

sounds of conflict were getting louder with frightening rapidity. Tatterdemalion and Corm anxiously watched the two of them, their eyes burning, one with supplication, the other with indecision.

"What I did, I did because I had to," Ryushi said. "I'd made a promise, and I had to keep that promise. Because my word is my bond, even to death." He took a breath. "But you must promise me this. If I let you go, you won't return to your father. If I let you go, you are his daughter no longer, and we'll never meet again as enemies. Do you understand?"

"I understand."

"Promise me."

"I promise," she said, lowering her eyes.

"*Mean* it!"

She raised her chin, meeting his gaze defiantly. "I promise, Ryushi! I promise. My word is *my* bond, and though it has never been tested as sorely as you profess yours to have been, you will find it every bit the equal."

Ryushi searched her face, seeking deceit and finding none. Then he stepped back and let her go. She did not go immediately, just took a pace away, such a mix of emotions written on her features that he could not tell what she was feeling as she did so.

+++ **My lady, we must go** +++ said Tatterdemalion. Neither he nor Corm were making any move to attack. They were still wary of Ryushi's power, even without his hostage. Outside, the noise of the conflict intensified suddenly, spilling towards them.

She turned away from him, walking slowly across to the mirror. There was still a good portion of it that was not shattered, for its impregnation of powdered spirit-stone had made it tough and resilient. Corm moved with her, taking her by the elbow, leading her towards where the Jachyra waited to take them through. Aurin did not turn, did not look back as they stepped through the mirror; and then the reflective surface flowed over her like molten metal and she was gone.

*

The battle ended quickly after that. Their palace overrun, the Princess's Riders decided to cut their losses and save their own skins, dispersing and heading for the keeps of other nobles. Most of the palace guns had fallen silent now, their operators slaughtered by the Keriags; and so the Parakkan wyverns were left free to obliterate the few remaining war-machines, finding the slow, lumbering things easy targets for their force-cannons. The Keriags scoured the corridors of Fane Aracq, killing without mercy or remorse, until finally the killing was done.

Calica hurried along the corridor, passing between patches of light and shade from alternately whole and shattered white glowstones. She had already become numbed to the sight of blood and bodies by the time she saw the smashed remains of the sentries that had tried to bar Ryushi's way into the Princess's chambers, and the horror could not penetrate the thick hide she had developed over years of Parakkan service. Hochi and Gerdi were close by her, and surrounding them were the rapid, angular movements of the Keriags that escorted them, bringing them to where the heartstone was, bringing them to. . .

"Ryushi!" Calica cried, and rushed across the rubble-strewn room to where he stood, leaning on the windowsill, looking out of the window. She walked up next to him, placing a hand on his shoulder. "Ryushi, are you alright?" Her relief and joy at seeing him alive was tempered by his silence.

Hochi and Gerdi followed her in. All around, the Keriags stood, their spears in their hands, waiting.

Ryushi muttered something.

"What?" Calica asked, leaning closer. He repeated himself again, this time in an even more mournful cadence. "You let her *go*?" she asked in disbelief. The Keriags stirred, reflecting the discomfiture of the hive-mind. "*Why*? You idiot, *why*?" she shouted. "Didn't you think to hold on to her? Do you know what will happen now if the heartstone *doesn't* match me?"

"What do you mean?" Ryushi asked suddenly, turning his head in alarm. "You? I'm supposed to give it to *you*? And you don't even know if it will *work*?"

The Keriags shuffled more animatedly, their joints clicking, their black eyes cold and intense.

"Have you got the heartstone, Ryushi?" Hochi said, stepping forward.

In answer, Ryushi slowly held out his hand and opened it. The silver double thread of Aurin's necklace spilled out, the three turquoise stones piled up in his palm. There was no vibration, no inner glow, no sign that it might crack and end the lives of thousands upon thousands of Keriags in a short second. The creatures around them went still.

"Put it on me," Calica said, turning around so that her back was to him. "The chain's broken. Tie it round my neck."

Ryushi hesitated a moment, then moved to comply. What if it didn't work? What if, even after everything, the Keriags died? He took a heavy breath, his eyes closing.

Father, Gerdi . . . I did my best for both of you. I tried my hardest to keep my promises. That's all I can do.

He brushed the straight fall of Calica's orange-gold hair aside, exposing her neck. He laid the heartstone against her heart, and tied the thin, double-chain of silver together behind her. He let go and stepped back.

For a time, Calica stood there, unmoving. Then she hitched in a sharp breath, suddenly, as if someone had placed something cold down her back. She closed her eyes, and kept them closed. All eyes were on her.

"Oh, for Cetra's sake, don't tell me it hasn't *worked*!" Gerdi exclaimed.

Calica's eyes flicked open, the olive of her irises misted by a sheen of saltwater. "Of course it's worked," she said, a terrible sadness in her eyes.

And all around her, the spiderlike Keriags lowered themselves until their low-slung torsos touched the creamstone floor, their spears held horizontally before them, a gesture unlike anything the others had ever seen before from the creatures. They were honouring her.

She lifted her head back, her spine straight and proud, and wiped the single tear from her face. "We've won only half the battle," she said, suddenly becoming again the leader she had always been. "Takami marches on Base Usido; he may already be there. Our friends are in danger. We have to go, if we're not already too late."

"Takami?" Ryushi said. "And where is Kia?"

Calica met his gaze unflinchingly, and Ryushi felt his stomach sink.

Kia.

27

The Path of the Bolt

"Get to cover! They're firing on us!" the Dominion man shouted, running from the small metal booth at the base of the cliffs that operated the lifts, dodging through the stabbing force-bolts that rained down from above. It was only by good fortune that one of the warriors who had escaped the clifftop massacre was the Overseer of Base Usido, a tall, gaunt man with a sparse black beard named Guji; he was one of the few people privy to the self-destruct mechanisms that the Machinists had installed in most of the sensitive devices in the Base.

Peliqua and Jaan retreated a little further, to where Iriqi stood, and watched as Guji ran with great, loping strides across the scarred clearing towards them. He took shelter behind a shattered hut, one that had been torn apart by the Snagglebacks a few cycles ago and had not yet been rebuilt. A few moments later, one of the larger lifts suddenly jarred into action, the chains and pulleys clanking as it began to rise up the cliff face, summoned by the Guardsmen above in a similar booth to the one that Guji had just come from. There was a breathless pause, as the Parakkans watched the lift wheeze higher and higher ... and then the booth imploded, folding in on itself with a thick *wham* and reducing to a heap of crushed metal. At the same time, several other mechanisms at various points up the cliff face followed suit, crumpling to a wrecked mess of components, and the ascending lift shuddered to a halt and was still.

"That'll hold them," Guji said, his voice bubbly with phlegm. "But only till they get ropes and cables to climb down with. Get yourselves ready; we want to make their descent as painful and costly as possible."

The defenders dispersed in a flurry of activity, finding themselves what ranged weapons they could and grabbing any cover that was available. The Guardsmen on the clifftop, tiny figures at such a huge distance, fired occasional bursts of concussion down at them; but they were too far away for the bombardment to be accurate, and it was more frightening than effective. The Parakkans formed themselves into a semicircle, using the shattered huts that surrounded the clearing to hide in, and waited for the Guardsmen to try and come down.

"Peliqua! You've gotta come with me!" said a voice that suddenly piped up at her shoulder where she crouched. As one, she and her brother turned from their flimsy barricade of broken wood and looked at Elani, dust-streaked and agitated.

"Oh! What is it?" she asked, her expression mirroring the younger girl's.

"Cousin Kia's just come in through the front gate. Ty's hurt! Come on!"

It did not even occur to her that there was probably nothing she could do to help; nor did she question how Elani had known where she was – not that this was unusual for the Resonant girl, for she was an endless mine of surprises. She simply acted, getting up to go with Elani. Jaan and Iriqi went with her. Together, the four of them left the semicircle of defenders and ran across the Base, between the shattered and smoking buildings and the craters, between the living and the dead and the still-dying.

It was what saved their lives.

Anaaca's spy in Takami's court had been useful in finding out many things, but he had been unable to provide them with more than a vague indication of the amount of troops that Takami possessed, the size of the garrisons given to him when he took over the thaneship of Maar. What information the spy had been able to glean had been further muddied by the army's trip through the Rifts, where it was uncertain how many men or vehicles they had lost. So nobody expected the second fleet of wyverns to arrive until they came screaming across the Base, loosing a terrific salvo of force-bolt fire across the settlement.

Elani shrieked as she and Peliqua leaped to the floor, closely followed by Jaan, and bundled themselves into a protective heap. Iriqi did not move, but seemed to brace itself as the backlash of the explosions hit them, using its own enormous body as a shield for the others. Splinters and divots of Kirin Taq earth blasted everywhere, dark shadows racing past them through the twilight; but in the lee of the huge creature, they were unharmed.

Jaan scrambled to his feet as the fury around them died, allowing the others to get up, their hair and eyes wild. He looked past Iriqi; and there, around the base of the cliffs, he saw that the huts they had been using for cover had been almost entirely destroyed, and the remains of those that had defended the clifftop had been destroyed with them. Anger welled up inside him, anger and helpless frustration. Such a loss of life! Even hardened as he was, he could not stop the cry of pain that he let out at the senseless waste; but nor could he deny the heady sense of relief that he had not been hiding there at the time, and he hated himself for feeling that way.

But now something new was happening. The wyverns were landing, soaring downward into the Base towards the spot that their cannons had cleared; and on their backs were many more Guardsmen, a small strike force that was being brought in to attack the Parakkans from the inside.

"What's happening?" Elani wailed in distress, looking around frantically.

"Come on," Jaan said grimly. "We'd better warn Kia. She'll know what to do."

They set off again, hurrying through the newly settling debris, forcing themselves to ignore the screams and cries for aid that floated to them from nearby, on the back of the ambient noise of the distant battle across the plains. In a short while, they reached the gate, where Kia was helping a dazed Ty to his feet, a pakpak standing next to them with its broad, flattish muzzle turning this way and that in alarm.

"Kia! Oh! Are you okay?" Peliqua asked, running up to her and taking Ty's other arm.

"What's going on over there?" Kia asked sharply, nodding towards the direction that they had just come from.

"We've been overrun! It's horrible, Kia! They're landing another load of Guardsmen to cover the cliff while the rest of them come down!"

"Have we got enough people to keep them out?" Kia demanded.

"I don't know! We've all been scattered!"

"How could—" Kia began, but cut herself off with a curse as she heard the first report of a Guardsman's halberd come from the cliffs, followed by another and another after it. Soon, the sounds of a new battle had begun, this one smaller and closer, as the isolated pockets of Parakkan resistance were swept up by Takami's Guardsmen, forcing them back so that the bulk of the army could abseil down the cliff face.

Kia looked around, a momentary despair gripping her. The Base had been all but levelled by the combination of the Banes' attack and then Takami's follow-up. Whatever happened now, there was little that could be salvaged from this place. Its location was known to their enemies, and nearly all their resources had been destroyed. If their companions had not managed to take Fane Aracq, then all was truly lost. But if they *had* . . . why, then there was a chance. Then they didn't *need* Base Usido anymore.

Then all they had to do was survive.

"Forget the Base!" she said. "Come on! It's safer on the plains, with the others! Are there any pakpaks left in the stable-yard?"

"Pregnant females, probably," Jaan said. "Everything else would have been taken to ride."

"Go get a couple. They'll die anyway if they're left here. You'll have to risk riding them."

"What about Iriqi?" Jaan protested, indicating the enormous shape of the Koth Taraan that stood silently next to him.

((I will go now. Catch me up)) it said, the last few words clothed in warm amusement as it used the characteristically human phrase for the first time. With that, it lumbered away from them with surprising speed, its huge forearms and claws carried close to the ground as it made its way out of the gate and towards the distant battle.

"Peliqua! Get the pakpaks!" Kia said. The Kirin girl released Ty and rushed off towards the stables, hoping that they would still be standing when she got there. Nearby, the sounds of the battle were getting closer.

Elani chewed her dark hair nervously, having fallen quiet since the recent blast had shaken them.

"We're running *away*?" Jaan asked.

"You have a problem with that?" Kia replied, a challenge in her voice.

"*I* don't," he said, truthfully. He had never been one for confrontation. "But it's not at all like you."

"Look," she said. "This Base is dead and gone. If we stay here, in small groups, the Guardsmen will just wipe us out. If we go back to the plains and join the main group, we can fight out in the open. We're *winning* out there." She hefted the weight of Ty against her shoulder. "And besides, I have more than just myself to think about."

The Guardsmen were spreading out from the cliff face into the Base. He could not see them through the obscuring mess of smashed buildings and smoke, but he could hear them coming closer. Kia was right. If they stood here, they would fall.

They helped Ty back into the saddle, and Kia got up behind him; then Peliqua was with them again, leading two pakpaks. How she had reined them so fast he would never know, but he was glad of her efficiency. One of the beasts was heavily pregnant, its belly swelled beneath its tiny forelimbs; but the other looked like it was in the early stages, and showed no bulge at all.

"These were all I could find," she said apologetically.

"I'm lighter," Jaan said, swinging himself up on to the

back of the larger one, hearing it murmur in discomfort as he got into the saddle. Peliqua mounted the other, picking Elani up with her.

"Ready?" Kia asked. "Then come on! We've got a fight to win!"

They urged their mounts forward, and the pakpaks obliged sluggishly, without any of the usual zeal of the species. Behind them, in the Base, they heard a screech and the *whoosh* of air as a number of wyverns launched themselves skyward, now that they had dropped off their cargo of troops. Bounding across the plain, their pakpak's muscular two-toed feet propelling them fast towards where Iriqi had a head start on them, Kia was suddenly conscious that they were terribly exposed out here. Between the Base and the fight that raged around the edges of the valley, there were only the dead and wounded; and there were not many of them, for they had a way to go before they reached the main battleground. She clutched harder to Ty's waist, and pushed her exhausted and overloaded pakpak onward, and sought safety in numbers.

"Cousin Kia! Up there!" Elani cried, pointing past Peliqua's stabilizing arm and up at where the forest canopy high above them peeled back to reveal a slice of velvet sky. Seven wyverns had taken wing, soaring from the Base and passing far overhead, making for the main mass of the battle. But as Kia looked, her expression suddenly changed to concern. One of the wyverns was dropping back and peeling away from the other six, banking in a shallow downward curve, turning towards them.

"They've seen us!" she barked. "Scatter!"

The three pakpaks split up, heading away from Iriqi as the wyvern neared at frightening velocity. It was coming from directly in front of them, intending to pass low overhead, but as the Parakkans spread further and further apart it became obvious who was its target. It was going for Kia and Ty.

Eyes narrowed against the wind of the sprinting pakpak, Kia fixed her gaze on the approaching beast, ready to gauge the moment it would strike. But her thoughts deserted her, her preparation dashed as the wyvern swooped low enough for her to see who occupied its harness. There was an Artillerist there, with a standard force-cannon on a pivot set into the pommel; but it was the sight of the rider that suddenly filled her mind.

The green, elegant, close-fitting armour. The silver mask, fashioned in the shape of a screaming spirit, its mouth distended in sorrowful agony. The long, black ponytail.

Takami.

The realization stunned her enough so that the hard swerve she had intended to execute never happened. But the Artillerist had no such hesitation. He loosed a bolt over Takami's shoulder a moment before the wyvern thundered past them like a hurricane, the force of its passing blowing their pakpak to a halt and almost making it tip over backwards. And a fraction of a second later the force-bolt hit the ground a few metres away and blasted them sideways, sending beast and riders flying. Kia landed hard and awkwardly, instinct making her put out one hand to try and break her dive. There was a sickening snap as her wrist gave, and her shriek of agony was knocked from her lungs as the rest of her body hit the bloodied grass. Her leg twisted under her and cracked like a twig, and unconsciousness boiled up from behind her eyes to claim her.

Nothingness. Then—

"Cousin Kia!" Elani was shouting distantly, but everything was fogged in pain as Kia's eyes opened, and she could not respond. She could only have been out for a few seconds, but it felt like lifetimes. Ignoring the burning fire in her leg, she tried to raise herself a little, knowing that they were still in danger, not allowing her body the respite it craved. Holding her broken wrist to her chest with her other hand, she lifted her head and peered through the waxy sheen of unreality that had suddenly descended upon her.

Their pakpak lay twitching some distance away, in its final death throes. Ty was next to it, mercifully conscious but unable to move, his shirt wet with blood, his eyes searching for hers in alarm. Faintly, she was aware that the wyvern would be looping around for another strike even now, and that it carried on its back her hated brother Takami. But it was as if, suddenly, all power to act had been taken from her, as if the fall had broken more than her bones but her will also. She was an observer now, powerless, and in one terrifying, heart-twisting moment, she saw everything that was about to happen and knew that the future had locked itself on course, that there was no way to avert it.

There was a screech as the wyvern closed in for the kill, the Artillerist sighting for the blast that would finish her and Ty. She looked up dazedly, an almost bewildered expression on her face, and saw the silver mask of her brother leaning low over the neck of the wyvern, plunging towards them like the spectre of death. From somewhere behind her, she heard the thunder of pakpak feet, felt the vibration through the ground. But her eyes had turned back to meet those of her lover: sweet, sensitive Ty, self-sacrificing Ty, Ty the Pilot's apprentice who had proved himself as good as any Master.

At least they'd die together, she thought. At least there was that.

"Cousin *Kia*!" A scream now, from the little nine-winter girl that had got them into all this in the first place.

History repeats itself, she thought, her inner voice speaking up clearly. *That's the way of war. Takami killed my father. Now he's killing Ty. It will never end.*

The Artillerist hit the firing stud. The force-cannon spat a ripple of energy, sending it racing towards where Kia and Ty lay helpless.

Peliqua's pakpak reached them at the same

moment, and the Kirin girl threw herself from the saddle, carrying Elani with her. Kia was suddenly aware of them as they hit the earth, aware that they had carried themselves into the path of the bolt, aware that—

"*No!*" she screamed as they flung themselves on to her, the agony of her broken and grating bones nothing to the agony that stabbed through every fibre of her being as she realized what was about to happen. She reached out for Ty with her good arm, but the distance between them might as well have been a mile. Her eyes never left his as the bolt hit, and between them passed a moment of understanding too great for words, a moment of tender parting and terrible sorrow.

And then they were gone, disappearing in the heart of the shattering concussion.

"*Peliquaaa!*" Jaan screamed, his voice ripping and going ragged. His yellow eyes stared in denial of what he had seen, saltwater stinging them as tears pricked at him. Takami's wyvern blasted overhead with a triumphant screech and soared away towards the battle, uninterested in the lone halfbreed boy on his pakpak or the rocklike creature that lumbered slowly back towards him.

Jaan did not turn to watch it leave. Panting, sobbing, he sat in his saddle and gazed mutely at the spot where the bolt had hit. Obliteration met his eyes. The earth had dented inwards and collapsed, opening a pit into the one of the bottomless faults that zigzagged across the rifts. Dirt and blood and rubble lay everywhere, scraps of pakpak fur and unidentifiable flesh. Ty had been blown clear, face down, and Jaan did not even need to look closely to see he was dead.

But his sister, along with the Resonant girl and Kia. Of them, there was no trace. If anything remained of their bodies, it was lost to the endless depths under the earth.

He had watched his sister die.

((Jaan)) said Iriqi, and the word was so heavy with the pastel colours of sorrow and sympathy that the halfbreed boy could not help but burst into tears. The Koth Taraan stood by him for a moment as he buried his face in his hands, his thick ropes of hair falling like a curtain, the ornaments and beads in them clacking together as they shifted.

((We are sorry, Jaan. Sorry that we came too late))

The words seemed not to come from Iriqi, but from another voice: deeper, wiser and immeasurably older, and through his uncontrollable grief Jaan suddenly understood what was meant.

The Koth Taraan had arrived.

The first to be hit were the clifftop defences. Like a thunder-head the creatures had moved through the forest, slow and looming and unstoppable. In all of the Base Usido, the only one who knew of their approach was Iriqi; and he had not even mentioned it to Jaan, for the Koth Macquai wanted secrecy. Nobody had expected the attack, and it came too suddenly for the

Guardsmen to react before the Koth Taraan came charging out of the treeline, gathering momentum as they came, like boulders rolling down a mountainside. Concussion-bolts thumped into them time and time again, but the halberds of the Guardsmen had little effect on the thick plates of armour that protected the creatures.

They smashed through the breach that the Guardsmen had made, hundreds upon hundreds of them, each a tower of immense strength and matchless power. Their claws went through the Guardsmen's black armour as if it were paper, and tore their bodies apart like they were held together by little more than air. The Artillerists in the force-cannon towers managed to bring their weapons to bear and began firing devastating shots off into the fray. Their more powerful weapons took the lives of several of the Koth Taraan before the enraged creatures toppled the towers and the wall with it, their combined might pushing the weakened structure outwards from the inside until it simply came apart.

It was a rampage. The Koth Taraan swatted aside Takami's Guardsmen like humans might wave off annoying insects, or clapped their huge claws together on their victims with enough force to shatter bones. They drove the terrified Guardsmen before them, pushing them to the cliff edge and over it, sending them spilling from the lip of the precipice to fall screaming to their deaths in the Base below.

In less than five Dominion minutes, it was over. Every Guardsman on the clifftop had been killed. The Koth Taraan waded in mud and gore, their wide black eyes intense as they stood in the aftermath of the slaughter. Then, silently, they moved on.

All around the cliffs that bordered the plain, a similar scene was being played. The secret reinforcements that Takami had kept back in the trees for a final surprise found themselves set upon with terrifying savagery, by creatures with such casual strength and power that they had no defence against them. Harried mercilessly, cut down at every turn, they could only run in the face of the stampede, to be driven howling over the cruel cliffs and sent plummeting on to their comrades far below.

For Takami's forces on the plains, it was impossible to tell exactly what was going on; but they knew that something had gone terribly wrong for them. Their back ranks – those closest to the feet of the cliffs – were being crushed by the falling bodies of their comrades; and the ropes and cables that they had been using to abseil from the clifftop were being cut loose, leaving them stranded in the valley with no way back up. Until then, despite the fact that the Parakkans had been beating them on the plain, they had fought with a vigour that was borne of the knowledge that they had a trick up their sleeves. Now, with their secret reinforcements gone, they had nothing.

It started in isolated pockets, but like spots of soap in a film of oil, it spread outwards, widening circles that joined other circles until, eventually, it encompassed them all. Takami's Guardsmen were surrendering, laying down their weapons and giving themselves up. His generals knew that they were beaten, and they would not allow their men to die senselessly. All across the plain, the fighting stuttered and ceased, and the cheer of Parakka's victory spread across the winners like a ripple, rising through the twilit forest.

But for Jaan, who sat with his face still in his hands on the back of his pakpak, there was no victory at all.

28

The Wounds Between the Worlds

Rain lashed the rock of the Fin Jaarek mountains, pounding at stone that had been there since the world had begun. It spattered and ran, dancing in rivulets or falling into pools whose surface jumped and splashed constantly with the excitement of new arrivals. The thin corona of the black sun of Kirin Taq was hidden behind a louring curtain of cloud, and thunder rumbled deafeningly around the peaks, humbling everything beneath its power. The sparse shivers of Glimmer plants were a muted purple, faint points of light in the darkness.

Ryushi stood in a wide gully, its uneven floor thirty feet across, banked up on three sides by hard, unforgiving rock. His back was to the roiling sky, for he was high up in the mountains. He had climbed long and hard to get here. At the end of the gully, a jagged slash of a cave mouth darkened the wet rock, many times his height. His hair hung dripping around his face, his clothes soaked, his cheeks and forehead beaded with water. The rain ran hard past his boots, plunging off the precipice behind him, inviting him to join it.

For a long time, he stood there, not feeling the rain, his blue eyes fixed on the cave mouth.

I am the last, he thought to himself. *Kia, Elani, Father, Mother, Ty. All gone. All dead. Only me left, of everything that used to be Osaka Stud. Me, and Takami.*

Ninety cycles had passed since Fane Aracq had fallen. Ninety cycles since Jaan had told him of his twin's death. Ninety cycles since he had lost Aurin. And so much had happened in that time . . . so much, and so little of it really mattered to him anymore.

For a time, he had held out hope that Kia might be alive, somehow, somewhere . . . but if she was alive, she would have returned, and as the cycles wore on he knew that he was entertaining a fool's dream. She was gone, her remains swallowed in death by the earth and soil that she had mastery over in life. Slowly, he had let his hope wither, until it had finally died completely.

The Keriags held the Ley Warrens now, the only means of transport to and from the Dominions without the use of Resonants. Those Keriags that lived in the Dominions had deserted Macaan and returned to their Warrens, where they had become an immovable force against his Guardsmen. Macaan was effectively cut off from Kirin Taq completely.

As to the forces that Aurin had commanded, they were dealt with swiftly. Aurin's nobles were deposed, for none of them had the manpower to hold out against the Keriag army. Most had been killed in Fane Aracq, as they had been gathered there for Festide; many of those who survived capitulated without a struggle. Perversely, it was the tyrannical measures that Aurin had used that made the handover of power so easy in the cities of Kirin Taq; the Keriags continued policing the land as they had always done until a suitable alternative could be found, and the Guardsmen were demobilized or turned to the use of Parakka. For the common folk, life was not vastly disrupted. The celebrations that had followed Aurin's downfall had lasted for thirty cycles, and though the new order was not without its troubles – there were riots, and uprisings over petty disputes that had festered unsettled over the years – it did not affect the daily routine of the people, and civilization went on.

And now the transition period was coming to a close, and the fledgling system of government was beginning to take root. Ryushi had no head for politics, but he knew vaguely what the leaders of Kirin Taq intended to do. Reinstate the thanes, to rule over the provinces as they had before, but replace the supreme rule of King or Queen or Princess with a Council, to choose thanes and to make decisions about the welfare of the land. A Council to which anyone could be elected, rich or poor, Kirin or Dominion-born. Like the Council of Parakka.

We've won a world, he thought. For a long time, he mulled over the enormity of the statement. Parakka had liberated a land. He had been instrumental in a revolution of a scale that had not been seen since

Macaan subjugated Kirin Taq, before he was born. *So why don't I care?*

So much lay unresolved behind him. Calica was still the bearer of the heartstone, carrying with her the lives of the entire Keriag species. Measures were being taken to deactivate the power of the necklace and free the Keriags once and for all, but in the interim Calica had submitted herself to the guardianship of the insectile creatures. The purpose of this was twofold: firstly, it was a sign of faith, to reassure the Keriags that they had not simply passed the reins of their civilization to a new tyrant but to one who genuinely would not use her influence to enslave them again; and secondly, because the Keriags were understandably concerned about the safety of the woman every thump of whose heart carried with it the continued survival of their race.

It was a move typical of Calica, the diplomat. She had refused the pressure from all sides to use the power of the heartstone to make the Keriags remove Macaan from the Dominions as well as Kirin Taq. That had not been part of the deal that had been made in the Ley Warren, and besides, Calica was adamant that she would not become like Aurin. Perhaps it was Calica consciously trying to distance herself from her Splitling, but more likely it had been what Ryushi had told her about the trap that the Princess had been caught in. If she made the Keriags act against their will, then she could never deactivate the stone for fear that they would kill her in reprisal; and unlike Aurin, she could not bear the responsibility of so many lives resting on her survival.

But all this meant that she, too, had been forced to leave Ryushi during his hour of need. Who was left for him? Hochi, Gerdi, Jaan and Iriqi. Perhaps he could have shared solace with Jaan's loss, but he had never been close to the halfbreed boy, and Jaan spent his time almost exclusively with Iriqi anyway. Hochi and Gerdi, then; but while they were fast friends, they were not people in which he could confide his deepest feelings. Gerdi was too flighty and inattentive, and Hochi had his own problems, obsessed as he was with his incomplete search for the true meaning of Broken Sky and the guilt he felt at Kia's death. He believed he had failed the memory of Banto by allowing one of his children to die, and Ryushi did not have the will to convince him otherwise, even though he did not believe it himself.

Of Takami or Aurin, there was no sign. The memory of the Princess and how he had been forced to betray her pained him anew every time he recalled it. And really, what had he gained by his betrayal? He thought of the ruin of grief that surrounded him and wondered if he had really done right in fulfilling his promise to Gerdi. After all, it could scarcely have turned out worse than it had from his point of view.

Elani. Oh, Father, I failed you. I lost the one thing I had left of you: my promise to protect her.

The only small consolation was that they had won. He smiled bitterly at the irony of the thought.

He blinked, and realized where he was again. Rain battered his face, dripping from the ends of the short, fat tentacles of his hair and plastering his clothes to his body. A booming wave of thunder broke across the mountains, the roar of the dark sky. The ache in his muscles from the chill and the long climb meant nothing to him. He savoured the physical pain, for it took his mind from the pain in his life, and made everything gloriously sharp and clear. In the ninety cycles since his sister's death he had taken to punishing his body more and more, and his lean frame was taut with muscle as a result. Perhaps he had, subconsciously, been preparing himself for this moment, for the raw exertion of the climb into the mountains to get to this cave.

There was something he had to do. He could not bear to be alone any longer.

He took a step towards the cave, and almost immediately heard the warning rumble from inside. Two bright points of amber light appeared in the darkness, cutting through the misty sheets of rain to fix on him with their pupilless glare. Something large shifted within the jagged black cave mouth.

Slowly, Ryushi reached into his shirt and drew out the Bonding-stone that hung there. He had worn it ever since he was five winters old, and it was as much a part of him as the skin of his chest. A small, diamond-shaped stone of an unremarkable grey-white colour. He raised it to his lips and whistled, half blowing on it and half forming the note himself. Whether by chance or by fate, he hit the right pitch first time, holding a high, pure note until the stone began to tremble between his fingers. A hum surrounded him, continuing even when he drew breath to keep the constant whistle going. The amber eyes in the darkness watched him intently, transfixed.

He walked forward, his steps measured and careful, non-threatening but confident. His gaze never left that of the creature in the cave, the great bull wyvern that protected the roost. It was a big one, this. And wild bulls were particularly aggressive when defending their mate and their young. The sky-blue spirit-stones that studded Ryushi's spine were gorged with energy, ready to release it at a moment's notice if the bull should attack. But as Ryushi neared, the bull seemed to be making no move to do so; instead, it watched the Bonding-stone, entranced by its hum, under the spell of its euphoric effect.

He went into the cave, and what little light there had been drew back as he was swallowed in the moist darkness. The pounding of the rain changed its tone as he stepped out of it, turning to a sodden rattle as it hammered on the rock all around. There was the sense of movement in front of him, the heavy click of claws on stone, the leathery rustle of wings. He did not fear. His fear was as stunted as the rest of his bushfired emotions at present. Still whistling, he reached into his belt pouch and drew out a glowstone, letting the rags that wrapped it fall free, holding it high in one hand, filling the cave with the dull orange light.

The bull that stood over him was enormous, its squat, powerful body thick with plates of bony armour. Its long neck craned towards him, the amber eyes studying him from within the protective skull-like mask of the species. It dwarfed him, huge in its power, but he stood defiant in its presence. Behind it, the cave ran further back into the mountain; and close by was the female, smaller and less bulky, its own eyes fixed on the Bonding-stone that Ryushi carried. Within the protective circle of the female's split tail, a fledgling was similarly mesmerized, its neck curled quizzically.

It was small, only the same height as Ryushi, and showed little of the shape that it would take when it was an adult. Its armour was soft, and its wings were fine and fragile and shot through with a tracery of thick veins. Its muzzle was more rounded, less defined than its parents'. A bull, though; he could tell by the bone structure already. The experience of growing up on a wyvern stud had not been entirely wasted on him.

As if at an unspoken signal, the mother wyvern shifted her powerful bulk, and her twin, club-tipped tail ends curled away from her fledgling, releasing it from her protection. The fledgling looked up at its mother, squawking in bewilderment, but the mother dipped her head and gently nosed it forward, urging it towards Ryushi. For a moment, it resisted; but eventually it acquiesced, shuffling on ungainly feet across the orange-stained cave, its gaze never once leaving the Bonding-stone that was held to Ryushi's lips. The bull loomed over them as the fledgeling approached the Dominion boy, close enough to touch.

This was not how the Bonding ceremony was supposed to be. Riders were Bonded to domesticated, selectively bred wyverns on a stud, with a solemn ritual accompanying the heavy responsibility that they took on. But Ryushi had no patience with ritual now; it was meaningless to him, as everything else had become meaningless. So he had climbed into the mountains, knowing that it had recently been birth-time, to seek a wild fledgling. It was part spite, part his need to be obtuse; his way of railing against the world that had let him down. He would fulfil the dream he had had ever since he was a child; but he would do it *his* way, and not by somebody else's rules. So what if he was still too young? It mattered nothing to him.

The air was charged with danger. This was no controlled ceremony. He had walked into the lair of a family of wyverns.

He stopped whistling. The hum of the stone continued for a few moments, and then tailed away to nothing. Beside him, the bull stirred its immense body at the change. The female screeched, the noise deafening in the confines of the cave. But neither made a move.

Putting down the glowstone, Ryushi took the small diamond of the Bonding-stone and held it between the fingers of both hands. It was completely smooth, and almost flat. With a sharp movement, he broke it along its edge, making two perfect diamonds of half the thickness of the stone. It came apart easily, as if his touch had suddenly polarized the two halves to repel each other. Slowly, he placed one diamond directly in the centre of his forehead. When he took his hand away, the stone stayed where it was.

He looked at the fledgling. The fledgling looked back at him with its clear amber gaze. Then, as if it had known all along what was to happen, it closed its eyes and dipped its head to him. Delicately, reverently, Ryushi positioned the stone on its forehead, between and a little above the eyes. And the link was made.

Ryushi had been told what to expect by some of the Parakkan Bonded, but words could only fall short of the experience as it hit him. The rush, the all-encompassing warmth, the giddying ecstasy of *togetherness*; the staggering complexity of assimilating the thought processes of a completely alien species; the womblike feeling of protection and support, of senseless reliance on another being for survival; and then finally, the understanding, as a level was reached, and the chain was forged.

Ryushi fell to his knees on the hard stone, sweating despite the freezing rain that had soaked his body. Panting hard, he hung his head for a moment. The link was there now, but they were not fully as one. That would take training, learning. That would come as the wyvern grew, as Ryushi grew with it. But he was Bonded. There was no going back now. It was for ever.

A smile broke out on his face, the movement of his muscles unfamiliar in his recent grief. He raised his head, and saw the fledgling looking back at him, its muzzle only inches from his nose, its breath hot on his face. Its Bonding-stone, like his, had turned from grey to a dark red.

"Your name is Araceil," he said, and it felt right. Suddenly, it all felt right. He got to his feet, a little shaken by his experience. The parent wyverns watched him closely, knowing instinctively that their fledgling was his now, and he was theirs.

Part of the family, Ryushi thought, and laughed softly.

He turned away and walked out of the cave, back into the rain, leaving the glowstone on the floor where he had put it down. The rain seemed cleansing now, its hard stripes slashing him again and again and washing him inside out. He walked to the edge of the short gully, where the cliff dropped away, and stood there for a long time, looking out over the storm-torn sky. A blaze of lightning flashed behind the peaks, and a shockwave of thunder tore across the mountains and rolled over him.

Everything was lost to him. But the game was not over yet. They had won Kirin Taq, but they had not won back their homeland. That was the true prize. Kia's deal with the Keriags had only extended as far as Kirin Taq; the insectile race were not interested in the

Dominions. Gradually, the Keriags would retreat back to their Warrens, and live as they had before Macaan had come; insular, self-sufficient, keeping to their own territory. So the Koth Macquai assured them, anyway. The truth of that remained to be seen.

Division with the eventual hope of unity, Ryushi thought. Maybe it was all part of Broken Sky. First Macaan merged Kirin Taq and the Dominions; unwittingly, he'd started it all off. Parakka could use that. An age-old hatred was beginning to heal, between the Keriags and the Koth Taraan, reunited by their shared struggle. Maybe the same was beginning to happen between the Kirins and the Dominion-folk. They'd won Kirin Taq; now they were sewing up the edges of the wounds between the worlds.

The Koth Taraan. They were the true victory. Many of them were willing to fight for Parakka, and that, at least, was something. For while Macaan massed his forces in the Dominions, Parakka would be massing their own in Kirin Taq.

Macaan. Takami, he thought, as he faced out over the dark, thunder-hammered mountains.

The real battle was yet to come.

So, this is the end of the second Act of **broken sky**

Parakka may well have won a world,
but they paid a high price for it.
And the war still isn't over.

Is Kia really dead?

There's only one way to find out. Read

broken sky 3
THE CITADEL

If you've enjoyed

broken sky

you'll love
these other incredible tales…

And don't forget to watch out for

MALICE

Chris Wooding's spine-tingling new novel.